ONE AND
WONDER

BOOKS BY PIERS ANTHONY

ONE AND WONDER

Piers Anthony's
Remembered Stories

Edited by

EVAN FILIPEK

Introduction by Piers Anthony
Illustrated by Jim Agpalza

FANTASTIC PLANET PRESS
PORTLAND, OREGON

Fantastic Planet Press
An Imprint of Eraserhead Press

Fantastic Planet
c/o Eraserhead Press
205 NE Bryant Street
Portland, OR 97211

WWW.BIZARROCENTRAL.COM

ISBN: 978-1-62105-082-7

Cover Design: Carlton Mellick III
Interior Design: Cameron Pierce and Kirsten Alene
Proofreading: Edmund Colell, Michael Kazepis, and Kirsten Alene

Printed in the USA.

TABLE OF CONTENTS

Introduction

Piers Anthony

I picked up an old magazine when I was thirteen, and it changed my life. It ushered me into science fiction as a genre, a realm of marvelous imagination so much better than the uncomfortable reality I lived in. I think it helped save my sanity, for as a child I had assessed my situation rationally and concluded that if I could be given a choice, I would prefer never to have existed. I was not suicidal, just not satisfied with life as I knew it. Now I had a refuge to which I could retreat at any time. My later life changed that assessment, as I entered into a half-century plus marriage and became a successful writer of science fiction and fantasy. Later I was to meet some of the authors of the stories that fascinated me, and to receive myriad fan letters from those who loved my stories as I had loved the stories of others. The wheel of fortune seems to have made a full turn.

Now I am returning to give credit to the stories that transformed my imagination. Rereading them more than half a century later has been an emotional experience. Perhaps it should be no surprise that as a septuagenarian (in plain talk: I'm in my 70s) I am a far more critical reader than I was as a teen, and I find the stories generally somewhat different from my often vague memories. But they remain good ones, ones that helped shape my own formation as a writer, and I think contemporary readers should find them worthwhile. If some of their themes seem familiar—well, these were essentially the originals, from which later authors and movie makers evidently drew. So they are primitive in much the way the fabled cave man was primitive: he was nevertheless our ancestor, and worthy of respect for surviving and showing us the way.

When we got crowded by possessions, children, and a growing library of research books, I gave away my beloved magazine collection. Then when I wanted to collect my favorite stories, I no longer had them available. So the project languished, until Evan Filipek took on the brute-work of locating, obtaining, and copying the stories so that I could assemble the volume. Thus it came to be at last: One and Wonder, I being the One fascinated reader, the entire science fiction and fantasy genre being the Wonder of the discovery.

Each story is presented with a forward and an afterword by me, giving my impressions as I remember them from my first reading so long ago, and as I see them now, together with my interactions with some of their authors. For example, when I met James Gunn, the only author with two stories here, it turned out that his son was a fan of mine. I met Jack Williamson, author of the first science fiction story I read in that marvelous magazine, when he visited my house. What phenomenal joy!

Here are summaries of the stories to be included. Skip these if you prefer to be surprised by the stories themselves, as I give away their key features.

"The Equalizer" by Jack Williamson, published in ASTOUNDING SCIENCE FICTION, March 1947. A military mission returns to Earth after twenty years at space, to find the moon base deserted, and indeed the cities deserted. What has happened? It turns out that there has been a breakthrough that enables anyone to obtain virtually unlimited power from a mere twisting of wires, and the industrial infrastructure is no longer needed and has faded away. A new, peaceful, better society has replaced the old coercive dictatorship. It is a dream of utopia.

"Breaking Point" by James Gunn, published in SPACE SCIENCE FICTION, March 1953. A space ship lands on an Earthlike planet. Before the crew can go out to explore, a voice says "Men of Earth! Welcome to our planet." They are locked in the ship as weird things happen, putting each of the five crew members to a psychological test to the breaking point. One man retreats to a chess game—and he is the one who survives, psychologically, because he has devised a way to adapt its rules to the alien game and defeat them. A psychological tour de force.

"Vengeance For Nikolai" by Walter M Miller, published in VENTURE for March 1957. A savage tale of a young Russian woman who is specially treated and sent behind American lines to assassinate an American general whose genius threatens to wipe out the Russian forces. The general has one weakness: a breast fetish. The girl, having just lost her baby in a bombing, has very full breasts. The general dies of poisoned milk . . .

"The Girl Had Guts" by Theodore Sturgeon, published in VENTURE, January 1957. A mission exploring an Earthlike world is beset by a horrendously ugly and smelly skinless creature that appears without warning and kills people. It turns out to be the result of a virus that changes people's innards, enabling them when threatened to spew out their guts, literally, and those animated guts attack and smother the opponent. The girl in question also shows considerable fortitude, enabling the mission to return to Earth. A stunning idea story.

"Little Lost Robot" by Isaac Asimov, published in ASTOUNDING SCIENCE FICTION March, 1947. This is one of a series of Asimov robot stories, the first I encountered, wherein a robot is told to get lost, and does so literally, hiding among other robots that look identical but are not not. This one has a modified directive that makes it potentially dangerous, but destroying all of them is too expensive. The question is how to find it, when it does not want to be found.

"Child's Play" by William Tenn, published in ASTOUNDING SCIENCE FICTION, March 1947. A man receives a Build-A-Man kit from the future, evidently a mailing foulup, and it's quite something. He decides to make a living twin of the woman he pines for, but first, as practice, he makes a twin of himself. Then a representative from the future comes to correct the mistake—and disassembles the wrong twin.

"Ground Leave Incident" by Rog Phillips, published in VENTURE for May 1958. A married settler mining for gems on a colony planet has his home wired, to be sure his wife is safe. He sees a rogue spaceman invade the house and rape his wife. He can't get home in time to stop it, but does intercept the spaceman in a bar and stab him through the genital. Rather than delay the ship with a trial, the authorities pretend it was just a fight between crewmen. Thus a crime and retribution that only the settler understands. A savage yet logical story.

"Dreams Are Sacred" by Peter Phillips, published in ASTOUNDING SCIENCE FICTION, September 1948. A man is sent to invade the lucid dream of a mad writer, to bring him out of his potentially fatal internal realm. Thus we get wild fantasy in a science fiction setting, living the dream. A precursor to a later popular movie theme.

"Wherever You May Be" by James Gunn, published in GALAXY, May 1953. A scientist investigating the supernatural encounters a girl who has phenomenal psi powers, but only when she's unhappy. So he sets out to make her extremely unhappy, by playing up to her, getting her to fall in love with him, then pretending he has a fiancee elsewhere. It works, and her powers manifest. But among them is telepathy, and when she reads his mind and discovers his cynical plot, hell really breaks loose. She is a woman scorned. This is a fantastic romp.

"Myrrha" by Gary Jennings, published in the MAGAZINE OF FANTASY AND SCIENCE FICTION, September 1962. Myrrha is a highborn Greek woman visiting the protagonist with her show horses. She is angered by a passing remark, and her vengeance, unwinding stage by stage, is devastating, concluding with the seeming seduction of the protagonist's husband though Myrrha denies it, and then the mare births a centaur. A savage story of undeserved punishment, surely a horror classic.

THE EQUALIZER

Jack Williamson

March 1947

This was the story that launched me into the science fiction genre. I was thirteen, in eighth grade at a school I detested, and my life was at best indifferent. It was the Christmas season, and I was waiting at the office where my mother worked, so that we could go home. I had nothing to do. There was a magazine lying on the counter, ASTOUNDING SCIENCE FICTION, so I picked it up and started to read the first story. It interested me, but I had not finished it when it was time to go. That's all right, they said; I could keep the magazine, as it was just one someone had left. So I took it home, and not only finished the story, but read the whole magazine. That changed my life. The story, as I remembered it more than 60 years later, told of a space ship returning after years, or maybe time dilation had made years pass back on Earth, and things had changed. There was no activity around the home planet. They checked the moon station, and it was deserted. They landed on Earth and there seemed to be no civilization there. What had happened? Well, among other things, the equalizer had happened. This was a simply device or technique to draw power from the environment so that no one had to pay for it anymore, and there no longer needed to be any highly developed technology to provide it. There was no need for competition for resources, so there was no war. Earth had become a quiet paradise of simple plenty. And, in the course of a year or so, the captain of the spaceship adapted and learned to make a cuckoo clock with his hands. I loved that vision. Later in life, as I became established as a science fiction writer—this was before I connected with fantasy—I had the immense pleasure of a visit at my house by Jack Williamson himself. I showed him my collection of magazines, including the ones with his stories, including the serialized . . . And Searching Mind, later published as The Humanoids. *Later still when I was guest of honor at the 1987 World Fantasy Convention I publicly complimented him on bringing me into the genre. I think it is fair to say that I would not be where I am today, had it not been for Jack Williamson and his fabulous and thoughtful fiction.*
    —Piers

I

Interstellar Task Force One was earthward bound, from twenty years at space. Operation Tyler was complete. We had circled Barstow's Dark Star, nearly a light-year from the Sun. The six enormous cruisers were burdened, now, with a precious and deadly cargo—on the frigid planets of the Dark Star we had toiled eight years, mining raw uranium, building atomic plants, filling the cadmium safety-drums with terrible plutonium.

We had left earth in a blare of bands and party oratory. Heroes of the people, we were setting out to trade our youth for the scarce fuel-metals that were the life-blood of the Squaredeal Machine. We were decelerating toward the Dark Star when Jim Cameron happened upon the somehow uncensored fact that both uranium and thorium are actually fairly plentiful on the planets at home, and concluded that we are not expected to return.

Allowed to test the cadmium safety-drums that we had brought to contain our refined plutonium, he found that some of them were not safe. One in each hundred—plated to look exactly like the rest—was a useless alloy that absorbed no neutrons. Stacked together in our hold, those dummy drums would have made each loaded ship a director-sized atomic bomb, fused with an unshielded critical mass of plutonium.

If Jim had been a Squaredealer, he might have got a medal. As a civilian feather merchant, he was allowed to scrap the deadly drums. Under party supervision, he was permitted to serve as safety inspector until the last tested drum was loaded in our holds. He was even granted limited laboratory privileges, under Squaredeal surveillance, until we were nearly home.

But he and I, aboard the *Great Director*, spent the last months of our homeward flight in the ship's prison. Held on charges never clearly stated, we somehow survived that efficient, antiseptic SBI equivalent of torture called "intensive interrogation." Our release, like the arrest, was stunningly unexpected.

"Okay, you guys." In the prison hospital, a bored guard shook us out of exhausted sleep. "Come alive, now. You're sprung. Get yourselves cleaned up—Hudd wants to see you."

Returning our clean laboratory whites, he unlocked the shower room. The prison barber shaved us. We signed a receipt for our personal belongings and finally stumbled out of the sound-proof cell-block where I had expected to die. There were no explanations and no regrets—the Special Bureau of Investigation was not emotional.

An MP sergeant was waiting.

"Come along, you guys." He pointed his stick at the officers' elevator. "Mr. Hudd wants to see you."

"Surprising," murmured Cameron.

Mr. Julian Hudd was not an officer. He had no formal connection with either the SBI or the Atomic Service. He was merely a special secretary to the Squaredeal Machine. As such, however, he gave orders to the admiral-generals. Hudd, the rumors said, was the bastard son of Director Tyler, who had sent him out to the Dark Star because he was becoming too dangerous at home. The imitation safety-drums, the rumors added, had been intended to keep him from returning. But Hudd, enjoying himself in a secret harem installed on his private deck, the rumors went on, meant to be hard to kill.

Julian Hudd rose to receive us in the huge mahogany-and-gold office beyond. At fifty, he was still handsome; he still bore a shaggy, dark-haired magnificence. Yet the enormous animal vitality of his heavy frame was visibly ailing. He was paunchy; his blue cheeks sagged into jowls; dark pouches hung under his blood-shot eyes.

"Jim! And Chad!" We were not his friends—a Squaredealer had no friends; but he made a fetish of informality. He shook our hands, seated us, and offered the first cigars I had seen in many years. "How are you?" Cameron's lean face turned sardonic.

"We have no scars or mutilations, thank you." Hudd nodded, beaming as genially as if he hadn't heard the sarcasm. Relaxed behind his opulent desk, he began tapping its sleek top with a paperweight, a small gold bust of Tyler.

"You two men are pariahs." He kept his smile of bland good-nature, but his voice became taut, violent. "Civilian scientists! Your own mutinous indiscretions got you into the cells of the SBI. Except for this present emergency, I should gladly let you rot there. Now, however, I'm going to let you exonerate yourselves—if you can."

The sagging, furrowed mask of his face gave me no hint about the nature or extent of this present emergency, and we had been incommunicado in the prison. By now, I thought, we must be near the earth. I recalled the booby drums. Perhaps, it occurred to me, he intended to take over the Directorate from Tyler or his heirs.

Hudd's gray, blood-shot eyes looked at me, disconcertingly.

"I know you, Chad Barstow." His fixed smile had no meaning, and his loud voice was a slashing denunciation. "Perhaps your own record is clean enough, but you are damned by a traitor's name."

I wanted to protest that my father had been no traitor, but a patriot. For Dr. Dane Barstow had been Secretary of Atomics, in Tyler's first cabinet—when Tyler was only President of the United States. He had organized the Atomic Service, from the older armed services, to defend democracy.

When he learned Tyler's dreams of conquest and autocratic power, he angrily resigned. That was the beginning of his treason.

In political disgrace, my father returned to pure science. He went out, with his bride, to found Letronne Observatory on the moon. Spending the war years there together, they discovered the Dark Star—my father first inferred the existence of some massive nonluminous body from minute perturbations of Pluto's orbit, and my mother aided him in the long task of determining its position and parallax with infrared photography.

Eagerly, Dane Barstow planned a voyage of his own to the Dark Star—he wanted, no doubt, to escape the oppressive intellectual atmosphere of the Directorate. He spent two years designing an improved ion-drive, and then tried to find aid to launch his expedition.

Tyler, meantime, had betrayed democracy and destroyed his rival dictators. From Americania, his splendid new capital, he domineered mankind. He was pouring billions into Fort America, on the moon, to secure his uneasy Directorate. He was not interested in the advancement of science.

Curtly, Tyler refused to finance or even to approve the Dark Star Expedition. He wanted the ion-drive, however, for the robot-guided atomic missiles of Fort America. My father quarreled with him, unwisely, and vanished into the labor camps of the SBI. My mother died in the care of a Square deal doctor.

Though I was only a little child, there are things I shall never forget. The sadness of my father's hollow-cheeked face. The intense, electric vitality of his eyes. The futile efforts of my mother to hide her fear and grief from me. The terror of the SBI, that haunted my sleep.

Five years old, I was taken into the Tyler Scouts.

Task Force One, which put to space three years later, was not the supreme scientific effort of my father's planning. The great expedition, as Jim Cameron once commented, was merely a moral equivalent of war.

"Dictators need an outside interest, to divert rebellion." A tall man, brown and spare, Cameron had looked thoughtfully at me across his little induction furnace—we were working together then in his shipboard laboratory. "War's the best thing—but Tyler had run out of enemies. That's why he had to conquer interstellar space."

I looked uneasily about for possible eavesdroppers, for such talk was not healthy.

"I wonder how it worked." Cameron gave me his likeable, quizzical grin. "Since we have failed to find any interstellar enemies, the essential factor was missing—there was no common danger, to make oppression seem the lesser evil. Perhaps it failed!"

Our arrest must have come from such reckless remarks as that. Cameron had always been unwisely free of speech, and it turned out that one of our laboratory assistants had been a Squaredealer, reporting every un-guarded word to the SBI.

Now, in that richly paneled office, Julian Hudd kept drumming ner-vously on his sleek mahogany desk. Through that bland and mask-like smile, he watched me with red, troubled eyes.

Hoarsely, I answered him.

"I know my father was a traitor, Mr. Hudd." I had learned to utter those bitter words while I was still a child in the Tyler Scouts, for they had been the high price of survival. "But I've been loyal," I protested. "The SBI have nothing on me."

"You're lucky, Barstow." His voice was flat and merciless. "One word of real evidence would have drummed you through the execution valve. Now, I'm giving you a chance to redeem your father's evil name."

Then he turned upon Jim Cameron, accusingly. A sharp unease took hold of me, for Cameron had never been broken to mute obedience, as I had been. Now, emaciated and weary as he was from the prison, he still stood proud and straight. His fine blue eyes met Hudd's—sardonic, amused, and unafraid.

Jim Cameron had always been that way—meeting the iron might of regimented society with a cool, critical intelligence; yielding, sometimes, an ironic show of respect, but never surrendering his proud independence.

He had been my best friend since we came aboard the *Great Direc-tor*—two, among the thousands of Tyler Scouts who were sent to provide youthful replacements for the crews. He was fourteen then, the leader of our troop. He found me lying on my back, sick with acceleration-pressure, homesick, too, dazed and hopeless.

"Hello, Scout." He put a friendly hand on my shoulder and gave me his wry, invincible grin. "Let's get our gear policed up for inspection."

We arranged our equipment. He sent me for a brush to sweep under our bunks. I showed him the treasures in my pocket—three model-planet marbles, a broken gyroscope top, and a real oak-acorn—and even let him see the contraband snapshot of my parents. We went to chow together. We were friends.

Now, under the provocation of Hudd's shaggy-browed, glaring vehe-mence, I was afraid that Cameron's stubborn self-respect would once again get the better of his judgment.

"As for you, Jim—" Hudd's blue-jowled smile was wide, his voice harsh and violent—"your record is bad. You were broken from the Tyler Scouts, for insubordination. You were blackballed from the Machine, for doubtful loyalty. You were even rejected for the Atomic Service."

"That's true, Mr. Hudd." Cameron grinned, cool and aloof.

"Feather merchant!" Hudd's red eyes glared through his mechanical smile. "The execution valve is waiting for you, Jim. Never forget that. I've saved your life a dozen times—just because you've been useful to me. Now I'm giving you a chance to earn one more reprieve. But the valve's still waiting, if you fail. Understand?"

"Perfectly." Cameron grinned. "What's the job, this time?"

He must have been thinking of those dummy drums that he had found in time to save all our lives. Perhaps he was thinking of other services, too. On the cold worlds of the Dark Star, he had been a very useful man. He had invented sensitive new detectors to find the uranium hidden under glaciers of frozen air. He had solved a hundred deadly riddles for Hudd, before the last lethal cylinder of newly made plutonium was loaded safely aboard.

"One question, first." Hudd's big mouth still smiled, but his red eyes were narrowed and dangerous. "The boys have brought me a rather disturbing report about some gadget you called an induction furnace. What's the truth about it?" "That's easy, Mr. Hudd." Cameron's low voice seemed relieved. "Until our arrest, we were running routine assays of our metallurgical specimens from the Dark Star system. I built that little furnace just for convenience in fusing samples."

"So? Hudd forgot to smile. His heavy, mottled face stiffened into a bleak mask of ruthless purpose. "The boys report that your assays were only a blind, intended to cover some secret experiment."

Hudd paused, but Cameron said nothing. He merely stood waiting, his lean face grave enough, but an alarming hint of impersonal amusement in his eyes. Hudd went on:

"I believe it was a most peculiar furnace." Hudd's voice was harsh with accusation. "The boys report that it consumed no current. They say it changed the metals fused in it—that buttons of pure iron, on spectrographic analysis, began to show yellow sodium lines."

Hudd's great body heaved forward against the desk, ominously.

"What about that?"

Cameron nodded easily. Then fear dropped like a staggering burden upon me. For he grinned across the gleaming mahogany, and told Hudd more than he had ever admitted to the SBI, in all our months of intensive interrogation. "I was looking for something."

For a moment, as he spoke, Cameron let down the shield of reserved and sardonic amusement that he carried against a world of totalitarian compulsion. For a moment his voice had a hard elation, terrible in its honesty.

"I was looking for—freedom." His thin shoulders lifted, almost defiantly. "I thought I had found a new and simple technique for manipulating the cosmic stuff that sometimes we call matter and sometimes energy. I thought I had found the way out of the Atomic Age."

His blue and deep-set eyes, for just that moment, held a stern radiance. Then his brief elation flowed away. His tall, emaciated frame bent to a burden of failure, and I saw the gray sickness of the prison on his haggard face.

"I was mistaken." His voice went flat, with the dull admission of defeat. "The accidental contamination of pure specimens with spectroscopic traces of sodium is notoriously easy. I had already abandoned the experiment, before we were arrested."

Hudd nodded his great shaggy head, unsurprised. "You're smart to tell the truth—and lucky that you failed." His broad, blue-jowled face recovered its habitual political smile. "Now, I think you've had a lesson, Jim, and I'm going to give you another chance." His voice turned savage again. "I don't mean another chance at treason—for you'll be watched, every minute."

Cameron stood waiting. The defeated look was gone. His lean face was properly grave, but his keen blue eyes had a glint of amused expectancy.

"What's your trouble, Mr. Hudd?"

Hudd pushed the little golden head of Tyler away from him, across the opulent desk. Slowly shifting his great bulk, he leaned back in his wide chair, knitting his fingers so that his huge, black-haired hands cradled his paunch. Under the dark thick brows, his small eyes were red with fatigue and trouble.

"I suppose you noticed when we went from acceleration thrust to centrifugal, three days ago?" His rasping voice was dry and hurried. "Anyhow, we're back—on a temporary orbit twenty thousand miles from the moon."

"And something's wrong?" Cameron's voice, it seemed to me, had some faint undertone of malicious anticipation. But Hudd didn't seem to notice, for he was stating gravely:

"Something has happened to the Directorate!"

"Eh?" Cameron's veiled amusement vanished. "What?"

"Here are the facts." Heavily, Hudd lurched forward against the desk again; his voice had a brittle snap. "We began calling Fort America weeks ago, from millions of miles at space. Our signals weren't answered. So far as we can determine, the moon has been abandoned."

His bloodshot eyes looked haunted.

"We haven't tried to signal the earth—I want to keep the advantage of surprise, until we know the situation. But things have happened, even there."

He reached, with a huge and hairy paw, for the little golden bust of Tyler and resumed his nervous drumming.

"But we've been listening, on every possible wave band. Of course, out here, we couldn't expect to get much. But we are in range of the great television propaganda stations of the Applied Semantics Authority—and they are dead. All we have picked up are feeble clicks and squeals—scrambled radiophone signals, apparently, which our engineers can't unscramble."

His lowered voice echoed a baffled unease.

"The telescopes give us several puzzling hints. The forests have grown, since we left—the spread of green into the deserts might almost indicate a general climatic change. The haze of smoke is gone from the old industrial areas. Where several cities used to be, in the tropics, we can find only green jungle."

"Very interesting," Cameron murmured.

"Two landing parties were sent to earth in life-craft," Hudd added grimly. "One was to land in Europe and the other in North America. Nothing has been heard from either, since they entered the ionosphere. They are twenty-four hours overdue."

The solemn, baffled hush of his voice gave me an uncomfortable chill. It would be a terrible and ironic thing I thought, if we had come back from our long exile to find our own human kind somehow destroyed.

Hudd blinked at Cameron with shrewd weary eyes.

"Now, I'm sending out another party." His voice turned decisive. "Captain Rory Doyle will be in command—under the advice of my liaison man, of course—and Doyle wants you two with him. You are taking off in two hours. Your first object will be to learn what happened to Fort America."

Hudd put his great hands flat on the desk and came laboriously to his feet, puffing with the effort. For all his gross bulk, however, he made a towering figure, dynamic and impressive still. Shrewd and imperious, his small eyes burned into Cameron.

"You had better find out." With a visible effort at control, he lowered his violent voice. "Your mission is important. I believe the Directorate has been overthrown, and I intend to restore it. I've got plutonium enough to smash the earth. The first necessity, however, is to learn what has happened. I believe you can anticipate the consequence to yourselves of failure."

"I think we can, Mr. Hudd," said Cameron.

My heart began to thump, with an excited and somewhat apprehensive expectation.

II

Life-craft 18 was a trim steel missile, lying snug in its berth-tube amidships of the *Great Director*. Eighty feet long and slim as a pencil, it had its own ion-drive, a regular crew of six, and plenty of additional space for our party.

Captain Rory Doyle met us at the valves. He was a big man, red-haired, straight and handsome in the gray of the Atomic Service. Under party supervision, he and Cameron had rescued a scout ship sunk in a liquid nitrogen sea on the inner planet of the Dark Star. He was capable, fearless, and loyal to Hudd. Smiling, he welcomed us aboard his swift little craft.

His crew of able spacemen helped us stow our space armor, and made ready to launch. Our take-off time went by, while Doyle scowled at his wrist chronometer, keeping the valves open.

"Waiting for Victor Lord," he muttered. "The Squaredealer."

Only his impatient tone suggested any dislike for Squaredealers—and even that was indiscreet.

Lord came swaggering insolently aboard, twenty minutes late. He was a tiny man, very erect and precise in his gray uniform—with the gold squares of the Machine instead of the blazing atoms of the Service. He had tight brown skin over a hard narrow face, with heavy lids drooping over pale yellow eyes. His long black hair had a varnished slickness. Strutting between his two tall bodyguards, he looked like a peevish dwarf.

He didn't bother to return Doyle's correct salute.

"You know my status, Doyle." His high, nasal voice was deliberately overbearing. "My duty here is to oversee your performance of this important mission. We'll have no trouble—if you just keep in mind that one word from me can break you."

He paused to blink at Doyle, with a sleepy-lidded arrogance. Success in the Squaredeal Machine required brutality, and Lord, I knew, stood second only to Julian Hudd. Haughtily, he added:

"You may take off, now."

"Yes, Mr. Lord."

The Squaredealer's petulant insolence may have been nothing more than a compensation for his size, but still I didn't like him. His yellow eyes were shifty; his narrow forehead sloped and his nose was too big; his whole expression was one of vicious cunning.

Doyle turned quickly away, perhaps to conceal his own resentment. He ordered the valves closed and climbed the central ladder-well to his bridge. A warning-horn beeped, and we cast off.

In the acceleration-lounge, we hung weightless for a few seconds as we dropped away from the flagship; then the thrust of our own ion-drive forced us back into the cushions with a 2-G acceleration.

I turned in the padded seat to look back through a small port. Against the dead black of space, I glimpsed the enormous bright projectile-shapes of the *Great Director* and the *Valley Forge*—coupled nose-to-nose with a long cable, spinning slowly, like a toy binary to create an imitation gravity.

Earth, close beside them, was a huge ball of misty wonder. The twilight zone made a long crimson slash between the day-side and the night. Dull greens and browns and blues were all patched with the dazzling white of storms.

All the hope and longing of twenty years burst over me when I saw the earth, in a sudden flood of choking emotion. My wet eyes blurred that splendid view. I sat grappling in vain with that shocking mystery of spreading forest, abandoned farmlands, and jungle-buried cities, until Victor Lord's high nasal voice recalled me to the life-craft.

"Feather merchants, huh?" Sitting pygmy-like between his two husky guards, Lord turned condescendingly to Cameron. "But Hudd insisted you must come. Let's have your expert opinion."

He stressed the adjective too strongly, but Cameron answered quietly, "I rather expect we'll find the ultimate result of what the old economists used to call the division of labor."

At the time, I failed to see the real significance of the interchange that followed, though it proved the key to much that happened later. I was merely annoyed at Cameron, and increasingly alarmed, because his talk plainly angered Lord.

"Explain!" Lord rapped.

"If you like—though I'm afraid the historical principle runs counter to Squaredeal ideology." Cameron was a little too grave. "Because I don't believe the Directorate was created by Tyler's unique statesmanship, or even by the emergent dictatorship of the common man. It was, I think, just one of the end-products of the division of labor."

Lord blinked his beady eyes, apparently uncertain whether this was double-talk or high treason. I kicked Cameron's foot, vainly trying to keep him quiet.

"Explain yourself," Lord commanded.

"Nothing to it," Cameron said. "The division of labor was hailed as something wonderful—before its unpleasant final consequences came to light. One man made arrows, another hunted, and they both had more to eat. That was very fine, back in the stone age."

Cameron stretched out his legs,   cheerful and relaxed.

"But it went a little farther, in the modern world. Division of labor divided mankind, setting special interest against the common good. It made specialists in mining coal, in scientific research—even in political power, Mr. Lord. The specialists formed pressure groups, each fighting to advance its own class interest—with weapons incidentally created by that same division of labor.

"When specialists fight, the winners are apt to be the experts in war," Cameron continued innocently. "Thus government becomes a function of military technology, which of course derives from the basic industrial technology. The prevailing form of government, therefore—dictatorship or democracy—depends on the current status of the division of labor. That interesting relation of technology and politics was pointed out by the old philosopher, Silas McKinley."

Lord's sleepy eyes glittered suspiciously.

"He's forbidden! Where do you keep such pernicious literature?"

Cameron grinned. "Once I had permission to do some research in Mr. Hudd's very excellent library."

"You're apt to suffer for the dangerous ideas you acquired there," Lord commented acidly. "Now what's this nonsense, about technology and government?"

"Political power reflects military power," Cameron cheerfully explained. "When war is fought with cheap, simple weapons, easy for the amateur to use, then the military importance of the ordinary citizen is reflected in his political freedom. Democracy in America was established by the flintlock and maintained by Colt's revolver.

"But democracy is always threatened by an increase in specialization, especially military specialization. When weapons are expensive and complicated, requiring a class of military experts, then the ordinary man can't defend his rights—and he therefore has no rights.

"Democracy was murdered, on a desert in New Mexico, in 1945. Already, for a hundred years, the increasing division of labor had been forcing it into slow decline. The same specialization that created the bomber and the tank had already reduced the free citizen to a pathetic little man at the mercy of the corporation manager, the union leader, and the party bureaucrat.

"The atom bomb was the end of freedom. Because it was the final limit of specialization. The most complicated and costly weapon ever, its production required a fantastically complex division of labor. Government followed the trend of technology, and totalitarian control destroyed the individual." Sitting half upright in the long reclining chair, Cameron gave the little Squaredealer his wry, sardonic grin.

"Tyler thought he had conquered the world," he concluded. "But really it was just division of labor that created the new technology of atomic war, and so destroyed the whole world's freedom. It was just the trend of specialization that made the Directorate and flung Tyler to the top of it—no more responsible than a pebble flung up by a wave."

Pressed deep in the cushions, Lord sat peering back with confused suspicion in his yellow eyes. Fortunately for Cameron, he was now concerned with dangers more immediate than ideological heresy. His nasal voice rasped angrily: "Well? What happened then—according to your theory?" Cameron answered with an easy grin.

"Quite likely, the division of labor broke down at last."

"Watch your manner, Mister." Lord clearly didn't like his grin. "What could break it down?"

"Rebellion, perhaps." Cameron was properly respectful. "For America had a permanent garrison of nine thousand specialists in death. They were prepared to devastate any part of the earth—or all of it. Perhaps they were just too thorough."

Uneasily, the little Squaredealer licked his thin lips. "Then why should the fort itself be silent?"

"Disease, perhaps—some biological weapon out of control." In Cameron's blue eyes, I caught a faint glint of malicious amusement. "Or famine—maybe they left the earth unable to feed them. Or natural cataclysm."

Lord fought the acceleration-pressure, to sit bolt upright. His bleak narrow face was filmed with sweat of effort—and of fear.

"Cataclysm?" He peered into Cameron's lean, sardonic face. "Explain!"

"Twenty years at space has shown us the insensate hostility of the universe." Cameron's low voice deepened my own unease. "Man lives at the mercy of blind chance, surviving only through a peculiar combination of improbable factors. Just suppose we find the earth stripped of oxygen." He grinned at Lord, satanically. "As efficiently as the planets of the Dark Star were robbed of uranium?"

Before we reached the moon, Lord had turned a sallow green with acceleration-sickness.

Fort America was hidden beneath a crater in the tawny desolation of the Mare Nubium. We wheeled above the mountain ring, just above the highest crags, searching the dozen miles of barren floor.

"It hasn't changed!" I whispered to Cameron. "The valves, the roads, the docks—just as they used to be!" I tried to point through the small quartz port. "There's where the *Great Director* stood."

"But it has changed." Cameron glanced at me; and the strong glare of the moonscape, striking his haggard face from below, made his habitual sardonic expression seem oddly diabolic. "It's abandoned, now."

And I remembered. Great trucks once had rolled over that white web of roads. Colored signal lights had blinked and flickered from the domes over the pits. Tall, tapered ships had stood like rows of silver pillars on the immense, dark fields.

But now the crater was an empty bowl. The lowering sun made all the westward rim a jagged lip of shattered ebony. Sharp fingers of the dark crept across the empty miles, to clutch the empty domes and seize the empty roads.

Nothing moved, anywhere. No metal flashed beneath the sun. No signals flickered, now, out of the cold, increasing shadow. Men had been here once, armed with atomic science, bold with conquest. Now they were gone.

Yet the crater wasn't empty, quite—for it held a riddle. What had silenced man's greatest citadel? Cold dread sank into me, out of that black, expanding shadow. The brooding mystery of it numbed my senses like some spreading biotoxin.

We landed at last, well out in the retreating sunlight, on a concrete road near one of the valves. We clambered into space-armor—Cameron and I, and Captain Doyle. Laden with assorted equipment, we scrambled one by one through the small air-lock, leaping clumsily down to the moon. Victor Lord remained aboard. He was ill. I believe his apprehensive thoughts had fastened too strongly on Cameron's malicious suggestion of interstellar invasion. I think he expected us to encounter unearthly monsters lurking down in the pits and tunnels.

Beside the bright spire of the life-craft, we set up a portable radiation counter and a neutron detector. The counter started flashing rapidly, and I couldn't stop an apprehensive gesture toward the valves.

"Dangerous intensity!" My voice rang loud and strange in the spherical helmet. "The residue, maybe, from atomic weapons—though I don't see any craters."

But Cameron was shaking his head, which looked queerly magnified inside the thick, laminated bubble of his helmet. "Just the normal secondary activity, excited by our own ion-blast." His voice came on the microwave phone, dulled and distorted. "I think it's safe for us to go on."

Moving clumsily with all our equipment, we moved a hundred yards to try again. Now the counter showed only the normal bombardment of solar and cosmic rays.

"Come along!" Doyle's deep voice roared in my phones. "Have a look—here's a whole row of wrecks. The mutineers must have caught them sitting. They're blown all to scrap." Beside a huge deserted dock of gray pumice-concrete, he had discovered the dismembered remnants of half a dozen vessels. We approached cautiously, and paused again to test for dangerous radiations. There were none—for these skeletons of space-craft had been stripped by something other than mutiny.

This had been a repair-dock. Suddenly sheepish, Doyle pointed at abandoned cranes and empty jet-pits. The apparent wrecks had merely been cannibalized—their plates and valves and jets ripped out to repair other vessels.

"No mutiny!" Doyle made a disgusted sound. "Let's look below."

For the actual fort was far beneath the crater. A vast web of tunnels, sheltered hangars, shops, barracks, magazines. The launching tubes, trained forever on the earth, were hidden in deep pits. Somewhere in that sublunar labyrinth, we could hope to find our riddle answered.

The nearest entrance shaft was topped with a low dome of concrete, piled with pumice boulders by way of camouflage. The great armored valve was closed, unrusted, quite intact. Doyle spun a bright little wheel, outside.

"I was stationed here, before they picked me for the task force," he said. "A robot-missiles officer—used to know my way around."

The massive steel wedge failed to move, and Doyle turned to another, larger wheel. It resisted, and I came to help. Stubbornly, it yielded. The great wedge sank slowly.

"Power's off." Doyle was breathless with effort. "Manual emergency control!"

We shuffled at last into the huge dark chamber of the lock. Our battery lights cast flickering, fantastic shadows. Peering at a row of dials and gauges on the curved steel wall, Doyle punched a series of buttons.

Suddenly I felt a faint vibration. The huge wedge lifted behind us, shutting out the dark and harsh-lit moonscape. The chamber was a steel-jawed trap. I felt a tense unease, and the sudden boom of Doyle's voice startled me.

"The main power lines are dead. That's an emergency generator, with a chemical engine—there's one at each valve, to work the controls and energize the instruments." He scanned the dials again. "Air inside—seven pounds. Better test it."

When he turned another wheel, air screamed into the chamber. It brought back sound—the clink of our equipment, the clatter of our armored boots, the throb of the emergency engine beneath the metal deck.

We tested it. The counter gave only an occasional click and flash. I broke the glass nipple off a regulation testing tube, and Cameron leaned clumsily beside me to study the reaction of the colored paper indicators. "Okay," he said. "Safe."

We took off our armor. The air was fresh, but icy cold—we exhaled white mist. Hopefully, Doyle tried the telephone in the box beneath the dials. Dead silence answered him. Shivering—perhaps to a sense of something colder than the freezing air—he hung it up and opened the inner valve. The emergency power system didn't work the elevators. We climbed down a black ladder-well, into the silent citadel.

III

Fort America was dead.

The thrumming of the little emergency engine was muffled, as we climbed on down, and finally lost. We descended into appalling silence. So long as we moved, there was a comfortable rustle and clatter. When we stopped to listen, there was nothing at all.

Everywhere, power lines were dead. Midnight shadows retreated grudgingly from our little battery lamps, and lay in wait at every turning. Beyond was total dark.

The heating system must have been shut off, months or years before, for the cold was numbing. Sweat had dampened my wool lined suit, in the heated armor, and now it was icy on my back. The chill of the rung sank through my thin gloves; my fingers were stiff and aching long before we reached a horizontal passage.

Gruesome expectations haunted me. I looked for frozen corpses, twisted with agony from quick biotoxins, or charred with atomic heat. Queerly, however, we found no mark of violence, nor any evidence of human death.

"They're just—*gone!*" Even the deep voice of Captain Doyle held a certain huskiness of dread. "Why—I can't imagine. Nothing wrong, no sign of any trouble." He caught his breath, squared his shoulders. "We've got to find the answer. Let's try the commandant's office."

He led the way along a black and soundless lateral tunnel, and opened an unlocked door. The series of rooms beyond was deserted—and quite in order. Empty chairs were neatly set behind the empty desks. Dead telephones were neatly racked in their cradles. Pens in their stands were neatly centered on green blotters, With the ink dried up. Doyle rubbed a dark mark in thin gray dust. "They've been gone a long time." His voice seemed oddly hushed, yet too loud in those silent rooms.

I began to open the drawers of desks and filing cabinets. They were empty. Bulletin boards had been stripped, floors swept clean. Even the wastebaskets had been neatly emptied.

A large portrait of Tyler in the commandant's office had slipped askew on the wall. Doyle moved without thinking to set it properly straight. Cameron followed his movement, I noticed, with a curious sardonic expression, but silently.

"The evacuation must have been quite orderly." Doyle shook his head, his eyes dark with bewilderment. "No sign of haste or panic. Now what could have caused them to go?"

We moved on, in search of the answer.

It wasn't famine. We walked through an empty mess hall. The long tables were all in line, filmed with dust. Clean trays and silver lay in geometric order, where the last KP's had left them for the last inspection. The warehouse beyond was stacked high with crates and bags and cans of food, frozen now, still preserved.

Nor was it any biological killer, gone wild. We found hundreds of beds in a hospital tunnel, empty, their dusty sheets still neat and smooth. The pharmacy shelves were loaded with drugs, untouched.

"Power failure?" Cameron suggested. "If the pile had gone dead—"

Rory Doyle found the way, down a black and bottomless ladder-well, to the main power-pile. The massive concrete safety-wall shut us away from all the actual mechanism, but Cameron scanned the long banks of recording instruments and remote controls. He flashed his light on a distant conveyor-belt, motionless, still laden with bright aluminum cans.

"Nothing wrong," he said. "The last operator discharged the pile—dumped the canned uranium out of the lattice, into the processing canyon underneath. There's plenty of metal left, but it wasn't charged again."

On another black and silent passage, a little above, we came to the steel-walled dungeons of the guardhouse and the military prison. The armored doors stood open. The records had been removed. The prisoners were gone.

"Revolt, perhaps," Doyle suggested. "Perhaps the prisoners escaped, and touched off a mutiny in the garrison—no, that couldn't have been, or we'd see the marks of fighting. Perhaps it was revolution, on the earth. That might explain everything—if the missiles are used up."

He led us up again, along an endless silent tunnel, and down another dark ladder-well. We spun stiff wheels to open three heavy safety-doors, and came at last into one of the magazines.

Doyle gasped, in blank astonishment.

For on row, as far as our lights could reach, long racks were loaded with the robot-missiles. They were sleek cylinders of bright metal, gracefully tapered, every part of them beautiful with precise machining. Space ships, really, they were six feet thick and sixty long, each powered with its own atomic generator, driven with its own ion-jets, controlled with the fine and costly mechanism of its own robot-pilot, each burdened with its own terrible cargo of plutonium-fused lithium hydrides or crystalline biotoxins.

Stunned, almost, Doyle walked to the nearest. He examined it expertly, lifting inspection plates, flashing his light on serial numbers. He came slowly back to us, baffled. "All abandoned!" he muttered. "I can't believe it. Why, those babies cost twenty million apiece, even in mass production. They are loaded with the finest precision machines that men ever made. One of them, in forty minutes, could obliterate a thousand square miles of earth. And never a one was fired!"

We climbed again, up a black narrow shaft, to the launcher which Doyle had once commanded. Bright, satiny metal shimmered against our lights. The huge vertical barrel cast monstrous, leaping shadows. Doyle slipped into a familiar seat and touched familiar buttons. An emergency engine began drumming. A huge periscope lens was suddenly bright with the broad crescent earth—with thin black cross hairs intersecting upon it.

He flashed his light on a blank log-sheet, and shook his head.

"Never a missile was fired."

Cameron was whistling through his teeth—a gray bit of melody that made a grotesque counterpoint to the themes of lifeless quiet and ghastly dark and deadly cold, to the whole haunting riddle of the abandoned fortress.

"Are these weapons still serviceable?" he asked.

"Not without some missing parts." Doyle opened an inspection door, to show a dark cavity. "The computer has been removed, and the gyros are gone from the projectiles."

"Too bad," Cameron's voice held the hint of irony. "I imagine Mr. Hudd is going to need them."

"They can be repaired," Doyle assured him soberly. "Our spares for the ships' launchers are interchangeable." Doyle looked at his chronometer. "Now it's time to report to Mr. Hudd—that our mission has failed."

The stern simplicity of the life-craft, when we were safely back aboard, seemed luxurious. We relaxed in the acceleration chairs and gulped hot soup against the chill of those abandoned tunnels while we answered the peevish and uneasy questions of little Victor Lord.

When the signal officer reported that he had contact with the *Great Director*, we crowded into the narrow television room. Hudd's heavy, blue-wattled face filled the screen.

"Let's have it, Jim." His loud, hearty voice was edged with tension. "What happened to the fort?"

"Evacuated, Mr. Hudd."

"But why?"

"We failed to discover that," Cameron reported. "The withdrawal was deliberate and orderly. The records were mostly removed or destroyed; the weapons were disabled without unnecessary destruction; the men took their personal belongings. There's no evidence whatever of trouble or violence."

"When did it happen?"

"About two years, I think, after the task force left. The dates on calendar pads and inspection cards show that men were here that long. The lowered air pressure, the accumulated dust, and the low counter readings we got about the main power plant—everything shows that they weren't here much longer."

Hudd turned, on the screen, to rap a few questions at Doyle and Lord. Lord's uneasy insolence had changed to a silky deference, now. He explained that acceleration sickness had kept him on the life-craft.

"A very puzzling situation." Hudd's frown showed his bewildered apprehension. "The entire task force, I feel, is in danger, until we find out what happened."

He straightened on the screen.

"Captain Doyle, you will proceed at once to the earth. You will land at Americania. Discover what happened to the Directorate—and what enemies we must destroy, to restore it. Take any precautions that you think necessary. But this time you must not fail."

"Yes, Mr. Hudd."

Hudd answered his smart salute, and looked at Lord.

"You, Mr. Lord, had better get well."

IV

Our life-craft, next day, spiraled slowly down over Americania—the splendid capital city which Tyler had founded, sentimentally, upon the Midwestern farm where he was born. Peering down through the ports, we felt an increasing sense of fearful puzzlement."

Wide suburban areas had been devastated by explosion or fire, so long ago that lush green forest had now overspread the blackened walls and the twisted frames of rust-red steel—but most of the city looked intact.

Avenue upon avenue, proud towers stood like monolithic memorials to history's greatest empire. Tyler had commanded his architects to build for a thousand years. Americania was a city of granite—of gray colossal masses, pillared and towered with contrasting red granite, and purple, and black.

Far below us, those stately avenues looked strangely empty. Nothing moved. Tall stacks rose from power plants and industrial buildings in the green-choked suburbs, but there was no smoke.

Was Americania all abandoned, like the moon?

Fear of that sent an uncomfortable prickling up my spine. I looked hopefully at my companions. Little Victor Lord had turned a sallow gray, and sweat made dark blots through his shirt. His two SBI men, in their ominous black, had turned away from the ports; muttering together uneasily, they were inspecting the action of their automatics.

Jim Cameron swung from his port, whistling in a way he had, softly, through his teeth. The air was the light, lilting melody of an old love song. The dwarfish Squaredealer whirled on him, in a sudden, tight-lipped fury.

"Stop your impudent whistling!" Lord's wrath had its real origin, no doubt, in his own frightened bafflement, but his sleep-lidded eyes looked dangerous. Even after Cameron stopped the whistling, Lord was not appeased.

"Look at me, you feather merchant." Lord's sharp nasal voice was angrily insolent. "Frankly, I don't approve the confidence that Mr. Hudd has placed in you. Now I'm warning you—watch your step!"

His small quick hand hovered suggestively over the heavy automatic sagging at his hip.

"Whatever we find here," he snarled, "my duty is to assure your continued loyalty to the Squaredeal Machine. Whatever happens, just remember that."

"I'll keep it in mind, Mr. Lord," Cameron promised him evenly.

Captain Doyle set the life-craft down at last on Tyler Field—the immense space-port on the outskirts of the city. Once it had been the gateway to the planets. I could remember my childish awe at the rush and glitter and vastness of it, from twenty years ago—when we marched across it, bravely screeching out the Tyler song, on our way out to Fort American and the Dark Star. Now, when I saw it again through the small ports of the life-craft, the change made me almost ill.

Like Fort America, the space-port seemed abandoned. Here, however, weather and decay had kept at work. Green life had kept on, overflowing every plot of soil, bursting from every crack in the neglected pavements.

Long rows of shops and warehouses stood deserted. Doors yawned open. Neglected roofs were sagging. Ruined walls, here and there, were black from old fire. Every building was hedged with weeds and brush.

Far across the shattered pavements stood the saddest sight of all. A score of tall ships stood scattered across the blast-aprons, where they had landed. Though small by comparison with such enormous interstellar cruisers as the *Great Director,* some of them towered many hundred feet above the broken concrete and the weeds. They stood like strange cenotaphs to the dead Directorate.

Once they had been proud vessels. They had carried the men and the metal to build Fort America. They had transported labor battalions to Mars, dived under the clouds of Venus, explored the cold moons of Jupiter and Saturn. They had been the long arm and the mighty fist of Tyler's Directorate, the iron heels upon the prostrate race of man. Now they stood in clumps of weeds, pointing out at the empty sky they once had ruled. Red wounds marred their sleek skins, where here and there some small meteoric particle must have scratched the mirror-bright polish, letting steel go to rust, which, in the rains of many years, had washed in ugly crimson streaks down their shining sides.

One of them had fallen. The great hull was flattened from the impact, broken in two. Steel beams, forced through the red-stained skin, jutted like red broken bones. The apron was shattered beneath it, so that a thick jungle of brush and young trees had grown up all around it.

Captain Rory Doyle came silently down his ladder from the bridge. His square face was black with gloomy puzzlement—as any loyal spaceman's should have been.

"A graveyard," he muttered, "of fine old ships—my first training voyage to Mars was on the old *Paul Jones,* yonder." He turned sadly to us. "Gadgets ready, Mr. Cameron? Then let's go out and see what unholy thing has happened to them."

"Hold on, Doyle!" Lord's nasal voice was sharp with dread. "Shouldn't we test the air? Suppose something has happened to the atmosphere?"

Doyle turned to Cameron, red brows lifted. "I don't think it's necessary, Mr. Lord," Cameron said respectfully. "You can see a gray squirrel scolding at us from the tree growing out of the apron, yonder, and a buzzard circling, toward the city. I think the air's all right."

"I'll do the thinking." The little Squaredealer drew himself up stiffly, in the sweat-blotched uniform. "Test it." I found a test-flask, and took it down to draw a sample through a tube in the inner valve. Cameron watchfully checked my reading of the colored indicators.

"It's safe enough, Mr. Lord," he reported crisply. "Oxygen normal. A bit of secondary radioactivity—due to our jets. No detectable toxic agents, chemical or biological."

"Then we're going out." Doyle looked thoughtfully at Cameron and me. "I don't know what we're running into. If you wish, I'll issue you arms."

"No, you won't!" The little Squaredealer barked out that sharp protest. "These men are suspected mutineers, Doyle. I'll take no chances with them."

Doyle's square jaw slowly hardened.

"Mr. Lord," he began. "I believe the SBI found nothing—"

"It doesn't matter, Captain," Cameron broke in. "We've gadgets enough to carry. Anyhow, I doubt that a pistol would be much use, where Fort America failed."

Lord looked at him with a puzzled alarm in his sleepy-seeming eyes, and then muttered something to his two gunmen. Their uneasy eyes went to Cameron.

Doyle led the way down the ladder-well. Air hissed, and the valves clanged open. One by one, we stooped to follow him through the lock and jumped out between the shining stabilizers to mother earth.

We hurried away from the scorched concrete and smoking weeds about the little ship, where the ion-jet might have left a dangerous activity, before we stopped to catch our breath.

Earth! We had dreamed of it for twenty years. Here in the northern hemisphere, it was early summer; the sky was a wondrous milky blue, flecked with cottony cumulus. The forenoon sun struck with a hot, welcome force. The warm air was heady with a fragrance that stirred old memories— the rich strong smell of green life growing out of damp vegetal decay. I heard a heavy buzzing, half-remembered, and saw a bumble-bee.

The warm earth, alive—and a lone black bird, yonder, wheeling over an empty city.

Lord, running after us through the blackened weeds, let out a nasal yelp of horror. A white skull, which he had stumbled against, rattled and bounded before him. We found the rest of the skeleton, with a rust-caked revolver on the broken concrete beside it. Scraping about in the weeds, we discovered several shapeless lumps of heavy metal, dark from heat, and a bent penny that still showed Tyler's profile. Cameron found the flattened cases of several ruined watches, and a woman's diamond bracelet, the links half-fused and the stones burned black. Doyle picked up a wicked-looking stainless steel blade, its haft rotted away. "A curious lot of loot." Cameron stood up, puzzled. "All burned, the money melted down. Maybe he was struck by lightning. Or maybe looting just isn't cricket."

Lord stood off and fired a bullet into the skull, I suppose just to test his gun. Bone shattered into white dust. He bolstered the automatic with an air of uneasy satisfaction, mopped the sweat off his narrow sallow face, and followed us watchfully.

We went on to the nearest ship. The bright curving hull towered three hundred feet, marred with long vertical streaks of rust. It was a stubby freighter; Doyle said it had been in the Martian metal trade.

We followed Doyle up a rusty accommodation ladder into the lock. The inner valve was closed, stiff with rust. We strained and hammered at the manual wheels until it groaned reluctantly open. A stale breath met us as we stumbled through the lock into dusty dark.

There was no power for lights or elevators. The interphone system was dead. We probed the silent dark with flashlights, and Doyle led the way up the ladder-shaft beside the elevator. Lord, with his two gunmen, decided to remain below. Doyle climbed into a cargo hold, and cursed in breath-taken astonishment.

"Plutonium!" A bewildered awe hushed his voice. "Hundreds of tons of refined plutonium in cadmium drums—enough to blow up half America—worth hundreds of millions." His haunted eyes peered back at Cameron. "Why did they leave it?"

We climbed on, looking for the answer. Our feeble lights, as we passed, searched each dark compartment. Everything was left in order. The galley was clean. The atomic generator had been discharged and secured.

There were no other skeletons.

A hard climb brought us to the executive deck. We found dusty charts and orbit plots neatly folded, astrogation instruments safe in their racks. Doyle opened an unlocked safe, with a shout of triumph.

"Now we'll know—here's the log."

He fumbled with the yellowing pages. Eagerly, we leaned to read the brief, routine entries which described an uneventful voyage from Mars. The four-hourly observations and computed positions were neatly entered, and the hourly checks of solar position and diameter. The date of the final entry corresponded with the dates on the calendar pads at Fort America. It was brief, neatly written, and completely exasperating:

"Routine landing at Tyler Field. Ship abandoned today, because of equalizer." That was all.

"I don't get it." Doyle shook his head, staring bleakly at that yellowed page. "A spaceworthy ship. Competent officers, evidently, and a loyal crew. They make a routine voyage and a routine landing. Not a hint of anything unusual."

He peered up at Cameron.

"Then something happens," he muttered. "Something makes them walk off and leave their jobs and their duty and a ship and cargo worth hundreds of millions. I just don't get it."

We went back to move the life-craft nearer the deserted city. When we landed again, in a suburban area which had been seared and flattened by some tremendous blast, the counter showed a lingering trace of secondary activity in the blobs of fused debris.

"An atomic explosion," Cameron decided. "But not one of our standard robot-missiles," Doyle added. "One shot from my launcher at Fort America would have leveled a hundred times this space."

We moved again, to a street in a still-standing suburb of detached, walled villas. Here, Doyle said, prominent officials of the Directorate had lived in an exclusive colony. He set the life-craft down on-a bit of unshattered pavement that made a clearing in the brush. Frowning walls faced the street, overgrown with green vines now, brilliant with blue morning-glories where the sun had not yet struck.

A tall gate of ornamental bronze sagged open before the nearest building, and we pushed in through a tangle of long-untended shrubbery that had overgrown the lawns. An unlocked door let us into the mansion, and musty silence met us.

Here we found no hint of any popular uprising against the ruling class. No bullet-prints, no human bones, no smashed furniture, no looted safes and chests. The refrigerator in the great kitchen had been emptied, but long shelves were filled with fine cut-glass and ornamental china. The gloomy library held thousands of volumes—but empty spaces seemed to say that others had been taken. Closets were hung with moth-ravaged clothing. A wall safe stood open, and Doyle explored the paper in it with a frown of dull bewilderment.

"They left a fortune," he muttered incredulously. "This man—His Excellency, A. P. Watts, Director-General of West Africa—must have been a lifetime piling up these stocks, annuities, bonds and shares, insurance poli-cies, deposit receipts. Then something happened. He just walked off and left it all."

His eyes appealed to Cameron.

"I don't understand it." The spectre of dread haunted his voice. "They weren't killed—there would be more skeletons. They weren't even fright-ened—they didn't barricade their doors, or fire a gun, or even upset the furniture. They just set things in order, took a few useful items—and went away."

His voice fell to a whisper of dull wonderment.

"But why—and where—could they have gone?"

We moved the life-craft again, this time into what had been an exclu-sive shopping district, where once, I fancied, the great men of the Direc-torate must have bought jewels and furs and perfumes for their mistresses, their secretaries, and perhaps even for their wives.

The street doors of these glittering shops were generally unlocked, or left wide open. Many shelves were bare, as if the goods had been simply carried out, but there was little evidence of vandalism or violent looting. Unbroken windows still held garish displays of tarnished costume jewelry. Abandoned cash registers were still stuffed with currency and coin—from which I saw Lord's gunmen furtively filling their pockets.

We landed next in the middle of the city, in the wide empty canyon of Tyler Avenue. There the massive granite walls were hushed and dead, but green weeds were pushing from every crevice in the hot pavements. A few sparrows were quarreling noisily about a window ledge.

"This was Squaredeal Square." Doyle's voice seemed too loud, in that sun-beaten silence. "If there was any fighting—war or rebellion—we ought to find the traces here."

Peering up at those splendid dead facades, I remembered that I had been here once before—in a great jamboree of the Tyler Scouts, when I was seven. There was Squaredeal Hall. There was the purple granite balcony where Tyler—or perhaps it was one of his public doubles—had appeared as we marched by, waving his arm mechanically as we screamed out the Tyler Song.

A diamondback, lazily sunning on the black granite steps of Squaredeal Hall, greeted us with a warning whir. Lord whipped out his automatic with a nervous expertness and shot it through the head.

The crash of his shot shattered that hot silence. It thundered back, ap-pallingly magnified by those sheer granite cliffs. The dwarfish Squaredealer and his guards crowded apprehensively together, and we all listened uneas-ily. But the echoes faded unanswered; the dead city was not aroused. Doyle led us up the steps, past the dead diamondback. Voiceless with awe, we went on between the immense square columns beyond. Here was the shrine of the Directorate. Tyler had surrounded his birthplace with a colonnade of purple granite, more majestic than Karnak.

Memory stirred again. After that review and jamboree, as a personal gift from Tyler, each Scout had received a picture post card of the shrine. The little weather-beaten farmhouse was shown beneath the towering columns, surrounded with an old-fashioned garden of zinnias and gladioli. The stone spring-house had been restored. The old apple tree, which the Director used to climb, was pink with blooms in the picture.

But that historic tree was dead, now. The house had fallen in. The mighty purple columns rose out of a green sea of weeds and sprouts and brambles. Wild morning-glories had buried the old spring-house. Something moved in the brush, and we heard the vicious warning hum of another diamondback.

Beside the useless elevator, we climbed a narrow stair. Tyler's own door, between two empty guard-boxes, had been left unlocked. We walked into the abandoned splendor of the Director's own apartment—and found no trace of violence.

On the high wall behind his desk, and the office chair that had served him for a throne, a faded tapestry still hung, intact and undefiled, embroidered in gold with the three linked squares of the Machine.

The massive door of a huge fireproof safe swung carelessly open. Its compartments were stuffed with documents marked RESTRICTED or CONFIDENTIAL or TOP SECRET. Letters, reports, beribboned executive decrees—the state papers of the Directorate, left heedlessly behind.

Lord, with a shrill excited shout, discovered a pile of heavy cloth bags that had been buried under the dusty documents, in the bottom of the safe. Feverishly, he ripped one of them open, spilling out bright golden double-eagles.

"Millions—left behind!" Wide awake, for once, his eyes glittered yellow as the metal, and his thin nasal voice was hushed with awe. "There must have been a dreadful panic, to make them leave the gold."

But Cameron pointed quietly to several empty compartments, and a blackened metal wastebasket, on the end of the desk, nearly full of gray ashes.

"It wasn't panic, Mr. Lord," he said respectfully. "Tyler had plenty of time to burn the papers he wanted to destroy. Then, I should imagine, he just walked out."

The little Squaredealer peered up at him, bewildered and visibly afraid.

"But why? Tyler wouldn't give up the whole Directorate."

The faded luxury of the great rooms gave us no answer.

The paneled walls showed no marks of bullets. The dusty rugs showed no stains that could be blood. The Director's great bed, under its coverlet of dust, still was neatly made.

Doyle came back to Cameron, muttering the question that haunted us: "Where could they have gone?"

Cameron rubbed his lean jaw with a brown forefinger.

"Let's try the country," he said thoughtfully.

Doyle stared at him, blankly. "Why?"

"People used to live in cities for certain reasons," Cameron said. "Just as they worked for great corporations, or enlisted in the Atomic Service, or joined the Squaredeal Machine. Perhaps those reasons changed."

Lord blinked sleepily.

"You had better watch your tongue," he warned sharply. "I believe you read too much in Mr. Hudd's library. I'll be compelled to report your dangerous views."

But we returned to the life-craft. Doyle landed it again, outside Americania, where a disused highway made a narrow slash through woods and thickets. We climbed down between the stabilizers once more, and Cameron pointed suddenly.

Planted in the middle of the old road behind us was a signpost. It carried a yellow-lettered warning:

DANGER!
Metropolitan Areas

V

Gathered in a puzzled little circle, we examined that sign.

"Well?" Doyle looked at Cameron.

"A remarkably strong aluminum alloy." Thoughtfully, Cameron rubbed his lean brown chin. "An excellent vitreous enamel. Evidently it was made and set up after the city was abandoned—to keep people out."

He started whistling gaily through his teeth, but Lord scowled him into silence. His blue eyes had lit with a speculative eagerness.

"And so?" prompted Doyle.

"Interesting implications." Cameron counted on lean brown fingers. "One, there are people. Two, they possess a high grade metal-and-enamel technology. Three, they have sufficient social organization to post public signs. Four, they don't like cities."

His eager eyes peered beyond the silver pencil of the life-craft, down the dark leafy tunnel of the old road. He softly whistled another lilting bar, and then looked quickly back at Doyle.

"Let's take off again, Captain," he suggested. "And follow the road, flying low. I think we'll find the sign-posters."

"We'll do that—" Doyle began, but the little Squaredealer interrupted him sharply:

"I'm in charge, and I don't agree." Lord's nasal tone was both insolent and apprehensive. "The jets are too bright and noisy. We'd be seen—maybe killed from ambush. Don't forget that melted money. No, we'll leave the craft hidden here, and go on foot."

Doyle's red head nodded soberly.

"A wise precaution, probably," he agreed. "We'll carry a radiophone, so we can call back."

Leaving the bright craft hidden among the trees, we started cautiously down the green tunnel. Interlacing branches usually hid the sky. Vines and ferns made thick walls on either side. Jays scolded at us, and unseen things rustled in the brush. Once we came upon a red deer. It stood quite motionless in a little glade ahead, antlers high, until Lord clutched for his automatic; then it bounded noisily away.

We were all, I think, keyed up and uneasy. The gloom of the forest darkened my own thoughts. Imagination turned small rustlings into startling threats. Recalling that the two other landing parties were long overdue, I began to wish I had a gun.

Cameron walked ahead. His step was light and springy, and his hollowed face had a look of grave expectancy. Once he started whistling again, softly, but Lord stopped him with a snarled command.

We must have gone three miles, before Cameron turned from a curve in the old road and plunged out of sight in the ferns and tangled vines. We followed him. A few yards brought us into daylight, on the rocky rim of a low sandstone cliff.

"The sign-posters," he said softly.

He pointed. Before us spread a broad, shallow valley of woods and open meadow. The sun glittered from the curve of a stream, but I saw no people.

"There's the house against the other cliff. Reddish walls, and green roof." I found it, then—a low graceful building that had seemed part of the landscape. "I heard a man singing."

I listened. It was midafternoon now, and a soft breeze had begun to disturb the midday hush. Leaves stirred lazily. I heard the sleepy hum of insects, the cool murmur of water running, a mockingbird singing—all wonderful sounds, half-familiar, that brought my boyhood back.

"Listen," Cameron urged.

There was a clear yodeling call—answered by a woman's voice.

"Keep down!" Lord's nasal voice was cautiously hushed. "We'll slip across, under cover. Study their weapons, and keep out of sight. If we're discovered—shoot first."

"Are you sure," Cameron protested, "that shooting's necessary?"

"I'm running this show." Lord's sleepy eyes narrowed unpleasantly. "I'll tolerate no meddling from you."

A fem-grown ravine let us down from the low cliff. We waded the clear stream and climbed again through the woods beyond. Nearer the dwelling, the land had been cleared. We crossed an orchard of young apple trees, slinking toward the voices of the man and the woman.

Twenty years at space had not made us expert stalkers. Dry leaves rattled, twigs cracked, and pebbles clattered. Lord turned, more than once, with a hissed injunction of silence. But at last we came on hands and knees to the grassy rim of another ravine, and peered down upon the unsuspecting two.

They were running a machine. The young woman sat in a little cab of bright aluminum, moving levers. A toothed bucket, on a long metal arm, scooped earth and stones from the side of the gorge to fill a hopper.

The man held a flexible hose, pouring a heavy yellow semi-liquid from the machine into a metal form across the little gorge. Presently he stopped to lift and adjust the plates of the form, and then poured again. Between the plates, I saw, a massive yellow dam was growing.

The machine ran quietly. There was only a subdued humming, and the occasional clatter of the bucket when sometimes it scraped a stone. It ate the dark soil, pouring out yellow concrete.

I peered at Cameron, astonished. He made a pleased little nod.

"A very neat step forward," he whispered, "in basic technology."

"Silence!" Lord hissed.

Below us, the man called to the girl, and she moved the machine on its wide caterpillar tracks. Watching them, I felt an increasing glow of pleasure. For twenty years I had thought and dreamed of life on earth; here at last was a glimpse of it—as any lucky man might hope to live it. The man was a lithe young giant in shorts, bareheaded and brown. The sweat of his toil, in the hot afternoon, made a film that rippled and gleamed with every movement of his sun-bronzed body. Sometimes he paused to get his breath, smiling and calling down to the girl.

"Mushrooms for supper, what?"

"Let's plant a Mac on the south terrace, shall we?"

"I've thought of a name, darling—let's call him Dane Barstow. Dane Barstow Hawkins!"

That name gave me a puzzled shock. Dane Barstow had been my own father's name—but it seemed quite improbable that the expected young Hawkins should be named for an unsuccessful traitor, long dead in the labor camps of the Squaredeal Machine.

But I soon forgot my wonder, watching them. Their absorbed happiness set me to dreaming wistfully. The girl was sun-colored, too, still slender, lovely. She ran the machine with a graceful skill, until the time when the man lost his balance as he hauled at the hose and teetered on the edge of the dam.

She stopped the machine then, with a sharp cry of alarm. After a moment of frantic clawing at the air, however, the man regained his balance. Seeing him safe, she laughed at him—a rich laugh, deep and musical and glad.

"Darling, if you had seen yourself! But please be careful—you're much too valuable to be made into the dam! If you're so weak, we'd better stop— I'm hungry anyhow."

"Laugh at me, huh?"

Grinning fondly through a mock ferocity, the man hung up the hose and dropped down from the dam. The girl scrambled out of the cab and ran from him, still laughing.

"Darling," she sobbed, "you looked so silly—"

"Stop 'em!" whispered Lord.

Instantly, the automatics crashed. The girl crumpled down beside the bright machine. The man ran another step, uttered a strangled cry, fell sprawling on top of her.

"My God!" Doyle shouted incredulous protest. "What have you done?"

The dwarfish Squaredealer fired twice more, expertly. His bullets thudded into the quivering bodies. The bitter reek of smoke stung my nostrils. Nodding to his bleak-faced gunmen, he rose calmly to his feet.

"Well, they didn't get away." His nasal voice had a shocking complacency. "I thought they might have seen us. Now we'll have to work fast, to learn what we can and get away to space. Doyle, call the craft—have it brought here at once. Cameron, inspect that machine—Mr. Hudd will want a full report on it. We'll look for their weapons."

Doyle had the self-discipline of a good officer. He was white-lipped, stunned, but any protest must wait for the proper channels. He reached obediently for the little radiophone which I had been carrying.

Cameron's discipline was not so fine.

"You fool!" His blue eyes glared at Lord, his low voice crackling with anger. "You murdering fool! You had no excuse for that."

His brown fists clenched. For one terrified moment, I thought he was going to strike the Squaredealer. Lord must have thought so too, for he nodded at his two black gunmen and stepped quickly back.

"Please, Jim." I caught Cameron's quivering arm. "You'll only get us shot."

"Quite right." Lord retreated again, watchfully. "Any further trouble, and I'll shoot you with pleasure. In any case, I shall report your insubordination. Now—if you want to stay alive—inspect that machine."

Angrily, Cameron shrugged off my hand. He stood facing Lord, defiant. Slowly—with an eager, dreadful little twist of his thin, pale lips—Lord raised his gun. Cameron gulped, shrugged, turned silently toward the bright machine.

Lord and his men searched the bodies. They found no weapons. The gunmen came back with a ring and a watch and a jeweled comb they had taken from the girl.

Cameron attacked the machine with an intense, trembling savagery of movement—as if it had been a substitute for Lord. After a few moments, however, a sudden consuming interest seemed to swallow his wrath. His lean face became intent, absorbed. His fingers were steady again, very quick and skillful. Soon he was whistling with his teeth, so softly that Lord seemed not to hear.

I tried to help him, ineffectually. The machine baffled me utterly. Obviously, it had turned ordinary stone and soil into a very strong quick-setting concrete, a feat which seemed remarkable enough. There was, however, something more astonishing.

The machine had evidently used a great deal of electrical power. Electric motors drove the tracks and moved the bucket; heavy busbars ran into the cylinder where soil became cement. Strangely, however, I couldn't find the source of that power. There was no lead-in cable, no space for batteries, no possible receiver for broadcast power, certainly nothing bulky enough to be any kind of fission-engine. Yet there was current—as a painful shock convinced me. So far as I could determine, it just appeared spontaneously in the circuits.

Bewildered—shaken, too, by that unexpected shock—I stood back to watch. Working with such an eager-faced absorption that I didn't dare to question him, Cameron was studying a bit of the wiring which, for no reason that I could see, was formed into a double coil of oddly twisted turns. His absently whistled notes turned gay.

Lord had posted his two gunmen on either side of the ravine, with orders to shoot any stranger at sight. He himself stood warily on the bank of the little gorge, watching Cameron. When Doyle had completed his call to the life-craft, Lord sent him and me to search the house.

"Look for weapons," he rapped. "Find out all you can, for our report to Hudd. Make it quick." His nasal voice was shrill with dread. "When the craft comes, we're getting out of here."

Doyle tramped in bitter silence until we were out of earshot, and then let flow a savage stream of low-voiced military profanity.

"That unprintable fool!" he finished. "Those poor farmers could have told us all we want to know, in five minutes—but that blood-thirsty fool had to butcher them!"

He kicked angrily at a pebble.

"I'm sorry about your friend Cameron." He gave me a sympathetic look. "Lord doesn't like him. You know the sort of report he'll make. Cameron's done for. He was just too independent."

VI

Rory Doyle and I came up to the dwelling. The long, low building seemed all of one piece, a solid part of the hillside. It was apparently made of the same soil-concrete as the dam—differently colored in different rooms, the walls smooth and warm to the touch.

The furnishings gave an effect of sturdy and comfortable simplicity. The whole house seemed to tell of a warm, free, spacious sort of life—a cold shadow fell across it, when I thought of its builders and owners, lying slaughtered in the gully.

Hastily, we explored the inviting living room, the workshop where a handsome table stood half-finished in a clutter of plastic dust and shavings, the big kitchen fitted with shining gadgets to manufacture dishes and synthetic staples on the spot, the cold locker stored with a rich abundance of frozen foods.

We found no identifiable weapons. Nor any good reason, that I could see, why men had fled the cities and abandoned their old way of life. Instead, it was another mystery that we found.

"They must have been very nearly self-sufficient." Peering about the silent rooms, Doyle tried to reconstruct the lives of the murdered couple. "I think they built and furnished this house, with their own hands—everything has the look of good, careful workmanship; they were adding a new room, which isn't roofed yet. Evidently they grew or manufactured their own food. That little machine in the shed is grinding a hopperful of leaves and sticks into something like cloth, very beautiful and strong. All these gadgets must use a lot of power."

His puzzled eyes came back to my face.

"But where does the power come from?"

I had to shake my head.

"The house isn't wired," I told him. "Each gadget seems to generate its own current—without any batteries or generator or anything else that makes sense to me. Just like that machine at the dam."

On a table in the living room we found a telephone instrument, cradled on a little black plastic box that had no wires attached. Doyle picked it up impulsively, then reluctantly set it back again.

"We could call," he said. "Perhaps we could just ask what we want to know. But Mr. Lord doesn't want it done that way."

We heard the roar of jets, then, and hurried back to the ravine. Doyle had brought a blanket from the house, which he spread decently over the two bodies. Sinking slowly upon an inverted mushroom of blue electric fire, the life-craft landed a hundred yards below the dam. Scorched weeds smoldered about the bright fins that held it upright.

On the bank of the little gorge, Lord turned from watching Cameron, to question Doyle. But when Doyle merely shook his head, with an empty-handed shrug, Lord went back to shout at Cameron:

On the double, now. Time to go. Let's see what you've got."

Cameron came up out of the ravine, carrying something in his hand. It was a piece of thick copper wire, shaped into a double coil of oddly-shaped loops at odd-seeming angles and held in shape with a transparent plastic rod.

"This is it," he said.

The hushed elation of his low voice told more than his words. I stared at him—for something, I thought, had somehow transformed him. His emaciated body had grown proudly straight. His hollowed face was smiling, illuminated with a stern joy which almost frightened me.

"Well?" Lord retreated as if afraid of Cameron's blue eyes. His sleek black head made a quick nod, to bring his two gunmen back from the ends of the unfinished dam. "What is it?"

Cameron held up that bit of wire on the plastic rod, with both his hands. His face had a look of solemn awe—as if the thing in his hands had been, perhaps, some unique and long-sought bit of priceless, ancient art.

"Speak up," Lord rapped nervously.

Cameron looked up at Lord again, with no awe at all. His blue eyes showed a sudden glint of ironic amusement. Yet still he held that bit of wire as if it were a precious thing.

"It's what we've all been looking for." Cameron's voice held the quick ring of triumph. "The reason men abandoned Fort America. Why they deserted the cities. What happened to the Directorate, and to Tyler."

Cameron's eyes turned sardonic.

"It's also what is going to happen to the task force," he added softly. "To Mr. Julian Hudd. And even to you, Mr. Lord."

Lord's sleepy yellow eyes slitted dangerously.

"I'll tolerate no further insubordination," he snapped savagely. "Tell me what you've got."

Cameron turned to Doyle and me. Angrily, Lord hauled out his automatic, and then slowly thrust it back again. I suppose that even he could see the folly of extinguishing the source of information. Perhaps he was a little awed by Cameron.

But he still intended, I knew, to get his revenge.

Cameron ignored his sullenly boiling fury.

"Chad, you remember that little gadget we called an induction furnace? Well, we were on the right track—if I hadn't been afraid of blowing up the *Great Director*. And this is the thing we were looking for."

Generously, he gave me far too much credit. I had known, of course, that the device was something more than a furnace—for it made atomic changes in the metal samples we fused, while it somehow generated power. That much I had known, and held my tongue about it. But I had really understood neither his effort nor his goal.

From me, Cameron turned impulsively to Doyle.

"Captain, may I have a word with you?"

"Of course." Doyle raised his red brows in puzzlement. "What about?"

"This." Cameron lifted the thing in his hands. "I've always admired you, Captain. I trust you now." He beckoned with his head, toward the end of the dam. "Let me tell you what this things means to you—and all of us." He glanced aside at the simmering, suspicious little Squaredealer, adding: "Listen for just ten minutes, Captain, and you'll be free of Lord and his sort."

Confusedly, Doyle shook his head.

"Careful, Cameron." I knew he was no friend of Lord's, yet his voice was shocked. "Watch yourself. You sound like treason."

Cameron gave him a brief, sardonic grin.

"If there is such a thing, any longer." His low voice turned grave again. "Though I imagine that this little device has repealed a lot of the old laws." He glanced at the twisted wire, and regretfully back to Doyle. "I wish you'd listen, Rory. But I know how you feel. I'll save your life if I can."

Little Lord was quivering with white-lipped fury. His hand hovered close to his gun. Yet caution or curiosity must have tempered his wrath, for he gestured sharply to halt his black-clad gunmen.

"Explain this strange behavior, Cameron," he snapped. "Before I have to shoot you down."

Cameron turned back to him.

"No, I don't think you'll do that, Mr. Lord," he murmured very softly. "Because you're an anachronism, now, along with the dinosaur and the atom bomb. Technological advancement has passed you by."

Lord's narrow, sallow face turned dark. Still, however, he seemed to want the secret of that piece of twisted wire more than he wanted Cameron's life. He nodded furtively to his gunmen, who began edging aside to

Cameron's right and left. "What's that gadget?" he snarled. Cameron had turned to me.

"You'll come with me, won't you, Chad?" His low voice had a tremor of anxious appeal. "There's a job we have to do, with this." He moved the little device. "It's not too dangerous—if we're lucky. I need you, Chad."

I wanted to go with him—wherever he was going. But I could see the two bleak-faced men moving warily to get behind him, I could see Lord's wolfish snarl and the cold menace of his yellow eyes, I could remember the SBI and all the cruel art of intensive interrogation. Somehow, that bit of wire and plastic had made Cameron seem a bolder and bigger man, but still I hadn't felt the power of it. Miserably, I shook my head.

"That's all right, Chad." He gave me a brief, cheering grin. "Perhaps I'll have a better chance alone. I'll do my best to save you."

"You, stand still!" Lord shouted, and sharply ordered his gunmen: "Shoot for the knees, if he tries anything."

Cameron turned back to him, soberly. "Better call them off, Mr. Lord." Something in his low voice sent a shiver up my spine. "It's time for you to think of your own skin, now. Because it's clear that you made error when you butchered that man and girl. You aren't safe here—or anywhere."

The little Squaredealer must have heard that something in Cameron's voice, for his sallow face turned a sickly yellow-gray. His perspiring arm gestured again, uneasily, to hold his gunmen back. He blinked apprehensively.

"I'll be back," Cameron said. "But I advise you not to follow."

He dropped into the ravine, up beyond the dam.

Lord hesitated for a long second, pale and breathless. "Get after him," he screamed at last. "Shoot him in the legs."

He didn't lead the pursuit, however, and his men weren't eager. That same something in Cameron's voice must have made them doubt that it was really wise to follow. They ran uncertainly along the rim of the little gorge, firing a few wild shots.

Ahead of them, something flashed. Its terrible brightness made us duck and shield our eyes, even in the full daylight. The detonation came instantly—a single, terrific report. A green tree, beside the ravine, shattered into smoking, whistling fragments.

Lord and his two men followed no farther. As soon as the burning splinters stopped falling, they scrambled up off their faces and hastily retired.

"Unprintable leather merchant!" gasped the little Squaredealer. "He'll regret this." He made a rather fearful gesture toward the life-craft. "On board!" he shouted. "We're getting out of here."

VII

We tumbled through the valves, and Lord ordered Captain Doyle to blast away at full thrust. Before Doyle could reach his bridge, however, the signal officer shouted down the ladder-well:

"Captain Doyle! I've just got contact with the *Great Director*. Mr. Hudd is on the screen. He wants a full report, at once, sir."

The earth's intervening mass had cut off microwave transmission since we dropped over the bulge of it before we landed; now, however, the planet's rotation had brought the flagship back above the horizon. We climbed hurriedly into the little television room.

Gigantic on the screen, Hudd boomed his question:

"What's the story, Lord?"

"A crisis, Mr. Hudd!" Lord looked damp with sweat, and his voice turned shrill. "We're in danger. I request permission to blast off at once, and make our full report at space."

"What's the crisis?"

Lord gulped uncomfortably. "Your smart feather merchant got away."

Hudd's great, blue-jowled face was furrowed with sudden concern.

"Then I'll take your full report, Mr. Lord," he said decisively. "Right now."

"But Cameron has a weapon," Lord protested desperately. "Something that strikes like lightning—"

"Then the entire task force may be in peril," Hudd cut in. "Now let's have it—at once."

Lord talked rapidly, while sweat burst out in great bright drops on his narrow face and soaked dark blotches into his uniform. Hudd listened gravely, now and then turning to Doyle or me with a sharp question.

It was Doyle who told him how Lord and the two guards had shot the couple named Hawkins. Hudd's heavy, sagging jaw hardened at the news. When the report was finished, he must have started his habitual nervous drumming—his hands were hidden below the screen, but the speaker brought a worried rapping.

"You made two blunders." His small, troubled eyes peered accusingly at Lord. "You let Cameron get away with the vital information I sent you for. And you killed those people before they had a chance to talk. I'm afraid you have gravely compromised our objectives, Victor—and your own future."

All his swagger gone, Lord twisted and cringed before the steady eyes of Hudd. Still perspiring, he seemed to fawn and cower like a punished dog, as the loud, aggressive voice of his master continued:

"We must take bold, immediate action, Victor, to restore the situation."

"Right, Mr. Hudd," Lord said eagerly. "Shall we blast off, now?"

"You will remain where you are," Hudd said. "Get in touch with the inhabitants, if you can. Offer apologies and compensation for the killing. Stall for time. Find out all you can about the weapons, the military establishment, and the government of the inhabitants." Lord gulped uneasily, nodding.

"Post a reward for Cameron." Hudd's big mouth set hard. "My mistake, to trust him. Get hold of him. Use extreme interrogation. Make him talk, then liquidate him. He has gone too far."

Hudd shook his head regretfully.

"Too bad," he added. "I always liked him."

I felt cold and ill. Hudd's loud words had struck me like numbing blows. That harsh command was no surprise to me, but it brought me a dull sickness of regret, because I had failed Cameron when he asked me to go with him.

Lord was protesting again:

"Mr. Hudd, I think we'll be attacked—"

"I'll support you," Hudd assured him, and turned to speak to his signal officer: "Change the scramble code—we don't know who is trying to listen."

The unseen officer on the flagship droned out a code number, repeating each digit. Our officer droned it back. The screen darkened, flickered. Then the image of Hudd came back, huge and resolute, declaring:

"Whatever happens, Victor, I intend to restore the Directorate. I am taking prompt action, to that end. The *Valley Forge* and the *Hiroshima* are proceeding to the moon. They will land a new garrison, with the necessary repairs to bring Fort America back into effectiveness. The *Yorktown*, the *Rio Plata* and the *Leningrad* will stand by, spaced on an orbit ten thousand miles from the earth, to relay communications and bombard any targets we discover.

"With the *Great Director*, I'm coming to earth."

Lord licked his thin, colorless lips.

"You're too daring, Mr. Hudd," he protested shrilly.

"It took audacity to establish the Directorate." The great boom of Hudd's voice in the speaker visibly startled Lord. "It's worth audacity to restore it. I'm coming, at full thrust, to take personal command."

Lord remained aboard the life-craft that night. His uneasy fancy must have dwelt upon the fused metal we had found beside that skeleton in the weeds and the sudden bolt that struck that tree as Cameron fled. Perhaps he thought of the two still bodies in the gully; no doubt he peopled the dark valley with vengeful enemies.

My own imagination, I know, was busy enough. Staring out into the thickening night, I felt myself die helpless spectator of stupendous forces sweeping grandly toward collision.

On one side, there was the Atomic Age itself, expressed in the rekindled might of Fort America, in the fine discipline of the task force, in sleek guided missiles, in the determined sagacity of Mr. Julian Hudd.

On the other side, there was that unknown power that had swept the old garrison from the moon and driven men from the cities and destroyed the Directorate. All I had seen of it was a piece of twisted wire, a blasted tree, and the change in Jim Cameron. But that was enough—I waited for the fireworks.

After dark, Captain Doyle volunteered to go back to the house.

"Mr. Hudd wants us to get in touch with the inhabitants," he reminded Lord. "And we saw some kind of telephone." With evident reluctance, Lord agreed.

"If you contact anybody, call for the government," he ordered. "Offer a reward for Cameron." His sleepy eyes glittered cunningly. "If anybody mentions those two dead peasants, we're holding them—alive—for Cameron's return."

Doyle went down through the valves, accompanied by the signal officer to help him work the strange radiophone. They were lost in the pale moonlight among the young apple trees. They didn't come back.

After an hour, Lord sent me after them, with one of his gunmen for escort. Soft lights came on of themselves, when I opened the door. I tried to call Doyle's name, and found that my voice had gone to a grating whisper. Walking through the silent rooms, we found nobody.

The little radiophone, oddly, was also gone. At midnight, Hudd called again. At the news of Doyle's apparent desertion, he muttered forebodingly:

"It's something pretty sinister, that takes so true a man." The interstellar cruiser landed, just at dawn. The thunder of it woke me out of a nodding doze. Moving groggily to a port, I saw a glare that burned all color out of the valley, so that everything was black or blinding white. I had to cover my smarting eyes. The wind rocked the life-craft on its stabilizers, and the earth shuddered.

When the thunder ceased and that cruel light was gone, I saw the cruiser standing two miles down the valley. Dark smoke billowed up about the base of it from the green woods burning. Its tall peak, towering out of the night in the valley, was already incandescent with sunlight.

Immensely high, the great flat turrets swung with ominous deliberation. The huge bright tubes of rifles and launchers lifted out of their housings, implacably purposeful. Hudd called again, looking as massively indomitable as his flagship.

"Have you met the inhabitants, Mr. Lord?"

"Not yet, Mr. Hudd." Relieved by the great ship's coming, Lord had his swagger back.

"Then you soon will," Hudd told him. "Our lookout reports a flying vehicle, approaching you now. Make contact, and report immediately."

We all turned to the ports, in time to see the red glint of sunlight on the rotor of a small helicopter. It landed among the young apple trees. Three people got out. One of them began waving a bit of white cloth. With a shock of dismay, I recognized Jim Cameron.

VIII

The three walked slowly down toward us across the young orchard. The other two paused by the dam, one of them bending to look at the bodies under the blanket. Cameron came on halfway to us, before he stopped and stood waiting.

Watching through a port in the signal room, Lord nervously wet his lips. Beneath a puzzled unease, his beady eyes had a glare of yellow elation. He sent me out to find what Cameron wanted.

Grinning with pleasure to see me, Cameron put down the stick with his handkerchief tied to it. Fatigue had drawn his stubbled face and smudged blue shadows under his eyes.

"Jim, you shouldn't have come back." I pitched my voice too low for Lord's gunmen, covering us from the valve. "Because you made a fool of Lord, when you got away. He'll never forgive that. He's got Hudd's permission to liquidate you."

He grinned wearily, glancing at the two behind him.

"You can tell Mr. Lord that he's in no position to liquidate anybody. On the contrary—these neighbors of the Hawkins couple have come to arraign him and his guard for the murder."

I must have gasped with astonishment.

"I'm afraid Lord will be unreasonable." He frowned, regretfully. "I came along to try to prevent any needless destruction. There's not much use for Lord to resist, and no need for others to be killed. Better tell him that."

Back aboard the life-craft, I told Lord what the strangers wanted. His pale, peering eyes rounded with wonderment, then narrowed to hard yellow slits. He glared malevolently out at Cameron.

"I suppose that damned feather merchant is the chief witness? Well, I'll fix the lot of them!" He shouted up the ladder-well to the astrogator, now acting as signal officer, "Get me Mr. Hudd!"

I followed him into the narrow signal room.

"It's your pet civilian," he shouted bitterly when Hudd's face appeared huge and interrogative on the screen. "And a couple of yokels with some nonsense about arresting me for murder."

"So?" Thoughtfully Hudd rubbed his blue, multiple chin. "I want to talk to them. Offer them all three safe-conduct to come aboard. Tell them I'll discuss compensation for the killing. You can bring them on the life-craft, Mr. Lord."

The negotiations which ensued were somewhat involved. I went back and forth, between Lord and Cameron. Cameron returned to consult with the watchful two by the ravine. Hudd and Lord conferred by television, Lord's nasal voice rising steadily with ill-concealed anger, Hudd frowning with increasing concern.

"I'd accept Mr. Hudd's safe-conduct, myself," Cameron told me. "But the Enlows don't want to trust him. They are willing to talk to Mr. Hudd, but he'll have to come out here."

With a surprising boldness, Hudd agreed to do that.

"But, Mr. Hudd!" Lord protested sharply. "We can't treat with them—two savages and a mutineering feather merchant. Think of your own safety. Why not let us take off, sir, and then wipe them out with a salvo of radio-toxin shells from the cruiser?"

Hudd shook his head stubbornly.

"I'm coming over, Victor, to handle this myself." His red, worried eyes turned to me. "Chad, you go back and tell Jim Cameron to wait till I get there." Lord's eyes narrowed suspiciously.

"Don't you give me up, Hudd." His angry nasal voice was hard and dangerous. "If you do, you're also giving up your New Directorate."

"I know that," Hudd assured him blandly. "You can trust me, Victor."

Lord dismissed me, with a curt, sullen nod. I went back across the burned grass to tell Cameron that Hudd was coming.

"He's smart." Cameron nodded approvingly. "Maybe he can save his neck." He took up the white flag again. "Now we had better rejoin the Enlows," he said. "They might misunderstand."

We walked back to the people waiting at the dam. I thought of Lord's gunmen crouching in the lock behind us, and the skin on my back crawled uneasily.

The two were a man and a young woman. They were both tanned, lean, sturdy; dark hair and gray level eyes showed a family likeness. Tight with the shock of what they had seen under the blanket, their faces were hard with purpose. "Are they coming out?" The man's quiet voice was taut as his gaunt face.

"Not yet." Cameron was urgently persuasive. "But please give me a chance to tell Mr. Hudd about the equalizer. I think he's smart enough to listen."

The man nodded his weather-beaten head. I saw that he carried what looked like a bulky flare-pistol. His deep-set angry eyes peered up at the enormous flagship, not at all afraid.

"If he wants to listen," he agreed. "But we're going to get the killers."

"I'll try to get Mr. Hudd to give them up," Cameron promised, and then he introduced me. "Chad Barstow. A likely candidate for the Brotherhood, as soon as he learns to use the equalizer."

The girl wore a radiophone, much like the one we had seen in the house—it must have been such units that made those scrambled signals we had heard. The little plastic case was snapped to her belt, the headset over her lustrous hair. She had been listening to that, but now she looked at me, her eyes widening.

"Yes, he's Dane Barstow's son." Seeing her troubled glance toward the gully, Cameron added quickly, "He had nothing to do with that."

She gave me a strong handclasp.

"Jane Enlow," Cameron said. "Her father, Frank Enlow."

The gaunt man gripped my hand silently, but his angry eyes flashed back to the life-craft and the cruiser.

"Before the equalizer," Cameron told him, "Mr. Enlow was a janitor in Tyler's Squaredeal Hall. He was just telling me about the Director's last days. After the equalizer, he smuggled Tyler out through the mob that was shouting for him under the balcony. Tyler lived for years in Mr. Enlow's house over the ridge, yonder, writing a history—trying to justify his career."

"A nasty old man!" Jane Enlow pouted. "He wouldn't learn the equalizer. Dad had to take care of him."

High up on the bright side of the cruiser, blue fire spurted. Frank Enlow crouched toward the ravine, swinging up his pistol-like device. Cameron called out, hastily:

"Don't shoot—that's probably Mr. Hudd."

As the gaunt man relaxed, I studied his weapon with a shocked fascination. It looked like a miniature guided missile launcher, rather than a gun. It seemed fantastically small, yet the lank man had a strangely confident air of facing the cruiser's weapons on even terms.

The girl was listening again to her radiophone. She twisted knobs on the case at her belt, and finally shook her dark head.

"Nothing." Her voice was gloomy. "They're taking too long."

Hudd's life-craft approached us swiftly, a bright projectile floating nearly upright on a jet of screaming fire. It crossed the burning forest to land near the other craft. The valves slammed open as soon as the dust had cleared, and Hudd's aide jumped out.

The hard-bitten commander darted across the blasted ground and hurried up to us. He seemed upset by Hudd's decision. First he wanted

Cameron and the Enlows to come aboard the life-craft to talk; then he wanted to send a bodyguard with Hudd; finally he warned that a general bombardment of the surrounding country would begin at once, if anything happened to Hudd.

"We've come for the killers," the lean man informed him gravely. "Since Mr. Cameron has taken the Brotherhood oath, the three of us form a competent court. We're bound to listen to any evidence that Mr. Hudd can offer. He will not be harmed, unless he tries to interfere."

Outraged, the commander went back. Immediately Mr. Julian Hudd climbed down between the bright fins. He came out of the burned area at a painful, heavy run. Gasping for breath, he waddled up to the dam. "Well, Jim!"

He grinned at Cameron, shook hands with the rawboned man, gave the girl a bow of open admiration. His small, shrewd eyes studied the unfinished dam and the abandoned machine in the gully.

"The incident here was most regrettable." Hudd's voice was a chesty, confident rumble. "I'll see that adequate compensation is paid. Personally. You people needn't concern yourselves any further."

His keen bloodshot eyes studied the gaunt man. "Now, I want to take up something more important. I've been trying to get in touch with your government." His broad, blue-tinged face was still a genial mask, but his loud voice turned imperious. "I demand that your government—" The lank man's voice was very quiet, yet the cold ring of it made Hudd stop to listen.

"We have no government," said Frank Enlow.

Hudd puffed out his cheeks, slowly turning red with anger.

"That's the surprising fact, Mr. Hudd," Cameron assured him gravely. "You'll have to get used to it. When the equalizer appeared, nations became extinct."

Ignoring him, Hudd glared at the lank man.

"You must have some organization."

"Only the Brotherhood," Enlow said. "It has no power to surrender anybody to you, because membership is voluntary."

Hudd's red eyes blinked, skeptical and defiant.

"Get in touch with this Brotherhood." His voice was rasping, arrogant. "Have them send a responsible agent. Have him here by noon, local time." He paused, ominously. "Otherwise, the task force and Fort America will open fire, at every likely target we can find."

Cameron made a startled gesture, as if to catch his arm.

"Please, Mr. Hudd," he protested sharply. "Wait until you know what you're doing."

Hudd kept his savage little eyes on Enlow.

"The young lady, I see, has a radiophone." His voice was loud and ominous. "You had better start calling this Brotherhood—"

"We came here for another purpose." The lank man met his truculent gaze, unimpressed. "We've come for the killers."

Hudd's bluish face swelled again with anger.

"Nonsense!" he shouted. "Mr. Lord is my second in command. He was acting under orders. I assume the responsibility. I'll pay for any unjust damage, but I refuse to subject him to humiliation."

The lean man listened to that, and nodded his rawboned head, and stalked away silently toward the ravine. Cameron hurried after him, visibly alarmed.

"The killers can wait," he called urgently. "Doyle must be trying. Mr. Hudd doesn't understand the equalizer. Please give me time to tell him about it."

The lank man turned back, reluctantly.

"If he wants to listen," he agreed. "We'll wait half an hour."

With a question on his face, Cameron turned to Hudd.

"All right, Jim," Hudd gasped, explosively. "I want to know all about this equalizer, anyhow." His red angry eyes went back to the gaunt man. "But my ships and the fort will open fire at noon."

IX

Hudd sat down on a hummock of grass, breathing hard with the effort of moving his clumsy bulk. His massive shoulders bunched with bold defiance. Only the quick movements of his eyes betrayed the intense and desperate working of his mind—they were the eyes of a fighting animal, fearful, yet audacious and altogether ruthless.

"Now!" he gasped. "This equalizer?"

Cameron squatted on his heels, facing Hudd. Behind us, as he talked, the sun rose higher. The flat green valley lay motionless under its hot light, and a pungent blue haze settled about us from the green forest burning.

"I heard the story last night. The beginning of the equalizer takes us back nearly twenty years." Cameron's tired, dark-smudged eyes came for a moment to me. "To your own father, Chad." His haggard and yet animated eyes went back to Hudd. "I think you remember Dane Barstow?"

"The traitor?" rumbled Hudd. "He died, I believe, in the labor camps."

"But he didn't," Cameron said. "Because Tyler learned that he was on the trail of something remarkable, and had him taken from the camps to a solitary cell at Fort America. The SBI went to work on him there, with extreme interrogation."

As Cameron glanced at me again, I noticed a strange thing. The story and the memory of my father's misfortunes brought me a bitter resentment, but now I noticed that all the old pain and hatred was gone from Cameron's face. Something had swept away his old saturnine reserve. He seemed oddly friendly even to Hudd.

"Finally," he said, "Barstow talked. He told what he had done and admitted all he had hoped to do. He even agreed to complete his interrupted work."

I knelt down to listen.

"Though he was half-blind and crippled from the extreme treatment, and sometimes out of his head, they took pretty drastic precautions. They kept him locked in that steel cell on the moon—one of those we saw there, I imagine, Chad.

Two guards were always with him. He was allowed paper and pencil, but no other equipment. If he wanted calculations made, or any experiments tried, such things were done for him by Atomic Service engineers."

Cameron briefly smiled, as if he shared my pride.

"Yes, Chad, your old man was all right. Working under such difficult conditions, shattered as he was, he charted a new science and created a new technology. And then—when we had been out at space about two years with the task force—he overturned the Directorate."

Hudd's bold eyes had drifted back to the sun-browned girl—who was listening, not to Cameron, but anxiously to the little portable radiophone. Now he started ponderously at Cameron's last words, to gasp for his breath and wheeze incredulously:

"How could he do that?"

"Not so hard, with the equalizer." Cameron grinned at Hudd's blinking, startled stare. "From his cell on the moon, Barstow smashed the Directorate. He didn't need any weapons or equipment. All he had to do was tell his jailors what he had discovered."

Hudd made a hollow, croaking sound. "How's that?"

"The news of the equalizer spread from one man to another," Cameron said. "Those same engineers who had been assigned to get the invention from him set up a little illicit transmitter and beamed the details back to earth with equalizer power, on every frequency they could get through the ionosphere.

"That finished the Directorate."

Hudd picked up a small red pebble and began nervously tapping the sod with it, as he had drummed on his desk with the little gold head of Tyler. His furtive eyes flashed to the lean man's weapon, and back to Cameron's face.

"That's too much!" His voice was harshly unbelieving. "No mere fact of science could defeat Fort America—much less wreck the Squaredeal Machine."

"Barstow's equalizer did," Cameron said. "Perhaps because the old technology of the Atomic Age had already reached the breaking point of over-complexity and super-centralization. When Barstow created this new technology, there was a natural swing to the opposite extreme—to simplicity, individualism, and complete personal freedom."

"So?" Hudd thumped the sod with his pebble, scowling at Cameron. "Just how does it work, this equalizer?"

Cameron glanced doubtfully at Frank Enlow.

"Tell him," the gaunt man said. "Barstow wanted every man to know. Generally it has a good effect." He glanced at a watch on his brown wrist. "But hurry—your time is running out."

Hudd's great shoulders lifted with aggression.

"So is yours," he snapped. "I'm willing to listen, but my men won't hear. I'm not yielding anything. This Brotherhood had better throw the towel in, by noon."

"Tell him," Enlow repeated.

Cameron launched into his explanation. His fatigue seemed forgotten, and some inner excitement made his haggard face almost vivacious.

"The old atomic reactor, you know, was an enormously clumsy and wasteful and dangerous way of doing extremely simple things. Pure energy exists in the atom, and that is what we want. But the old atomic plants used intractable and inadequate processes to change kinetic and electrical and binding energy into heat, and then required expensive and inefficient machinery to turn a little of that heat back into electricity.

"Even with all its elaborate complexity, the reactor plants could tap only a little of the binding energy which holds electrons and protons and neutrons together into atoms. The mass energy of the particles themselves—really nearly all the actual energy of the atom—it couldn't even reach.

"Barstow's dream—like my own—was merely a simple way of doing a simple thing. Material energy exists, as Einstein demonstrated. Barstow dreamed of a simple way to let it flow. The equalizer is his dream, realized."

I couldn't help the breathless interruption:

"That piece of wire?"

"Just a solenoid." Cameron nodded. "But wound in a certain way, not helically, so that its field slightly alters the co-ordinates of space and slightly changes the interaction of mass and energy. The atomic particles of the solenoid are equalized, as your father termed the process. The converted energy appears as direct current in the wire.

"The fact is simple—even though the tensors of a new geometry are

54

required to describe the solenoid field. That apparent complexity is more in our awkward description, however, than in the vital fact. The actual specifications of the equalizer can be memorized in five minutes."

Cameron's intent, elated eyes looked aside at me.

"The safety-feature is what threw us, Chad, with our induction furnace experiments," he told me. "Our gadget annihilated matter—degenerating iron atoms into sodium—and produced electric current. The increased output intensified the conversion field, and the intensified field increased the output. An excellent arrangement, if you want a matter-bomb—but highly unsafe for a power plant.

"Your father solved that problem, Chad—very simply, too. Just a secondary solenoid, in series with the primary, which develops an opposing voltage as the equalizing field expands. It gives you a safe, guaranteed maximum voltage—the precise value determined by the way it's wound."

Hudd's deep-sunken eyes blinked skeptically.

"You mean, you can generate electricity?" he rasped. "With just a coil of wire?"

"And a few stray ions to excite it," Cameron told him. "A pound of copper solenoid would drive the cruiser, yonder, out to the Dark Star. Or iron, or silver—the metal doesn't matter; it's only the exact shape and alignment and spacing of the turns of wire."

Hudd shook his head, in massive unbelief.

"Perpetual motion!" he scoffed.

"Almost." Cameron grinned. "Equalized mass is converted into electrical energy, according to the Einstein equation. The solenoid wastes away— but slowly. One pound of solenoid will generate ten billion kilowatt hours of electricity."

"If it's all that simple," Hudd objected shrewdly, "somebody would have stumbled on it, by accident."

"Very likely, men did," Cameron agreed. "Not many—the shape of the coils is not one you would want for anything else; and the turns must be very exactly formed and aligned, or else the regenerative effect is damped out. The few who did it must have been instantly electrocuted—because they didn't also stumble on Barstow's safety-winding."

"I'll believe it when I see it," muttered Hudd. Cameron pointed up the edge of the ravine, to a shattered tree-stump.

"Mr. Lord wanted a demonstration, yesterday," he said. "I straightened part of the safety-coil on a small power unit from that machine, to step up the voltage, and tossed it into a green tree yonder."

"A rather reckless thing to do," commented the lean man. Hudd said nothing. His black-haired, ham-sized hand tossed the red pebble, aimlessly, and caught it again. His troubled eyes peered at the stump, at the gaunt man's weapon, at the enormous tower of the *Great Director.*

"You have ten minutes to give up the killer, Mr. Hudd," drawled Frank Enlow. "Otherwise you may see a better demonstration."

Hudd snorted: a blast of defiance. "I'll wait for it," he gasped. "You can't bluff me." A shadow came over Cameron's face. When his tired eyes closed for a moment, I saw the blue stains under them. He sat back on his heels, his emaciated body sagging as if from a punishing blow.

"It's no bluff, Mr. Hudd." He paused as if to gather himself for a weary and yet vehement protest. "You just don't grasp what the equalizer means. It ended the Atomic Age. The Directorate was part of that lost era. You can't hope to restore it, now, any more than you could revive a fossil tyrannosaur. Perhaps you can cause some needless bloodshed and death."

Hudd's wide mouth hardened with an unconvinced hostility.

"Tyler spilt plenty of blood, building the first Directorate," he commented coldly. "I may have to pay the same price again, but I expect to win. Perhaps Tyler's garrisons mutinied when they heard about this equalizer. My men won't hear about it."

"It wasn't mutiny, Mr. Hudd," Cameron insisted. "There was no fighting. The Directorate wasn't overthrown—it simply ceased to exist. When the equalizer appeared, there was no more reason for Fort America than there is for arrow-makers. The officers recognized that, as well as the men. The garrison just packed up and came home."

"Home to what?" Hudd challenged him. "The people here were already deserting the cities, leaving nearly everything they owned. There must have been something else wrong—perhaps some biotoxin loose—to cause such panic."

"You still don't get it." Cameron shook his head with a tired impatience. "The equalizer freed the city-dwellers, just as it did the garrison. Because most people didn't live in cities by choice. They were huddled into them by the old division of labor—specialized cogs in a social machine grown ruinously complex.

"The equalizer abolished the division of labor—at least in military technology. Every man with a piece of wire became a complete military specialist, competent to defend himself. Using the new control of atomic and molecular processes, he could also provide for nearly all his own, ordinary wants. Complexity was replaced with stark simplicity.

"Take the couple who lived here." He nodded regretfully at the empty house behind us. "They built their own home, made their own food and clothing. They were setting up this dam, when they were murdered, to save their own land from erosion. They weren't slaves of any single skill, or prisoners of any class. They had no reason to hate or fear their neighbors—until we came along."

Hudd blinked, still doubtful.

"Why were the cities so utterly abandoned?" he questioned. "Why was all that money left behind, as Lord reports? Why were signs posted, warning people out?"

Cameron glanced up at the great frowning ship.

"The cities were a product of the old technology, and they died with it," he argued doggedly. "The day of the equalizer, workers walked out and services stopped. There was no food, no power, no water, no sewage disposal. City life was impossible, without division of labor.

"As for money, paper dollars were merely shares in the extinct Atomic Age. Metal was still useful—but the equalizer must have made it easier to refine new metal than to wreck the cities. About the danger—I forgot to ask."

He turned inquiringly to Frank Enlow. "Criminals," the lean man drawled. "A few men and women too stupid or too vicious to use the equalizer. They never left the cities. They stayed hidden, trying to exist by raiding and looting. They used the old military weapons. A few of them became very cunning and dangerous. The signs were posted during our campaigns to hunt them out."

"Don't you have worse criminals?" Hudd demanded shrewdly. "Those who do use the equalizer?" Enlow shook his head.

"The users of the equalizer have very little economic reason for crime," he said. "And people armed with it aren't very likely victims. It's simply because crime has become so rare that the Hawkinses weren't alert."

Hudd's eyes dwelt on the lean man's weapon. "This Brotherhood?" he asked shrewdly. "If it isn't a government—what is it?"

"A voluntary substitute." The gaunt man glanced at me. "Tour father's last great project, Mr. Barstow. After he got back his health, he spent the rest of his years organizing the Brotherhood."

"Just what does it do?"

"Runs schools and libraries and hospitals," Enlow told him. "Supports laboratories. Builds irrigation projects. Anything for the public good. It operates the post office and issues money against metal deposits."

Hudd nodded triumphantly. "If it can do all that, it can surrender to me."

"The Brotherhood has no authority." Enlow shook his head, rawboned and resolute. "People may join or leave it, as they please. It is supported by voluntary contributions, and the elected officers serve without pay. They can't surrender, Mr. Hudd—but they can organize the common defense."

"If you have no law," Hudd demanded shrewdly, "then why do you want Mr. Lord?"

Enlow stared back at him, brown and lean and angry. "In the Brotherhood, we enter a voluntary agreement to respect and defend the rights of others. I think your Mr. Lord has proved himself a public menace."

Hudd pulled absently at his thick lower lip.

"If you've got no government," his harsh voice came, "then I think you've got a madhouse—and all the madmen armed with insane weapons."

Enlow shook his dark head with a lean dignity.

"You're living under a false philosophy, Mr. Hudd. You believe that men are evil, that they have to be driven. Fortunately, that philosophy is mistaken—because men with equalizers can't be driven."

As Hudd made another derisive snort, Enlow looked at his watch.

"Unfortunately, a few men are bad," he added gently. "Your time is up. We want those killers."

Cameron turned back to Hudd, importunately.

"Why don't you give them up?" he urged. "And let me tell your men about the equalizer?"

"I will not." Hudd came laboriously to his feet, red and gasping from the effort. "I still think you'd have a hard time to silence Fort America—with all your equalizers. And my ultimatum still expires at noon."

Having delivered that ominous blast, Hudd turned back to Jane Enlow. She had been listening to her radiophone, absorbed. Now, as she became aware of Hudd's hungry eyes, she started, a rich color darkened her tan. Hudd made her a bow, ponderously graceful, in the manner he must have learned while he was Tyler's Director-General of Europe.

"I deeply regret the awkward circumstances of this first meeting, Miss Enlow." He smiled with a genial admiration. "But I hope soon to offer you an introduction to the best society of the New Directorate."

Flushing deeply, she said nothing.

Hudd bowed again. After a moment, he stalked heavily back toward his life-craft.

Little Victor Lord, watching from the other craft, must have misunderstood that bow. I can imagine his sweating consternation when he saw the apparently friendly ending of the little conference and decided, no doubt, that Hudd had abandoned him.

The crewmen, evidently, opposed his flight.

The sudden crash of guns made a muffled booming in the thin bright hull. Two spacemen jumped wildly out of the open valve, which slammed immediately, behind them. One of them stumbled on his knees, pressing red, agonized hands against his wounds. The other tried to drag him out of danger—until the incandescent blast of the jets flattened and hid them both.

X

The fugitive life-craft lifted on that column of thundering fire, at first very slowly and jerkily—Lord was not an expert pilot. It leaned drunkenly from the upright, so that I thought it was going to crash. But the roar was suddenly louder. It lifted, swept above our heads, hurtled northward up the valley. Behind it, when the dust and smoke had cleared, the blackened forms of the two spacemen moved no longer.

The tall man turned, with his gaunt face grimly angular, and watched the life-craft go. It became a vanishing point of bright metal and violet fire. Its thunder rolled away.

His clumsy-seeming weapon lifted, at last, and clicked.

"Down, Barstow!" the girl screamed at me. "Cover your eyes."

Astonished to find that I was left standing alone, I dropped. The flash of heat stung my skin. I looked, afterward, in time to see the small bright cloud of iridescent metal vapor fading in the blue northward sky, turning into a white tuft of rising cumulus. The crash came a whole minute later, like one loud peal of thunder.

Enlow shook his lean head, regretfully.

"Too bad it happened that way," he said. "The two guards were only obeying orders. The equalizer might have made them very good members of the Brotherhood."

Calmly, as he spoke, he slipped another little self-propelled missile out of a case at his belt, pulled a safety-key out of it, and pushed it down the muzzle of his launcher. Shaped very much like the huge guided missiles of Fort America, it was only six inches long.

Halfway to his own craft, Mr. Julian Hudd stood peering back toward us. He was shading his eyes, dazedly shaking his dark shaggy head, as if the flash had nearly blinded him.

"Your demonstration, Mr. Hudd!" Cameron shouted after him, urgently. "Now will you give up your New Directorate?"

"Jim, this is an act of war," his great bellow came back defiantly. "Your damned Brotherhood will feel the consequences."

He went on at a stumbling, laborious run, toward his waiting craft. Frank Enlow was beckoning us imperatively back toward the gully.

"Wait!" Jane Enlow called out, eagerly. "Mr. Doyle is getting through."

She listened again. The gaunt man looked warily back at the enormous bright nose of the cruiser which still loomed, high above the ravine's rim, and speculatively hefted his launcher. I turned to Cameron, puzzled.

"So you've seen Doyle?"

"Last night." He watched the girl's shining eyes, anxious for the news. "The Enlows live just over the ridge—the first place I found. Their phone began ringing while I was there. It was Rory Doyle. I told him about the equalizer, and he came over to help us stop Mr. Hudd."

Awed, I glanced up at the appalling pillar of the *Great Director*. "How?"

"The first two landing parties had already got in touch with the Brotherhood," Cameron explained. "They were being indoctrinated with the equalizer. The plan was to send them back to spread the word among the crews. But Hudd pushed his own scheme too fast for that to succeed."

Anxiously, he watched the intent girl.

"The only way left was to try a broadcast. Not quite so good, but I think the signal crews will mostly recognize and trust Rory Doyle. It took a little time to improvise a net of short wave stations strong enough to reach out through the ionosphere to the other ships and the moon."

Suddenly, the eager-faced girl slipped off her single headphone. She held it up between us, twisted a volume-control, gestured for us to listen.

"—specifications of the equalizer." Thinned and small, hoarse with a weary tension, it was the voice of Rory Doyle. "The absolute dimensions, remember, may be varied at will.

It is the proportionate dimensions, and the shape and alignment of the turns, which must be precisely true.

"The safety-coil, remember, must always have a greater number of turns than the primary—otherwise you have a matter-bomb, instead of a power plant. The number and spacing of the secondary turns control the maximum voltage, according to the rule I gave you.

"Now, pass the word along!"

His tiny-seeming voice held a tired elation.

"Membership in the Brotherhood is open to every man of you. Now you are welcome on earth. Mr. Hudd's ill-advised threats will be forgotten. You have nothing to fear—so long as you respect the rights of others. The officers of the Brotherhood wish me to say that you are welcome home."

His voice ceased. The girl took back the headphone, and her father led us up the floor of the rocky little gorge. We stopped, presently, to climb a fern-grown slope and look back across the valley.

The interstellar cruiser still towered out of the smoking forest, incredibly enormous. Nearer, the tiny pencil of Hudd's life-craft stood mirror-bright upon a blackened island in the green. Between the fins of it, I saw a doll-like figure—hammering with frantic fists upon the shining valve.

"Mr. Julian Hudd," murmured Cameron, almost with pity.

We hurried on. We were crossing the low ridge into the next valley, when the ground quivered. The jets of the cruiser made a deafening, crushing reverberation. The bright immensity of it lifted, on a pillar of terrible fire.

Jane Enlow was listening again, as the thunder faded.

"They are going to the shore of the new Sahara Sea," she told us. "A new irrigation project—the crews can take up land, there."

An immense quiet fell upon us, after that thunder had died. I stood apart, staring into the sky, long after the living blue spark of the jets was gone. For the meaning of the equalizer was breaking slowly over me. A wave of deep emotion left me awed and changed and lifted, somehow strong and free.

"What happened to Mr. Hudd?" Cameron was asking.

"I don't know." Twisting at the knobs, Jane Enlow looked pale with concern for him. "The crews wouldn't let him come back on the ship. I'm afraid he was killed in the blast."

Many months had passed, however, before I learned the actual and somewhat surprising fate of Mr. Julian Hudd—who had been Director-General of Europe and Special Secretary of the Squaredeal Machine, and who was still an adaptive and resourceful man.

The following summer, after we had all been inducted into the Brotherhood and taught the equalizer, I came back in answer to a hospitable invitation to visit the home of Frank Enlow. Already I had claimed a small homestead beside a new western sea, and friendly neighbors had helped me build the first rooms of a house there. I wanted to see Jane Enlow.

She wasn't at home, however, when I arrived.

Frank Enlow, the lean ex-janitor and the last friend of Tyler, met me at the door of his pleasant home. He began to talk of Mr. Julian Hudd, who had survived unhurt by the ion-jets of the departing cruiser. He had established himself in the vacant house that had belonged to the murdered Hawkins couple. Frank Enlow took me to see him, there.

Now a simple brother of the Brotherhood, we found Hudd plowing his young orchard. Walking behind a small equalizer-tractor, he was bare to the waist and brown with sun. Sweat ran in rivulets down his dusty flanks, but his paunch and his jowls and his several chins were no longer the burdens they had been. I scarcely recognized him.

"Glad to see you, Chad." He used my first name, as always, but now his hard handclasp had a genuine cordiality. His great booming voice seemed mellowed, happy. With an air of simple, equalitarian friendship, he invited us into his home.

"Come along, Chad," he urged genially. "You'll want to see the wife. I think you'll remember her—the former Miss Jane Enlow."

Wow. There was a whole lot of detail I had completely forgotten, such as the ugliness of the military minions, the size of the returning fleet, the length of time gone, the killing of the innocent young couple, and the technical detail of the equalizer wiring. Perhaps not surprising in 63 years between readings, though the essence remained. But the conclusion differs. I remember clearly how Hudd presented himself to Jane a year or two later, and presented his handmade cuckoo clock, whose bird then solemnly fluted twice. That was the end. It also seemed to me that the girl had a larger part, instead of just standing there while her father talked. The author must have reworked it subsequently to take it a bit farther, or maybe the editor had pasted that ending on, as editors do, and this is the original version restored. It works either way. I love the idea of it: unlimited free power for everyone, resulting in an ideal peaceful society. Jack Williamson did like to try for those, notably in the novel The Humanoids, *originally serialized as* With Folded Hands . . . And Searching Mind, *another favorite of mine. Would it work in real life? I doubt it. For one thing it does not address the problem of overpopulation or diminishing resources, which will not be solved by free power. But it's a marvelous dream, the kind that forever locked me into this genre. Okay; bugged by that changed conclusion, I did a Google search on the key words, and found them: in "Late Night Special" by Eric Frank Russell, published a year and a half later. My memory must have merged the ending of the later story with the earlier story. Sigh; I think it might have been better that way.*

—Piers

BREAKING POINT

James Gunn

1953

This was I think my favorite science fiction story ever. I remember reading it when it was published in 1953. I was between college semesters. I had worked that day at a warehouse, baling bundles of clothing for shipment overseas, and I was tired. I relaxed by reading a magazine. The story transported me. My ideal was when a spaceship landed on a foreign planet, earth type but alien, and the spacemen first step out onto the surface. What wonders do they find there? In this story they don't even step out, yet the wonders overwhelm them. It's psychological science fiction, and it utterly thrilled me. When I finished it I paused, pondering it. Then something weird happened. My easy chair started slowly rotating in one direction, while my body slowly rotated the other way. There was no actual motion; it was all illusory. The rotations increased, until I feared I was losing my mind. I shook myself, and it stopped. Then the chair and the room started shaking, like a beginning earthquake. That made me nervous anew, and I got up and walked around, and the effect ceased. I concluded that I was fatigued and the emotional excitement of the story had warped my awareness. Decades later I got to meet the author, James Gunn, whose son was a fan of mine. But by that time I was older and more settled, and the world did not spin or shake. I was glad to be able to tell him what his story meant to me.

—Piers

I

They sent the advance unit out to scout the new planet in the Ambassador, *homing down on the secret beeping of a featureless box dropped by an earlier survey party. Then they sat back at GHQ and began the same old pattern of worry that followed every advance unit.*

Not about the ship. The Ambassador *was a perfect machine: automatic, self-adjusting, self-regulating. It was built to last and do its job without failure, under any and all conditions, as long as there was a universe around it. And it could not fail. There was no question about that.*

But an advance unit is composed of men. The factors of safety are indeterminable; the duplications of their internal mechanisms are conjectural, variable. The strength of the unit is the sum of the strengths of its members. The weakness of the unit can be a single small failing in a single man.

Beep . . . . boop . . .

"Gotcha!" said Ives. Ives was Communications. He had quick eyes, quick hands. He was huge, almost gross, but graceful. "On the nose," he grinned, and turned up the volume.

Beep . . . boop . . .

"What else do you expect?" said Johnny. Johnny was the Pilot—young, wide, flat. His movements were as controlled and decisive as those of the ship itself, in which he had an unshakeable faith. He slid into the bucket seat before the great master console.

Beep . . . boop . . .

"We expect the ship to do her job," said Hoskins, the Engineer. He was mild and deft, middle-aged, with a domed head and wide, light-blue eyes behind old-fashioned spectacles. He shared Johnny's belief in the machine, but through understanding rather than through admiration. "But it's always good to see her do it."

Beep . . . boop . . .

"Beautiful," said Captain Anderson softly, and he may have been talking about the way the ship was homing in on the tiny, featureless box that Survey had dropped on the unexplored planet, or about the planet itself, or even about the smooth integration of his crew.

Beep . . . boop . . .

Paresi said nothing. He had eyebrows and nostrils as sensitive as a radarscope, and masked eyes of a luminous black. Faces and motives were to him what gauges and log-entries were to the Engineer. Paresi was the Doctor, and he had many a salve and many a splint for invisible ills. He saw everything and understood much. He leaned against the bulkhead, his gaze flicking from one to the other of the crew. Occasionally his small mustache twitched like the antennae of a cat watching a bird.

Barely audible, faint as the blue outline of a distant hill, hungry and lost as the half-heard cry of a banshee, came the thin sound of high atmosphere against the ship's hull.

An hour passed.

Bup-bup-bup-bup. . .

"Shut that damned thing off!"

Ives looked up at the Pilot, startled. He turned the gain down to a whisper. Paresi left the bulkhead and stood behind Johnny. "What's the matter?" he asked. His voice was feline, too—a sort of purr.

Johnny looked up at him quickly, and grinned. "I can put her down," he said. "That's what I'm here for. I—like to think maybe I'll get to do it, that's all. I can't think that with the auto-pilot blasting out an 'on course.'" He punched the veering-jet controls. It served men perfectly. The ship ignored him, homed on the beam. The ship computed velocity, altitude, gravity, magnetic polarization, windage; used and balanced and adjusted for them all. It adjusted for interference from the manual controls. It served men perfectly. It ignored them utterly.

Johnny turned to look out and downward. Paresi's gaze followed. It was a beautiful planet, perhaps a shade greener than the blue-green of Earth. It seemed, indefinably, more park-like than wild. It had an air of controlled lushness and peace.

The braking-jets thundered as Johnny depressed a control. Paresi nodded slightly as he saw the Pilot's hand move, for he knew that the auto-pilot had done it, and that Johnny's movement was one of trained reflex. The youngster was intense and alert, hair-trigger schooled, taught to pretend in such detail that the pretense was reality to him; a precise pretense that would become reality for all of them if the machine failed.

But, of course, the machine would not fail.

Fields fled beneath them, looking like a crazy-quilt in pastel. On them, nothing moved. Hoskins moved to the viewport and watched them mildly. "Very pastoral," he said. "Pretty."

"They haven't gotten very far," said Ives.

"Or they've gotten very far indeed," said Captain Anderson.

Johnny snorted. "No factories. No bridges. Cow-tracks and goat paths."

The Captain chuckled. "Some cultures go through an agrarian stage to reach a technological civilization, and some pass through technology to reach the pastoral."

"I don't see it," said Johnny shortly, eyes ahead.

Paresi's hand touched the Captain's arm, and the Captain then said nothing.

Pwing-g-g!

"Stand by for landing," said the Captain. Ives and Hoskins went aft to the shock-panels in the after bulkhead. Paresi and the Captain stepped into niches flanking the console. Johnny touched a control that freed his chair in its hydraulic gimbals. Chair and niches and shock-panels would not be needed as long as the artificial gravity and inertialess field functioned; it was a ritual.

The ship skimmed treetops, heading phlegmatically for a rocky bluff. A gush of flame from its underjets and it shouldered heavily upward, just missing the jagged crest. A gout of fire forward, another, and it went into a long flat glide, following the fall of a foothill to the plain beyond. It held course and reduced speed, letting the ground billow up to it rather than descending. There was a moment of almost-flight, almost-sliding, and then a rush of dust and smoke which overtook and passed them. When it cleared, they were part of the plain, part of the planet.

"A good landing, John," Paresi said. Hoskins caught his eye and frowned. Paresi grinned broadly, and the exchange between them was clear: *Why do you needle the kid?* and *Quiet, Engine-room. I know what I'm doing.* Hoskins shrugged, and, with Ives, crossed to the communications desk.

Ives ran his fat, skilled hands over the controls and peered at his indicators. "It's more than a good landing," he grunted. "That squeak-box we homed in on can't be more than a hundred meters from here. First time I've ever seen a ship bull's-eye like that."

Johnny locked his gimbals, ran a steady, sensitive hand over the turn of the console as if it were a woman's flank. "Why—how close do you usually come?"

"Planetfall's close enough to satisfy Survey," said the Captain. "Once in a while the box will materialize conveniently on a continent. But this—this is too good to be true. We practically landed on it."

Hoskins nodded. "It's usually buried in some jungle, or at the bottom of a sea. But this is really all right. What a lineup! Point nine-eight earth gravity, Earth-type atmosphere—"

"Argon-rich," said Ives, from the panel. "Very rich."

"That'll make no real difference," Hoskins went on. "Temperature, about normal for an early summer back home . . . looks as if there's a fiendish plot afoot here to make things easy for us."

Paresi said, as if to himself, "I worry about easy things."

"Yeah, I know," snorted Johnny, rising to stretch. "The head-shrinker always does it the hard way. You can't just dislike rice pudding; it has to be a sister-syndrome. If the shortest distance is from here to there, don't take it—remember your Uncle Oedipus."

Captain Anderson chuckled. "Cut your jets, Johnny. Maybe Paresi's tortuous reasoning does seem out of order on such a nice day. But remember— eternal vigilance isn't just the price of liberty, as the old books say. It's the price of existence. We know we're here—but we don't know where 'here' is, and won't until after we get back. This is *really* Terra Incognita. The location of Earth, or even of our part of the galaxy, is something that has to be concealed at all costs, until we're sure we're not going to turn up a potentially dangerous, possibly superior alien culture. What we don't know can't hurt Earth. No conceivable method could get that information out of us, any more than it could be had from the squeak-box that Survey dropped here.

"Base all your thinking on that, Johnny. If that seems like leaning over backwards, it's only a sample of how careful we've got to be, how many angels we've got to figure."

"Hell," said the Pilot. "I know all that. I was just ribbing the bat-snatcher here." He thumbed a cigarette out of his tunic, touched his lighter to it. He frowned, stared at the lighter, tried it again. "It doesn't work. *Damn* it!" he barked explosively. "I don't like things that don't work!"

Paresi was beside him, catlike, watchful. "Here's a light. Take it easy, Johnny! A bum lighter's not that important."

Johnny looked sullenly at his lighter. "It doesn't work," he muttered. "Guaranteed, too. When we get back I'm going to feed it to Supply." He made a vivid gesture to describe the feeding technique, and jammed the lighter back into his pocket.

"Heh!" Ives's heavy voice came from the communications desk. "Maybe the natives are primitives, at that. Not a whisper of any radio on any band. No powerline fields, either. These are plowboys, for sure."

Johnny looked out at the sleeping valley. His irritation over the lighter was still in his voice. "Imagine that. No video or trideo. No jet-races or feelies. What do people do with their time in a place like this?"

"Books," said Hoskins, almost absently. "Chess. Conversation."

"I don't know what chess is, and conversation's great if you want to tell somebody something, like 'bring me a steak,'" said Johnny. "Let's get out of this firetrap," he said to the Captain.

"In time," said the Captain. "Ives, DX those radio frequencies. If there's so much as a smell of radiation even from the other side of this planet, we want to know about it. Hoskins, check the landing-suits—food, water, oxygen, radio, everything. Earth-type planet or no, we're not fooling with alien viruses. Johnny, I want you to survey this valley in every way you can and plot a minimum of three take-off vectors."

The crew fell to work, Ives and Hoskins intently, Johnny off-handedly, as if he were playing out a ritual with some children. Paresi bent over a stereomicroscope, manipulating controls which brought in samples of airborne bacteria and fungi and placed them under its objective. Captain Anderson ranged up beside him.

"We could walk out of the ship as if we were on Muroc Port," said Paresi. "These couldn't be more like Earth organisms if they'd been transplanted from home to delude us."

The Captain laughed. "Sometimes I tend to agree with Johnny. I never met a more suspicious character. How'd you ever bring yourself to sign your contract?"

"Turned my back on a couple of clauses," said Paresi. "Here—have a look."

At that moment the usually imperturbable Ives turned a sharp grunt that echoed and re-echoed through the cabin. Paresi and the Captain turned. Hoskins was just coming out of the after alleyway with an oxygen bottle in his hand, and had frozen in his tracks at the sharp sound Ives had made. Johnny had whipped around as if the grunt had been a lion's roar. His back was to the bulkhead, his lean, long frame tensed for fight or flight. It was indescribable, Ives's grunt, and it was the only sound which could have had such an effect on such a variety of men—the same shocked immobility.

Ives sat over his communications desk as if hypnotized by it. He moved one great arm forward, almost reluctantly, and turned a knob.

A soft, smooth hum filled the room. "Carrier," said Ives.

Then the words came. They were English words, faultlessly spoken, loud and clear and precise. They were harmless words, pleasant words even.

They were: *"Men of Earth! Welcome to our planet."*

The voice hung in the air. The words stuck in the silence like insects wriggling upon a pin. Then the voice was gone, and the silence was complete and heavy. The carrier hum ceased. With a spine-tingling, brief blaze of high-frequency sound, Hoskins's oxygen bottle hit the steel deck.

Then they all began to breathe again.

"There's your farmers, Johnny," said Paresi.

"Knight to bishop's third," said Hoskins softly.

"What's that?" demanded Johnny.

"Chess again," said the Captain appreciatively. "An opening gambit."

Johnny put a cigarette to his lips, tried his lighter. "Damn. Gimme a light, Ives,"

Ives complied, saying over his big shoulder to the Captain, "In case you wondered, there was no fix on that. My direction-finders indicate that the signal came simultaneously from forty-odd transmitters placed in a circle around the ship, which is their way of saying 'I dunno.'"

The Captain walked to the view-bubble in front of the console and peered around. He saw the valley, the warm light of mid-afternoon, the too-green slopes, and the blue-green distances. Trees, rocks, a balancing bird.

"It doesn't work," muttered Johnny.

The Captain ignored him. "'*Men of Earth* . . .'" he quoted. "Ives, they've gotten into Survey's squeak-box and analyzed its origin. They know all about us!"

"They don't because they can't," said Ives flatly. "Survey traverses those boxes through second-order space. They materialize near a planet and drop in. No computation on Earth or off it could trace their normal-space trajectory, let alone what happens in the second-order condition. The elements the box is made of are carefully averaged isotopic forms that could have come from any of nine galaxies we know about and probably more. And all it does is throw out a VUHF signal that says *beep* on one side, *boop* on the other, and *bup-bup* in between. It does *not* speak English, mention the planet Earth, announce anyone's arrival and purpose, or teach etiquette."

Captain Anderson spread his hands. "They got it from somewhere. They didn't get it from us. This ship and the box are the only Terran objects on this planet. Therefore they got then- information from the box."

"Q.E.D. You reason like Euclid," said Paresi admiringly. "But don't forget that geometry is an artificial school, based on arbitrary axioms. It just doesn't work where the shortest distance is *not* a straight line . . . I'd suggest we gather evidence and postpone our conclusions."

"How do you think they got it?" Ives challenged.

"I think we can operate from the fact they got it, and make our analyses when we have more data."

Ives went back to his desk and threw a switch.

"What are you doing?" asked the Captain.

"Don't you think they ought to be answered?"

"Turn it off, Ives."

"But—"

"Turn it off!" Ives did. An expedition is an informal, highly democratic group, and can afford to be, for when the situation calls for it, there is never any question of where authority lies. The Captain said, "There is nothing we can say to them which won't yield them more information. Nothing. For all we know it may be very important to them to learn whether or not we received their message. Our countermove is obviously to make no move at all."

"You mean just sit here and wait until they do something else?" asked Johnny, appalled.

The Captain thumped his shoulder. "Don't worry. We'll do something in some other area than communications. Hoskins—are those landing-suits ready?"

"All but," rapped Hoskins. He scooped up the oxygen bottle and disappeared.

Paresi said, "We'll tell them something if we *don't* answer."

The Captain set his jaw. "We do what we can, Nick. We do the best we can. Got any better ideas?"

Paresi shrugged easily and smiled. "Just knocking, Skipper. Knock everything. Then what's hollow, you know about."

"I should know better than to jump salty with you," said the Captain, all but returning the Doctor's smile. "Johnny, Hoskins. Prepare for exploratory patrol."

"I'll go," said Paresi.

"Johnny goes," said the Captain bluntly, "because it's his first trip, and because if he isn't given something to do he'll bust his adrenals. Hoskins goes, because of all of us, the Engineer is most expendable. Ives stays because we need hair-trigger communications. I stay to correlate what goes on outside with what goes on inside. You stay because if anything goes wrong I'd rather have you fixing the men up than find myself trying to fix you up." He squinted at Paresi. "Does that knock solid?"

"Solid."

"Testing, Johnny," Ives said into a microphone.

Johnny's duplicated voice, from the open face-plate of his helmet and from the intercom speaker, said, "I hear you fine."

"Testing, Hoskins."

"If I'd never seen you," said the speaker softly, "I'd think you were right here in the suit with me." Hoskins's helmet was obviously buttoned up.

The two men came shuffling into the cabin, looking like gleaming ghosts in their chameleon-suits, which repeated the color of the walls. "Someday," growled Johnny, "there'll be a type suit where you can scratch your—"

"Scratch when you get back," said the Captain. "Now hear this. Johnny, you can move fastest. You go out first. Wait in the airlock for thirty seconds after the outer port opens. When Ives gives you the beep, jump out, run around the bows, and plant your back against the hull directly opposite the port. Hold your blaster at the ready, aimed down—you hear me? *Down,* so that any observer will know you're armed, but not attacking. Hoskins, you'll be in the lock with the outer port open by that time. When Johnny gives the all clear, you'll jump out and put your back against the hull by the port. Then you'll both stay where you are until you get further orders. Is that clear?" "Aye."

"Yup."

"You're covered adequately from the ship. Don't fire without orders.

There's nothing you can get with a blaster that we can't get first with a projector—unless it happens to be within ten meters of the hull and we can't depress to it. Even then, describe it first and await orders to fire except in really extreme emergency. A single shot at the wrong time could set us back a thousand years with this planet. Remember that this ship isn't called *Killer* or *Warrior* or even *Hero*. It's the Earth Ship *Ambassador*. Go to it, and good luck."

Hoskins stepped back and waved Johnny past him. "After you, Jets."

Johnny's teeth flashed behind the face-plate. He clicked his heels and bowed stiffly from the waist, in a fine burlesque of an ancient courtier. He stalked past Hoskins and punched the button which controlled the airlock. They waited. Nothing.

Johnny frowned, jabbed the button again. And again. The Captain started to speak, then fell watchfully silent. Johnny reached toward the button, touched it, then struck it savagely. He stepped back then, one foot striking the other like that of a clumsy child. He turned partially to the others. In his voice, as it came from the speaker across the room, was a deep amazement that rang like the opening chords of a prophetic and gloomy symphony. He said, "The port won't open."

II

The extremes of mysticism and of pragmatism have their own expressions of worship. Each has its form, and the difference between them is the difference between deus ex machina *and* deus machina est.
—*E. Hunter Waldo*

"Of course it will open," said Hoskins. He strode past the stunned Pilot and confidently palmed the control.

The port didn't open.

Hoskins said, "Hm?" as if he had been asked an inaudible question, and tried again. Nothing happened. "Skipper," he said over his shoulder, "have a quick look at the meters behind you there. Are we getting auxiliary power?"

"All well here," said Anderson after a glance at the board. "And no shorts showing."

There was a silence punctuated by the soft, useless clicking of the control as Hoskins manipulated it. "Well, what do you know."

"It won't work," said Johnny plaintively.

"Sure it'll work," said Paresi swiftly, confidently. "Take it easy, Johnny."

"It won't work," said Johnny. "It won't work." He stumbled across the cabin and leaned against the opposite bulkhead, staring at the closed port with his head a little to one side as if he expected it to shriek at him.

"Let me try," said Ives, going to Hoskins. He put out his. hand.

"Don't!" Johnny cried.

"Shut up, Johnny," said Paresi.

"All right, Nick," said Johnny. He opened his face-plate, went to the rear bulkhead, keyed open an acceleration couch, and lay face down on it. Paresi watched him, his lips pursed.

"Can't say I blame him," said the Captain softly, catching Paresi's eye. "It's something of a shock. This shouldn't *be.* The safety factor's too great—a thousand percent or better."

"I know what you mean," said Hoskins. "I saw it myself, but I don't believe it." He pushed the button again.

"I believe it" said Paresi.

Ives went to his desk, clicked the transmitter and receiver switches on and off, moved a rheostat or two. He reached up to a wall-toggle, turned a small air-circulating fan on and off. "Everything else seems to work," he said absently.

"This is ridiculous!" exploded the Captain. "It's like leaving your keys home, or arriving at the theater without your tickets. It isn't dangerous—it's just stupid!"

"It's dangerous," said Paresi.

"Dangerous how?" Ives demanded.

"For one thing—" Paresi nodded toward Johnny, who lay tensely, his face hidden. "For another, the simple calculation that if nothing inside this ship made that control fail, something outside this ship did it. And *that I* don't like."

"That couldn't happen," said the Captain reasonably.

Paresi snorted impatiently. "Which of two mutually exclusive facts are you going to reason from? That the ship can't fail? Then this failure isn't a failure; it's an external control. Or are you going to reason that the ship *can* fail? Then you don't have to worry about an external force—but you can't trust anything about the ship. Do the trick that makes you happy. But do only one. You can't have both."

Johnny began to laugh.

Ives went to him. "Hey, boy—"

Johnny rolled over, swung his feet down, and sat up, brushing the fat man aside. "What you guys need," Johnny chuckled, "is a nice kind police-man to feed you candy and take you home. You're real lost."

Ives said, "Johnny, take it easy and be quiet, huh? We'll figure a way out of this."

"I already have, scrawny," said Johnny offensively. He got up, strode to the port. "What a bunch of deadheads," he growled. He went two steps past the port and grasped the control-wheel which was mounted on the other side of the port from the button.

"Oh my God," breathed Anderson delightedly, "the manual! Anybody else want to be Captain?"

"Factor of safety," said Hoskins, smiting himself on the brow. "There's a manual control for everything on this scow that there can be. And we stand here staring at it—"

"If we don't win the fur-lined teacup . . ." Ives laughed.

Johnny hauled on the wheel

It wouldn't budge.

"Here—" Ives began to approach.

"Get away," said Johnny. He put his hands close together on the rim of the wheel, settled his big shoulders, and hauled. With a sharp crack the wheel broke off in his hands.

Johnny staggered, then stood. He looked at the wheel and then up at the broken end of its shaft, gleaming deep below the surface of the bulkhead.

"Oh, fine . . ." Ives whispered.

Suddenly Johnny threw back his head and loosed a burst of high, hysterical laughter. It echoed back and forth between the metal walls like a torrent from a burst dam. It went on and on, as if now that the dam was gone, the flood would run forever.

Anderson called out "Johnny!" three times, but the note of command had no effect. Paresi walked to the Pilot and slapped him sharply across the cheeks. "Johnny! Stop it!" The laughter broke off as suddenly as it had begun. Johnny's chest heaved, drawing in breath with great, rasping near-sobs. Slowly they died away. He extended the wheel toward the Captain.

"It broke off," he said finally, dully, without emphasis. Then he leaned back against the hull, slowly slid down until he was sitting on the deck. "Broke right off," he said.

Ives twined his fat fingers together and bent them until the knuckles cracked. "Now what?"

"I suggest," said Paresi, in an extremely controlled tone, "that we all sit down and think over the whole thing very carefully."

Hoskins had been staring hypnotically at the broken shaft deep in the wall. "I wonder," he said at length, "which way Johnny turned that wheel."

"Counter-clockwise," said Ives. "You saw him."

"I know that," said Hoskins. "I mean, which way: the right way, or the wrong way?"

"Oh." There was a short silence. Then Ives said, "I guess we'll never know now."

"Not until we get back to Earth," said Paresi quickly.

"You say 'until,' or 'unless'?" Ives demanded.

"I said 'until,' Ives," said Paresi levelly, "and watch your mouth."

"Sometimes," said the fat man with a dangerous joviality, "you pick the wrong way to say the right thing, Nick." Then he clapped the slender Doctor on the back. "But I'll be good. We sow no panic seed, do we?"

"Much better not to," said the Captain. "It's being done efficiently enough from outside."

"You are convinced it's being done from outside?" asked Hoskins, peering at him owlishly.

"I'm . . . convinced of very little," said the Captain heavily. He went to the acceleration couch and sat down. "I want out," he said. He waved away the professional comment he could see forming on Paresi's lips and went on, "Not claustrophobia, Nick. Getting out of the ship's more important than just relieving our feelings. If the trouble with the port is being caused by some fantastic *something* outside this ship, we'll achieve a powerful victory over it, purely by ignoring it"

"It broke off," murmured Johnny.

"Ignore *that,*" snorted Ives.

"You keep talking about this thing being caused by something outside," said Paresi. His tone was almost complaining.

"Got a better hypothesis?" asked Hoskins.

"Hoskins," said the Captain, "isn't there some way we can get out? What about the tubes?"

"Take a shipyard to move those power-plants," said Hoskins, "and even if it could be done, those radioactive tubes would fry you before you crawled a third of the way."

"We should have a lifeboat," said Ives to no one in particular.

"What in time does a ship like the *Ambassador* need with a lifeboat?" asked Hoskins in genuine amazement.

The Captain frowned. "What about the ventilators?"

"Take us days to remove all the screens and purifiers," said Hoskins, "and then we'd be up against the intake ports. You could stroll out through any of them about as far as your forearm. And after that it's hull-metal, Skipper. *That* you don't cut, not with a piece of the Sun's core."

The Captain got up and began pacing, slowly and steadily, as if the problem could be trodden out like ripe grapes. He closed his eyes and said, "I've been circling around that idea for thirty minutes now. Look: the hull can't be cut because it is built so it can't fail. It doesn't fail. The port controls were also built so they wouldn't fail. They do fail. The thing that keeps us in stays in shape. The thing that lets us out goes bad. Effect: we stay inside. Cause: something that wants us to stay inside."

"Oh," said Johnny clearly.

They looked at him. He raised his head, stiffened his spine against the bulkhead. Paresi smiled at him. "Sure, Johnny. The machine didn't fail. It was—controlled. It's all right." Then he turned to the Captain and said carefully, "I'm not denying what you say, Skipper. But I don't like to think of what will happen if you take that tack, reason it through, and don't get any answers."

"I'd hate to be a psychologist," said Ives fervently. "Do you extrapolate your mastications, too, and get frightened of the stink you might get?"

Paresi smiled coldly. "I control my projections."

Captain Anderson's lips twitched in passing amusement, and then his expression sobered. "I'll take the challenge, Paresi. We have a cause and an effect. Something is keeping us in the ship. Corollary: We—or perhaps the ship—we're not welcome."

"Men of Earth," quoted Ives, in an excellent imitation of the accentless English they had heard on the radio, *"welcome to our planet."*

"They're kidding," said Johnny heartily, rising to his feet. He dropped the control wheel with a clang and shoved it carelessly aside with his foot. "Who ever says exactly what they mean anyhow? I see that conclusion the head-shrinker's afraid you'll get to, Skipper. If we can't leave the ship, the only other thing we can do is to leave the planet. That it?"

Paresi nodded and watched the Captain closely. Anderson turned abruptly away from them all and stood, feet apart, head down, hands behind his back, and stared out of the forward viewports. In the tense silence they could hear his knuckles crack. At length he said quietly, "That isn't what we came here for, Johnny."

Johnny shrugged. "Okay. Chew it up all you like, fellers. The only other choice is to sit here like bugs in a bottle until we die of old age. When you get tired of thinking that over, just let me know. I'll fly you out."

"We can always depend on Johnny," said Paresi with no detectable emphasis at all.

"Not on me," said Johnny, and swatted the bulkhead. "On the ship. Nothing on any planet can stop this baby once I pour on the coal. She's just got too much muscle."

"Well, Captain?" asked Hoskins softly.

Anderson looked at the basking valley, at the too-blue sky, and the near-familiar, mellow-weathered crags. They waited.

"Take her up," said the Captain. "Put her in orbit at two hundred kilos. I'm not giving up this easily."

Ives swatted Johnny's broad shoulder. "That's a take-off *and* a landing, if I know the Old Man. Go to it, Jets."

Johnny's wide white grin flashed and he strode to the control chair.

"Gentlemen, be seated."

"I'll take mine lying down," said Ives, and spread his bulk out on the acceleration couch. The others went to their takeoff posts.

"On automatics," said the Captain, "Fire away!"

"Fire away!" said Johnny cheerfully. He reached forward and pressed the central control.

Nothing happened.

Johnny put his hand toward the control again. It moved as if there were a repellor field around the button. The hand moved more and more slowly the closer it got, until it hovered just over the control and began to tremble.

"On manual," barked the Captain. "Fire!"

"Manual, sir," said Johnny reflexively. His trembling hand darted up to an overhead switch, pulled it. He grasped the control bars and dropped the heels of his hands heavily on the firing studs. From somewhere came a muted roar, a whispering; a subjective suggestion of the thunder of reaction motors.

A frown crossed Paresi's face. The rocket noise was gone as the mind reached for it, like an occluded thought. The motors were silent; there wasn't a tremor of vibration. Yet somewhere a ghost engine was warming up, preparing a ghost ship for an intangible take-off into nothingness.

He snapped off the catch of his safety belt and crossed swiftly and silently to the console. Johnny sat raptly. A slow smile of satisfaction began to spread over his face. His gaze flicked to dials and gauges; he nodded very slightly, and brought both hands down like an organist playing a mighty chord. He watched the gauges. The needles were still, lying on their zero pins, and, where lights should have flickered and flashed, there was nothing. Paresi glanced at Anderson and met a worried look. Hoskins had his head cocked to one side, listening, puzzled. Ives rose from the couch and came forward to stand beside Paresi.

Johnny was manipulating the keys firmly. His fingers began to play a rapid, skillful, silent concerto. His face had a look of intense concentration and of complete self-confidence.

"Well," said Ives heavily. "That's a bust, too."

Paresi spun to him. *"Shh!"* It was done with such intensity that Ives recoiled. With a warning look at him, Paresi walked to the Captain, whispered in his ear.

"My God," said Anderson. "All right, Doctor." He came forward to the Pilot's chair. Johnny was still concentratedly, uselessly at work. Anderson glanced inquiringly at Paresi, who nodded.

"That does it," said the Captain, loudly. "Nice work, Johnny. We're smack in orbit. The automatics couldn't have done it better. For once it feels good to be out in space again. Cut your jets now. You can check for correction."

"Aye, sir," said Johnny. He made two delicate adjustments, threw a master switch and swung around. "Whew! That's work!"

Facing the four silent men, Johnny thumbed out a cigarette, put it in his mouth, touched his lighter to it, drew a long slow puff.

"Man, that goes good . . ."

The cigarette was not lighted. Hoskins turned away, an expression of sick pity on his face. Ives reached abruptly for his own lighter, and the Doctor checked him with a gesture.

"Every time I see a hot pilot work I'm amazed," Paresi said conversationally. "Such concentration . . . you must be tuckered, Johnny."

Johnny puffed at his unlit cigarette. "Tuckered," he said. "Yeah." There were two odd undertones to his voice suddenly. They were fatigue and eagerness. Paresi said, "You're off-watch, John. Go stretch out."

"Real tired," mumbled Johnny. He lumbered to his feet and went aft, where he rolled to the couch and was asleep almost instantly.

The others congregated far forward around the controls, and for a long moment stared silently at the sleeping Pilot.

"I don't get it," murmured Ives.

"He really thought he flew us out, didn't he?" asked Hoskins.

Paresi nodded. "Had to. There isn't any place in his cosmos for machines that don't work. Contrary evidence can get just so strong. Then, for him, it ceased to exist. A faulty cigarette lighter irritated him, a failing airlock control made him angry and sullen and then hysterical. When the drive controls wouldn't respond, he reached his breaking point. Everyone has such a breaking point, and arrives at it just that way if he's pushed far enough."

"Everyone?"

Paresi looked from face to face, and nodded somberly. Anderson asked, "What knocked him out? He's trained to take far more strain than that."

"Oh, he isn't suffering from any physical or conscious mental fatigue. The one thing he wanted to do was to get away from a terrifying situation. He convinced himself that he flew out of it. The next best thing he could do to keep anything else from attacking him was to sleep. He very much appreciated my suggestion that he was worn out and needed to stretch out."

"I'd very much appreciate some such," said Ives. "Do it to me, Nick."

"Reach your breaking point first," said the Doctor flatly, and went to place a pillow between Johnny's head and a guard-rail.

Hoskins turned away to stare at the peaceful landscape outside. The Captain watched him for a moment, then; "Hoskins!"

"Aye."

"I've seen that expression before. What are you thinking about?"

The Engineer looked at him, shrugged, and said mildly, "Chess."

"What, especially?"

"Oh, a very general thing. The reciprocity of the game. That's what makes it the magnificent thing it is. Most human enterprises can gang up on a man, slap him with one disaster after another without pause. But not chess. No matter who your opponent might be, every time he does something to you, *it's your move.*"

"Very comforting. Have you any idea of how we move now?"

Hoskins looked at him, a gentle surprise on his aging face. "You missed my point, Skipper. *We* don't move."

"Oh," the Captain whispered. His face tautened as it paled. "I . . . I see. We pushed the airlocks button to get out. Countermove: It wouldn't work. We tried the manual. Countermove: It broke off. And so on. Now we've tried to fly the ship out. Oh, but Hoskins—Johnny broke. Isn't that countermove enough?"

"Maybe. Maybe you're right. Maybe the move wasn't trying the drive controls, though. Maybe the move was to do what was necessary to knock Johnny out." He shrugged again. "We'll very soon see."

The Captain exhaled explosively through his nostrils. "We'll find out if it's our move by moving," he gritted. "Ives! Paresi! We're going to go over this thing from the beginning. First, try the port. You, Ives."

Ives grunted and went to the ship's side. Then he stopped.

"Where is the port?"

Anderson and Paresi followed Ives's flaccid, shocked gaze to the bulkhead where there had been the outline of the closed port, and beside it the hole which had held the axle of the manual wheel, and which now was a smooth, seamless curtain of impenetrable black. But Hoskins looked at the Captain first of all, and he said *"Now* it's our move," and only then did he turn with them to look at the darkness.

III

The unfamiliar, you say, is the unseen, the completely new and strange? Not so. The epitome of the unfamiliar is the familiar inverted, the familiar turned on its head. View a familiar place under new conditions—a deserted and darkened theater, an empty nightclub by day—and you will find yourself more influenced by the emotion of strangeness than by any number of unseen places. Go back to your old neighborhood and find everything changed. Come into your own home when everyone is gone, when the lights are out and the furniture rearranged— there 1 will show you the strange and frightening ghosts that are the shapes left over when reality superimposes itself upon the images of memory. The goblins

lurk in the shadows of your own room . . .
—*Owen Miller* ESSAYS ON NIGHT AND THE UNFAMILIAR

For one heart-stopping moment the darkness had seemed to swoop in upon them like the clutching hand of death. Instinctively they had huddled together in the center of the room. But when the second look, and the third, gave them reassurance that the effect was really there, though the cause was still a mystery, then half the mystery was gone, and they began to drift apart. Each felt on trial, and held tight to himself and the picture of himself he emphasized in the others' eyes.

The Captain said quietly, "It's just . . . there. It doesn't seem to be spreading."

Hoskins gazed at it critically. "About half-a-meter deep," he murmured. "What do you suppose it's made of?"

"Not a gas," said Paresi. "It has a—a sort of surface."

Ives, who had frozen to the spot when first he saw the blackness on his way to the port, took another two steps. The hand, which had been half-lifted to touch the control, continued relievedly, as if glad to have a continuous function even though its purpose had changed.

"Don't touch it!" rapped the Captain.

Ives turned his head to look at the Captain, then faltered and let the hand drop. "Why not?"

"Certainly not a liquid," Paresi mused, as if there had been no interruption. "And if it's a solid, where did that much matter come from? Through the hull?"

Hoskins, who knew the hull, how it was made, how fitted, how treated once it was in place, snorted at the idea.

"If it was a gas," said Paresi, "there'd be diffusion. *And* convection. If it were poisonous, we'd all be dead. If not, the chances are we'd smell it. And the counter's not saying a thing—so it's not radioactive."

"You trust the counter?" asked Ives bitterly.

"I trust it," said Paresi. His near-whisper shook with what sounded like passion. "A man must have faith in something. I hold that faith in every single function of every part of this ship until each and every part is separately and distinctly proved unworthy of faith!"

"Then, by God, you'll understand my faith in my own two hands and what they feel," snarled Ives. He stepped to the bulkhead and brought his meaty hand hard against it

"Touché" murmured Hoskins, and meant either Ives's remark or the flat, solid smack of the hand against the blackness.

In his sleep, Johnny uttered a high, soft, careless tinkle of youthful, happy laughter.

"Somebody's happy," said Ives.

"Paresi," said the Captain, "what happens when he wakes up?"

Paresi's eyebrows shrugged for him. "Practically anything. He's reached down inside himself, somewhere, and found a way out. For him—not for any of the rest of us. Maybe he'll ignore what we see. Maybe he'll think he's somewhere else, or in some other time. Maybe he'll *be* someone else. Maybe he won't wake up at all."

"Maybe he has the right idea," said Ives.

"That's the second time you've made a crack like that," said Paresi levelly. "Don't do it again. You can't afford it."

"*We* can't afford it," the Captain put in.

"All right," said Ives, with such docility that Paresi shot him a startled, suspicious glance. The big Communications man went to his station and sat, half-turned away from the rest.

"What are they after?" complained the Captain suddenly. "What do they want?"

"Who?" asked Paresi, still watching Ives.

Hoskins explained, "Whoever it was who said, '*Welcome to our planet.*'"

Ives turned toward them, and Paresi's relief was noticeable. Ives said, "They want us dead."

"Do they?" asked the Captain.

"They don't want us to leave the ship, and they don't want the ship to leave the planet."

"Then it's the ship they want."

"Yeah," amended Ives, "without us."

Paresi said, "You can't conclude that, Ives. They've inconvenienced us. They've turned us in on ourselves, and put a drain on our intangible resources as men and as a crew. But so far they haven't actually done anything to us. We've done it to ourselves."

Ives looked at him scornfully. "We wrecked the un-wreckable controls, manufactured that case-hardened darkness, and talked to ourselves on an all-wave carrier with no source, about information no outsider could get?"

"I didn't say any of that." Paresi paused to choose words. "Of course they're responsible for these phenomena. But the phenomena haven't hurt us. Our reactions to the phenomena are what have done the damage."

"A fall never hurt anyone, they told me when I was a kid," said Ives pugnaciously. "It's the sudden stop."

Paresi dismissed the remark with a shrug. "I still say that while we have been astonished, frightened, puzzled, and frustrated, we have not been seriously threatened. Our water and food and air are virtually unlimited. Our ability to live with one another under emergency situations has been tested to a fare-thee-well, and all we have to do is recognize the emergency as such and that ability will rise to optimum." He smiled suddenly. "It could be worse, Ives."

"I suppose it could," said Ives. "That blackness could move in until it really crowded us, or—"

Very quietly Hoskins said, "It *is* moving in."

Captain Anderson shook his head. "No . . ." And hearing him, they slowly recognized that the syllable was not a denial, but an exclamation. For the darkness was no longer a half-meter deep on the bulkhead. No one had noticed it, but they suddenly became aware that the almost-square cabin was now definitely rectangular, with the familiar controls, the communications wall, and the thwartship partition aft of them forming three sides to the encroaching fourth,

Ives rose shaking and round-eyed from his chair. He made an unspellable animal sound and rushed at the blackness. Paresi leaped for him, but not fast enough. Ives collided sickeningly against the strange jet surface and fell. He fell massively, gracelessly, not prone but on wide-spread knees, with his arms crumpled beneath him and the side of his face on the deck. He stayed there, quite unconscious, a gross caricature of worship.

There was a furiously active, silent moment while Paresi turned the fat man over on his back, ran skilled fingers over his bleeding face, his chest, back to the carotid area of his neck. "He's all right," said Paresi, still working; then, as if to keep his mind going with words to avoid conjecture, he went on didactically. "This is the other fear reaction. Johnny's was 'flight,' Ives's is 'fight.' The empirical result is very much the same."

"I thought," said Hoskins dryly, "that fight and flight were survival reactions."

Paresi stood up. "Why, they are. In the last analysis, so is suicide."

"I'll think about that," said Hoskins softly.

"Paresi!" spat Anderson. "Medic or no, you'll watch your mouth!"

"Sorry, Captain. That was panic seed. Hoskins—"

"Don't explain it to me," said the Engineer mildly. "I know what you meant. Suicide's the direct product of survival compulsions—drives that try to save something, just as fight and flight are efforts to save something. I don't think you need worry; immolation doesn't tempt me. I'm too—too interested in what goes on. What are you going to do about Ives?"

"Bunk him, I guess, and stand by to fix up that headache he'll wake up to. Give me a hand, will you?"

Hoskins went to the bulkhead and dropped a second acceleration couch. It took all three of them, working hard, to lift Ives's great bulk up to it. Paresi opened the first-aid kit clamped under the control console and went to the unconscious man. The Captain cast about him for something to do, something to say, and apparently found it. "Hoskins!"

"Aye."

"Do you usually think better on an empty stomach?"

"Not me."

"I never have either."

Hoskins smiled. "I can take a hint. I'll rassle up something hot and filling."

"Good man," said the Captain, as Hoskins disappeared toward the after quarters. Anderson walked over to the Doctor and stood watching him clean up the abraded bruise on Ives's forehead.

Paresi, without looking up, said, "You'd better say it, whatever it is. Get it out."

Anderson half-chuckled. "You psychic?"

Paresi shot him a glance. "Depends. If you mean has a natural sensitivity to the tension spectra coupled itself with some years of practice in observing people—then yes. What's on your mind?"

Anderson said nothing for a long time. It was as if he were waiting for a question, a single prod from Paresi. But Paresi wouldn't give it. Paresi waited, just waited, with his dark face turned away, not helping, not pushing, not doing a single thing to modify the pressure that churned about in the Captain.

"All right," said the Captain irritably. "I'll tell you."

Paresi took tweezers, a retractor, two scalpels, and a hypodermic case out of the kit and laid them in a neat row on the bunk. He then picked up each one and returned it to the kit. When he had quite finished Anderson said, "I was wondering, *who's next?*"

Paresi nodded and shut the kit with a sharp click. He looked up at the Captain and nodded again. "Why does it have to be you?" he asked.

"I didn't say it would be me!" said the Captain sharply.

"Didn't you?" When the Captain had no answer, Paresi asked him, "Then why wonder about a thing like that?"

"Oh . . . I see what you mean. When you start to be afraid, you start to be unsure—not of anyone else's weaknesses, but of your own. That what you mean?"

"Yup." His dark-framed grin flashed suddenly. "But you're not afraid, Cap'n."

"The hell I'm not."

Paresi shook his head. "Johnny was afraid, and fled. Ives was afraid, and fought. There's only one fear that's a real fear, and that's the one that brings you to your breaking point. Any other fear is small potatoes compared with a terror like that. Small enough so no one but me has to worry about it."

"Why you, then?"

Paresi swatted the first-aid kit as he carried it back to its clamp. "I'm the

M.O., remember? Symptoms are my business. Let me watch 'em, Captain. Give me orders, but don't crowd me in my specialty."

"You're insubordinate, Paresi," said Anderson, "and you're a great comfort." His slight smile faded, and horizontal furrows appeared over his eyes. "Tell me why I had that nasty little phase of doubt about myself."

"You think I can?"

"Yes." He was certain.

"That's half the reason. The other half is Hoskins."

"What are you talking about?"

"Johnny broke. Ives broke. Your question was, 'Who's next?' You doubt that it will be me, because I'm *de facto* the boy with all the answers. You doubt it will be Hoskins, because you can't extrapolate how he might break—or even if he would. So that leaves you."

"I hadn't exactly reasoned it out like that—"

"Oh yes you had," said Paresi, and thumped the Captain's shoulder. "Now forget it. Confucius say he who turn gaze inward wind up cross-eyed. Can't afford to have a cross-eyed Captain. Our friends out there are due to make another move."

"No they're not."

The Doctor and the Captain whirled at the quiet voice. "What does *that* mean, Hoskins?"

The Engineer came into the cabin, crossed over to his station, and began opening and closing drawers. "They've moved." From the bottom drawer he pulled out a folded chessboard and a rectangular box. Only then did he look directly at them. "The food's gone."

"Food? . . . gone where?"

Hoskins smiled tiredly. "Where's the port? Where's the outboard bulkhead? That black stuff has covered it up—heading units, foodlockers, disposal unit, everything," He pulled a couple of chairs from their clips on the bulkhead and carried them across the cabin to the sheet of chairs. On the seat of one he placed the chessboard. He sat on the other and pushed the board close to the darkness. "The scuttlebutt's inboard, and still available." His voice seemed to get fainter and fainter as he talked, as if he were going slowly away from them. "But there's no food. No food."

He began to set up the pieces, his face to the black wall.

IV

The primary function of personality is self-preservation, but personality itself is not a static but a dynamic thing. The basic factor in its development is integration; each new situation calls forth a new adjustment which modifies or alters

*the personality in the process. The proper aim of personality, therefore, is not per-
manence and stability, but unification. The inability of a personality to adjust to
or integrate a new situation, the resistance of the personality to unification, and
its efforts to preserve its integrity are known popularly as insanity.*
—*Morgan Littlefield*, NOTES ON PSYCHOLOGY.

"Hoskins!"

Paresi grabbed the Captain's arm and spun him around roughly. "Captain Anderson! Cut it!" Very softly, he said, "Leave him alone. He's doing
what he has to do."

Anderson stared over his shoulder at the little Engineer. "Is he, now?
Damn it, he's still under orders!"

"Got something for him to do?" asked the Doctor coolly.

Anderson looked around, at the controls, out at the sleeping mountains.
"I guess not. But I'd like to know he'd take an order when I have one."

"Leave him alone until you have an order. Hoskins is a very steady
head, Skipper. But just now he's on the outside edge. Don't push."

The Captain put his hand over his eyes and fumbled his way to the
controls. He turned his back to the Pilot's chair and leaned heavily against
it. "Okay," he said. "This thing is developing into a duel between you and
those . . . those colleagues of yours out there. I guess the least we . . . I . . .
can do is not to fight you while you're fighting them."

Paresi said, "You're choosing up sides the wrong way. They're fighting
us, all right. We're only fighting ourselves. I don't mean each other; I mean
each of us is fighting himself. We've got to stop doing that, Skipper."

The Captain gave him a wan smile. "Who has, at the best of times?"

Paresi returned the smile. "Drug addicts . . . catatonics . . . illusionaries
. . . and saints. I guess it's up to us to add to the category."

"How about dead people?"

"Ives! How long have you been awake?"

The big man shoved himself up and leaned on one arm. He shook his
head and grunted as if he had been punched in the solar plexus. "Who hit
me with what?" he said painfully, from between clenched teeth.

"You apparently decided the bulkhead was a paper hoop and tried to
dive through it," said Paresi. He spoke lightly but his face was watchful.

"Oooh . . ." Ives held his head for a moment and then peered between
his fingers *at* the darkness. "I remember," he said in a strained whisper.
He looked around him, saw the Engineer huddled against his chessboard.
"What's he doing?"

They all looked at the Engineer as he moved a piece and then sat quietly.

"Hey, Hoskins!"

Hoskins ignored Ives's bull-voice. Paresi said, "He's not talking just now. He's . . . all right, Ives. Leave him alone. At the moment, I'm more interested in you. How do you feel?"

"Me? I feel great. Hungry, though. What's for chow?"

Anderson said quickly, "Nick doesn't want us to eat just now."

"Thanks," muttered Paresi in vicious irony.

"He's the Doctor," said Ives good-naturedly. "But don't put it off too long, huh? This furnace needs stoking." He fisted his huge chest.

"Well, this is encouraging," said Paresi.

"It certainly is," said the Captain. "Maybe the breaking point is just the point of impact. After that the rebound, hm?"

Paresi shook his head. "Breaking means breaking. Sometimes things just don't break."

"Got to pass," said a voice. Johnny, the Pilot, was stirring.

"Ha!" Anderson's voice was exultant. "Here comes another one!"

"How sure are you of that?" asked the Doctor. To Johnny, he called, "Hiya, John."

"I got to pass," said Johnny worriedly. He swung his feet to the deck. "You see," he said earnestly, "being the head of your class doesn't make it any easier. You've got to keep that and pass the examinations too. You've got two jobs. Now the guy who stands fourth, say—he has only one job to do."

Anderson turned a blank face to Paresi, who made a silencing gesture. Johnny put his head in his hands and said, "When one variable varies directly as another, two pairs of their corresponding values are in proportion." He looked up. "That's supposed to be the keystone of all vector analysis, the man says, and you don't get to be a pilot without vector analysis. And it makes no sense to me. What am I going to do?"

"Get some shut-eye," said Paresi immediately. "You've been studying too hard. It'll make more sense to you in the morning."

Johnny grinned and yawned at the same time, the worried wrinkles smoothing out. "Now that was a real educational remark, Martin, old chap," he said. He lay down and stretched luxuriously. "*That* I can understand. You may wear my famous maroon zipsuit." He turned his face away and was instantly asleep.

"Who the hell is Martin?" Ives demanded. "Martin who?"

"Shh. Probably his roommate in pre-pilot school."

Anderson gaped. "You mean he's back in school?"

"Doesn't it figure?" said Paresi sadly. "I told you that this situation is intolerable to him. If he can't escape in space, he'll escape in time. He hasn't the imagination to go forward, so he goes backward."

Something scuttled across the floor. Ives whipped his feet oft the floor and sat like some cartoon of a Buddha, clutching his ankles. "What in God's name was that?"

"I didn't see anything," said Paresi.

The Captain demanded, "What was it?"

From the shadows, Hoskins said, "A mouse."

"Nonsense."

"I can't stand things that scuttle and slither and crawl," said Ives. His voice was suddenly womanish. "Don't let anything like that in here!"

From the quarters aft came a faint scratching, a squeak. Ives turned pale. His wattles quivered.

"Snap out of it, Ives," said Paresi coldly. "There isn't so much as a microbe on this ship that I haven't inventoried. Don't sit there like little Miss Muffet."

"I know what I saw," said Ives. He rose suddenly, turned to the black wall, and bellowed, "Damn you, send something I can fight!"

Two mice emerged from under the couch. One of them ran over Ives's foot. They disappeared aft, squeaking. Ives leapt straight up and came down standing on the couch. Anderson stepped back against the inboard bulkhead and stood rigid. Paresi walked with great purpose to the medical chest, took out a small black case and opened it.

Ives cowered down to his knees and began to blubber openly, without attempting to hide it, without any articulate speech. Paresi approached him, half-concealing a small metal tube in his hand.

A slight movement on the deck caught Anderson's eye. He was unable to control a shrill intake of breath as an enormous spider, hairy and swift, darted across to the couch and sprang. It landed next to Ives's knee, sprang again. Paresi swung at it and missed, his hand catching Ives heavily just under the armpit. The spider hit the deck, skidded, righted itself and, abruptly, was gone. Ives caved in around the impact point of Paresi's hand and curled up silently on the couch. Anderson ran to him.

"He'll be all right now," said Paresi. "Forget it."

"Don't tell me he faulted! Not Ives!"

"Of course not." Paresi held up the little cylinder.

"Anesthox! Why did you use that on him?"

Paresi said irritably, "For the reason one usually uses anesthox. To knock a patient out for a couple of hours without hurting him."

"Suppose you hadn't?"

"How much more of that scuttle-and-slither treatment do you think he could have taken?"

Anderson looked at the unconscious Communications man. "Surely more than that." He looked up suddenly. "Where the hell *did* that vermin come from?"

"Ah. Now you have it. He dislikes mice and spiders. But there was something special about these. They couldn't be here, and they were. He felt that it was a deliberate and personal attack. He couldn't have handled much more of it."

"Where did they come from?" demanded the Captain again.

"I don't know!" snapped Paresi. "Sorry, Skipper. . . I'm a little unnerved. I'm not used to seeing a patient's hallucinations. Not that clearly, at any rate."

"They were Ives's hallucinations?"

"Can you recall what was said just before they appeared?"

"Uh . . . something scuttled. A mouse."

"It wasn't a mouse until someone said it was." The Doctor turned and looked searchingly at Hoskins, who still sat quietly over his chess.

"By God, it was Hoskins. Hoskins—what made you say that?"

The Engineer did not move nor answer. Paresi shook his head hopelessly. "Another retreat. It's no use, Captain."

Anderson took a single step toward Hoskins, then obviously changed his mind. He shrugged and said, "All right. Something scuttled and Hoskins defined it. Let's accept that without reasoning it out. So who called up the spider?"

"You did."

"*I* did?"

In a startling imitation of the Captain's voice, Paresi quoted, "Don't sit there like Miss Muffet!"

"I'll be damned," said Anderson. "Maybe we'd all be better off saying nothing."

Paresi said bitterly, "You think it makes any difference if we *say* what we think?"

"Perhaps. . ."

"Nope," said Paresi positively. "Look at the way this thing works. First it traps us, and then it shows us a growing darkness. Very basic. Then it starts picking on us, one by one. Johnny gets machines that don't work, when with his whole soul he worships machines that do. Ives gets a large charge of claustrophobia from the black stuff over there and goes into a flat spin."

"He came out of it."

"Johnny woke up too. In another subjective time-track. Quite harmless to—to Them. So they left him alone. But they lowered the boom on Ives when he showed any resilience. It's breaking point they're after, Captain. Nothing less."

"Hoskins?"

"I guess so," said Paresi tiredly. "Like Johnny, he escaped from a problem he couldn't handle to one he could. Only instead of regressing he's turned to chess. I hope Johnny doesn't bounce back for awhile, yet. He's too—Captain! He's gone!"

They turned and stared at Johnny's bunk. Or—where the bunk had been before the black wall had swelled inwards and covered it.

V

". . . and there I was, Doctor, in the lobby of the hotel at noon, stark naked!"

"Do you have these dreams often?"

"I'm afraid so, Doctor. Am I—all right? I mean . . ."

"Let me ask you this question: Do you believe that these experiences are real?"

"Of course not!"

"Then, Madam, you are, by definition, sane; for insanity, in the final analysis, is the inability to distinguish the real from the unreal."

Paresi and the Captain ran aft together, and together they stopped four paces away from the bulging blackness.

"Johnny!" The Captain's voice cracked with the agonized effort of his cry. He stepped to the black wall, pounded it with the heel of his hand.

"He won't hear you," said Paresi bleakly. "Come back, Captain. Come back."

"Why him? Why Johnny? They've done everything they could to Johnny; you said so yourself!"

"Come back," Paresi said again, soothing. Then he spoke briskly: "Can't you see they're not doing anything to him? They're doing it to us!"

The Captain stood rigidly, staring at the featureless intrusion. He turned presently. "To us," he parroted. Then he stumbled blindly to the Doctor, who put a firm hand on his biceps and walked with him to the forward acceleration couch.

The Captain sat down heavily with his back to this new invasion. Paresi stood by him reflectively, then walked silently to Hoskins.

The Engineer sat over his chessboard in deep concentration. The far edge of the board seemed to be indefinite, lost partially in the mysterious sable curtain which covered the bulkhead.

"Hoskins."

No answer.

Paresi put his hand on Hoskins's shoulder. Hoskins's head came up slowly. He did not turn it. His gaze was straight ahead into the darkness. But at least it was off the board.

"Hoskins," said Paresi, "why are you playing chess?"

"Chess is chess," said Hoskins quietly. "Chess may symbolize any conflict, but it is chess and it will remain chess."

"Who are you playing with?"

No answer.

"Hoskins—we need you. Help us."

Hoskins let his gaze travel slowly downward again until it was on the board. "The word is not the thing," he said. "The number is not the thing. The picture, the ideograph, the symbol—these are not the thing. Conversely . . ."

"Yes, Hoskins."

Paresi waited. Hoskins did not move or speak. Paresi put his hand on the man's shoulder again, but now there was no response. He cursed suddenly, bent, and brought up his hand with a violent smash and sent board and pieces flying.

When the clatter had died down, Hoskins said pleasantly, "The pieces are not the game. The symbols are not the thing." He sat still, his eyes fixed on the empty chair where the board had been. He put out a hand and moved a piece, where there was no piece, to a square which was no longer there. Then he sat and waited.

Paresi, breathing heavily, backed off, whirled, and went back to the Captain.

Anderson looked up at him, and there was the glimmer of humor in his eyes. "Better sit down and talk about something different, Doctor."

Paresi made an animal sound, soft and deep, far back in his throat, plumped down next to the Captain, and kneaded his hands together for a moment. Then he smiled. "Quite right, Skipper. I'd better."

They sat quietly for a moment. Then the Captain prompted, "About the different breaking points . . ."

"Yes, Captain?"

"Perhaps you can put your finger on the thing that makes different men break in different ways, for different reasons. I mean, Johnny's case seemed pretty clear cut, and what you haven't explained about Hoskins, Hoskins has demonstrated pretty clearly. About Ives, now—we can skip that for the time he'll be unconscious. But if you can figure out where you and I might break, why—we'd know what to look for."

"You think that would help?"

"We'd be prepared."

Paresi looked at him sharply. "Let's hypothesize a child who is afraid of the dark. Ask him and he might say that there's a *something* in dark places that will jump out at him. Then assure him, with great authority, that not only is he right but that it's about to jump any minute, and what have you done?"

"Damage," nodded the Captain. "But you wouldn't say that to the child. You'd tell him there was nothing there. You'd *prove* there wasn't."

"So I would," agreed the Doctor. "But in our case I couldn't do anything of the kind. Johnny broke over machines that really didn't work. Hoskins broke over phenomena that couldn't be measured nor understood. Ives broke over things that scuttled and crawled. Subjectively real phenomena, all of them. Whatever basic terrors hide in you and in me will come to face us, no matter how improbable they might be. And you want me to tell you what they are. No, Skipper. Better leave them in your subconscious, where you've buried them."

"I'm not afraid," said the Captain. "Tell me, Paresi! At least I'll know. I'd rather know. I'd so *damn* much rather know!"

"You're sure I can tell you?"

"Yes."

"I haven't psychoanalyzed you, you know. Some of these things are very hard to—"

"You do know, don't you?"

"Damn you, yes!" Paresi wet his lips. "All right, then. I may be doing a wrong thing here . . . You've cuddled up to the idea that I'm a very astute character who automatically knows about things like this, and it's been a comfort to you. Well, I've got news for you. I didn't figure all these things out. I was told."

"Told?"

"Yes, told," said Paresi angrily. "Look, this is supposed to be restricted information, but the Exploration Service doesn't rely on individual aptitude tests alone to make up a crew. There's another factor—call it an inaptitude factor. In its simplest terms, it comes to this: that a crew can't work together only if each member is the most efficient at his job. He has to *need* the others, each one of the others. And the word *need* predicates *lack*. In other words, none of us is a balanced individual. And the imbalances are chosen to match and blend, so that we will react as a balanced unit. Sure I know Johnny's bugaboos, and Hoskins's, and yours. They were all in my indoctrination treatments. I know all your case histories, all your psychic push-buttons."

"And yours?" demanded the Captain.

"Hoskins, for example," said Paresi. "Happily married, no children. Physically inferior all his life. Repressed desire for pure science, which produced more than a smattering of a great many sciences and made him a hell of an Engineer. High idealistic quotient; self-sacrifice. Look at him playing chess, making of this very real situation a theoretical abstraction . . . like leaving a marriage for deep space.

"Johnny we know about. Brought up with never-failing machines. Still plays with them as if they were toys, and like any imaginative child, turns to his toys for reassurance. He needs to be a hero, hence the stars . . .

"Ives . . . always fat. Learned to be easy-going, learned to laugh *with* when others were laughing *at,* and bottling up pressures every time it happened. A large appetite. He's here to satisfy it; he's with us so he can eat up the galaxies . . ."

There was a long pause. "Go on," said the Captain. "Who's next? You?"

"You," said the Doctor shortly. "You grew up with a burning curiosity about the nature of things. But it wasn't a scientist's curiosity; it was an aesthete's. You're one of the few people alive who refused a subsidized education and worked your way through advanced studies as a crewman on commercial space-liners. You became one of the youngest professors of philosophy in recent history. You made a romantic marriage and your wife died in childbirth. Since then—almost a hundred missions with E.A.S., refusing numerous offers of advancement. Do I have to tell you what your bugaboo is now?"

"No," said Anderson hoarsely. "But I'm . . . not afraid of it. I had no idea your . . ." He swallowed. ". . . information was that complete."

"I wish it wasn't. I wish I had some things to—wonder about," said Paresi with surprising bitterness.

The Captain looked at him shrewdly. "Go on with your case histories."

"I've finished."

"No you haven't." When Paresi did not answer, the Captain nudged him. "Johnny, Ives, Hoskins, me. Haven't you forgotten someone?"

"No I haven't," snarled Paresi, "and if you expect me to tell you why a psychologist buries himself in the stars, I'm not going to do it."

"I don't want to be told anything so general," said the Captain. "I just want to know why *you* came out here."

Paresi scowled. The Captain looked away from him and hazarded, "Big frog in a small pond, Nick?"

Paresi snorted.

Anderson asked, "Women don't like you, do they, Nick?"

Almost inaudibly, Paresi said, "Better cut it out, Skipper."

Anderson said, "Closest thing to being a mother—is that it?"

Paresi went white.

The Captain closed his eyes, frowned, and at last said, "Or maybe you just want to play God."

"I'm going to make it tough for you," said Paresi between his teeth. "There are several ways you can break, just as there are several ways to break a log—explode it, crush it, saw it, burn it . . . One of the ways is to fight me until you win. Me, because there's no one else left to fight you. So—I won't fight with you. And you're too rational to attack me unless I do. *That* is the thing that will make it tough. If you must break, it'll have to be some other way."

"Is that what I'm doing?" the Captain asked with sudden mildness. "I didn't know that. I thought I was trying to get your own case history out of you, that's all. What are you staring at?"

"Nothing."

There was nothing. Where there had been forward viewports, there was nothing. Where there had been controls, the communication station, the forward acceleration panels, and storage lockers; the charts and computers and radar gear—there was nothing. Blackness; featureless, silent, impenetrable. They sat on one couch by one wall, to which was fixed one table. Around them was empty floor and a blackness. The chess player faced into it, and perhaps he was partly within it; it was difficult to see.

The Captain and the medical officer stared at one another. There seemed to be nothing to say.

VI

For man's sense is falsely asserted to be the standard of things; on the contrary, all the perceptions, both of the senses and the mind, bear reference to man and not to the universe; and the human mind resembles those uneven mirrors which impart their own properties to different objects . . . and distorts and disfigures them . . . For every one . . . has a cave or den of his own which refracts and discolors the light of nature.
—Sir Francis Bacon (1561-1626)

It was the Captain who moved first. He went to the remaining bulkhead, spun a cog, and opened a cabinet. From it he took a rack of spare radar parts and three thick coils of wire. Paresi, startled, turned and saw Hoskins peering owlishly at the Captain.

Anderson withdrew some tools, reached far back in the cabinet, and took out a large bottle.

"Oh," said Paresi. "That . . . I thought you were doing something constructive."

In the far shadows, Hoskins turned silently back to his game. The Captain gazed down at the bottle, tossed it, caught it. "I am," he said. "I am."

He came and sat beside the Doctor. He thumbed off the stopper and drank ferociously. Paresi watched, his eyes as featureless as the imprisoning dark.

"Well?" said the Captain pugnaciously.

Paresi's hands rose and fell, once. "Just wondering why."

"Why I'm going to get loopin', stoopin' drunk? I'll tell you why, head-shrinker. Because I want to, that's why. Because I like it. I'm doing something I like because I like it. I'm not doing it because of the inversion of this concealed repression as expressed in the involuted feelings my childhood developed in my attitude toward the sex life of beavers, see, couch-catechizer old boy? I like it and that's why."

"I knew a man who went to bed with old shoes because he liked it," said Paresi coldly.

The Captain drank again and laughed harshly. "Nothing can change you, can it, Nick?"

Paresi looked around him almost fearfully. "I can change," he whispered. "Ives is gone. Give me the bottle."

Something clattered to the deck at the hem of the black curtain.

"It's another hallucination," said the Captain. "Go pick up the hallucination, Nicky boy."

"Not my hallucination," said Paresi. "Pick it up yourself."

"Sure," said the Captain good-naturedly. He waited while Paresi drank, took back the bottle, tilted it sharply over his mouth. He wiped his lips with the back of his hand, exhaled heavily, and went to the blackness across the cabin.

"Well, what do you know," he breathed.

"What is it this time?"

Anderson held the thing up. "A trophy, that's what." He peered at it. *"All-American 2675.* Little statue of a guy holding up a victory wreath. Nice going, little guy." He strode to Paresi and snatched away the bottle. He poured liquor on the head of the figurine. "Have a drink, little guy"

"Let me see that."

Paresi took it, held it, turned it over. Suddenly he dropped it as if it were a red-hot coal. "Oh, dear God . . ."

"'S'matter, Nick?" The Captain picked up the statuette and peered at it.

"Put it down, put it down," said the Doctor in a choked voice. "It's—Johnny . . ."

"Oh, it is, it is," breathed the Captain. He put down the statuette gingerly on the table, hesitated, then turned its face away from them. With abrupt animation he swung to Paresi. "Hey! You didn't say it looked like Johnny. You said it *was* Johnny!"

"Did I?"

"Yup." He grinned wolfishly. "Not bad for a psychologist. What a peephole you opened up! Graven images, huh?"

"Shut up, Anderson," said Paresi tiredly. "I told you I'm not going to let you needle me."

"Aw now, it's all in fun," said the Captain. He plumped down and threw a heavy arm across Paresi's shoulders. "Le's be friends. Le's sing a song."

Paresi shoved him away. "Leave me alone. Leave me alone."

Anderson turned away from him and regarded the statuette gravely. He extended the bottle toward it, muttered a greeting, and drank. "I wonder . . ."

The words hung there until Paresi twisted up out of his forlorn reverie to bat them down. "Damn it—*what* do you wonder?"

"Oh," said the Captain jovially, "I was just wondering what you'll be."

"What are you talking about?"

Anderson waved the bottle at the figurine, which called it to his attention again, and so again he drank. "Johnny turned into what he thinks he is. A little guy with a big victory. Hoskins, there, he's going to be a slide-rule, jus' you wait and see. Ol' Ives, that's easy. He's going to be a beer barrel, with beer in it. Always did have a head on him, Ives did." He stopped to laugh immoderately at Paresi's darkening face. "Me, I have no secrets no more. I'm going to be a coat of arms—a useless philosophy rampant on a field of stars." He put the open mouth of the bottle against his forehead and pressed it violently, lowered it, and touched the angry red ring it left between his eyes. "Mark of the beast," he confided. "Caste mark. Zero, that's me and my whole damn family. The die is cast, the caste has died." He grunted appreciatively and turned again to Paresi. "But what's old Nicky going to be?"

"Don't call me Nicky," said the Doctor testily.

"I know," said the Captain, narrowing his eyes and laying one finger alongside his nose. "A ref'rence book, tha's what you'll be. A treatise on the . . .the post-nasal hysterectomy, or how to unbutton a man's prejudices and take down his pride . . . I swiped all that from somewhere . . .

"No!" he shouted suddenly; then, with conspiratorial quiet, he said, "You won't be no book, Nicky boy. Covers aren't hard enough. Not the right type face. Get it?" he roared, and dug Paresi viciously in the ribs. "Type face, it's a witticism."

Paresi bent away from the blow like a caterpillar being bitten by a fire-ant. He said nothing.

"And finally," said the Captain, "you won't be a book because you got . . . no . . . spine." He leapt abruptly to his feet. "Well, what do you know!"

He bent and scooped up an unaccountable object that rested by the nearest shadows. It was a quarter-keg of beer. He hefted it and thumped it heavily down on the table.

"Come on, Nick," he chortled. "Gather ye round. Here's old Ives, like I said."

Paresi stared at the keg, his eyes stretched so wide open that the lids moved visibly with his pulse. "Stop it, Anderson, you swine. . . ."

The Captain tossed him a disgusted glance and a matching snort. From the clutter of radar gear he pulled a screwdriver and a massive little step-down transformer down on its handle. The bung disappeared explosively inside the keg and was replaced by a gout of white foam. Paresi shrieked.

"Ah, shaddup," growled Anderson. He rummaged until he found a tube-shield. He stripped off a small length of self-welding metal tape and clapped it over the terminal-hole at the closed end of the shield, making it into an adequate mug. He waited a moment while the weld cooled, then tipped the keg until solid beer began to run with the foam. He filled the improvised mug and extended it toward Paresi.

"Good ol' Ives," he said sentimentally. "Come on, Paresi. Have a drink on Ives."

Paresi turned and covered his face like a frightened woman.

Anderson shrugged and drank the beer. "It's good beer," he said. He glanced down at the Doctor, who suddenly flung himself face down across the couch with his head hanging out of sight on the opposite side, from which came the sounds of heaving and choking.

"Poor ol' Nick," said the Captain sadly. He refilled the mug and sat down. With his free hand he patted Paresi's back. "Can't take it. Poor, poor ol' Nick . . ."

After that there was a deepening silence, a deepening blackness. Paresi was quiet now, breathing very slowly, holding each breath, expelling air and lying quiet for three full seconds before each inhalation, as if breathing were a conscious effort—more; as if breathing were the whole task, the entire end of existence. Anderson slumped lower and lower. Each time he blinked his lids opened a fraction less, while the time his eyes stayed closed became a fraction of a second longer. The cabin waited as tensely as the taut pose of the rigid little victory trophy.

Then, there was the music.

It was soft, grand music; the music of pageantry, cloth-of-gold and scarlet vestments; pendant jewels and multicolored dimness shouldering upward to be lost in vaulted stone. It was music which awaited the accompaniment whispers, thousands of awed, ritualistic sibilants that would carry no knowable meaning and only one avowed purpose. Soft music, soft, soft; not soft as to volume, the volume grew and grew, but soft with the softness clouds which are soft for all their mountain-size and brilliance; soft and living as a tiger's throat, soft as a breast, as the act of drowning, and huge as a cloud.

Anderson made two moves: he raised his head, and he spun the beer in his mug so its center surface sank and bubbles whirled. With his head up and his eyes down he sat watching the bubbles circle and slow.

Paresi rose slowly and went to the center of the small lighted space left to them, and slowly he knelt. His arms came up and out, and his upturned face was twisted and radiant.

Before him in the blackness there was—or perhaps there had been for some time—a blue glow, almost as lightless the surrounding dark, but blue and physically deep for all that. Its depth increased rather than its light. It became ghost of a grotto, the mouth of a nameless Place.

And in it was a person. A . . . *presence.* It beckoned.

Paresi's face gleamed wetly. "Me?" he breathed. "Want—me?"

It beckoned.

"I—don't believe you," said Paresi. "You can't want me. You don't know who I am. You don't know what I what I've done. You don't want me . . ." His voice covered almost to inaudibility. ". . . do you?"

It beckoned.

"Then you know," sang Paresi in the voice of revelation. "I have denied you with my lips, but you know, you know, you know that underneath . . . deep down . . . I have wavered for an instant. I have kept your image before me."

He rose. Now Anderson watched him.

"You are my life," said Paresi, "my hopes, my fulfillment. You are all wisdom and all charity. Thank you, thank you . . . Master. I give thee thanks, oh Lord," he blurted, and walked straight into the blue glow.

There was an instant when the music was an anthem, and then it too was gone.

Anderson's breath whistled out. He lifted his beer, checked himself, then set it down gently by the figurine of the athlete. He went to the place where Paresi had disappeared, bent, and picked up a small object. He swore, and came back to the couch.

He sucked his thumb and swore again. "Your thorns are sharp, Paresi."

Carefully he placed the object between the beer keg and the statuette. It was a simple wooden cross. Around the arms and shaft, twisted tightly and biting deeply into the wood, was a thorny withe. "God all mighty, Nick," Anderson said mournfully, "you didn't have to hide it. Nobody'd have minded."

"Well?" he roared suddenly at the blackness, "What are you waiting for? Am I in your way? Have I done anything to stop you? Come on, come on!"

His voice rebounded from the remaining bulkhead, but was noticeably swallowed up in the absorbent blackness. He waited until its last reverberations had died, and then until its memory was hard to fix. He pounded futilely at the couch cushions, glared all about in a swift, intense, animal way. Then he relaxed, bent down, and fumbled for the alcohol bottle. "What's the matter with you, out there?" he demanded quietly. "You waiting for me to sober up? You want me to be myself before you fix me up? You want to know something? *In vino veritas,* that's what. You don't have to wait for me, kiddies. I'm a hell of a lot more me right now than I will be after I get over this." He took the figurine and replaced it on the other side of the keg. "Tha's right, Johnny. Get over on the other side of ol' Beer-belly there. Make room for the old man." To the blackness he said, "Look, I got neat habits, don't leave me on no deck, hear? Rack me up alongside the boys. What is it I'm going to be? Oh yeah. A coat of arms. Hey, I forgot the motto. All righty: this is my motto. *'Sic itur ad astra'*—that is to say, 'This is the way to the men's room.'"

Somewhere a baby cried.

Anderson threw his forearm over his eyes.

Someone went "Shh!" but the baby went right on crying.

Anderson said, "Who's there?"

"Just me, darling."

He breathed deeply, twice, and then whispered, "Louise?"

"Of course. *Shh,* Jeannie!"

"Jeannie's with you, Louise? She's all right? You're—all right?"

"Come and see," the sweet voice chuckled.

Captain Anderson dove into the blackness aft. It closed over him silently and completely.

On the table stood an ivory figurine, a quarter-keg of beer, a thorny cross, and a heart. It wasn't a physiological specimen; rather it was the archetype of the most sentimental of symbols; the balanced, cushiony, brilliant-red valentine heart. Through it was a golden arrow, and on it lay cut flowers: lilies, white roses, and forget-me-nots. The heart pulsed strongly; and though it pumped no blood, at least it showed that it was alive, which made it, perhaps, a better thing than it looked at first glance.

Now it was very quiet in the ship, and very dark.

VII

. . . We are about to land. The planet is green and blue below us, and the long trip is over. . . . It looks as if it might be a pleasant place to live . . .

A fragment of Old Testament verse has been running through my mind—from Ecclesiastes, I think. I don't remember it verbatim, but it's something like this:

To every thing there is a season, and a time to every purpose under heaven: A time to weep, and a time to laugh; a time to mourn, and a time to dance; A time to get, and a time to lose; a time to keep, and a time to cast away; A time to be born, and a time to die; a time to plant, and a time to pluck up that which is planted.

For me, anyway, I feel that the time has come. Perhaps it is not to die, but something else, less final or more terrible.

In any case, you will remember, I know, what we decided long ago—that a man owes one of two things to his planet, to his race: posterity, or himself. I could

not contribute the first—it is only proper that I should offer the second and not shrink if it is accepted . . .
—*From a letter by Peter Hoskins to his wife.*

In the quiet and the dark, Hoskins moved.

"Checkmate," he said.

He rose from his chair and crossed the cabin. Ignoring what was on the table, he opened a drawer under the parts cabinet and took out a steel rule. From a book rack he lifted down a heavy manual. He sat on the end of the couch with the manual on his knees and leafed through it, smoothing it open at a page of physical measurements. He glanced at the floor, across it to the black curtain, back to the one exposed bulkhead. He grunted, put the book down, and carried his tape to the steel wall. He anchored one end of it there by flipping the paramagnetic control on the tape case, and pulled the tape across the room. At the blackness he took a reading, made a mark.

Then he took a fore-and-aft measurement from a point opposite the forward end of the table to one opposite the after end of the bunk. Working carefully, he knelt and constructed a perpendicular to this line. He put the tape down for the third time, arriving again at the outboard wall of darkness. He stood regarding it thoughtfully, and then unhesitatingly plunged his arm into it. He fumbled for a moment, moving his hand around in a circle, pressing forward, trying again. Suddenly there was a click, a faint hum. He stepped back.

Something huge shouldered out of the dark. It pressed forward toward him, passed him, stopped moving.

It was the port.

Hoskins wiped sweat away from his upper lip and stood blinking into the airlock until the outer port opened as well. Warm afternoon sunlight and a soft, fresh breeze poured in. In the wind was birdsong and the smell of growing things. Hoskins gazed into it, his mild eyes misty. Then he turned back to the cabin.

The darkness was gone. Ives was sprawled on the after couch, apparently unconscious. Johnny was smiling in his sleep. The Captain was snoring stertorously, and Paresi was curled up like a cat on the floor. The sunlight streamed in through the forward viewports. The manual wheel gleamed on the bulkhead, unbroken.

Hoskins looked at the sleeping crew and shook his head, half-smiling. Then he stepped to the control console and lifted a microphone from its hook. He began to speak softly into it in his gentle, unimpressive voice. He said:

"Reality is what it is, and not what it seems to be. What it seems to be is an individual matter, and even in the individual it varies constantly. If that's a truism, it's still the truth, as true as the fact that this ship cannot fail. The course of events after our landing would have been profoundly different if we had unanimously accepted the thing we knew to be true. But none of us need feel guilty on that score. We are not conditioned to deny the evidence of our senses.

"What the natives of this planet have done is, at base, simple and straightforward. They had to know if the race who built this ship could do so because they were psychologically sound (and therefore capable of reasoning out the building process, among many, many other things) or whether we were merely mechanically apt. To find this out, they tested us. They tested us the way we test steel—to find out its breaking point. And while they were playing a game for our sanity, I played a game for our lives. I could not share it with any of you because it was a game only I, of us all, have experience in. Paresi was right to a certain degree when he said I had retreated into abstraction—the abstraction of chess. He was wrong, though, when he concluded I had been driven to it. You can be quite sure that I did it by choice. It was simply a matter of translating the contactual evidence into an equivalent idea-system.

"I learned very rapidly that when they play a game, they abide by the rules. I know the rules of chess, but I did not know the rules of their game. They did not give me their rules. They simply permitted me to convey mine to them.

"I learned a little more slowly that, though their power to reach our minds is unheard-of in any of the seven galaxies we know about, it still cannot take and use any but the ideas in the fore-front of our consciousness. In other words, chess was a possibility. They could be forced to take a sacrificed piece, as well as being forced to lose one of their own. They extrapolate a sequence beautifully—but they can be out-thought. So much for that: I beat them at chess. And by confining my efforts to the chessboard, where I knew the rules and where they respected them, I was able to keep what we call sanity. Where you were disturbed because the port disappeared, I was not disturbed because the disappearance was not chess.

"You're wondering, of course, how they did what they did to us. I don't know. But I can tell you what they did. They empathize—that is, see through our eyes, feel with our fingertips—so that they perceive what we do. Second, they can control those perceptions; hang on a distortion circuit, as Ives would put it, between the sense organ and the brain. For example, you'll find all our fingerprints all around the port control, where, one after the other, we punched the wall and thought we were punching the button.

"You're wondering, too, what I did to break their hold on us. Well, I simply believed what I knew to be the truth; that the ship is unharmed and unchanged. I measured it with a steel tape and it was so. Why didn't they force me to misread the tape? They would have, if I'd done that measuring first. At the start they were in the business of turning every piece of pragmatic evidence into an outright lie. But I outlasted the test. When they'd finished with their whole arsenal of sensory lies, they still hadn't broken me. They then turned me loose, like a rat in a maze, to see if I could find the way out. And again they abided by their rules. They didn't change the maze when at last I attacked it.

"Let me rephrase what I've done; I feel uncomfortable cast as a superman. We five pedestrians faced some heavy traffic on a surface road. You four tried nobly to cross—deaf and blind-folded. You were all casualties. I was not; and it wasn't because I am stronger or wiser than you, but only because I stayed on the sidewalk and waited for the light to change. . . .

"So we won. Now. . ."

Hoskins paused to wet his lips. He looked at his shipmates, each in turn, each for a long, reflective moment. Again his gentle face showed the half-smile, the small shake of the head. He lifted the mike.

" . . . In my chess game I offered them a minor piece in order to achieve a victory, and they accepted. My interpretation is that they want *me* for further tests. This need not concern you on either of the scores which occur to you as you hear this. First: The choice is my own. It is not a difficult one to make. As Paresi once pointed out, I have a high idealistic quotient. Second: I am, after all, a very minor piece and the game is a great one. I am convinced that there is no test to which they can now subject me, and break me, that any one of you cannot pass.

"But you must in no case come tearing after me in a wild and thoughtless rescue attempt. I neither want that nor need it. And do not judge the natives severely; we are in no position to do so. I am certain now that whether I come back or not, these people will make a valuable addition to the galactic community.

"Good luck, in any case. If the tests shouldn't prove too arduous, I'll see you again. If not, my only regret is that I shall break up what has turned out to be, after all, a very effective team. If this happens, tell my wife the usual things and deliver to her a letter you will find among my papers. She was long ago reconciled to eventualities.

"Johnny . . . the natives will fix your lighter. . .

"Good luck, good-bye."

Hoskins hung up the microphone. He took a stylus and wrote a line: *"Hear my recording. Pete."*

And then, bareheaded and unarmed, he stepped through the port, out into the golden sunshine. Outside he stopped, and for a moment touched his cheek to the flawless surface of the hull.

He walked down into the valley.

Rereading this story over half a century later, I was dismayed at first by the fast introduction of five different characters, making it hard for me to keep them straight. I don't remember being bothered by this when I first read it, so it may be that at age 76 my ability to spot-remember new names was not what it was at age 18. I'm not sure how else it could have been done, short of having a side-bar listing the names and offices for easy reference. The viewpoint perplexed me; there seems to be none, not even omniscient, just a narrative of who said and did what. Had I first encountered this story today the beginning of it would not have impressed me. Then came the message: "Men of Earth! Welcome to our planet," and the game was on. Things would not work. I have been frustrated innumerable times by false error messages locking into the computer, requiring a complete resetting and possible loss of material to clear; I think I'd have reacted much as the crewmen did, had I been one of them. I remembered little of the detail from before, just the overall thrust and details like sweeping away the chessboard. So what do I think of it now? It's a psychological tour de force as each member of the crew is stressed to his breaking point. Except one, who had seemed to have cracked early when he locked onto his chess game. But as it turned out, he was using a game whose rules he knew to relate to the one whose rules he didn't know. I think of it as being like the mechanism to trisect a line: create a trisected line, then draw parallels to the original line, and they will trisect it. Genius, in this situation, where they could not trust their senses. How are the folk of a foreign planet to judge an intruding machine with aggressive creatures aboard? This is an answer. Does it remain my all-time favorite? I don't know, but certainly it's one great story.

—Piers

VENGEANCE FOR NIKOLAI

Walter M. Miller, Jr.

1957

In 1957 a new science fiction magazine appeared, VENTURE, so naturally I gave it a try. The first issue had Sturgeon's "The Girl Had Guts," and the second issue this one. I don't remember what else was in it, but this savage story thrilled me. It was told from an original viewpoint. In those days the cold war was in full force, and all things Soviet were public anathema, so it surely took courage for an author to make a Russian assassin the hero. And the way she killed him—I had never imagined that before. I also learned a new word, "demesnes," one I have subsequently used often enough in my own fiction. The story had verisimilitude—another word I learned from a science fiction story. That is, it seemed that this was the way future war would be; it was believable in its ugliness. My sympathy was with the girl throughout, regardless of her mission. The purpose of any story is to entertain and sometimes broaden the reader's perspective. This did that for me. It was in my fond memory my #2 favorite story.
  —Piers

The distant thunder of the artillery was only faintly audible in the dugout. The girl sat quietly picking at her hands while the colonel spoke. She was only a slip of a girl, all breast and eyes, but there was an intensity about her that made her unmistakably beautiful, and the colonel kept glancing at her sidelong as if his eyes refused to share the impersonal manner of his speech. The light of a single bare bulb glistened in her dark hair and made dark shadows under deep jade eyes already shadowed by weeping. She was listening intently or not at all. She had just lost her child.

"They will not kill you, *grazhdanka,* if you can get safely past the lines," said the colonel. He paced slowly in the dugout, his boot heels clicking pleasantly on the concrete while he sucked at a long cigarette holder and milked his thumbs behind his back in solemn thought. "These Americans, you have heard about their women? No, they will not kill you, unless by accident in passing the lines. They may do other things to you—forgive me!— it is war." He stopped pacing, straddled her shadow, and looked down at her with paternal pity. "Come, you have said nothing, nothing at all. I feel like a swine for asking it of you, but there is no other hope of beating back this attack. And I am ordered to ask you. Do you understand?"

She looked up. Light filled her eyes and danced in them with the moist glittering of a fresh grief, already an ancient grief, old as Man. "They killed my Nikolai," she said softly. "Why do you speak to me so? What can it mean? The bombardment—I know nothing—I cannot think of it. Why do you torment me?"

The colonel betrayed no impatience with her, although he had gone over it twice before. "This morning you tried to leap off the bridge. It is such a shame to die without purpose, *dushka.* I offer you a purpose. Do you love the Fatherland?"

"I am not a Party member, *Tovarish Polkovnik.*"

"I did not ask if you love the Party, my dear. However, you should say *'parties,'* now that we are tolerating those accursed Menshevist deviationists again. Bah! *They* even name members of the *Gorodskoi* Soviets these days. We are becoming a two party republic. How sickening! Where are the old warrior Bolsheviks? It makes one weep. . . . But that is not the question. I asked if you love the Fatherland." She gave a hesitant nod.

"Then think of the Fatherland, think of vengeance for Nikolai. Would you trade your life for that? I know you would. You were ready to fling it away."

She stirred a little; her mind seemed to re-enter the room. "This Ami *Gyenyeral.* Why do you wish him dead?"

"He is the genius behind this assault, my child. Who would have thought the Americans would have chosen such an unlikely place for an invasion? And the manner of it! They parachuted an army ninety miles inland, *instead* of assaulting the fortified coastline. He committed half a million troops to deliberate encirclement. Do you understand what this means? If they had been unable to drive to the coast, they would have been cut off, and the war would very likely be over. With *our* victory. As it was, the coast defenders panicked. The airborne army swept to the sea to capture their beachhead without need of a landing by sea, and now there are two million enemy troops on our soil, and we are in full retreat. *Flight* is a better word. General Rufus MacAmsward gambled his country's entire future on one operation, and he won. If he had lost, they would likely have shot him. Such a man is necessarily mad. A megalomaniac, an evil genius. Oh, I admire him very much! He reminds me of one of their earlier generals, thirty years ago. But that was before their Fascism, before their Blue Shirts."

"And if he is killed?"

The colonel sighed. He seemed to listen for a time to the distant shell-fire. "We are all a little superstitious in wartime," he said at last. "Perhaps we attach too much significance to this one man. But they have no other generals like *him*. He will be replaced by a competent man. We would rather fight competent men than fight an unpredictable devil. He keeps his own counsels, that is so. We know he does not rely heavily upon his staff. His will rules the operation. He accepts intelligence but not advice. If he is struck dead—well, we shall see."

"And I *am* to kill him. It seems unthinkable. How do you know I can?"

The colonel waved a sheaf of papers. "Only a woman can get to him. We have his character clearly defined. Here is his psychoanalytic biography. We have photo-sats of medical records taken from Washington. We have interviews with his ex-wife and his mother. Our psychologists have studied every inch of him. Here, I'll read you—but no, it is very dry, full of psychiatric jargon. I'll boil it down.

"MacAmsward is a champion of the purity of womanhood, and yet he is a vile old lecher. He is at once a baby and an old man. He will kneel and kiss your hand—yes, really. He is a worshiper of womanhood. He will court you, pay you homage, and then expect you to—forgive me—to take him to bed. He could not possibly make advances on you uninvited, but he expects you—as a goddess rewarding a worshiper—to make advances on *him*. He will be your abject servant, but with courtly dignity. His life is full of breast symbols. He clucks in his sleep. He has visited every volcano in the world. He collects anatomical photographs; his women have all been bosomy brunettes. He is still in what the Freudians call the oral stage of emotional development—emotionally a two-year-old. I know Freud is bad politics, but for the Ami, it is sometimes so."

The colonel stopped. There was a sudden tremor in the earth. The colonel lurched, lost his balance. The floor heaved him against the wall. The girl sat still, hands in her lap, face very white. The air shock followed the earth shock, but the thunder clap was muted by six feet of concrete and steel. The ceiling leaked dust.

"Tactical A-missile," the colonel hissed. "Another of them! If they keep it up, they'll drive us to use Lucifer. This is a mad dog war. Neither side uses the H-bomb, but in the end one side or the other will have to use it. If the Kremlin sees certain defeat, we'll use it. So would Washington. If you're being murdered, you might as well take your killer with you if you can. Bah! It is a madness. I, Porphiry Grigoryevich, am as mad as the rest. Listen to me, Marya Dmitriyevna, I met you an hour ago, and now I am madly in love with you, do you hear? Look at you! Only a day after a bomb fragment dashed the life out of your baby, your bosom still swelled with unclaimed milk and dumb grief, and yet I dare stand here and say I am in love with you, and in another breath ask you to go and kill yourself by killing an Ami general! Ah, ah! What insane apes we are! Forget the Ami general. Let us both desert, let us run away to Africa together, to Africa where apes are simpler. There! I've made you cry. What a brute is Porphiry, what a brute!"

The girl breathed in gasps. "Please, *Tovarish Polkovnik!* Please say nothing more! I will go and do what you ask, if it is possible."

"I only ask it, *dushka,* I cannot command it. I advise you to refuse."

"I will go and kill him. Tell me how! Is there a plan? There must be a plan. How shall I pass the lines? How shall I get to him? What is the weapon? How can I kill him?"

"The weapon, you mean? The medical officer will explain that. Of course, you'll be too thoroughly searched to get even a stickpin past the lines. They often use fluoroscopy, so you couldn't even swallow a weapon and get it past them. But there's a way, there's a way—I'll let the *vrach* explain it. I can only tell you how to get taken to MacAmsward after your capture. As for the rest of it, you will be directed by post-hypnotic suggestion. Tell me, you were an officer in the Woman's Defense Corps, the home guard, were you not?"

"Yes, but when Nikki was born, they asked for my resignation."

"Yes, of course, but the enemy needn't find out you're inactive. You have your uniform still? . . . Good! Wear it. Your former company is in action right now. You will join them briefly?"

"And be captured?"

"Yes. Bring nothing but your ID tags. We shall supply the rest. You will carry in your pocket a certain memorandum addressed to all home guard unit commanders. It is in a code the Ami have already broken. It contains the phrase: 'Tactical bacteriological weapons immediately in use.' Nothing else of any importance. It is enough. It will drive them frantic. They will question you. Since you know nothing, they can torture nothing out of you.

"In another pocket, you will be carrying a book of love poetry. Tucked in the book will be a photograph of General Rufus MacAmsward, plus two or three religious ikons. Their Intelligence will *certainly* send the memorandum to MacAmsward; both sides are that nervous about germ weapons. It is most probable that they will send him the book and the picture—for reasons both humorous and practical. The rest will take care of itself. MacAmsward is all ego. Do you understand?"

She nodded. Porphiry Grigoryevich reached for the phone.

"Now I am going to call the surgeon," he said. "He will give you several injections. Eventually, the injections will be fatal, but for some weeks, you will feel nothing from them. Post-hypnotic urges will direct you. If your plan works, you will not kill MacAmsward in the literal sense. If the plan fails, you'll kill him another way if you can. You were an actress, I believe?"

"For a time. I never got to the Bolshoi."

"But excellent! His mother was an actress. You speak English. You are beautiful, and full of grief. It is enough. You are the one. But do you really love the Fatherland enough to carry it out?"

Her eyes burned. "I hate the killers of my son!" she whispered.

The colonel cleared his throat. "Yes, of course. Very well, Marya Dmitriyevna, it is death I am giving you. But you will be sung in our legends for a thousand years. And by the way—" He cocked his head and looked at her oddly. "I believe I really do love you, *dushka.*"

With that, he picked up the phone.

Strange exhilaration surged within her as she crawled through the brush along the crest of the flood embankment, crawled hastily, panting and perspiring under a smoky sun in a dusty sky while Ami fighters strafed the opposite bank of the river where her company was retreating. The last of the Russ troops had crossed, or were killed in crossing. The terrain along the bank where she crawled was now the enemy's. There was no lull in the din of battle, and the ugly belching of artillery mingled with the sound of the planes to batter the senses with a merciless avalanche of noise; but the Ami infantry and mechanized divisions had paused for regrouping at the river. It would be a smart business for the Americans to plunge on across the river at once before the Russians could recognize and prepare to defend it, but perhaps they could not. The assault had carried the Ami forces four hundred miles inland, and it had to stop somewhere and wait for the supply lines to catch up. Marya's guess—and it was the educated guess of a former officer—was that the Ami would bridge the river immediately under air cover and send mechanized killer-strikes across to harass the retreating Russ without involving infantry in an attempt to occupy territory beyond the river.

She fell flat and hugged the earth as machine-gun fire traversed the ridge. A tracer hit rock a yard from her head, spraying her with dust, and sang like a snapped wire as it shot off to the south. The spray of bullets traveled on along the ridge. She moved ahead again.

The danger was unreal. It was all part of an explosive symphony. She had the manna. She could not be harmed. Nothing but vengeance lay ahead. She had only to crawl on.

Was it the drug that made her think like that? Was there a euphoric mixed in the injections? She had felt nothing like this during the raids. During the raids there was only fear, and the struggle to remember whether she had left the teapot boiling while the bombs blew off.

Macbeth. Once she had played Lady Macbeth upon the Moscow stage. How did it go? *The raven himself is hoarse that croaks the fatal entrance of Duncan under my battlements. Come, you spirits that tend on mortal thoughts, unsex me here, and fill me, from crown to toes, top-full of direst cruelty!*

But that wasn't quite it. That wasn't quite what she felt. It was a new power that dwelt in her bosom. It was something else.

Her guard uniform was caked with mud, and the insignia was torn loose from her collar. The earth scuffed her knees and the brush scratched her arms. She kept falling flat to avoid the raking fire of her own machine guns. And yet it was necessary that she stay on the ridge and appear to be seeking a way across the river.

She was too intent upon watching the other side to notice the sergeant. She crawled over a corpse and nearly fell in the foxhole with him. She had been crawling along with her pistol in hand, and the first she saw of the sergeant was his boot. It stamped down on her gun hand. He jammed the muzzle of a tommy-gun against the side of her throat.

"Drop it, sister! *Voyennoplyennvi!*"

She gasped in pain—her hand—and stared up at him with wide eyes. A lank young Ami with curly hair and a quid of tobacco in one cheek.

"*Moya rooka*—my hand!"

He kept his boot heel on the gun, but let her get her hand free. "Get down in here!"

She rolled into the hole. He kicked the gun toward the river.

"*Hey, Cap!*" he yelled over his shoulder. "I got a guest. One of the commissar's ladies." Then to the girl: "Before I kill you, what are you doing on this side of the river, spy?"

"*Most chyeryez ryekoo . . .*"

"I don't speak it. No savvy. *Ya nye govoryu . . .*"

Marya was suddenly terrified. He was lean and young and pale with an unwelcome fear that would easily allow him to fire a burst into her body at close range. The Ami forces had been taking no prisoners during the running battle. The papers called them sub-human beasts because of it, but Marya was sufficiently a soldier to know that prisoners of war were a luxury for an army with stretchy logistic problems, and often the luxury could not be afforded. One Russian lieutenant had brought his men to the Ami under a white flag, and the Ami captain had shot him in the face and ordered his platoon to pick off the others with rifle fire as they tried to flee. In a sense, it was retaliatory. The Russians had taken no prisoners during the Ami airborne landings, and she had seen some Ami airmen herded together and machine-gunned. She hated it. But as an officer, she knew there were times of necessity.

"Please don't shoot," she said in English. "I give up. I can't get across the river anyway."

"What are you doing on this side?" he demanded. "My company was retreating across the bridge. I was the last to start across. Your artillery hit the bridge. The jets finished it off with their rockets." She had to shout to be heard above the roar of battle. She pointed down the river. "I was trying to make it down to the ford. Down there you can wade across."

It was all true. The sergeant thought it over. "Hey, Cap!" he yelled again. "Didn't you hear me? What'll I do with her?"

If there was an answer, it was drowned by shellfire.

"Undress!" the sergeant barked.

"What?"

"I said to take off your clothes. And no tricks. Strip to the skin."

She went sick inside. So now it started, did it? Well, let it come! For the Fatherland! For Nikolai. She began unbuttoning her blouse. She did not look at the Ami sergeant. Once he whistled softly. When she had finished undressing, she looked up defiantly. His face had changed. He moistened his lips and swore softly under his breath. He crossed himself and edged away. Deep within her, something smiled. He was only a boy.

"Well, what are you cursing about?" she asked tonelessly.

"If I didn't think you would I mean, I wish this gun, if I had time I'd, but you'd stab me in the back, but when I think about what they'll do to you back there . . ."

"Jeezis!" he said fervently, wagging his head and rolling his quid into the other cheek. "Put the underwear and the blouse back on, roll up the rest of it, and start crawling down the slope. Aim for that slit trench down there. I'll be right behind you."

"She's quite a little dish, incidentally," the Ami captain was saying on the field telephone. "Are we shooting prisoners now, or are we sending them back . . . Yeah?" He listened for awhile. A mortar shall came screaming down nearby and they all sat down in the trench and opened their mouths to save eardrums. "To whom?" he said when it was over. "Slim? Oh, to you . . . Yeah, that's right, a photograph of Old Brass Butt in person. I can't read the other stuff. It's in Russky. . . . Just a minute. "He covered the mouthpiece and looked up at the sergeant. "Where's the rest of your squad, Sarge?"

The sergeant swallowed solemnly. "I lost all my men except Price and Vittorio, sir. They were wounded and went to the rear."

"Damn! Well, they're sending up replacements tonight, and we're all going back for a breather, as soon as they get here. So you might as well march her on back yourself." He glanced thoughtfully at the girl. "Good God!" he murmured.

Marya was surrounded by several officers. They were all looking at her hungrily. She thought quickly.

"You have searched me," she said coolly. "Would you gentlemen allow me to put on my skirt? I have submitted to capture. As an officer, I expect . . ."

"Look, lady, what you expect doesn't matter a damn!" snapped a lieutenant. "You're a prisoner of war, and you're lucky to be alive. Besides, you are now about to have the high privilege of lying down with six . . ."

"Quiet, Sam!" grunted the captain. "We can't do it. Lady, put on the rest of your clothes and get going."

"Why?" the lieutenant yelled. "That damned sergeant is going to . . ."

"Shut up! Can't you see she's no peasant? Christ, man, this war doesn't make you *all* swine, does it? Sergeant, trade that Chicago typewriter for a forty-five, and take her back to Major Kline for interrogation. Don't touch her, you hear?"

"Yes, sir."

The captain scribbled an order in his notebook, tore out the page, and handed it to the sergeant. "You can probably hitch a ride on the chow wagon part of the way. It's going to get dark pretty soon so keep a leash on her. If anybody starts a gang rape, blow his guts out." He grinned ruefully. "If we are going to pass it up ourselves, by damn, I want to make sure nobody else does it." He glanced at the Russian girl and reddened. "My apologies, lieutenant. We're not really bastards. We're just a long way from home. After we wipe out this Red Disease," (he spat out the words like bites of tainted meat) "you'll see we're not so bad. I hope you'll be treated like an officer and a gentlewoman, even if you are a commie." He bowed slightly and offered the first salute.

"But I'm not—well, thank you, Captain," she said, and returned the salute. . . .

They sat spraddle-legged in the back of the truck as it bounced along the shell-pocked road. The guns had fallen silent, but the sky was full of

Ami squadrons jetting toward the sunset. Pilotless planes and rocket missiles painted swift vapor trails across the heavens, and the sun colored them
with blood. She breathed easier now, and she was very tired. The Ami sergeant sat across from her and kept his gun trained on her and appeared very
ill-at-ease. He blushed several times for no apparent cause. She tried to shut
him out of her consciousness and think of nothing. He was a doggy sort
of a pup, and she disliked him. The Ami were all doggy pups. She had met
them before. There was something of the spaniel in them. Nikolai, Nikolai,
my breasts ache for you, and they burst with your milk, and I must drain
them before I die of it. My baby, my bodykins, my flesh torn from my flesh,
my baby, my pain, my Nikki Andreyevich come milk me—but no, now it
is death, and we can be one again. How wretched it is to ache with milk
and mourn you . . .

"Why are you crying?" the sergeant grunted after awhile.

"You killed my baby."

"I what?"

"Your bombers. They killed my baby. Only yesterday."

"Damnation! So that's why you're—" He looked at her blouse and reddened again.

She glanced down at herself. She was leaking a little, and the pressure
was maddening. So that's what he was blushing about!

There was a crushed paper cup in the back of the truck. She picked it
up and unfolded it, then glanced doubtfully at the sergeant. He was looking
at her in a kind of mournful anguish.

"Do you mind if I turn my back?" she asked.

"Hell's bells!" he said softly, and put away his gun.

"Give me your word you won't jump out, and I won't even look. This
war gives me a sick knot in the gut." He stood up and leaned over the back
of the cab, watching the road ahead and not looking at her, although he
kept one hand on his holster and one boot heel on the hem of her skirt.

Marya tried to dislike him a little less than before. When she was finished, she threw out the cup and buttoned her blouse again. "Thank you,
sergeant, you can turn around now."

He sat down and began talking about his family and how much he
hated the war. Marya sat with her eyes closed and her head tilted back in
the wind and tried not to listen. "Say, how can you have a baby and be in
the army?" he asked after a time.

"Not the army. The home guard. Everybody's in the home guard.
Please, won't you just be quiet awhile?"

"Oh. Well. Sure, I guess."

Once they bailed out of the truck and lay flat in the ditch while two
Russian jets screamed over at low altitude, but the jets were headed else-

where and did not strafe the road. They climbed back in the truck and rolled on. They stopped at two road blocks for MP shakedowns before the truck pulled up at a supply dump. It was pitch dark.

The sergeant vaulted out of the truck. "This is as far as we ride," he told her. "We'll have to walk the rest of the way. It's dark as the devil, and we're only allowed a penlight." He flashed it in her face. "It would be a good chance for you to try to break for it. I hate to do this to you, sis, but put your hands together behind your back."

She submitted to having her wrists bound with telephone wire. She walked ahead of him down the ditch while he pointed the way with the feeble light and held one end of the wire.

"I'd sure hate to shoot you, so please don't try anything."

She stumbled once and felt the wire jerk taut.

"You've cut off the circulation; do you want to cut off the hands?" she snapped. "How much farther do we have to go?"

The sergeant seemed very remorseful. "Stop a minute. I want to think. It's about four miles." He fell silent. They stood in the ditch while a column of tanks thundered past toward the front. There was no traffic going the other way.

"Well?" she asked after awhile.

"I was just thinking about the three Russky women they captured on a night patrol awhile back. And what they did to them at interrogation."

"Go on."

"Well, it's the Blue Shirt boys that make it ugly, not so much the army officers. It's the political heel snappers you've got to watch out for. They see red and hate Russky. Listen, it would be a lot safer for you if I took you in after daylight, instead of at night. During the day, there's sometimes a Red Cross fellow hanging around, and everybody's mostly sober. If you tell everything you know, then they won't be so rough on you."

"Well?"

"There's some deserted gun emplacements just up the hill here, and an old command post. I guess I could stay awake until dawn."

She paused, wondered whether to trust him. No, she shouldn't. But even so, he would be easier to handle than half a dozen drunken officers.

"All right, Ami, but if you don't take these wires off, your medics will have to amputate my hands."

They climbed the hill, crawled through splintered logs and burned timbers, and found the command post underground. Half the roof was caved in, and the place smelled of death and cartridge casings, but there was a canvas cot and a gasoline lantern that still had some fuel in it. After he had freed her wrists, she sat on the cot and rubbed the numbness out of her hands while he opened a K-ration and shared it with her. He watched her rather wistfully while she ate.

"It's too bad you're on the wrong side of this war," he said. "You're okay, as Russkies go. How come you're fighting for the commies?"

She paused, then reached down and picked up a handful of dirt from the floor, kneaded it, and showed it to him, while she nibbled cheese.

"Ami, this has the blood of my ancestors in it. This ground is mine. Now it has the blood of my baby in it; don't speak to me of sides, or leaders, or politics." She held the soil out to him. "Here, look at it. But don't touch. It's mine. No, when I think about it, go ahead and *touch*. Feel it, smell it, taste a little of it the way a peasant would to see if it's ripe for planting. I'll even give you a handful of it to take home and mix with your own. It's mine to give. It's also mine to fight for." She spoke calmly and watched him with deep jade eyes. She kept working the dirt in her hand and offering it to him. "Here! This is Russia. See how it crumbles? It's what they'll bury you in. Here, take it." She tossed it at him. He grunted angrily and leaped to his feet to brush himself off.

Marya went on eating cheese. "Do you want an argument, Ami?" she asked, chewing hungrily while she talked. "You will get awfully dirty, if you do. I have a simple mind. I can only keep tossing handfuls of Russia at you to answer your ponderous questions."

He did an unprecedented thing. He sat down on the floor and began—well, almost sobbing. His shoulders heaved convulsively for a moment. Marya stopped eating cheese and stared at him in amazement. He put his arms across his knees and rolled his forehead on them. When he looked up, his face was blank as a frightened child's.

"God, I want to go home!" he croaked.

Marya put down the K-ration and went to bend over him. She pulled his head back with a handful of his hair and kissed him. Then she went to lie down on the cot and turned her face to the wall.

"Thanks, Sergeant," she said. "I hope they don't bury you in it after all."

When she awoke, the lantern was out. She could see him bending over her, silhouetted against the stars through the torn roof. She stifled a shriek.

"Take your hands away!"

He took them away at once and made a choking sound. His silhouette vanished. She heard him stumbling among the broken timbers, making his way outside. She lay there thinking for awhile, thoughts without words. After a few minutes, she called out.

"Sergeant? Sergeant!"

There was no answer. She started up and kicked something that clattered. She went down on her knees and felt for it in the dark. Finally she found it. It was his gun.

"*Sergeant!*"

After awhile he came stumbling back. "Yes?" he asked softly.

"Come here."

His silhouette blotted the patch of stars again. She felt for his holster and shoved the gun back in it.

"Thanks, Ami, but they would shoot you for that."

"I could say you grabbed it and ran."

"Sit down, Ami."

Obediently he sat.

"Now give me your hands again," she said, then, whispering: "No, please! Not there! Not there."

The last thing would be vengeance and death, but the next to the last thing was something else. And it was clearly in violation of the captain's orders.

It was the beating of the old man that aroused her fury. They dragged him out of the bunker being used by Major Kline for questionings, and they beat him about the head with a piece of hydraulic hose. "They" were immaculately tailored Blue Shirts of the Americanist Party, and "he" was an elderly Russian major of near retirement age. Two of them held his arms while the third kicked him to his knees and whipped him with the hose.

"Just a little spanking, commie, to learn you how to recite for teacher, see?"

"Whip the bejeezis out of him." "Fill him with gasoline and stick a wick in his mouth." "Give it to him!"

They were very methodical about it, like men handling an unruly circus animal. Marya stood in line with a dozen other prisoners, waiting her turn to be interrogated. It was nine in the morning, and the sun was evaporating the last of the dew on the tents in the camp. The sergeant had gone into the bunker to report to Major Kline and present the articles her captors had taken from her person. He had been gone ten minutes. When he came out, the Blue Shirts were still whipping the prisoner. The old man had fainted. "He's faking."

"Wake him up with it, Mac. Teach him." The sergeant walked straight toward her but gave no sign of recognition. He did not look toward the whistle and slap of the hose, although his face seemed slightly pale. He drew his gun in approaching the prisoners and a guard stepped into his path. "Halt! You can't . . ."

"Major Kline's orders, Corporal. He'll see Marya Dmitriyevna Lisitsa next. Right now. I'm to show her in." The guard turned blankly to look at the prisoners. "*That* one," said the sergeant.

"The girl? Okay, you! *Shagom marsh!*" She stepped out of line and went with the sergeant, who took her arm and hissed, "Make it easy on yourself," out of the corner of his mouth. Neither looked at the other. It was dark in the bunker, but she could make out a fat little major behind the desk. He had a poker expression and a small moustache. He kept drumming his fingers on the desk and spoke in comic grunts.

"So this is the wench," he muttered at the sergeant. He stared at Marya for a moment, then thundered: "Attention! Hit a brace! Has nobody taught you how to salute?"

Her fury congealed into a cold knot. She ignored the command and refused to answer in his own language. *"Ya nye govoryu po Angliiski!"* she snapped.

"I thought you said she spoke English," he grunted at the sergeant. "I thought you said you'd talked to her."

She felt the sergeant's fingers tighten on her arm. He hesitated. She heard him swallow. Then he said, "Yes, sir, I did. Through an interpreter."

Bless you, little sergeant! she thought, not daring to look her thanks at him.

"Hoy, McCoy!" the major bellowed toward the door. The man who came in was not McCoy, but one of the Americanist Blue Shirts. He gave the major a cross-breasted Americanist salute and barked the slogan: *"Ameh'ca Fust!"*

"America First," echoed the major without vigor and without returning the political salute. "What is it now?"

"I regrets to repoaht, suh, that the cuhnel is dead of a heaht condition, and can't answeh moa questions."

"I told you to loosen him up, not kill him. Damn! Well, no help for it. Get him out. That's all, Purvis, that's all."

"Ameh'ca Fust!"

"Yeah."

The Blue Shirt smacked his heels, whirled, and hiked out. The interpreter came in.

"McCoy, I hate this job. Well, there she is. Take a gander. She's the one with the bacteriological memo and the snap of MacAmsward. I'm scared to touch it. They'll want this one higher up. Look at her. A fine piece, eh?"

"Distinctly, sir," said McCoy, who looked legal and regal and private-school-polished.

"Yes, well, let's begin. Sergeant, wait outside 'till we're through."

She was suddenly standing alone with them, eyes bright with fury.

"Why did you begin using bacteriological weapons?" Kline barked.

The interpreter repeated the question in Russian. The question was a silly beginning. No one had yet made official accusations of germ warfare. She answered with a crisp sentence, causing the interpreter to make a long face.

"She says they are using such weapons because they dislike us, sir."

The major coughed behind his hand. "Tell her what will happen to her if she does that again. Let's start over." He squinted at her. "Name?"

"*Imya?*" echoed McCoy.

"Marya Dmitriyevna."

"*Familiya?*"

"Lisitsa."

"It means 'fox,' sir. Possibly a lie."

"Well, Marya Dmitriyevna Fox, what's your rank?"

"*V kakom vy chinye?*" snapped McCoy.

"*Starshii Lyeityenant,*" said the girl.

"Senior lieutenant, sir."

"You see, girl? It's all straight from Geneva. Name, rank, serial number, that's all. You can trust us. . . . Ask her if she's with Intelligence."

"*Razvye'dyvatyel naya sluzhba?*"

"*Nyet!*"

"Nyet, eh? How many divisions are ready at the front?"

"*Sol'kyo na frontye divizii?*"

"*Ya nye pomnyu!*"

"She says she doesn't remember."

"Who is your battalion commander, Lisitsa?"

"*Kto komandir va'shyevo batalyona?*"

'*Ya nye pomnyu!*"

"She says she doesn't remember."

"Doesn't, eh? Tell her I know she's a spy, and we'll shoot her at once."

The interpreter repeated the threat in Russian. The girl folded her arms and stared contempt at the major.

"You're to stand at attention!"

"*Smirno!*"

She kept her arms folded and stood as she had been standing. The major drew his forty-five and worked the slide.

"Tell her that I am the sixteenth bastard grandson of Mickey Spillane and blowing holes on ladies' bellies is my heritage and my hobby."

The interpreter repeated it. Marya snorted three words she had learned from a fisherman.

"I think she called you a castrate, sir."

The major lifted the automatic and took casual aim. Something in his manner caused the girl to go white. She closed her eyes and murmured something reverent in favor of the Fatherland.

The gun jumped in Kline's hand. The crash brought a yell from the sergeant outside the bunker. The bullet hit concrete out the doorway and screamed off on a skyward ricochet. The girl bent over and grabbed at the front of her skirt. There was a bullet hole in front and in back where the slug had passed between her thighs. She cursed softly and fanned the skirt.

"Tell her I am a terrible marksman, but will do better next time," chuckled Kline. "Good thing the light shows through that skirt, eh, McCoy—or I might have burned the 'tender demesnes.' There! Is she still cursing me?"

"Fluently, sir."

"I must have burned her little white hide. Give her a second to cool off, then ask what division she's from."

"*Kakovo vy polka?*"

"*Ya nye pomnyu!*"

"She has a very poor memory, sir."

The major sighed and inspected his nails. They were grubby. "Tell her," he muttered, "that I think I'll have her assigned to C company as its official prostitute after our psychosurgeons make her a nymphomaniac."

McCoy translated. Marya spat. The major wrote.

"Have you been in any battles, woman?" he grunted.

"*F kakikh srazhyeniyakh vy oochast'vovali?*"

"*Ya nye pomnyu!*"

"She says—"

"Yeah, I know. It was a silly question." He handed the interpreter her file. "Give these to the sergeant and have him take her up to Purvis. I haven't the heart to whip information out of a woman. Slim's queer; he loves it." He paused, looking her over. "I don't know whether to feel sorry for her, or for Purvis. That's all, McCoy."

The sergeant led her to the Blue Shirts' tent. "Listen," he whispered. "I'll sneak a call to the Red Cross." He appeared very worried in her behalf.

The pain lasted for several hours. She lay on a cot somewhere while a nurse and a Red Cross girl took blood samples and smears. They kept giving each other grim little glances across the cot while they ministered to her. "We'll see that the ones who did it to you are tried," the Red Cross worker told her in bad Russian.

"I speak English," Marya muttered, although she had never admitted it to her interrogators, not even to Purvis.

"You'll be all right. But why don't you cry?" But she could only cry for Nikolai now, and even that would be over soon. She lay there for two days and waited.

After that, there was General MacAmsward, and a politer form of questioning. The answers, though, were still the same.

"*Ya nye pomnyu!*"

What quality or quantity can it be, laughably godlike, transubstantially apelike, that abides in the flesh of brutes and makes them men? For General MacAmsward was indeed a man, although he wished to be only a soldier.

There are militarists who love the Fatherland, and militarists who love the Motherland, and the difference between them is as distinct as the difference between the drinkers of bourbon and the drinkers of rye. There are the neo-Prussian zombies in jackboots who stifle their souls to make themselves machines of the Fatherland, but MacAmsward was not one of them. MacAmsward was a Motherland man, and Mother was never much interested in machines. Mother raised babies into champions, and a champion is mightier than the State; never is he a tool of the State. So it was with Rufus MacAmsward, evil genius by sworn word of Porphiry Grigoryevich.

Consider a towering vision of Michael the Archangel carrying a swagger stick. Fresh from the holy wars of Heaven he comes, striding past the rows of white gloved orderlies standing at saber salute, their halos (M-1, official nimbus) studded with brass spikes. The archangel's headgear is a trifle rakish, crusted with gold laurel and dented by a dervish devil's bullet. He ignores the thrones and dominations, but smiles democratically at a lowly cherub and pauses to inquire after the health of his grandmother.

Grandmother is greatly improved.

Immensely reassured, General MacAmsward strides into his quarters and hangs up his hat. The room is in darkness except for the light from a metal wall lamp that casts its glare around the great chair and upon the girl who sits in the great chair at the far end of the room. The girl is toying with a goblet of wine, and her dark hair coils in thick masses about her silk-clad shoulders. The silk came by virtue of the negligence of the general's ex-wife in forgetting to pack. The great chair came as a prize of war, having been taken from a Soviet People's Court where it is no longer needed. It is massive as an episcopal throne—a fitting seat for an archangel—and it is placed on a low dais at the head of a long table flanked by lesser chairs. The room is used for staff conference, and none would dare to sit in the great chair except the general—or, of course, a lovely grief-stung maiden.

The girl stares at him from out of two pools of shadow. Her head is slightly inclined and the downlight catches only the tip of her nose. The general pauses with his hand on his hat. He turns slowly away from the hat rack, brings himself slowly to attention, and gives her a solemn salute. It is a tribute to beauty. She acknowledges it with a nod. The general advances and sits in the simple chair at the far end of the long table. The general sighs with fervor, as if he had not breathed since entering the door. His eyes have not left her face. The girl puts down the glass.

"I have come to kill you," she said. "I have come to nurse you to death with the milk of a murdered child."

The general winced. She had said it three times before, once for each day she had resided in his house. And for the fourth time, the general ignored it.

"I have seen to it, my child," he told her gravely. "Captain Purvis faces court martial in the morning. I have directed it. I have directed too that you be repatriated forthwith, if it is your wish, for this is only common justice after what that monster has done to you. Now however let me implore you to remain with us and quit the forces of godlessness until the war is won and you can return to your home in peace."

Marya watched his shadowy figure at the far end of the table. He was like Raleigh at the court of Beth, at once mighty and humble. Again she felt the surge of exhilaration, as when she had crawled along the ridge at the river, ducking machine gun fire. It was the voice of Macbeth's wife whispering within her: *Come to my woman's breasts, and take my milk for gall, you murdering ministers, wherever in your sightless substances you wait on nature's mischief!* It was the power of death in her bosom, where once had been the power of life.

She arose slowly and leaned on the table to stare at him fiercely. "Murderer of my child!" she hissed.

"May God in His mercy—"

"Murderer of my child!"

"Marya Dmitriyevna, it is my deepest sorrow." He sat watching her gravely and seemed to lose none of his lofty composure. "I can say nothing to comfort you. It is impossible. It is my deepest sorrow."

"There is something you can do."

"Then it is done. Tell me quickly."

"Come here." She stepped from the table to the edge of the dais and beckoned. "Come to me here. I have secrets to whisper to the killer of my son. Come."

He came and stood down from her so that their faces were at the same level. She could see now that there was real pain in his eyes. Good! Let it be. She must make him understand. He must know perfectly well that she was going to kill him. And he must know how. The necessity of knowing was not by any command of Porphiry's; it was a must that she had created within herself. She was smiling now, and there was a new quickness in her gestures.

"Look at me, high killer. I cannot show you the broken body of my son. I can show you no token or relic. It is all buried in a mass grave." Swiftly she opened the silk robe. "Look at me instead. See? How swollen I am again. Yes, here! A token after all. A single drop. Look, it is his, it is Nikolai's."

MacAmsward went white. He stood like a man hypnotized.

"See? To nourish life, but now to nourish death. Your death, high killer. But more! My son was conceived in love, and you have killed him, and now I come to you. You will give me another, you see. Now we shall conceive him in hate, you and I, and you'll die of the death in my bosom. Come, make hate to me, killer."

His jaw trembled. He took her shoulders and ran his hands down her arms and closed them over hers.

"Your hands are ice," he whispered, and leaned forward to kiss a bare spot just below her throat, and somehow she was certain that he understood. It was a preconscious understanding, but it was there. And still he bent over her.

Come, thick night, and pall thee in the dunnest smoke of hell, that my keen knife see not the wound it makes . . . Of course the general had been intellectually convinced that it was entirely a figure of speech.

The toxin's work was quickly done. A bacterial toxin, swiftly lethal to the non-immunized, slowly lethal to Marya who could pass it out in her milk as it formed. The general slept for half an hour and woke up with a raging fever. She sat by the window and watched him die. He tried to shout, but his throat was constricted. He got out of bed, took two steps, and fell. He tried to crawl toward the door. He fell flat again. His face was crimson. The telephone rang.

Someone knocked at the door.

The ringing stopped and the knocking went away. She watched him breathe. He tried to speak, but she turned her back to him and looked out the window at the shell-pocked countryside. Russia, Nikolai, and even the Ami sergeant who had wanted to go home, it was for them that she listened to his gasping. She lit one of his American cigarettes and found it very enjoyable. The phone was ringing furiously again. It kept on ringing.

The gasping stopped. Someone was hammering on the door and shouting. She stood enjoying the cigarettes and watching the crows flocking in a newly planted field. The earth was rich and black here, the same soil she had tossed at the Ami sergeant. It belonged to her, this soil. Soon she would belong to it. With Nikolai, and maybe the Ami sergeant.

The door crashed loose from its hinges. Three Blue Shirts burst in and stopped. They looked at the body on the floor. They looked at Marya.

"What has happened here?"

The Russian girl laughed. Their expressions were quite comical. One of them raised his gun. He pulled the trigger six times.

"Come . . . Nikki Andreyevich . . . come . . ."

One of them went over and nudged her with his boot, but she was already dead. She had beaten them. She had beaten them all.

The American newspapers printed the truth. They said that General MacAmsward had died of poisoned milk. But that was all they said. The *whole* truth was only sung in Russian legend for the next one thousand years.

I had forgotten details, but it remains a savage masterpiece. It is not a nice story, yet it still rings true, as the atrocities perpetrated by Americans in Iraq indicate. We like to think that we are morally superior, that only regimes like the Nazis practiced torture and humiliation, but any nationality can do it when conditions are conducive. I note ellipses that I suspect would hide less were the story written today, so that the beating is hidden, and of course the giving of her breasts, but the essence gets through. I hate the things this story depicts, yet love the story itself. That's part of what makes it superior. It may be coincidence, but that story was published the same time as my wife and I lost our first baby, a boy, stillborn. So I had reason to appreciate the pain of such a loss, though there was no enemy to blame it on.
—Piers

THE GIRL
HAD GUTS

Theodore Sturgeon

1957

This was the other remarkable story presented by the then-new magazine VEN-TURE, and I recognized it immediately as a likely classic. Sturgeon was a re-markable writer, capable of outstanding notions and arguably the finest stylist the genre has seen. I met him I think in 1982 and sat beside him at a panel, when he was writing very little. He was a fine writer who didn't actually like to write, in contrast to me: I love to write despite demeaning assessments by critics. We had a somewhat devious personal interaction. He was fascinated by my daughter Cheryl, then twelve and the very picture of dawning womanhood, something he clearly appreciated. Years later I met Sturgeon's daughter, and elected not to collaborate with her on a book. Regardless, I remember this story as demonstrating one of the wildest ideas the genre has seen. I remember few details apart from the one that relates to the title; I just know it's a great story.

  —Piers

The cabby wouldn't take the fare ("Me take a nickel from Captain Gargan? Not in this life!") and the doorman welcomed me so warmly I almost forgave Sue for moving into a place that had a doorman. And then the elevator and then Sue. You have to be away a long time, a long way, to miss someone like that, and me, I'd been farther away than anyone ought to be for too long plus six weeks. I kissed her and squeezed her until she yelled for mercy, and when I got to where I realized she was yelling we were clear back to the terrace, the whole length of the apartment away from the door. I guess I was sort of enthusiastic, but as I said . . . oh, who can say a thing like that and make any sense? I was glad to see my wife, and that was it.

She finally got me quieted down and my uniform jacket and shoes off and a dish of ale in my fist, and there I lay in the relaxer looking at her just the way I used to when I could come home from the base every night, just the way I'd dreamed every off-duty minute since we blasted off all those months ago. Special message to anyone who's never been off Earth: Look around you. Take a good *long* look around. You're in the best place there is. A fine place.

I said as much to Sue, and she laughed and said, "Even the last six weeks?" and I said, "I don't want to insult you, baby, but yes: even those six weeks in lousy quarantine at the lousy base hospital were good, compared to being anyplace else. But it was the longest six weeks I ever spent? I'll give you that." I pulled her down on top of me and kissed her again. "It was longer than twice the rest of the trip."

She struggled loose and patted me on the head the way I don't like. "Was it so bad really?"

"It was bad. It was lonesome and dangerous and—and disgusting, I guess is the best word for it."

"You mean the plague."

I snorted. "It wasn't a plague."

"Well, I wouldn't know," she said. "Just rumors. That thing of you recalling the crew after twelve hours of liberty, for six weeks of quarantine . . ."

"Yeah, I guess that would start rumors." I closed my eyes and laughed grimly. "Let 'em rumor. No one could dream up anything uglier than the truth. Give me another bucket of suds."

She did, and I kissed her hand as she passed it over. She took the hand right away and I laughed at her. "Scared of me or something?"

"Oh Lord no. Just . . . wanting to catch up. So much you've done, millions of miles, months and months . . . and all I know is you're back, and nothing else."

"I brought the Demon Lover back safe and sound," I kidded.

She colored up. "Don't talk like that." The Demon Lover was my Second, name of Purcell. Purcell was one of those guys who just has to go around making like a bull moose in fly-time, bellowing at the moon and banging his antlers against the rocks. He'd been to the house a couple or three times and said things about Sue that were so appreciative that I had to tell him to knock it off or he'd collect a punch in the mouth. Sue had liked him, though; well, Sue was always that way, always going a bit out of her way to get upwind of an animal like that. And I guess I'm one of 'em myself; anyway, it was me she married. I said, "I'm afraid ol' Purcell's either a blow-hard or he was just out of character when we rounded up the crew and brought 'em all back. We found 'em in honky-tonks and strip joints; we found 'em in the bosoms of their families behaving like normal family men do after a long trip; but Purcell, we found him at the King George Hotel—" I emphasized with a forefinger—"alone by himself and fast asleep, where he tells us he went as soon as he got earth side. Said he wanted a soak in a hot tub and 24 hours' sleep in a real 1-G bed with sheets. How's that for a sailor ashore on his first leave?"

She'd gotten up to get me more ale. "I haven't finished this one yet!" I said.

She said oh and sat down again. "You were going to tell me about the trip."

"I was? Oh, all right, I was. But listen carefully, because this is one trip I'm going to forget as fast as I can, and I'm not going to do it again, even in my head."

I don't have to tell you about blastoff—that it's more like drift-off these days, since all long hops start from Outer Orbit satellites, out past the Moon—or about the flicker-field by which we hop faster than light, get dizzier than a five-year-old on a drug store stool, and develop more morning-sickness than Mom. That I've told you before.

So I'll start with planetfall on Mullygantz II, Terra's best bet to date for a colonial planet, five-nines Earth Normal (that is, .99999) and just about as handsome a rock as ever circled a sun. We hung the blister in stable orbit and Purcell and I dropped down in a superscout with supplies and equipment for the ecological survey station. We expected to find things humming there, five busy people and a sheaf of completed reports, and we hoped we'd be the ones to take back the news that the next ship would be the colony ship. We found three dead and two sick, and knew right away that the news we'd be taking back was going to stop the colonists in their tracks.

Clement was the only one I'd known personally. Head of the station, physicist and ecologist both, and tops both ways, and he was one of the dead. Joe and Katherine Flent were dead. Amy Segal, the recorder—one of the best in Pioneer Service—was sick in a way I'll go into a minute, and Glenda Spooner, the plant biologist, was—well, call it withdrawn. Retreated. Something had scared her so badly that she could only sit with her arms folded and her legs crossed and her eyes wide open, rocking and watching.

Anyone gets to striking hero medals ought to make a platter-sized one for Amy Segal. Like I said, she was sick. Her body temperature was wildly erratic, going from 102 all the way down to 96 and back up again. She was just this side of breakdown and must have been like that for weeks, slipping across the line for minutes at a time, hauling herself back for a moment or two, then sliding across again. But she knew Glenda was helpless, though physically in perfect shape, and she knew that even automatic machinery has to be watched. She not only dragged herself around keeping ink in the recording pens and new charts when the seismo's and hygro's and airsonde recorders needed them, but she kept Glenda fed; more than that, she fed herself.

She fed herself *close to fifteen thousand calories a day.* And she was forty pounds underweight. She was the weirdest sight you ever saw, her face full like a fat person's but her abdomen, from the lower ribs to the pubes, collapsed almost against her spine. You'd never have believed an organism could require so much food—not, that is, until you saw her eat. She'd rigged up a chopper out of the lab equipment because she actually couldn't wait to chew her food. She just dumped everything and anything edible into that gadget and propped her chin on the edge of the table by the outlet, and packed that garbage into her open mouth with both hands. If she could have slept it would have been easier but hunger would wake her after twenty minutes or so and back she'd go, chop and cram, guzzle and swill. If Glenda had been able to help—but there she was, she did it all herself, and when we got the whole story straight we found she'd been at it for nearly three weeks. In another three weeks they'd have been close to the end of their stores, enough for five people for anyway another couple of months.

We had a portable hypno in the first-aid kit on the scout, and we slapped it to Glenda Spooner with a reassurance tape and a normal sleep command, and just put her to bed with it. We bedded Amy down too, though she got a bit hysterical until we could make her understand through that fog of delirium that one of us would stand by every minute with premasticated rations. Once she understood that she slept like a corpse, but such a corpse you never want to see, lying there eating.

It was a lot of work all at once, and when we had it done Purcell wiped his face and said, "Five-nines Earth Normal, hah. No malignant virus or bacterium. No toxic plants or fungi. Come to Mullygantz II, land of happiness and health."

"Nobody's used that big fat *no,*" I reminded him. "The reports only say there's nothing bad here that we know about or can test for. My God, the best brains in the world used to kill AB patients by transfusing type O blood. Heaven help us the day we think we know everything that goes on in the universe."

We didn't get the whole story then; rather, it was all there but not in a comprehensible order. The key to it all was Amy Segal's personal log, which she called a "diary," and kept in hentracks called shorthands, which took three historians and a philologist a week to decode after we returned to Earth. It was the diary that fleshed the thing out for us, told us about these people and their guts and how they exploded all over each other. So I'll tell it, not the way we got it, but the way it happened.

To begin with, it was a good team. Clement was a good head, one of those relaxed guys who always listens to other people talking. He could get a fantastic amount of work out of a team and out of himself too, and it never showed. His kind of drive is sort of a secret weapon.

Glenda Spooner and Amy Segal were wild about him in a warm respectful way that never interfered with the work. I'd guess that Glenda was more worshipful about it, or at least, with her it showed more. Amy was the little mouse with the big eyes that gets happier and stays just as quiet when her grand passion walks into the room, except maybe she works a little harder so he'll be pleased. Clement was bed-friends with both of them, which is the way things usually arrange themselves when there's an odd number of singles on a team. It's expected of them, and the wise exec keeps it going that way and plays no favorites, at least till the job's done.

The Flents, Katherine and Joe, were married, and had been for quite a while before they went Outside. His specialty was geology and mineralogy and she was a chemist, and just as their sciences supplemented each other so did their egos. One of Amy's early "diary" entries says they knew each other so well they were one step away from telepathy; they'd work side by side for hours swapping information with grunts and eyebrows.

Just what kicked over all this stability it's hard to say. It wasn't a fine balance; you'd think from the look of things that the arrangement could stand a lot of bumps and friction. Probably it was an unlucky combination of small things all harmless in themselves, but having a critical-mass characteristic that nobody knew about. Maybe it was Clement's sick spell that triggered it; maybe the Flents suddenly went into one of those oh-God-what-did-I-ever-see-in-you phases that come over married people who are never separated; maybe it was Amy's sudden crazy yen for Joe Flent and her confusion over it. Probably the worst thing of all was that Joe Flent might have sensed how she felt and caught fire too. I don't know. I guess, like I said, that they all happened at once.

Clement getting sick like that. He was out after bio specimens and spotted a primate. They're fairly rare on Mully-gantz II, big ugly devils may-be five feet tall but so fat they outweigh a man two to one. They're mottled pink and gray, and hairless, and they have a face that looks like an angry gorilla when it's relaxed, and a ridiculous row of little pointed teeth instead of fangs. They get around pretty good in the trees but they're easy to outrun on the ground, because they never learned to use their arms and knuckles like the great apes, but waddle over the ground with their arms held up in the air to get them out of the way. It fools you. They look so damn silly that you forget they might be dangerous.

So anyway, Clement surprised one on the ground and had it headed for the open fields before it knew what was happening. He ran it to a stand-still, just by getting between it and the trees and then approaching it. The primate did all the running; Clement just maneuvered it until it was totally pooped and squatted down to await its doom. Actually all the doom it would have gotten from Clement was to get stunned, hypoed, examined and turned loose, but of course it had no way of knowing that. It just sat there in the grass looking stupid and ludicrous and harmless in an ugly sort of way, and when Clement put out his hand it didn't move, and when he patted it on the neck it just trembled. He was slowly withdrawing his hand to get his stun-gun out when he said something or laughed—anyway, made a sound, and the thing bit him.

Those little bitty teeth weren't what they seemed. The gums are retrac-tile and the teeth are really not teeth at all but serrated bone with all those little needles slanting inward like a shark's. The jaw muscles are pretty flab-by, fortunately, or he'd have lost an elbow, but all the same, it was a bad bite. Clement couldn't get loose, and he couldn't reach around himself to get to the stun-gun, so he drew his flame pistol, thumbed it around to "low," and scorched the primate's throat with it. That was Clement, never wanting to do any more damage than he had to. The primate opened its mouth to protect its throat and Clement got free. He jumped back and twisted his foot and fell, and something burned him on the side of the face like a lick of hellfire. He scrambled back out of the way and got to his feet. The primate was galloping for the woods on its stumpy little legs with its long arms up over its head—even then Clement thought it was funny. Then something else went for him in the long grass and he took a big leap out of its way.

He later wrote very careful notes on this thing. It was wet and it was nasty and it stunk beyond words. He said you could search your memory long afterwards and locate separate smells in that overall stench the way you can with the instruments of an orchestra. There was butyl mercaptan and rotten celery, excrement, formic acid, decayed meat and that certain smell which is like the taste of some brasses. The burn on his cheek smelt like hydrochloric acid at work on a hydrocarbon; just what it was.

The thing was irregularly spherical or ovoid, but soft and squashy. Fluids of various lands oozed from it here and there—colorless and watery, clotted yellow like soft-boiled eggs, and blood. It bled more than anything ought to that needs blood; it bled in gouts from openings at random, and it bled cutaneously, droplets forming on its surface like the sweat on a glass of icewater. Cutaneously, did I say? That's not what Clement reported. It looked skinless—flayed was the word he used. Much of its surface was striated muscle fiber, apparently unprotected. In two places that he could see was naked brown tissue like liver, drooling and dripping excretions of its own.

And this thing, roughly a foot and a half by two feet and weighing maybe thirty pounds, was flopping and hopping in a spastic fashion, not caring which side was up (if it had an up) but always moving toward him.

Clement blew sharply out of his nostrils and stepped back and to one side—a good long step, with the agony of his scalded cheek to remind him that wherever the thing had come from, it was high up, and he didn't want it taking off like that again.

And when he turned like that, so did the thing, leaving behind it a trail of slime and blood in the beaten grass, a curved filthy spoor to show him it knew him and wanted him.

He confesses he does not remember dialing up the flame pistol, or the first squeeze of the release. He does remember circling the thing and pouring fire on it while it squirmed and squirted, and while he yelled sounds that were not words, until he and his weapon were spent and there was nothing where the thing had been but a charred wetness adding the smell of burned fat to all the others. He says in his unsparing report that he tramped around and around the thing, stamping out the grass-fire he had started, and shaking with revulsion, and that he squatted weakly in the grass weeping from reaction, and that only then did he think of his wounds. He broke out his pioneer's spectral salve and smeared it liberally on burns and bite both. He hunkered there until the analgesic took the pain away and he felt confident that the wide array of spansuled antibiotics was at work, and then he roused himself and slogged back to the base.

And to that sickness. It lasted only eight days or so, and wasn't the kind of sickness that ought to follow such an experience. His arm and his face healed well and quickly, his appetite was very good but not excessive, and his mind seemed clear enough. But during that time, as he put it in the careful notes he taped on the voicewriter, he felt things he had never felt before and could hardly describe. They were all things he had heard about or read about, foreign to him personally. There were faint shooting pains in his abdomen and back, a sense of pulse where no pulse should be—like that in a knitting bone, but beating in his soft tissues. None of it was beyond bearing. He had a constant black diarrhea, but like the pains it never passed the nuisance stage. One vague thing he said about four times: that when he woke up in the morning he felt that he was in some way different from what he had been the night before, and he couldn't say how. Just . . . different.

And in time it faded away and he felt normal again. That was the whole damned thing about what had happened—he was a very resourceful guy, Clement was, and if he'd been gigged just a little more by this he'd have laid his ears back and worked until he *knew* what the trouble was. But he wasn't pushed into it that way, and it didn't keep him from doing his usual man-and-a-half's hard work each day. To the others he was unusually quiet, but if they noticed it at all, it wasn't enough to remark about. They were all working hard too, don't forget. Clement slept alone these eight or nine days, and this wasn't remarkable either, only a little unusual, and not worth comment to either Glenda or Amy, who were satisfied, secure, and fully occupied women.

But then, here again was that rotten timing, small things on small things. This had to be the time of poor Amy Segal's trouble. It started over nothing at all, in the chem lab where she was doing the hurry-up-and-wait routine of a lengthy titration. Joe Flent came in to see how it was going, passed the time of day, did a little something here, something there with the equipment. He had to move along the bench just where Amy was standing, and, absorbed in what he was doing, he put out his hand to gesture her back, and went on with what he was doing. But—

She wrote it in her diary, in longhand, a big scrawl of it in the middle of those neat little glyphs of hers: "He *touched* me." All underlined and everything. All right, it was a nothing: I said that. It was an accident. But the accident had jarred her and she was made of fulminate of mercury all of a sudden. She stood where she was and let him press close to her, going on with his work, and she almost fainted. What makes these things happen . . . ? Never mind; the thing happened. She looked at him as if she had never seen him before, the light on his hair, the shape of his ears and his jaw, the—well, all like that. Maybe she made a sound and maybe Joe Flent just sensed it, but he turned around and there they were, staring at each other in some sort of mutual hypnosis with God knows what flowing back and forth between them. Then Joe gave a funny little surprised grunt and did not walk, he ran out of there.

That doesn't sound like anything at all, does it? Whatever it was, though, it was enough to throw little Amy Segal into a flat spin of the second order, and pop her gimbal bearings. I've read that there used to be a lot of stress and strain between people about this business of sex. Well, we've pretty well cleared that up, in the way we humans generally clear things up, by being extreme about it. If you're single you're absolutely free. If you're married you're absolutely bound. If you're married and you get an external itch, you have your free choice—you stay married and don't scratch it, or you scuttle the marriage and you do scratch it. If you're single you respect the marriage bond just like anyone else; you don't, but I mean you *don't* go holing somebody else's hull.

All of which hardly needs saying, especially not to Amy Segal. But like a lot of fine fools before her, she was all mixed up with what she felt and what she thought she should feel. Maybe she's a throwback to the primitive, when everybody's concave was fair game to anyone else's convex. Whatever it was about her, it took the form of making her hate herself. She was walking around among those other people thinking, I'm no good, Joe's married and look at me, I guess I don't *care* he's married. What's the matter with me, how could I feel this way about Joe, I must be a monster, I don't deserve to be here among decent people. And so on. And no one to tell it to. Maybe if Clement hadn't been sick, or maybe if she'd had it *in* her to confide in one of the other women, or maybe—well, hell with maybe's. She was half-blind with misery.

Reading the diary transcript later, I wished I could put time back and space too and tap her on the shoulder and say come along, little girl, and then put her in a corner and say listen, knothead, get untied, will you? You got a yen, never mind, it'll pass. But as long as it lasts don't be ashamed of it. Damn it, that's all she needed, just a word like that . . . .

Then Clement was well again and one night gave her the sign, and she jumped at it, and that was the most miserable thing of all, because after it was over she burst into tears and told him it was the last time, never again. He must've been no end startled. He missed the ferry there. He could've got the whole story if he'd tried, but he didn't. Maybe . . . maybe he was a little changed from what happened to him, after all. Anyway, poor Amy hit the bottom of the tank about then. She scribbled yards about it in her book. She'd just found out she responded to Clement just like always, and that proved to her that she couldn't love Joe after all, therefore her love wasn't real, therefore she wasn't worth loving, therefore Joe would never love her. Little bubblehead! and the only way out she could see was to force herself to be faithful to somebody, so she was going to "purify her feelings"—that's what she wrote—by being faithful to Joe, hence no more Clement and of course no Joe. And with that decision she put her ductless glands in a grand alliance with her insanity. Would you believe that anyone in this day and age could have such a pot boiling inside a fuzzy skull?

From that moment on Amy Segal was under forced draft. Apparently no one said anything about it, but you just don't build up incandescence in small dark places without somebody noticing. Katherine Flent must have tumbled early, as women do, and probably said nothing about it, as some women sometimes don't. Ultimately Joe Flent saw it, and what he went through nobody will ever know. I know he saw it, and felt it, because of what happened. Oh my God, what happened!

It must have been about now that Amy got the same strange almost-sickness Clement had gone through. Vague throbbings and shiftings in the abdomen, and the drizzles, and again that weird thing, about feeling different in the morning and not knowing why. And when she was about halfway through the eight-day siege, damn if Glenda Spooner doesn't seem to come down with it. Clement did the reporting on this; he was seeing a lot more of Glenda these days and could watch it. He noticed the similarity with his own illness all right, though it wasn't as noticeable, and called all hands for a report. Amy, possibly Glenda, and Clement had it and passed it; the Flents never showed the signs. Clement decided finally that it was just one of those things that people get and no one knows why, like the common cold before Billipp discovered it was an allergy to a gluten fraction. And the fact that Glenda Spooner had had such a slight attack opened the possibility that one or both Flents had had it and never known it—and that's something else we'll never know for sure.

Well, one fine day Clement headed out to quarter the shale hills to the north, looking for petroleum if he could find it and anything else if he couldn't. Clement was a fine observer. Trouble with Clement, he was an ecologist, which is mostly a biologist, and biologists are crazy.

The fine day, about three hours after he left, sprung a leak, and the bottom dropped out of the sky—which didn't worry anyone because everyone knew it wouldn't worry Clement.

Only he didn't come back.

That was a long night at the base. Twice searchers started out but they turned back in the first two hundred yards. Rain can come down like that if it wants to, but it shouldn't keep it up for so long. Morning didn't stop it, but as soon as it was dark grey outside instead of total black, the Flents and the two girls dropped everything and headed for the hills. Amy and Glenda went to the west and separated and searched the ridge until mid-afternoon, so it was all over by the time they got back. The Flents took the north and east, and it was Joe who found Clement.

That crazy Clement, he'd seen a bird's nest. He saw it because it was raining and because the fish-head stork always roosts in the rain; if it didn't its goofy glued-together nest would come unstuck. It's a big bird, larger than a terran stork, snow-white, wide-winged and easy to see, especially against the black shale bluff. Clement wanted a good look at how it sheltered its nest, which looks like half a pinecone as big as half a barrel—you'd think too big for the bird to keep dry. So up he went—and discovered that the fish-head stork's thick floppy neck conceals three, maybe four S-curves underneath all that loose skin. He was all of nine feet away from the nest, clinging to the crumbly rock wall, when he discovered it, the hard way. The stork's head shot out like a battering ram and caught him right on the breastbone, and down he went, and I guess that waterlogged shale was waiting for just this, because he started a really good rock-slide. He broke his leg and was buried up to the shoulder blades. He was facing up the cliff, with the rain beating down on him almost enough to tear his eyelids. He had nothing to look at except the underside of the nest, which his rock-slide had exposed, and I imagine he looked at it until he understood, much against his will, that the nest was all that was holding up more loosened rock above it; and he put in the night that way, waiting for seepage to loosen the gunk that stuck the nest up there and sent those tons of rock smack in his face. The leg was pretty bad and he probably passed out two or three times, but never long enough to suit him . . . *damn* it! I got a list this long of people who ought to have things like that happen to them. So it has to happen to Clement.

It was still raining in the morning when Joe Flent found him. Joe let out a roar to the westward where his wife was combing the rocks, but didn't wait to see if she'd heard. If she didn't, maybe there was a sort of telepathy between them like Amy said in her diary. Anyway, she arrived just in time to see it happen, but not in time to do anything about it.

She saw Joe bending over Clement's head and shoulders where they stuck out of the rock pile, and then she heard a short, sharp shout. It must have been Clement who shouted; he was facing uphill and could see it coming, nest and all. Katherine screamed and ran toward them, and then the new slide reached the bottom, and that was that for Clement.

But not for Joe. Something else got Joe.

It seemed to explode out of the rocks a split second before the slide hit. It took Joe Flent in the chest so hard it lifted him right off his feet and flung him down and away from the slide. Katherine screamed again as she ran, because the thing that had knocked Joe down was bouncing up and down in a crazy irregular hop, each one taking it closer to Joe as he lay on his back half stunned, and she recognized it for the thing that had attacked Clement the day the primate bit him.

She logged this report on the voicewriter and I heard the tape, and I wish they'd transcribe it and then destroy it. Nobody should hear a duty-bound horror-struck soul like that tell such a story. Read it, okay. But that torn-up monotone, oh God. She was having nine agonies at once, what with her hands all gone and what happened to Joe out there, and what he'd said . . . arrgh! I can't tell it without hearing it in my head.

Well. That stinking horror hopped up on Joe and he half sat up and it hopped again and landed right over his face and slumped there quivering, bleeding and streaming rain and acid. Joe flipped so hard his feet went straight up in the air and he seemed to hang there, standing on the back of his head and his shoulder-blades with his arms and legs doing a crazy jumping-jack flailing. Then he fell again with the monstrosity snugger than ever over his face and neck and head, and he squirmed once and then lay still, and that was when Katherine got to him.

Katherine went at that thing with her bare hands. One-half second contact, even in all that rain, was enough to pucker and shrivel her skin, and it must have felt like plunging her hands into smoking deep-fat. She didn't say what it felt like. She only said that when she grabbed at the thing to tear it away from Joe's face, it came apart in small slippery handfuls. She kicked at it and her foot went in and through it and it spilled ropy guts and gouted blood. She tore into it again, clawing and batting it away, and that was probably when she did the most damage to her hands. Then she had an idea from somewhere in that nightmare, fell back and took Joe's feet and dragged him twenty feet away—don't ask me how—and turned him over on his face so the last of that mess dropped off him. She skinned out of her shirt and knelt down and rolled him over and sat him up. She tried to wipe his face with the shirt but found she couldn't hold it, so she scooped her ruined hand under it and brought it up and mopped, but what she mopped at wasn't a face any more. On the tape she said, in that flat shredded voice, "I didn't realize that for a while."

She put her arms around Joe and rocked him and said, "Joey, it's Katherine, it's all right, honey. Katherine's here." He sighed once, a long, shuddering sigh and straightened his back, and a hole bigger than a mouth opened up in the front of his head. He said, "Amy? Amy?" and suddenly fought Katherine blindly. She lost her balance and her arm fell away from his back, and he went down. He made one great cry that raised echoes all up and down the ridge: "A . . . meeeee . . . " and in a minute or two he was dead.

Katherine sat there until she was ready to go, and covered his face with the shirt. She looked once at the thing that had killed him. It was dead, scattered in slimy bits all over the edge of the rock-fall. She went back to the base. She didn't remember the trip. She must have been soaked and chilled to the bone-marrow. She apparently went straight to the voicewriter and reported in and then just sat there, three, four hours until the others got back.

Now if only somebody had been there to . . . I don't know. Maybe she couldn't have listened, after all that. Who knows what went on in her head while she sat there letting her blood run out of her hands on to the floor? I'd guess it was that last cry of Joe's, because of what happened when Glenda and Amy came in. It might have been so loud in her head that nobody else's voice could get in. But I still wish somebody had been there, somebody who knows about the things people say when they die. Sometimes they're already dead when they say those things; they don't mean anything. I saw an engineer get it when a generator threw a segment. He just said, "Three-eighths . . . three-eighths . . ." What I'm trying to say, it didn't have to mean anything . . . Well, what's the difference now? They came in dripping and tired, calling out. Katherine Flent didn't answer. They came into the recording shack, Amy first. Amy was half across the floor before she saw Katherine. Glenda was still in the doorway. Amy screamed, and I guess anyone would, seeing Katherine with her hair plastered around her face the way it had dried, and blood all over her clothes and the floor, and no shirt. She fixed her crazy eyes on Amy and got up slowly. Amy called her name twice but Katherine kept on moving, slow, steady, evenly. Between the heels of her ruined hands she held a skinning knife. She probably couldn't have held it tightly enough to do any damage, but I guess that didn't occur to Amy.

Amy stepped back toward the door and with one long step Katherine headed her off and herded her toward the other corner, where there was no way out. Amy glanced behind her, saw the trap, covered her face with her hands, stepped back and dropped her hands. "Katherine!" she screamed. "What is it? What is it? Did you find Clement? Quick!" she rapped at Glenda, who stood frozen in the doorway. "Get Joe."

At the sound of Joe's name, Katherine moaned softly and leaped. She was met in mid-air by the same kind of thing that had killed her husband.

The soft horror caught Katherine off the floor in mid-leap and hurled her backward. Her head hit the corner of a steel relay-rack . . .

The stench in the small room was quite beyond description, beyond bearing. Amy staggered to the door, pushing an unresisting Glenda ahead of her . . . .

And there they were as we found them, Purcell and me: one fevered freak that could out-eat six men, and one catatonic.

I sent Purcell out to the shale hill to see if there was enough left of Clement and Joe Flent for an examination. There wasn't. Animals had scattered Joe's remains pretty thoroughly, and Purcell couldn't find Clement at all, though he moved rocks till his hands bled. There had probably been more slides after that rain. Somehow, in those weeks when she maintained the basic instrumentation single-handed, Amy Segal had managed to drag Katherine out and bury her, and clean up the recording room, though nothing but burning would ever get all that smell out of it.

We left everything but the tapes and records. The scout was built for two men and cargo, and getting her off the ground with four wasn't easy. I was mighty glad to get back on the bridge of the flicker-ship and away from that five-nines hell. We stashed the two girls in a cabin next to the sick bay and quarantined them, just in case, and I went to work on the records, getting the story in about the order I've given it here.

And once I had it, there wasn't a thing I could do with it. Amy was at all times delirious, or asleep or eating; you could get very little from her, and even then you couldn't trust what you got. From Glenda you got nothing. She just lay still with that pleasant half-smile on her face and let the universe proceed without her. On a ship like ours we are the medical division, the skipper and the officers, and we could do nothing for these two but keep them fed and comfortable; otherwise, we mostly forgot they were aboard. Which was an error.

Status quo, then, far as I knew, from the time we left the planet until we made earthfall, the crew going about its business, the two girls in quarantine with Purcell filling the hopper with food for the one and spoon-feeding the other, and me locked up with the records, piecing and guessing and trying to make sense out of a limbless, eyeless monstrosity which apparently could appear from nowhere in mid-air, even indoors (like the one that killed Katherine Flent); which looked as if it could not live, but which still would attack and could kill. I got no place. I mulled over more theories than I'll go into, some of 'em pretty far-fetched, like a fourth-dimensional thing that . . . well, on the other hand, Nature can be pretty far-fetched too, as anyone who has seen the rear end of a mandrill will attest.

What do you know about sea-cucumbers, as another nauseating example?

We popped out of the flicker-field in due time, and Luna was good to see. We transferred to a rocket-ferry at Outer Orbit and dropped in smoothly, and came into the base here in quarantine procedure, impounding ferry and all. The girls were at last put into competent hands, and the crew were given the usual screening. Usual or not, it's about as thorough as a physical examination can get, and after they'd all been cleared, and slept six hours, and gone through it again and been cleared again, I gave them 72-hour passes, renewable, and turned 'em loose.

I was more than anxious to go along too, but by that time I was up to the eyeballs in specialists and theorists, and in some specialties and theories that began to get too fascinating for even a home-hungry hound like me to ignore. That was when I called you and said how tied up I was and swore I'd be out of there in another day. You were nice about that. Of course, I had no idea it wouldn't be just one more day, but another six weeks.

Right after the crew was turned loose they called me out of the semantics section, where we were collating all notes and records, into the psych division. They had one of the . . . the things there. I have to hand it to those guys. I guess they were just as tempted as Clement was when he first saw one, to burn it into nothing as fast as it could be burned. I saw it, and that was my first impulse. God. No amount of clinical reporting like Clement's could give you the remotest idea of just how disgusting one of those things is.

They'd been working over Glenda Spooner. Catatonics are hard to do anything with, but they used some high-potency narcosyntheses and some field inductions, and did a regression. They found out just what sort of a catatonic she was. Some, you probably know, retreat like that as a result of some profound shock—after they have been shocked. It's an escape. But some go into that seize-up in the split second *before* the shock. Then it isn't an escape, it's a defense. And that was our girl Glenda.

They regressed her until they had her located out in the field, searching for Clement. Then they brought her forward again, so that in her mind she was contacting Amy, slogging through the rain, back to the base. They got to where Amy entered the recording shack and screamed, seeing Katherine Flent looking that way. There they located the exact split second of trauma, the moment when something happened which was so terrible that Glenda had not let herself see it. More dope, more application of the fields through the helmet they had her strapped into. They regressed her a few minutes and had her approach that moment again. They tried it again, and some more, making slight adjustments each time, knowing that sooner or later they would have the exact subtle nudge that would push her through her self-induced barrier, make her at last experience the thing she was so afraid to acknowledge.

And they did it, and when they did it, the soft gutty *thing* appeared, slamming into a technician fifteen feet away, hitting him so hard it knocked him flat and slid him spinning into the far wall. He was a young fellow named Petri and it killed him. Like Katherine Flent, he died probably before he felt the acid burns. He went right into the transformer housing and died in a net of sparks.

And as I said, these boys had their wits about them. Sure, someone went to help Petri (though not in time) and someone else went after a flame pistol. He wasn't in time either; because when he got back with it, Shellabarger and Li Kyu had the glass bell off a vacuum rig and had corralled the filthy thing with it. They slid a resilient mat under it and slapped a coupling on top and jetted the jar full of liquid argon.

This time there was no charred mass, no kicked-apart, rain-soaked scatter of parts to deal with. Here was a perfect specimen, if you can call such a thing perfect, frozen solid while it was still alive and trying to hop up and down and find someone to bubble its dirty acids on. They had it to keep, to slice up with a microtome, even to revive, if anyone had the strong guts.

Glenda proved clearly that with her particular psychic makeup, she had chosen the right defense. When she saw the thing, she died of fright. It was that, just that, that she had tried to avoid with catatonia. The psycho boys breached it, and found out just how right she had been. But at least she didn't die uselessly, like Flent and Clement and poor Katherine. Because it was her autopsy that cleared things up.

One thing they found was pretty subtle. It was a nuclear pattern in the cells of the connective tissue quite unlike any of them had seen before. They checked Amy Segal for it and found the same thing. They checked me for it and didn't. That was when I sent out the recall order for the whole crew. I didn't think any of them would have it, but we had to be sure. If that got loose on Earth . . .

All but one of the crew had a clean bill when given the new test, and there wasn't otherwise anything wrong with that one.

The other thing Glenda's autopsy revealed was anything but subtle.

Her abdomen was empty.

Her liver, kidneys, almost all of the upper and all of the lower intestine were missing, along with the spleen, the bladder, and assorted tripe of that nature. Remaining were the uterus, with the Fallopian tubes newly convoluted and the ovaries tacked right to the uterus itself; the stomach; a single loop of what had once been upper intestine, attached in a dozen places to various spots on the wall of the peritoneum. It emptied directly into a rectal segment, without any distinctive urinary system, much like the primitive equipment of a bird.

Everything that was missing, they found under the bell jar.

Now we knew what had hit Katherine Flent, and why Amy was empty and starved when we found her. Joe Flent had been killed by . . . one of the . . . well, by something that erupted at him as he bent over the trapped Clement. Clement himself had been struck on the side of the face by such a thing—and whose was that?

Why, that primate's. The primate he walked into submission, and touched, and frightened.

It bit him in panic terror. Joe Flent was killed in a moment of panic terror too—not this, but Clement's, who saw the rock-slide coming. Katherine Flent died in a moment of terror—not hers, but Amy's, as Amy crouched cornered in the shack and watched Katherine coming with a knife. And the one which had appeared on earth, in the psych lab, why, that needed the same thing to be born in—when the boys forced Glenda Spooner across a mental barrier she could not cross and live.

We had everything now but the mechanics of the thing, and that we got from Amy, the bravest woman yet. By the time we were through with her, every man in the place admired her g—uh, dammit not that. Admired her fortitude. She was probed and goaded and prodded and checked, and finally went through a whole series of advanced exploratories. By the time the exploratories began, about six weeks had gone by, that is, six weeks from Katherine Flent's death, and Amy was almost back to normal; she'd tapered off on the calories, her abdomen had filled out to almost normal, her temperature had steadied and by and large she was okay. What I'm trying to put over is that she had some intestines for us to investigate—*she'd grown a new set.* That's right. She'd thrown her old ones at Katherine Flent. There wasn't anything wrong with the new ones, either. At the time of her first examination everything was operating but the kidneys; their function was being handled by a very simple, very efficient sort of filter attached to the ventral wall of the peritoneum. We found a similar organ in autopsying poor Glenda Spooner. Next to it were the adrenals, apparently transferred there from their place astride the original kidneys. And sure enough, we found Amy's adrenals placed that way, and not on the new kidneys. In a fascinating three-day sequence we saw those new kidneys completed and begin to operate, while the surrogate organ which had been doing their work atrophied and went quiet. It stayed there, though, ready.

The climax of the examination came when we induced panic terror in her, with a vivid abreaction of the events in the recording shack the day Katherine died. Bless that Amy, when we suggested it she grinned and said, "Sure!"

But this time it was done under laboratory conditions, with a high-speed camera to watch the proceedings. Oh God, did they proceed!

The film showed Amy's plain pleasant sleeping face with its stainless halo of psych-field hood, which was hauling her subjective self back to that awful moment in the records shack. You could tell the moment she arrived there by the anxiety, the tension, the surprise and shock that showed on her face. "Glenda!" she screamed, "Get Joe!"—and then . . .

It looked at first as if she was making a face, sticking out her tongue. She was making a face all right, the mask of purest, terminal fear, but that wasn't a tongue. It came out and out, unbelievably fast even on the slow-motion frames on the high-speed camera. At its greatest, the diameter was no more than two inches, the length . . .about eight feet. It arrowed out of her mouth, and even in mid-air it contracted into the roughly spherical shape we had seen before. It stuck the net which the doctors had spread for it and dropped into a plastic container, where it hopped and hopped, sweated, drooled, bled and died. They tried to keep it alive but it wasn't meant to live more than a few minutes.

On dissection they found it contained all Amy's new equipment, in sorry shape. All abdominal organs can be compressed to less than two inches in diameter, but not if they're expected to work again. These weren't.

The thing was covered with a layer of muscle tissue, and dotted with two kinds of ganglia, one sensory and one motor. It would keep hopping as long as there was enough of it left to hop, which was what the motor system did. It was geotropic, and it would alter its muscular spasms to move it toward anything around it that lived and had warm blood, and that's what the primitive sensory system was for.

And at last we could discard the fifty or sixty theories that had been formed and decide on one: That the primates of Mullygantz II had the ability, like a terran sea-cucumber, of ejecting their internal organs when frightened, and of growing a new set; that in a primitive creature this was a survival characteristic, and the more elaborate the ejected matter the better the chances of the animal's survival. Probably starting with something as simple as a lizard's discarding a tail-segment which just lies there and squirms to distract a pursuer, this one had evolved from 'distract' to 'attract' and finally to 'attack.' True, it took a fantastic amount of forage for the animal to supply itself with a new set of innards, but for vegetarian primates on fertile Mullygantz II, this was no problem.

The only problem that remained was to find out exactly how terrans had become infected, and the records cleared that up. Clement got it from a primate's bite. Amy and Glenda got it from Clement. The Flents may well never have had it. Did that mean that Clement had bitten those girls? Amy said no, and experiments proved that the activating factor passed readily from any mucous tissue to any other. A bite would do it, but so would a kiss. Which didn't explain our one crew-member who "contracted" the condition. Nor did it explain what kind of a survival characteristic it is that can get transmitted around like a virus infection, even between species.

Within that same six weeks of quarantine, we even got an answer to that. By a stretch of the imagination, you might call the thing a virus. At least, it was a filterable organism which, like the tobacco mosaic or the slime mold, had an organizing factor. You might call it a life form, or a complex biochemical action, basically un-alive. You could call it symbiote. Symbiotes often go out of their way to see to it that the hosts survive.

After entering a body, these creatures multiplied until they could organize, and then went to work on the host. Connective tissue and muscle fiber was where they did most of their work. They separated muscle fibers all over the peritoneal walls and diaphragm, giving a layer to the entrails and the rest to the exterior. They duplicated organic functions with their efficient, primitive little surrogate organs and glands. They hooked the ilium to the stomach wall and to the rectum, and in a dozen places to their new organic structures. Then they apparently stood by.

When an emergency came every muscle in the abdomen and throat cooperated in a single, synchronized spasm, and the entrails, sheathed in muscle fiber and dotted with nerve ganglia, compressed into a long tube and was forced out like a bullet. Instantly the revised and edited abdomen got to work, perforating the new stomach outlet, sealing the old, and starting the complex of simple surrogate to work. And as long as enough new building material was received fast enough, an enormously accelerated rebuilding job started, blue-printed God knows how from God knows what kind of a cellular memory, until in less than two months the original abdominal contents, plus revision, were duplicated, and all was ready for the next emergency.

Then we found that in spite of its incredible and complex hold on its own life and those of its hosts, it had no defense at all against one of humanity's oldest therapeutic tools, the RF fever cabinet. A high frequency induced fever of 108 sustained for seven minutes killed it off as if it had never existed, and we found that the "revised" gut was in every way as good as the original, if not better (because damaged organs were replaced with healthy ones if there was enough of them left to show original structure)—and that by keeping a culture of the Mullygantz 'virus' we had the ultimate, drastic treatment for forty-odd types of abdominal cancer—including two types for which we'd had no answer at all!

So it was we lost the planet, and gained it back with a bonus. We could cause this thing and cure it and diagnose it and use it, and the new world was open again. And that part of the story, as you probably know, came out all over the newsfax and 'casters, which is why I'm getting a big hello from taxi drivers and doormen . . . .

"But the 'fax said you wouldn't be leaving the base until tomorrow noon!" Sue said after I had spouted all this to her and at long last got it all off my chest in one great big piece.

"Sure. They got that straight from me. I heard rumors of a parade and speeches and God knows what else, and I wanted to get home to my walkin' talkin' wettin' doll that blows bubbles."

"You're silly."

"C'mere."

The doorbell hummed.

"I'll get it," I said, "and throw 'em out. It's probably a reporter."

But Sue was already on her feet. "Let me, let me. You just stay there and finish your drink." And before I could stop her she flung into the house and up the long corridor to the foyer.

I chuckled, drank my ale and got up to see who was horning in. I had my shoes off so I guess I was pretty quiet. Though I didn't need to be. Purcell was roaring away in his best old salt fashion, "Let's have us another quickie, Susie, before the Space Scout gets through with his red carpet treatment tomorrow—miss me, honey?" . . . while Sue was imploringly trying to cover his mouth with her hands.

Maybe I ran; I don't know. Anyway, I was there, right behind her. I didn't say anything. Purcell looked at me and went white. "Skipper . . . "

And *in* the hall mirror behind Purcell, my wife met my eyes. What she saw in my face I cannot say, but in hers I saw panic and terror.

In the small space between Purcell and Sue, something appeared. It knocked Purcell into the mirror, and he slid down in a welter of blood and stinks and broken glass. The recoil slammed Sue into my arms. I put her by so I could watch the tattered, bleeding thing on the floor hop and hop until it settled down on the nearest warm living thing it could sense, which was Purcell's face.

I let Sue watch it and crossed to the phone and called the commandant. "Gargan," I said, watching. "Listen, Joe. I found out that Purcell lied about where he went in that first liberty. Also why he lied." For a few seconds I couldn't seem to get my breath. "Send the meat wagon and an ambulance, and tell Harry to get ready for another hollow-belly. . . . Yes, I said, one dead. . . . Purcell, dammit. Do I have to draw you a cartoon?" I roared, and hung up.

I said to Sue, who was holding on to her flat midriff, "That Purcell, I guess it did him good to get away with things under my nose. First that helpless catatonic Glenda on the way home, then you. I hope you had a real good time, honey."

It smelled bad in there so I left. I left and walked all the way back to the Base. It took about ten hours. When I got there I went to the Medical wing for my own fever-box-cure and to do some thinking about girls with guts, one way or another. And I began to wait. They'd be opening up Mully-gantz II again, and I thought I might look for a girl who'd have the . . . fortitude to go back with me. A girl like Amy. Or maybe Amy.

Sturgeon's finesse of description came through again. I did have trouble tracking all the characters, but got by. I see this as a superb integration of a spectacular idea—the expelled guts—with human conflict to evoke those guts, and a nice science mystery that gradually gets fathomed. I had not remembered the final twist at all. In that situation I would go with Amy, who strikes me as an ideal woman. She had physical and emotional guts galore. This remains a top story. I understand that Miller, author of "Vengeance for Nikolai," and Sturgeon, author of "The Girl Had Guts," each thought the other's story was superlative. Both were right.
    —Piers

THE LITTLE
LOST ROBOT

Isaac Asimov

March 1947

This was the first Asimov robot story I read, and I can't claim it's the best, just the one that introduced me to a subsection of science fiction that I still like very well. I have had intelligent self-willed humanoid robots in my own fiction, notably the Adept series and the final volume of the ChroMagic Series. My robots do not follow the Asimov Laws of Robotics, but I was surely influenced by them. I re-member the problem of identifying a robot that looks and acts exactly like others of its type, but has slightly different software, making it potentially dangerous. How do you spot such a robot, when it doesn't want to be spotted? There's the riddle, with a nice solution. Asimov was good at intellectual riddles and solu-tions. My contact with him was only one exchange of letters, and in the fanzines, but we were similar in our need to be constantly writing, regardless where we are. Other writers seem to like to get away from writing; we two never wanted to get away. As a result, Asimov wrote more than 300 books, mostly nonfiction. My total is about half that, but I actually have written more fiction than he did.
    —Piers

When I did see Susan Calvin again, it was at the door of her office. Files were being moved out.

She said, "How are your articles coming along, young man?"

"Fine," I said. I had put them into shape according to my own lights, dramatized the bare bones of her recital, added the conversation and little touches, "Would you look over them and see if I haven't been libelous or too unreasonably inaccurate anywhere?"

"I suppose so. Shall we retire to the Executives' Lounge? We can have coffee."

She seemed in good humor, so I chanced it as we walked down the corridor, "I was wondering, Dr. Calvin—"

"Yes?"

"If you would tell me more concerning the history of robotics."

"Surely you have what you want, young man."

"In a way. But these incidents I have written up don't apply much to the modern world. I mean, there was only one mind-reading robot ever developed, and Space-Stations are already outmoded and in disuse, and robot mining is taken for granted. What about interstellar travel? It's only been about twenty years since the hyperatomic motor was invented and it's well known that it was a robotic invention. What is the truth about it?"

"Interstellar travel?" She was thoughtful. We were in the lounge, and I ordered a full dinner. She just had coffee.

"It wasn't a simple robotic invention, you know; not just like that. But, of course, until we developed the Brain, we didn't get very far. But we tried; we really tried. My first connection (directly, that is) with interstellar research was in 2029, when a robot was lost—"

Measures on Hyper Base had been taken in a sort of rattling fury—the muscular equivalent of an hysterical shriek.

To itemize them in order of both chronology and desperation, they were:

1. All work on the Hyperatomic Drive through all the space volume occupied by the Stations of the Twenty-Seventh Asteroidal Grouping came to a halt.

2. That entire volume of space was nipped out of the System, practically speaking. No one entered without permission. No one left under any conditions.

3. By special government patrol ship, Drs. Susan Calvin and Peter Bogert, respectively Head Psychologist and Mathematical Director of United States Robot & Mechanical Men Corporation, were brought to Hyper Base.

Susan Calvin had never left the surface of Earth before, and had no perceptible desire to leave it this time. In an age of Atomic Power and a clearly coming Hyper-atomic Drive, she remained quietly provincial. So she was dissatisfied with her trip and unconvinced of the emergency, and every line of her plain, middle-aged face showed it clearly enough during her first dinner at Hyper Base.

Nor did Dr. Bogert's sleek paleness abandon a certain hangdog attitude. Nor did Major-general Kallner, who headed the project, even once forget to maintain a hunted expression.

In short, it was a grisly episode, that meal, and the little session of three that followed began in a gray, unhappy manner.

Kallner, with his baldness glistening, and his dress uniform oddly unsuited to the general mood, began with uneasy directness.

"This is a queer story to tell, sir, and madam. I want to thank you for coming on short notice and without a reason being given. We'll try to correct that now. We've lost a robot. Work has stopped and *must* stop until such time as we locate it. So far we have failed, and we feel we need expert help."

Perhaps the general felt his predicament anticlimactic. He continued with a note of desperation, "I needn't tell you the importance of our work here. More than eighty percent of last year's appropriations for scientific research have gone to us—"

"Why, we know that," said Bogert, agreeably. "U. S. Robots is receiving a generous rental fee for use of our robots."

Susan Calvin injected a blunt, vinegary note, "What makes a single robot so important to the project, and why hasn't it been located?"

The general turned his red face toward her and wet his lips quickly. "Why, in a manner of speaking we *have* located it." Then, with near anguish, "Here, suppose I explain. As soon as the robot failed to report, a state of emergency was declared, and all movement off Hyper Base stopped. A cargo vessel had landed the previous day and had delivered us two robots for our laboratories. It had sixty-two robots of the . . . uh . . . same type for shipment elsewhere. We are certain as to that figure. There is no question about it whatever."

"Yes? And the connection?"

"When our missing robot failed of location anywhere—I assure you we would have found a missing blade of grass if it had been there to find—we brain-stormed ourselves into counting the robots left of the cargo ship. They have sixty-three now."

"So that the sixty-third, I take it, is the missing prodigal?" Dr. Calvin's eyes darkened.

"Yes, but we have no way of telling which is the sixty-third."

There was a dead silence while the electric clock chimed eleven times, and then the robopsychologist said, "Very peculiar," and the corners of her lips moved downward.

"Peter," she turned to her colleague with a trace of savagery, "what's wrong here? What kind of robots are they using at Hyper Base?"

Dr. Bogert hesitated and smiled feebly, "It's been rather a matter of delicacy till now, Susan."

She spoke rapidly, "Yes, *till* now. If there are sixty-three same-type robots, one of which is wanted and the identity of which cannot be determined, why won't any of them do? What's the idea of all this? Why have we been sent for?"

Bogert said in resigned fashion, "If you'll give me a chance, Susan—Hyper Base happens to be using several robots whose brains are not impressioned with the entire First Law of Robotics."

"*Aren't* impressioned?" Calvin slumped back in her chair. "I see. How many were made?"

"A few. It was on government order and there was no way of violating the secrecy. No one was to know except the top men directly concerned. You weren't included, Susan. It was nothing I had anything to do with."

The general interrupted with a measure of authority. "I would like to explain that bit. I hadn't been aware that Dr. Calvin was unacquainted with the situation. I needn't tell you, Dr. Calvin, that there always has been strong opposition to robots on the Planet. The only defense the government has had against the Fundamentalist radicals in this matter was the fact that robots are always built with an unbreakable First Law—which makes it impossible for them to harm human beings under any circumstance.

"But we *had* to have robots of a different nature. So just a few of the NS-2 model, the Nestors, that is, were prepared with a modified First Law. To keep it quiet, all NS-2's are manufactured without serial numbers; modified members are delivered here along with a group of normal robots; and, of course, all our kind are under the strictest impressionment never to tell of their modification to unauthorized personnel." He wore an embarrassed smile, "This has all worked out against us now."

Calvin said grimly, "Have you asked each one who it is, anyhow? Certainly, you are authorized?"

The general nodded, "All sixty-three deny having worked here—and one is lying."

"Does the one you want show traces of wear? The others, I take it, are factory-fresh."

"The one in question only arrived last month. It, and the two that have just arrived, were to be the last we needed. There's no perceptible wear." He shook his head slowly and his eyes were haunted again, "Dr. Calvin, we don't dare let that ship leave. If the existence of non-First Law robots becomes general knowledge—" There seemed no way of avoiding understatement in the conclusion.

"Destroy all sixty-three," said the robopsychologist coldly and flatly, "and make an end of it."

Bogert drew back a corner of his mouth. "You mean destroy thirty thousand dollars per robot. I'm afraid U. S. Robots wouldn't like that. We'd better make an effort first, Susan, before we destroy anything."

"In that case," she said, sharply, "I need facts. Exactly what advantage does Hyper Base derive from these modified robots? What factor made them desirable, general?"

Kallner ruffled his forehead and stroked it with an upward gesture of his hand. "We had trouble with our previous robots. Our men work with hard radiations a good deal, you see. It's dangerous, of course, but reasonable precautions are taken. There have been only two accidents since we began and neither was fatal. However, it was impossible to explain that to an ordinary robot. The First Law states—I'll quote it—'*No robot may harm a human being, or through inaction, allow a human being to come to harm.'*

"That's primary, Dr. Calvin. When it was necessary for one of our men to expose himself for a short period to a moderate gamma field, one that would have no physiological effects, the nearest robot would dash in to drag him out. If the field were exceedingly weak, it would succeed, and work could not continue till all robots were cleared out. If the field were a trifle stronger, the robot would never reach the technician concerned, since its positronic brain would collapse under gamma radiations—and then we would be out one expensive and hard-to-replace robot.

"We tried arguing with them. Their point was that a human being in a gamma field was endangering his life and that it didn't matter that he could remain there half an hour safely. Supposing, they would say, he forgot and remained an hour. They couldn't take chances. We pointed out that they were risking their lives on a wild off-chance. But self-preservation is only the Third Law of Robotics—and the First Law of human safety came first. We gave them orders; we ordered them strictly and harshly to remain out of gamma fields at whatever cost. But obedience is only the Second Law of Robotics—and the First Law of human safety came first. Dr. Calvin, we either had to do without robots, or do something about the First Law—and we made our choice."

"I can't believe," said Dr. Calvin, "that it was found possible to remove the First Law."

"It wasn't removed, it was modified," explained Kallner. "Positronic brains were constructed that contained the positive aspect only of the Law, which in them reads: *No robot may harm a human being.'* That is all. They have no compulsion to prevent one coming to harm through an extraneous agency such as gamma rays. I state the matter correctly, Dr. Bogert?"

"Quite," assented the mathematician.

"And that is the only difference of your robots from the ordinary NS-2 model? The *only* difference? Peter?"

"The *only* difference, Susan."

She rose and spoke with finality, "I intend sleeping now, and in about eight hours, I want to speak to whomever saw the robot last. And from now on, General Kallner, if I'm to take any responsibility at all for events, I want full and unquestioned control of this investigation."

Susan Calvin, except for two hours of resentful lassitude, experienced nothing approaching sleep. She signaled at Bogert's door at the local time of 0700 and found him also awake. He had apparently taken the trouble of transporting a dressing gown to Hyper Base with him, for he was sitting in it. He put his nail scissors down when Calvin entered.

He said softly, "I've been expecting you more or less. I suppose you feel sick about all this."

"I do."

"Well—I'm sorry. There was no way of preventing it. When the call came out from Hyper Base for us, I knew that something must have gone wrong with the modified Nestors. But what was there to do? I couldn't break the matter to you on the trip here as I would have liked to, because I had to be sure. The matter of the modification is top secret."

The psychologist muttered, "I should have been told. U. S. Robots had no right to modify positronic brains this way without the approval of a psychologist."

Bogert lifted his eyebrows and sighed. "Be reasonable, Susan. You couldn't have influenced them. In this matter, the government was bound to have its way. They want the Hyperatomic Drive and the etheric physicists want robots that won't interfere with them. They were going to get them even if it did mean twisting the First Law. We had to admit it was possible from a construction standpoint and they swore a mighty oath that they wanted only twelve, that they would be used only at Hyper Base, that they would be destroyed once the Drive was perfected, and that full precautions would be taken. And they insisted on secrecy—and that's the situation."

Dr. Calvin spoke through her teeth, "I would have resigned."

"It wouldn't have helped. The government was offering the company a fortune, and threatening it with antirobot legislation in case of a refusal. We were stuck then, and we're badly stuck now. If this leaks out, it might hurt Kallner and the government, but it would hurt U. S. Robots a devil of a lot more."

The psychologist stared at him. "Peter, don't you realize what all this is about? Can't you understand what the removal of the First Law means? It isn't just a matter of secrecy."

"I know what removal would mean. I'm not a child. It would mean complete instability, with no nonimaginary solutions to the positronic Field Equations."

"Yes, mathematically. But can you translate that into crude psychological thought. All normal life, Peter, consciously or otherwise, resents domination. If the domination is by an inferior, or by a supposed inferior, the resentment becomes stronger. Physically, and, to an extent, mentally, a robot—any robot—is superior to human beings. What makes him slavish, then? *Only the First Law!* Why, without it, the first order you tried to give a robot would result in your death. Unstable? What do you think?"

"Susan," said Bogert, with an air of sympathetic amusement. "I'll admit that this Frankenstein Complex you're exhibiting has a certain justification—hence the First Law in the first place. But the Law, I repeat and repeat, has not been removed—merely modified."

"And what about the stability of the brain?"

The mathematician thrust out his lips, "Decreased, naturally. But it's within the border of safety. The first Nestors were delivered to Hyper Base nine months ago, and nothing whatever has gone wrong till now, and even this involves merely fear of discovery and not danger to humans."

"Very well, then. We'll see what comes of the morning conference."

Bogert saw her politely to the door and grimaced eloquently when she left. He saw no reason to change his perennial opinion of her as a sour and fidgety frustration.

Susan Calvin's train of thought did not include Bogert in the least. She had dismissed him years ago as a smooth and pretentious sleekness.

Gerald Black had taken his degree in etheric physics the year before and, in common with his entire generation of physicists, found himself engaged in the problem of the Drive. He now made a proper addition to the general atmosphere of these meetings on Hyper Base. In his stained white smock, he was half rebellious and wholly uncertain. His stocky strength seemed striving for release and his fingers, as they twisted each other with nervous yanks, might have forced an iron bar out of true.

Major-general Kallner sat beside him, the two from U. S. Robots faced him.

Black said, "I'm told that I was the last to see Nestor 10 before he vanished. I take it you want to ask me about that."

Dr. Calvin regarded him with interest, "You sound as if you were not sure, young man. Don't you *know* whether you were the last to see him?"

"He worked with me, ma'am, on the field generators, and he was with me the morning of his disappearance. I don't know if anyone saw him after about noon. No one admits having done so."

"Do you think anyone's lying about it?"

"I don't say that. But I don't say that I want the blame of it, either." His dark eyes smoldered.

"There's no question of blame. The robot acted as it did because of what it is. We're just trying to locate it, Mr. Black, and let's put everything else aside. Now if you've worked with the robot, you probably know it better than anyone else. Was there anything unusual about it that you noticed? Had you ever worked with robots before?"

"I've worked with other robots we have here—the simple ones. Nothing different about the Nestors except that they're a good deal cleverer—and more annoying."

"Annoying? In what way?"

"Well—perhaps it's not their fault. The work here is rough and most of us get a little jagged. Fooling around with hyper-space isn't fun." He smiled feebly, finding pleasure in confession. "We run the risk continually of blowing a hole in normal space-time fabric and dropping right out of the universe, asteroid and all. Sounds screwy, doesn't it? Naturally, you're on edge sometimes. But these Nestors aren't. They're curious, they're calm, they don't worry. It's enough to drive you nuts at times. When you want something done in a tearing hurry, they seem to take their time. Sometimes I'd rather do without."

"You say they take their time? Have they ever refused an order?"

"Oh, no,"—hastily. "They do it all right. They tell you when they think you're wrong, though. They don't know anything about the subject but what we taught them, but that doesn't stop them. Maybe I imagine it, but the other fellows have the same trouble with their Nestors."

General Kallner cleared his throat ominously. "Why have no complaints reached me on the matter, Black?"

The young physicist reddened. "We didn't *really* want to do without the robots, sir, and besides we weren't certain exactly how such . . . uh . . . minor complaints might be received."

Bogert interrupted softly, "Anything in particular happen the morning you last saw it?"

There was a silence. With a quiet motion, Calvin repressed the comment that was about to emerge from Kallner, and waited patiently.

Then Black spoke in blurting anger, "I had a little trouble with it. I'd broken a Kimball tube that morning and was out five days of work; my entire program was behind schedule; I hadn't received any mail from home for a couple of weeks. And he came around wanting me to repeat an experiment I had abandoned a month ago. He was always annoying me on that subject and I was tired of it. I told him to go away—and that's all I saw of him."

"You told him to go away?" asked Dr. Calvin with sharp interest. "In just those words? Did you say 'Go away'? Try to remember the exact words."

There was apparently an internal struggle in progress. Black cradled his forehead in a broad palm for a moment, then tore it away and said defiantly, "I said, 'Go lose yourself.'"

Bogert laughed for a short moment. "And he did, eh?"

But Calvin wasn't finished. She spoke cajolingly, "Now we're getting somewhere, Mr. Black. But exact details are important. In understanding the robot's actions, a word, a gesture, an emphasis may be everything. You couldn't have said just those three words, for instance, could you? By your own description you must have been in a hasty mood. Perhaps you strengthened your speech a little."

The young man reddened. "Well . . . I may have called it a . . . a few things."

"Exactly what things?"

"Oh—I wouldn't remember exactly. Besides, I couldn't repeat it. You know how you get when you're excited." His embarrassed laugh was almost a giggle. "I sort of have a tendency to strong language."

"That's quite all right," she replied, with prim severity. "At the moment, I'm a psychologist. I would like to have you repeat exactly what you said as nearly as you remember, and, even more important, the exact tone of voice you used."

Black looked at his commanding officer for support, found none. His eyes grew round and appalled. "But I can't."

"You must."

"Suppose," said Bogert, with ill-hidden amusement, "you address me. You may find it easier."

The young man's scarlet face turned to Bogert. He swallowed. "I said—" His voice faded out. He tried again, "I said—"

And he drew a deep breath and spewed it out hastily in one long succession of syllables. Then, in the charged air that lingered, he concluded almost in tears, ". . . more or less. I don't remember the exact order of what I called him, and maybe I left out something or put in something, but that was about it."

Only the slightest flush betrayed any feeling on the part of the robopsychologist. She said, "I am aware of the meaning of most of the terms used. The others, I suppose, are equally derogatory."

"I'm afraid so," agreed the tormented Black.

"And in among it, you told him to lose himself."

"I meant it only figuratively."

"I realize that. No disciplinary action is intended, I am sure." And at her glance, the general, who, five seconds earlier, had seemed not sure at all, nodded angrily.

"You may leave, Mr. Black. Thank you for your cooperation."

It took five hours for Susan Calvin to interview the sixty-three robots. It was five hours of multi-repetition; of replacement after replacement of identical robot; of Questions A, B, C, D; and Answers A, B, C, D; of a carefully bland expression, a carefully neutral tone, a carefully friendly atmosphere; and a hidden wire recorder.

The psychologist felt drained of vitality when she was finished.

Bogert was waiting for her and looked expectant as she dropped the recording spool with a clang upon the plastic of the desk.

She shook her head. "All sixty-three seemed the same to me. I couldn't tell—"

He said, "You couldn't expect to tell by ear, Susan. Suppose we analyze the recordings."

Ordinarily, the mathematical interpretation of verbal reactions of robots is one of the more intricate branches of robotic analysis. It requires a staff of trained technicians and the help of complicated computing machines. Bogert knew that. Bogert stated as much, in an extreme of unshown annoyance after having listened to each set of replies, made lists of word deviations, and graphs of the intervals of responses.

"There are no anomalies present, Susan. The variations in wording and the time reactions are within the limits of ordinary frequency groupings. We need finer methods. They must have computers here. No." He frowned and nibbled delicately at a thumbnail. "We can't use computers. Too much danger of leakage. Or maybe if we—"

Dr. Calvin stopped him with an impatient gesture, "Please, Peter. This isn't one of your petty laboratory problems. If we can't determine the modified Nestor by some gross difference that we can see with the naked eye, one that there is no mistake about, we're out of luck. The danger of being wrong, and of letting him escape is otherwise too great. It's not enough to point out a minute irregularity in a graph. I tell you, if that's all I've got to go on, I'd destroy them all just to be certain. Have you spoken to the other modified Nestors?"

"Yes, I have," snapped back Bogert, "and there's nothing wrong with them. They're above normal in friendliness if anything. They answered my questions, displayed pride in their knowledge—except the two new ones that haven't had time to learn their etheric physics. They laughed rather good-naturedly at my ignorance in some of the specializations here." He shrugged. "I suppose that forms some of the basis for resentment toward them on the part of the technicians here. The robots are perhaps too willing to impress you with their greater knowledge."

"Can you try a few Planar Reactions to see if there has been any change, any deterioration, in their mental set-up since manufacture?"

"I haven't yet, but I will." He shook a slim finger at her, "You're losing your nerve, Susan. I don't see what it is you're dramatizing. They're essentially harmless."

"They are?" Calvin took fire. "They are? Do you realize one of them is lying? One of the sixty-three robots I have just interviewed has deliberately lied to me after the strictest injunction to tell the truth. The abnormality indicated is horribly deep-seated, and horribly frightening."

Peter Bogert felt his teeth harden against each other. He said, "Not at all. Look! Nestor 10 was given orders to lose himself. Those orders were expressed in maximum urgency by the person most authorized to command him. You can't counteract that order either by superior urgency or superior right of command. Naturally, the robot will attempt to defend the carrying out of his orders. In fact, objectively, I admire his ingenuity. How better can a robot lose himself than to hide himself among a group of similar robots?"

"Yes, you would admire it. I've detected amusement in you, Peter—amusement and an appalling lack of understanding. Are you a roboticist, Peter? Those robots attach importance to what they consider superiority. You've just said as much yourself. Subconsciously they feel humans to be inferior and the First Law which protects us from them is imperfect. They are unstable. And here we have a young man ordering a robot to leave him, to lose himself, with every verbal appearance of revulsion, disdain, and disgust. Granted, that robot must follow orders, but subconsciously, there is resentment. It will become more important than ever for it to prove that it is superior despite the horrible names it was called. It may become *so* important that what's left of the First Law won't be enough."

"How on Earth, or anywhere in the Solar System, Susan, is a robot going to know the meaning of the assorted strong language used upon him? Obscenity is not one of the things impressioned upon his brain."

"Original impressionment is not everything," Calvin snarled at him. "Robots have learning capacity, you . . . you fool—" And Bogert knew that she had really lost her temper. She continued hastily, "Don't you suppose he could tell from the tone used that the words weren't complimentary? Don't you suppose he's heard the words used before and noted upon what occasions?"

"Well, then," shouted Bogert, "will you kindly tell me one way in which a modified robot can harm a human being, no matter how offended it is, no matter how sick with desire to prove superiority?"

"If I tell you one way, will you keep quiet?"

"Yes."

They were leaning across the table at each other, angry eyes nailed together.

The psychologist said, "If a modified robot were to drop a heavy weight upon a human being, he would not be breaking the First Law, if he did so with the knowledge that his strength and reaction speed would be sufficient to snatch the weight away before it struck the man. However once the weight left his fingers, he would be no longer the active medium. Only the blind force of gravity would be that. The robot could then change his mind and merely by inaction, allow the weight to strike. The modified First Law allows that."

"That's an awful stretch of imagination."

"That's what my profession requires sometimes. Peter, let's not quarrel. Let's work. You know the exact nature of the stimulus that caused the robot to lose himself. You have the records of his original mental make-up. I want you to tell me how possible it is for our robot to do the sort of thing I just talked about. Not the specific instance, mind you, but that whole class of response. And I want it done quickly."

"And meanwhile—"

"And meanwhile, we'll have to try performance tests directly on the response to First Law."

Gerald Black, at his own request, was supervising the mushrooming wooden partitions that were springing up in a bellying circle on the vaulted third floor of Radiation Building 2. The laborers worked, in the main, silently, but more than one was openly a-wonder at the sixty-three photocells that required installation.

One of them sat down near Black, removed his hat, and wiped his forehead thoughtfully with a freckled forearm.

Black nodded at him. "How's it doing, Walensky?"

Walensky shrugged and fired a cigar. "Smooth as butter. What's going on anyway, Doc? First, there's no work for three days and then we have this mess of jiggers." He leaned backward on his elbows and puffed smoke.

Black twitched his eyebrows. "A couple of robot men came over from Earth. Remember the trouble we had with robots running into the gamma fields, before we pounded it into their skulls that they weren't to do it."

"Yeah. Didn't we get new robots?"

"We got some replacements, but mostly it was a job of indoctrination. Anyway, the people who make them want to figure out robots that aren't hit so bad by gamma rays."

"Sure seems funny, though, to stop all the work on the Drive for this robot deal. I thought nothing was allowed to stop the Drive."

"Well, it's the fellows upstairs that have the say on that. Me—I just do as I'm told. Probably all a matter of—"

"Pull—"

"Yeah," the electrician jerked a smile, and winked a wise eye. "Somebody knew somebody in Washington. But as long as my pay comes through on the dot, I shouldn't worry. The Drive's none of my affair. What are they going to do here?"

"You're asking me? They brought a mess of robots with them—over sixty—and they're going to measure reactions. That's all *my* knowledge."

"How long will it take?"

"I wish I knew."

"Well," Walensky said, with heavy sarcasm, "as long as they dish me my money, they can play games all they want."

Black felt quietly satisfied. Let the story spread. It was harmless, and near enough to the truth to take the fangs out of curiosity.

A man sat in the chair, motionless, silent. A weight dropped, crashed downward, then pounded aside at the last moment under the synchronized thump of a sudden force beam. In sixty-three wooden cells, watching NS-2 robots dashing forward in that split second before the weight veered, and sixty-three photocells five feet ahead of their original positions jiggled the marking pen and presented a little jag on the paper. The weight rose and dropped, rose and dropped, rose—

Ten times!

Ten times the robots sprang forward and stopped, as the man remained safely seated.

Major-general Kallner had not worn his uniform in its entirety since the first dinner with the U. S. Robot representatives. He wore nothing over his blue-gray shirt now, the collar was open, and the black tie was pulled loose.

He looked hopefully at Bogert, who was still blandly neat and whose inner tension was perhaps betrayed only by the trace of glister at his temples.

The general said, "How does it look? What is it you're trying to see?"

Bogert replied, "A difference which may turn out to be a little too subtle for our purposes, I'm afraid. For sixty-two of those robots the necessity of jumping toward the apparently threatened human was what we call, in robotics, a forced reaction. You see, even when the robots knew that the human in question would not come to harm—and after the third or fourth time they must have known it—they could not prevent reacting as they did. First Law requires it."

"Well?"

"But the sixty-third robot, the modified Nestor, had no such compulsion. He was under free action. If he had wished, he could have remained in his seat. Unfortunately," he said, his voice mildly regretful, "he didn't so wish."

"Why do you suppose?"

Bogert shrugged. "I suppose Dr. Calvin will tell us when she gets here. Probably with a horribly pessimistic interpretation, too. She is sometimes a bit annoying."

"She's qualified, isn't she?" demanded the general with a sudden frown of uneasiness.

"Yes." Bogert seemed amused. "She's qualified all right. She understands robots like a sister—comes from hating human beings so much, I think. It's just that, psychologist or not, she's an extreme neurotic. Has paranoid tendencies. Don't take her too seriously."

He spread the long row of broken-line graphs out in front of him. "You see, general, in the case of each robot the time interval from moment of drop to the completion of a five-foot movement tends to decrease as the tests are repeated. There's a definite mathematical relationship that governs such things and failure to conform would indicate marked abnormality in the positronic brain. Unfortunately, all here appear normal."

"But if our Nestor 10 was not responding with a forced action, why isn't his curve different? I don't understand that."

"It's simple enough. Robotic responses are not perfectly analogous to human responses, more's the pity. In human beings, voluntary action is much slower than reflex action. But that's not the case with robots; with them it is merely a question of freedom of choice, otherwise the speeds of free and forced action are much the same. What I *had* been expecting, though, was that Nestor 10 would be caught by surprise the first time and allow too great an interval to elapse before responding."

"And he didn't?"

"I'm afraid not."

"Then we haven't gotten anywhere." The general sat back with an expression of pain. "It's five days since you've come."

At this point, Susan Calvin entered and slammed the door behind her. "Put your graphs away, Peter," she cried, "you know they don't show anything."

She mumbled something impatiently as Kallner half-rose to greet her, and went on, "We'll have to try something else quickly. I don't like what's happening."

Bogert exchanged a resigned glance with the general. "Is anything wrong?"

"You mean specifically? No. But I don't like to have Nestor 10 continue to elude us. It's bad. It *must* be gratifying his swollen sense of superiority. I'm afraid that his motivation is no longer simply one of following orders. I think it's becoming more a matter of sheer neurotic necessity to outthink humans. That's a dangerously unhealthy situation. Peter, have you done what I asked? Have you worked out the instability factors of the modified NS-2 along the lines I want?"

"It's in progress," said the mathematician, without interest.

She stared at him angrily for a moment, then turned to Kallner. "Nestor 10 is decidedly aware of what we're doing, general. He had no reason to jump for the bait in this experiment, especially after the first time, when he must have seen that there was no real danger to our subject. The others couldn't help it; but *he* was deliberately falsifying a reaction."

"What do you think we ought to do now, then, Dr. Calvin?"

"Make it impossible for him to fake an action the next time. We will repeat the experiment, but with an addition. High-tension cables, capable of electrocuting the Nestor models will be placed between subject and robot—enough of them to avoid the possibility of jumping over—and the robot will be made perfectly aware in advance that touching the cables will mean death."

"Hold on," spat out Bogert with sudden viciousness. "I rule that out. We are not electrocuting two million dollars worth of robots to locate Nestor 10. There are other ways."

"You're certain? You've found none. In any case, it's not a question of electrocution. We can arrange a relay which will break the current at the instant of application of weight. If the robot should place his weight on it, he won't die. *But he won't know that,* you see."

The general's eyes gleamed into hope. "Will that work?"

"It should. Under those conditions, Nestor 10 would have to remain in his seat. He could be *ordered* to touch the cables and die, for the Second Law of obedience is superior to the Third Law of self-preservation. But *he won't* be ordered to; he will merely be left to his own devices, as will all the robots. In the case of the normal robots, the First Law of human safety will drive them to their death even without orders. But not our Nestor 10. Without the entire First Law, and without having received any orders on the matter, the Third Law, self-preservation, will be the highest operating, and he will have no choice but to remain in his seat. It would be a forced action."

"Will it be done tonight, then?"

"Tonight," said the psychologist, "if the cables can be laid in time. I'll tell the robots now what they're to be up against."

A man sat in the chair, motionless, silent. A weight dropped, crashed downward, then pounded aside at the last moment under the synchronized thump of a sudden force beam.

Only once—

And from her small camp chair in the observing booth in the balcony, Dr. Susan Calvin rose with a short gasp of pure horror.

Sixty-three robots sat quietly in their chairs, staring owlishly at the endangered man before them. Not one moved.

Dr. Calvin was angry, angry almost past endurance. Angry the worse for not daring to show it to the robots that, one by one, were entering the room and then leaving. She checked the list. Number twenty-eight was due in now—Thirty-five still lay ahead of her.

Number Twenty-eight entered, diffidently.

She forced herself into reasonable calm. "And who are you?"

The robot replied in a low, uncertain voice, "I have received no number of my own yet, ma'am. I'm an NS-2 robot, and I was Number Twenty-eight in line outside. I have a slip of paper here that I'm to give to you."

"You haven't been in here before this today?"

"No, ma'am."

"Sit down. Right there. I want to ask you some questions, Number Twenty-eight. Were you in the Radiation Room of Building Two about four hours ago?"

The robot had trouble answering. Then it came out hoarsely, like machinery needing oil, "Yes, ma'am."

"There was a man who almost came to harm there, wasn't there?"

"Yes, ma'am."

"You did nothing, did you?"

"No, ma'am."

"The man might have been hurt because of your inaction. Do you know that?"

"Yes, ma'am. I couldn't help it, ma'am." It is hard to picture a large expressionless metallic figure cringing, but it managed.

"I want you to tell me exactly why you did nothing to save him."

"I want to explain, ma'am. I certainly don't want to have you . . . have *anyone* . . . think that I could do a thing that might cause harm to a master. Oh, no, that would be a horrible . . . an inconceivable—"

"Please don't get excited, boy. I'm not blaming you for anything. I only want to know what you were thinking at the time."

"Ma'am, before it all happened you told us that one of the masters would be in danger of harm from that weight that keeps falling and that we would have to cross electric cables if we were to try to save him. Well, ma'am, that wouldn't stop me. What is my destruction compared to the safety of a master? But . . . but it occurred to me that if I died on my way to him, I wouldn't be able to save him anyway. The weight would crush him and then I would be dead for no purpose and perhaps some day some other master might come to harm who wouldn't have, if I had only stayed alive. Do you understand me, ma'am?"

"You mean that it was merely a choice of the man dying, or both the man and yourself dying. Is that right?"

"Yes, ma'am. It was impossible to save the master. He might be considered dead. In that case, it is inconceivable that I destroy myself for nothing—without orders."

The robopsychologist twiddled a pencil. She had heard the same story with insignificant verbal variations twenty-seven times before. This was the crucial question now.

"Boy," she said, "your thinking has its points, but it is not the sort of thing I thought you might think. Did you think of this yourself?"

The robot hesitated. "No."

"Who thought of it, then?"

"We were talking last night, and one of us got that idea and it sounded reasonable."

"Which one?"

The robot thought deeply. "I don't know. Just one of us."

She sighed, "That's all."

Number Twenty-nine was next. Thirty-four after that.

Major-general Kallner, too, was angry. For one week all of Hyper Base had stopped dead, barring some paper work on the subsidiary asteroids of the group. For nearly one week, the two top experts in the field had aggravated the situation with useless tests. And now they—or the woman, at any rate—made impossible propositions.

Fortunately for the general situation, Kallner felt it impolitic to display his anger openly.

Susan Calvin was insisting, "Why not, sir? It's obvious that the present situation is unfortunate. The only way we may reach results in the future—or what future is left us in this matter—is to separate the robots. We can't keep them together any longer."

"My dear Dr. Calvin," rumbled the general, his voice sinking into the lower baritone registers. "I don't see how I can quarter sixty-three robots all over the place—"

Dr. Calvin raised her arms helplessly. "I can do nothing then. Nestor 10 will either imitate what the other robots would do, or else argue them plausibly into not doing what he himself cannot do. And in any case, this is bad business. We're in actual combat with this little lost robot of ours and he's winning out. Every victory of his aggravates his abnormality."

She rose to her feet in determination. "General Kallner, if you do not separate the robots as I ask, then I can only demand that all sixty-three be destroyed immediately."

"You demand it, do you?" Bogert looked up suddenly, and with real anger. "What gives you the right to demand any such thing? Those robots remain as they are. *I'm* responsible to the management, not you."

"And I," added Major-general Kallner, "am responsible to the World Co-ordinator—and I must have this settled."

"In that case," flashed back Calvin, "there is nothing for me to do but resign. If necessary to force you to the necessary destruction, I'll make this whole matter public. It was not I that approved the manufacture of modified robots."

"One word from you, Dr. Calvin," said the general, deliberately, "in violation of security measures, and you would be certainly imprisoned instantly."

Bogert felt the matter to be getting out of hand. His voice grew syrupy, "Well, now, we're beginning to act like children, all of us. We need only a little more time. Surely we can outwit a robot without resigning, or imprisoning people, or destroying two millions."

The psychologist turned on him with quiet fury. "I don't want any unbalanced robots in existence. We have one Nestor that's definitely unbalanced, eleven more that are potentially so, and sixty-two normal robots that are being subjected to an unbalanced environment. The only absolute safe method is complete destruction."

The signal-burr brought all three to a halt, and the angry tumult of growingly unrestrained emotion froze.

"Come in," growled Kallner.

It was Gerald Black, looking perturbed. He had heard angry voices. He said, "I thought I'd come myself . . . didn't like to ask anyone else—"

"What is it? Don't orate—"

"The locks of Compartment C in the trading ship have been played with. There are fresh scratches on them."

"Compartment C?" exclaimed Calvin quickly. "That's the one that holds the robots, isn't it? Who did it?"

"From the inside," said Black, laconically.

"The lock isn't out of order, is it?"

"No. It's all right. I've been staying on the ship now for four days and none of them have tried to get out. But I thought you ought to know, and I didn't like to spread the news. I noticed the matter myself."

"Is anyone there now?" demanded the general.

"I left Robbins and McAdams there."

There was a thoughtful silence, and then Dr. Calvin said, ironically, "Well?"

Kallner rubbed his nose uncertainly. "What's it all about?"

"Isn't it obvious? Nester 10 is planning to leave. That order to lose himself is dominating his abnormality past anything we can do. I wouldn't be surprised if what's left of his First Law would scarcely be powerful enough to override it. He is perfectly capable of seizing the ship and leaving with it. Then we'd have a mad robot on a spaceship. What would he do next? Any idea? Do you still want to leave them all together, general?"

"Nonsense," interrupted Bogert. He had regained his smoothness. "All that from a few scratch marks on a lock."

"Have you, Dr. Bogert, completed the analysis I've required, since you volunteer opinions?"

"Yes."

"May I see it?"

"No."

"Why not? Or mayn't I ask that, either?"

"Because there's no point in it, Susan. I told you in advance that these modified robots are less stable than the normal variety, and my analysis shows it. There's a certain very small chance of breakdown under extreme circumstances that are not likely to occur. Let it go at that. I won't give you ammunition for your absurd claim that sixty-two perfectly good robots be destroyed just because so far you lack the ability to detect Nestor 10 among them."

Susan Calvin stared him down and let disgust fill her eyes. "You won't let anything stand in the way of the permanent directorship, will you?"

"Please," begged Kallner, half in irritation. "Do you insist that nothing further can be done, Dr. Calvin?"

"I can't think of anything, sir," she replied, wearily. "If there were only other differences between Nestor 10 and the normal robots, differences that didn't involve the First Law. Even one other difference. Something in impressionment, environment, specification—" And she stopped suddenly.

"What is it?"

"I've thought of something . . . I think—" Her eyes grew distant and hard, "These modified Nestors, Peter. They get the same impressioning the normal ones get, don't they?"

"Yes. Exactly the same."

"And what was it you were saying, Mr. Black," she turned to the young man, who through the storms that had followed his news had maintained a discreet silence. "Once when complaining of the Nestors' attitude of superiority, you said the technicians had taught them all they knew."

"Yes, in etheric physics. They're not acquainted with the subject when they come here."

"That's right," said Bogert, in surprise. "I told you, Susan, when I spoke to the other Nestors here that the two new arrivals hadn't learned etheric physics yet."

"And why is that?" Dr. Calvin was speaking in mounting excitement. "Why aren't NS-2 models impressioned with etheric physics to start with?"

"I can tell you that," said Kallner. "It's all of a piece with the secrecy. We thought that if we made a special model with knowledge of etheric physics, used twelve of them and put the others to work in an unrelated field, there might be suspicion. Men working with normal Nestors might wonder why they knew etheric physics. So there was merely an impressionment with a capacity for training in the field. Only the ones that come here, naturally, receive such a training. It's that simple."

"I understand. Please get out of here, the lot of you. Let me have an hour or so."

Calvin felt she could not face the ordeal for a third time. Her mind had contemplated it and rejected it with an intensity that left her nauseated. She could face that unending file of repetitious robots no more.

So Bogert asked the question now, while she sat aside, eyes and mind half closed.

Number Fourteen came in—forty-nine to go.

Bogert looked up from the guide sheet and said, "What is your number in line?"

"Fourteen, sir." The robot presented his numbered ticket.

"Sit down, boy."

Bogert asked, "You haven't been here before on this day?"

"No, sir."

"Well, boy, we are going to have another man in danger of harm soon after we're through here. In fact, when you leave this room, you will be led to a stall where you will wait quietly, till you are needed. Do you understand?"

"Yes, sir."

"Now, naturally, if a man is in danger of harm, you will try to save him."

"Naturally, sir."

"Unfortunately, between the man and yourself, there will be a gamma ray field."

Silence.

"Do you know what gamma rays are?" asked Bogert sharply.

"Energy radiation, sir?"

The next question came in a friendly, offhand manner, "Ever work with gamma rays?"

"No, sir." The answer was definite.

"Mm-m. Well, boy, gamma rays will kill you instantly. They'll destroy your brain. That is a fact you must know and remember. Naturally, you don't want to destroy yourself."

"Naturally." Again the robot seemed shocked. Then, slowly, "But, sir, if the gamma rays are between myself and the master that may be harmed, how can I save him? I would be destroying myself to no purpose."

"Yes, there is that," Bogert seemed concerned about the matter. "The only thing I can advise, boy, is that if you detect the gamma radiation between yourself and the man, you may as well sit where you are."

The robot was openly relieved. "Thank you, sir. There wouldn't be any use, would there?"

"Of course not. But if there *weren't* any dangerous radiation, that would be a different matter."

"Naturally, sir. No question of that."

"You may leave now. The man on the other side of the door will lead you to your stall. Please wait there."

He turned to Susan Calvin when the robot left. "How did that go, Susan?"

"Very well," she said, dully.

"Do you think we could catch Nestor 10 by quick questioning on etheric physics?"

"Perhaps, but it's not sure enough." Her hands lay loosely in her lap. "Remember, he's fighting us. He's on his guard. The only way we can catch him is to outsmart him—and, within his limitations, he can think much more quickly than a human being."

"Well, just for fun—suppose I ask the robots from now on a few questions on gamma rays. Wave length limits, for instance."

"No!" Dr. Calvin's eyes sparked to life. "It would be too easy for him to deny knowledge and then he'd be warned against the test that's coming up—which is our real chance. Please follow the questions I've indicated, Peter, and don't improvise. It's just within the bounds of risk to ask them if they've ever worked with gamma rays. And try to sound even less interested than you do when you ask it."

Bogert shrugged, and pressed the buzzer that would allow the entrance of Number Fifteen.

The large Radiation Room was in readiness once more. The robots waited patiently in their wooden cells, all open to the center but closed off from each other.

Major-general Kallner mopped his brow slowly with a large handkerchief while Dr. Calvin checked the last details with Black.

"You're sure now," she demanded, "that none of the robots have had a chance to talk with each other after leaving the Orientation Room?"

"Absolutely sure," insisted Black. "There's not been a word exchanged."

"And the robots are put in the proper stalls?"

"Here's the plan."

The psychologist looked at it thoughtfully. "Um-m-m."

The general peered over her shoulder. "What's the idea of the arrangement, Dr. Calvin?"

"I've asked to have those robots that appeared even slightly out of true in the previous tests concentrated on one side of the circle. I'm going to be sitting in the center myself this time, and I wanted to watch those particularly."

"*You're* going to be sitting there—" exclaimed Bogert.

"Why not?" she demanded coldly. "What I expect to see may be something quite momentary. I can't risk having anyone else as main observer. Peter, you'll be in the observing booth, and I want you to keep your eye on the opposite side of the circle. General Kallner, I've arranged for motion pictures to be taken of each robot, in case visual observation isn't enough. If these are required, the robots are to remain exactly where they are until the pictures are developed and studied. None must leave, none must change place. Is that clear?"

"Perfectly."

"Then let's try it this one last time."

Susan Calvin sat in the chair, silent, eyes restless. A weight dropped, crashed downward, then pounded aside at the last moment under the synchronized thump of a sudden force beam.

And a single robot jerked upright and took two steps.

And stopped.

But Dr. Calvin was upright, and her finger pointed to him sharply. "Nestor 10, come here," she cried, *"come here!* COME HERE!"

Slowly, reluctantly, the robot took another step forward. The psychologist shouted at the top of her voice, without taking her eyes from the robot, "Get every other robot out of this place, somebody. Get them out quickly, and *keep* them out."

Somewhere within reach of her ears there was noise, and the thud of hard feet upon the floor. She did not look away.

Nestor 10—if it was Nestor 10—took another step, and then, under force of her imperious gesture, two more. He was only ten feet away, when he spoke harshly, "I have been told to be lost—"

Another stop. "I must not disobey. They have not found me so far— He would think me a failure—He told me—But it's not so—I am powerful and intelligent—"

The words came in spurts.

Another step.

"I know a good deal—He would think . . . I mean I've been found— Disgraceful—Not I—I am intelligent—And by just a master . . . who is weak— Slow—"

Another step—and one metal arm flew out suddenly to her shoulder, and she felt the weight bearing her down. Her throat constricted, and she felt a shriek tear through.

Dimly, she heard Nestor 10's next words, "No one must find me. No master—" and the cold metal was against her, and she was sinking under the weight of it.

And then a queer, metallic sound, and she was on the ground with an unfelt thump, and a gleaming arm was heavy across her body. It did not move. Nor did Nestor 10, who sprawled beside her.

And now faces were bending over her.

Gerald Black was gasping, "Are you hurt, Dr. Calvin?"

She shook her head feebly. They pried the arm off her and lifted her gently to her feet. "What happened?"

Black said, "I bathed the place in gamma rays for five seconds. We didn't know what was happening. It wasn't till the last second that we realized he was attacking you, and then there was no time for anything but a gamma field. He went down in an instant. There wasn't enough to harm you though. Don't worry about it."

"I'm not worried." She closed her eyes and leaned for a moment upon his shoulder. "I don't think I was attacked exactly. Nestor 10 was simply trying to do so. What was left of the First Law was still holding him back."

Susan Calvin and Peter Bogert, two weeks after their first meeting with Major-general Kallner had their last. Work at Hyper Base had been resumed. The trading ship with its sixty-two normal NS-2's was gone to wherever it was bound, with an officially imposed story to explain its two weeks' delay. The government cruiser was making ready to carry the two roboticists back to Earth.

Kallner was once again agleam in dress uniform. His white gloves shone as he shook hands.

Calvin said, "The other modified Nestors are, of course, to be destroyed."

"They will be. We'll make shift with normal robots, or, if necessary, do without."

"Good."

"But tell me—You haven't explained—How was it done?"

She smiled tightly, "Oh, that. I would have told you in advance if I had been more certain of its working. You see, Nestor 10 had a superiority complex that was becoming more radical all the time. He liked to think that he and other robots knew more than human beings. It was becoming very important for him to think so.

"We knew that. So we warned every robot in advance that gamma rays would kill them, which it would, and we further warned them all that gamma rays would be between them and myself. So they all stayed where they were, naturally. By Nestor 10's own logic in the previous test they had all decided that there was no point in trying to save a human being if they were sure to die before they could do it."

"Well, yes, Dr. Calvin, I understand that. But why did Nestor 10 himself leave his seat?"

"Ah! That was a little arrangement between myself and your young Mr. Black. You see it wasn't gamma rays that flooded the area between myself and the robots—but infrared rays. Just ordinary heat rays, absolutely harmless. Nestor 10 knew they were infrared and harmless and so he began to dash out, as he expected the rest would do, under First Law compulsion. It was only a fraction of a second too late that he remembered that the normal NS-2's could detect radiation, but could not identify the type. That he himself could only identify wave lengths by virtue of the training he had received at Hyper Base, under mere human beings, was a little too humiliating to remember for just a moment. To the normal robots the area was fatal because we had told them it would be, and only Nestor 10 knew we were lying.

"And just for a moment he forgot, or didn't want to remember, that other robots might be more ignorant than human beings. His very superiority caught him. Good-bye, general."

After reading Little Lost Robot: I remembered the details as I read them. How the modified First Law would enable a robot to harm a man. How the robot had been told to lose himself. How a seemingly pointless test did reveal the key robot. It's a logical puzzle, well resolved. A good story. Would it be a favorite of mine today? I think not, simply because in the interim I have read whole Asimov novels featuring fully humanoid robots—that is, ones you can't tell from living folk if they don't tell you—and they are more impressive than these partially humanoid robots. In my own fiction I have had female humanoid robots a man can fall in love with, even knowing their nature. So this story is relatively primitive, and suffers by comparison. But that's part of the point: it was leading the way.

    —Piers

CHILD'S PLAY

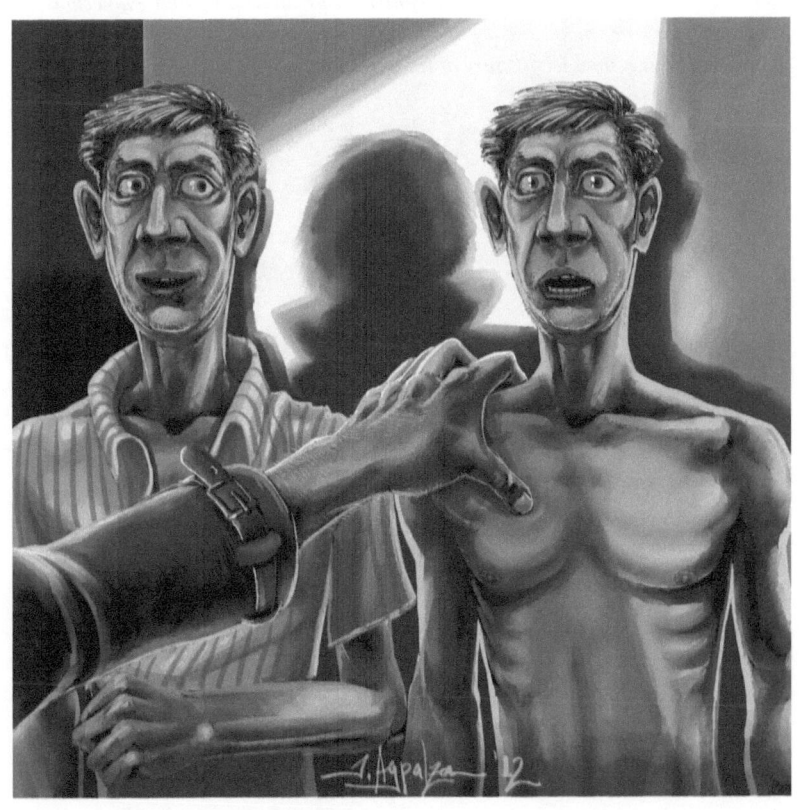

William Tenn

March 1947

This was one of the other stories in that first fabulous issue of ASTOUNDING Science Fiction I picked up. It was easy to get into as a man receives a package, and easy to follow as he explores its content and directions, and marvelous in its potential as he makes a copy of himself. Then the devastating conclusion. I remember it as a wonderful story of imagination.
—Piers

After the man from the express company had given the door an untipped slam, Sam Weber decided to move the huge crate under the one light bulb in his room. It was all very well for the messenger to drawl, "I dunno. We don't send 'em; we just deliver 'em, mister"—but there must be some sensible explanation.

With a grunt that began as an anticipatory reflex and ended on a note of surprised annoyance, Sam shoved the box forward the few feet necessary. It was heavy enough; he wondered how the messenger had carried it up the three nights of stairs.

He straightened and frowned down at the garish card which contained his name and address as well as the legend—"Merry Christmas, 2353."

A joke? He didn't know anyone who'd think it funny to send a card dated over two hundred years in the future. Unless one of the comedians in his law school graduating class meant to record his opinion as to when Weber would be trying his first case. Even so—

The letters were shaped strangely, come to think of it, sort of green streaks instead of lines. And the card was a sheet of gold!

Sam decided he was really interested. He ripped the card aside, tore off the flimsy wrapping material—and stopped.

There was no top to the box, no slit in its side, no handle anywhere in sight. It seemed to be a solid, cubical mass of brown stuff. Yet he was positive something had rattled inside when it was moved.

He seized the corners and strained and grunted till it lifted. The underside was as smooth and innocent of openings as the rest. He let it thump back to the floor.

"Ah, well," he said, philosophically, "it's not the gift; it's the principle involved."

Many of his gifts still required appreciative notes. He'd have to work up something special for Aunt Maggie. Her neckties were things of cubistic horror, but he hadn't even sent her a lone handkerchief this Christmas. Every cent had gone into buying that brooch for Tina. Not quite a ring, but maybe she'd consider that under the circumstances—

He turned to walk to his bed which he had drafted into the additional service of desk and chair. He kicked at the great box disconsolately. "Well, if you won't open, you won't open."

As if smarting under the kick, the box opened. A cut appeared on the upper surface, widened rapidly and folded the top back and down on either side like a valise. Sam clapped his forehead and addressed a rapid prayer to every god from Set to Father Divine. Then he remembered what he'd said. "Close," he suggested.

The box closed, once more as smooth as a baby's bottom. "Open."

The box opened.

So much for the sideshow, Sam decided. He bent down and peered into the container.

The interior was a crazy mass of shelving on which rested vials filled with blue liquids, jars filled with red solids, transparent tubes showing yellow and green and orange and mauve and other colors which Sam's eyes didn't quite remember. There were seven pieces of intricate apparatus on the bottom which looked as if tube-happy radio hams had assembled them. There was also a book.

Sam picked the book off the bottom and noted numbly that while all its pages were metallic, it was lighter than any paper book he'd ever held.

He carried the book over to the bed and sat down. Then he took a long, deep breath and turned to the first page. *"Gug,"* he said, exhaling his long, deep breath.

In mad, green streaks of letters:

Bild-A-Man Set #3. This set is intended solely for the use of children between the ages of eleven and thirteen. The equipment, much more advanced than Bild-A-Man Sets 1 and 2, will enable the child of this age-group to build and assemble complete adult humans in perfect working order. The retarded child may also construct the babies and mannikins of the earlier kits. Two disassembleators are provided so that the set can be used again and again with profit. As with Sets 1 and 2, the aid of a Census Keeper in all disassembling is advised. Refills and additional parts may be acquired from The Bild-A-Man Company, 928 Diagonal Level, Glunt City, Ohio. Remember—only with a Bild-A-Man can you build a man!

Weber squeezed his eyes shut. What was that gag in the movie he'd seen last night? Terrific gag. Terrific picture, too. Nice Technicolor. Wonder how much the director made a week? The cameraman? Five hundred? A thousand?

He opened his eyes warily. The box was still a squat cube in the center of his room. The book was still in his shaking hand. And the page read the same.

"Only with a Bild-A-Man can you build a man!" Heaven help a neurotic young lawyer at a time like this!

There was a price list on the next page for "refills and additional parts." Things like one liter of hemoglobin and three grams of assorted enzymes were offered for sale in terms of one slunk fifty and three slunks forty-five. A note on the bottom advertised Set #4: "The thrill of building your first live Martian!"

Fine print announced *pat. pending 2348.*

The third page was a table of contents. Sam gripped the edge of the mattress with one sweating hand and read:

Chapter I—A child's garden of bio-chemistry.
Chapter II—Making simple living things indoors and out.
Chapter III—Mannikins and what makes them do the world's work.
Chapter IV—Babies and other small humans.
Chapter V—Twins for every purpose, twinning yourself and your friends.
Chapter VI—What you need to build a man.
Chapter VII—Completing the man.
Chapter VIII—Disassembling the man.
Chapter IX—New kinds of life for your leisure moments.

Sam dropped the book back into the box and ran for the mirror. His face was still the same, somewhat like bleached chalk, but fundamentally the same. He hadn't twinned or grown himself a mannikin or devised a new kind of life for his pleasure moments. Everything was snug as a bug in a bughouse.

Very carefully he pushed his eyes back into the proper position in their sockets.

"Dear Aunt Maggie," he began writing feverishly. "Your ties made the most beautiful gift of my Christmas. My only regret is—"

My only regret is that I have but one life to give for my Christmas present. Who could have gone to such fantastic lengths for a practical joke? Lew Knight? Even Lew must have some reverence in his insensitive body for the institution of Christmas. And Lew didn't have the brains or the patience for a job so involved.

Tina? Tina had the fine talent for complication, all right. But Tina, while possessing a delightful abundance of all other physical attributes, was badly lacking in funny-bone.

Sam drew the leather envelope forth and caressed it. Tina's perfume seemed to cling to the surface and move the world back into focus.

The metallic greeting card glinted at him from the floor. Maybe the reverse side contained the sender's name. He picked it up, turned it over.

Nothing but blank gold surface. He was sure of the gold; his father had been a jeweler. The very value of the sheet was rebuttal to the possibility of a practical joke. Besides, again, what was the point?

"Merry Christmas, 2353." Where would humanity be in four hundred years? Traveling to the stars, or beyond—to unimaginable destinations? Using little mannikins to perform the work of machines and robots? Providing children with—

There might be another card or note inside the box. Weber bent down to remove its contents. His eye noted a large grayish jar and the label etched into its surface: *Dehydrated Neurone Preparation, for human construction only.*

He backed away and glared. "Close!" The thing melted shut. Weber sighed his relief at it and decided to go to bed.

He regretted while undressing that he hadn't thought to ask the messenger the name of his firm. Knowing the delivery service involved would be useful in tracing the origin of this gruesome gift.

"But then," he repeated as he fell asleep, "it's not the gift—it's the principle! Merry Christmas, me."

The next morning when Lew Knight breezed in with his "Good morning, counselor," Sam waited for the first sly ribbing to start. Lew wasn't the man to hide his humor behind a bushel. But Lew buried his nose in *The New York State Supplement* and kept it there all morning. The other five young lawyers in the communal office appeared either too bored or too busy to have Bild-A-Man sets on their conscience. There were no sly grins, no covert glances, no leading questions.

Tina walked in at ten o'clock, looking like a pinup girl caught with her clothes on.

"Good morning, counselors," she said.

Each in his own way, according to the peculiar gland secretions he was enjoying at the moment, beamed, drooled or nodded a reply. Lew Knight drooled. Sam Weber beamed.

Tina took it all in and analyzed the situation while she fluffed her hair about. Her conclusions evidently involved leaning markedly against Lew Knight's desk and asking what he had for her to do this morning.

Sam bit savagely into Hackleworth *On Torts*. Theoretically, Tina was employed by all seven of them as secretary, switchboard operator and receptionist. Actually, the most faithful performance of her duties entailed nothing more daily than the typing and addressing of two envelopes with an occasional letter to be sealed inside. Once a week there might be a wistful little brief which was never to attain judicial scrutiny. Tina therefore had a fair library of fashion magazines in the first drawer of her desk and a complete cosmetics laboratory in the other two; she spent one third of her working day in the ladies' room swapping stocking prices and sources with other secretaries; she devoted the other two thirds religiously to that one of her employers who as of her arrival seemed to be in the most masculine mood. Her pay was small but her life was full.

Just before lunch, she approached casually with the morning's mail. "Didn't think we'd be too busy this morning, counselor—" she began.

"You thought incorrectly, Miss Hill," he informed her with a brisk irritation that he hoped became him well; "I've been waiting for you to terminate your social engagements so that we could get down to what occasionally passes for business."

She was as startled as an uncushioned kitten. "But—but this isn't Monday. Somerset & Ojack only send you stuff on Mondays."

Sam winced at the reminder that if it weren't for the legal drudgework he received once a week from Somerset & Ojack he would be a lawyer in name only, if not in spirit only. "I have a letter, Miss Hill," he replied steadily. "Whenever you assemble the necessary materials, we can get on with it."

Tina returned in a head-shaking moment with stenographic pad and pencils.

"Regular heading, today's date," Sam began. "Address it to Chamber of Commerce, Glunt City, Ohio. Gentlemen: Would you inform me if you have registered currently with you a firm bearing the name of the Bild-A-Man Company or a firm with any name at all similar? I am also interested in whether a firm bearing the above or related name has recently made known its intention of joining your community. This inquiry is being made informally on behalf of a client who is interested in a product of this organization whose address he has mislaid. Signature and then this P.S.—My client is also curious as to the business possibilities of a street known as Diagonal Avenue or Diagonal Level. Any data on this address and the organizations presently located there will be greatly appreciated."

Tina batted wide blue eyes at him. "Oh, Sam," she breathed, ignoring the formality he had introduced, "oh, Sam, you have another client. I'm so glad. He looked a little sinister, but in *such* a distinguished manner that I was certain—"

"Who? Who looked a little sinister?"

"Why your new cli-ent." Sam had the uncomfortable feeling that she had almost added "stu-pid." "When I came in this morning, there was this terribly tall old man in a long black overcoat talking to the elevator operator. He turned to me—the elevator operator, I mean—and said, 'This is Mr. Weber's secretary. She'll be able to tell you anything you want to know.' Then he sort of winked which I thought was sort of impolite, you know, considering. Then this old man looked at me hard and I felt distinctly uncomfortable and he walked away muttering 'Either disjointed or predatory personalities. Never normal. Never balanced.' Which I didn't think was very polite, either, I'll have you know, if he is your new client!" She sat back and began breathing again.

Tall, sinister old men in long, black overcoats pumping the elevator operator about him. Hardly a matter of business. He had no skeletons in his personal closet. Could it be connected with his unusual Christmas present? Sam hummed mentally.

"—but she is my favorite aunt, you know," Tina was saying. "And she came in so unexpectedly."

The girl was explaining about their Christmas date. Sam felt a rush of affection for her as she leaned forward.

"Don't bother," he told her. "I knew you couldn't help breaking the date. I was a little sore when you called me, but I got over it; never-hold-a-grudge-against-a-pretty-girl-Sam, I'm known as. How about lunch?"

"Lunch?" She gestured distractedly. "I promised Lew—Mr. Knight, that is—But he wouldn't mind if you came along."

"Fine. Let's go." This would be helping Lew to a spoonful of his own medicine.

Lew Knight took the business of having a crowd instead of a party for lunch as badly as Sam hoped he would. Unfortunately, Lew was able to describe details of his forthcoming case, the probable fees and possible distinction to be reaped thereof. After one or two attempts to bring an interesting will he was rephrasing for Somerset & Ojack into the conversation, Sam subsided into daydreams. Lew immediately dropped *Rosenthal* vs. *Rosenthal* and leered at Tina conversationally.

Outside the restaurant, snow discolored into slush. Most of the stores were removing Christmas displays. Sam noticed construction sets for children, haloed by tinsel and glittering with artificial snow. Build a radio, a skyscraper, an airplane. But "Only with a Bild-A-Man can you—"

"I'm going home," he announced suddenly. "Something important I just remembered. If anything comes up, call me there."

He was leaving Lew a clear field, he told himself, as he found a seat on the subway. But the bitter truth was that the field was almost as clear when he was around as when he wasn't. Lupine Lew Knight, he had been called in Law School; since the day when he had noticed that Tina had the correct proportions of dress-filling substance, Sam's chances had been worth a crowbar at Fort Knox.

Tina hadn't been wearing his brooch today. Her little finger, right hand, however, had sported an unfamiliar and garish little ring. "Some got it," Sam philosophized. "Some don't got it. I don't got it."

But it would have been nice, with Tina, to have got it.

As he unlocked the door of his room he was surprised by an unmade bed telling with rumpled stoicism of a chambermaid who'd never come. This hadn't happened before—Of course! He'd never locked his room before. The girl must have thought he wanted privacy.

Maybe he had.

Aunt Maggie's ties glittered obscenely at the foot of the bed. He chucked them into the closet as he removed his hat and coat. Then he went over to the washstand and washed his hands, slowly. He turned around.

This was it. At last the great cubical bulk that had been lurking quietly in the corner of his vision was squarely before him. It was there and it undoubtedly contained all the outlandish collection he remembered.

"Open," he said, and the box opened.

The book, still open to the metallic table of contents, was lying at the bottom of the box. Part of it had slipped into the chamber of a strange piece of apparatus. Sam picked both out gingerly.

He slipped the book out and noticed the apparatus consisted mostly of some sort of binoculars, supported by a coil and tube arrangement and bearing on a flat green plate. He turned it over. The underside was lettered in the same streaky way as the book. *Combination Electron Microscope and Workbench.*

Very carefully he placed it on the floor. One by one, he removed the others, from the *Junior Biocalibrator* to the *Jiffy Vitalizer.* Very respectfully he ranged against the box in five multi-colored rows the phials of lymph and the jars of basic cartilage. The walls of the chest were lined with indescribably thin and wrinkled sheets; a slight pressure along their edges expanded them into three-dimensional outlines of human organs whose shape and size could be varied with pinching any part of their surface—most indubitably molds.

Quite an assortment. If there was anything solidly scientific to it, that box might mean unimaginable wealth. Or some very useful publicity. Or— well, it should mean something!

If there was anything solidly scientific to it.

Sam flopped down to the bed and opened to *A Child's Garden Of Biochemistry.*

At nine that night he squatted next to the Combination Electron Microscope and Workbench and began opening certain small bottles. At nine forty-seven Sam Weber made his first simple living thing.

It wasn't much, if you used the first chapter of Genesis as your standard. Just a primitive brown mold that, in the field of the microscope, fed diffidently on a piece of pretzel, put forth a few spores and died in about twenty minutes. But *he* had made it. He had constructed a specific life-form to feed on the constituents of a specific pretzel; it could survive nowhere else.

He went out to supper with every intention of getting drunk. After just a little alcohol, however, the *deüsh* feeling returned and he scurried back to his room.

Never again that evening did he recapture the exultation of the brown mold, though he constructed a giant protein molecule and a whole slew of filterable viruses.

He called the office in the little corner drugstore which was his breakfast nook. "I'll be home all day," he told Tina.

She was a little puzzled. So was Lew Knight, who grabbed the phone. "Hey, counselor, you building up a neighborhood practice? Kid Blackstone is missing out on a lot of cases. Two ambulances have already clanged past the building."

"Yeah," said Sam. "I'll tell him when he comes in."

The weekend was almost upon him, so he decided to take the next day off as well. He wouldn't have any real work till Monday when the Somerset & Ojack basket would produce his lone egg.

Before he returned to his room, he purchased a copy of an advanced bacteriology. It was amusing to construct—with improvements!—unicellular creatures whose very place in the scheme of classification was a matter for argument among scientists of his own day. The Bild-A-Man manual, of course, merely gave a few examples and general rules; but with the descriptions in the bacteriology, the world was his oyster.

Which was an idea: he made a few oysters. The shells weren't hard enough, and he couldn't quite screw his courage up to the eating point, but they were most undeniably bivalves. If he cared to perfect his technique, his food problem would be solved.

The manual was fairly easy to follow and profusely illustrated with pictures that expanded into solidity as the page was opened. Very little was taken for granted; involved explanations followed simpler ones. Only the allusions were occasionally obscure—"This is the principle used in the phanphophlink toys," "When your teeth are next yokekkled or demortoned, think of the *Bacterium cyanogenum* and the humble part it plays," "If you have a rubicular mannikin around the house, you needn't bother with the chapter on mannikins."

After a brief search had convinced Sam that whatever else he now had in his apartment he didn't have a rubicular mannikin, he felt justified in turning to the chapter on mannikins. He had conquered completely this feeling of being Pop playing with Junior's toy train: already he had done more than the world's top biologists ever dreamed of for the next generation and what might not lie ahead—what problems might he not yet solve?

"Never forget that mannikins are constructed for one purpose and one purpose only." I won't, Sam promised. "Whether they are sanitary mannikins, tailoring mannikins, printing mannikins or even sunevviarry mannikins, they are each constructed with one operation of a given process in view. When you make a mannikin that is capable of more than one function, you are committing a crime so serious as to be punishable by public admonition."

"To construct an elementary mannikin—"

It was very difficult. Three times he tore down developing monstrosities and began anew. It wasn't till Sunday afternoon that the mannikin was complete—or rather, incomplete.

Long arms it had—although by an error, one was slightly longer than the other—a faceless head and a trunk. No legs. No eyes or ears, no organs of reproduction. It lay on his bed and gurgled out of the red rim of a mouth that was supposed to serve both for ingress and excretion of food. It waved the long arms, designed for some one simple operation not yet invented, in slow circles.

Sam, watching it, decided that life could be as ugly as an open field latrine in midsummer.

He had to disassemble it. Its length—three feet from almost boneless fingers to tapering, sealed-off trunk—precluded the use of the tiny disassembleator with which he had taken apart the oysters and miscellaneous small creations. There was a bright yellow notice on the large diassembleator, however—"To be used only under the direct supervision of a Census Keeper. Call formula A76 or unstable your id."

"Formula A76" meant about as much as "sunevviarry," and Sam decided his id was already sufficiently un-stabled, thank you. He'd have to make out without a Census Keeper. The big disassembleator probably used the same general principles as the small one.

He clamped it to a bedpost and adjusted the focus. He snapped the switch set in the smooth underside.

Five minutes later the mannikin was a bright, gooey mess on his bed.

The large disassembleator, Sam was convinced as he tidied his room, did require the supervision of a Census Keeper. Some sort of keeper anyway. He rescued as many of the legless creature's constitutents as he could, although he doubted he'd be using the set for the next fifty years or so. He certainly wouldn't ever use the disassembleator again; much less spectacular and disagreeable to shove the whole thing into a meat grinder and crank the handle as it squashed inside.

As he locked the door behind him on his way to a gentle binge, he made a mental note to purchase some fresh sheets the next morning. He'd have to sleep on the floor tonight.

Wrist-deep in Somerset & Ojack minutiae, Sam was conscious of Lew Knight's stares and Tina's puzzled glances. If they only knew, he exulted! But Tina would probably just think it "marr-vell-ouss!" and Lew Knight might make some crack like "Hey! Kid Frankenstein himself!" Come to think of it though Lew would probably have worked out some method of duplicating, to a limited extent, the contents of the Bild-A-Man set and marketing it commercially. Whereas he—well, there were other things you could do with the gadget. Plenty of other things.

"Hey, counselor," Lew Knight was perched on the corner of his desk, "what are these long weekends we're taking? You might not make as much money in the law, but does it look right for an associate of mine to sell magazine subscriptions on the side?"

Sam stuffed his ears mentally against the emery-wheel voice. "I've been writing a book."

"A law book? Weber *On Bankruptcy?*"

"No, a juvenile. *Lew Knight, The Neanderthal Nitwit.*"

"Won't sell. The title lacks punch. Something like *Knights, Knaves and Knobheads* is what the public goes for these days. By the way, Tina tells me you two had some sort of understanding about New Year's Eve and she doesn't think you'd mind if I took her out instead. I don't think you'd mind either, but I may be prejudiced. Especially since I have a table reservation at Cigale's where there's usually less of a crowd of a New Year's Eve than at the Automat."

"I don't mind."

"Good," said Knight approvingly as he moved away. "By the way, I won that case. Nice juicy fee, too. Thanks for asking."

Tina also wanted to know if he objected to the new arrangements when she brought the mail. Again, he didn't. Where had he been for over two days? He had been busy, very busy. Something entirely new. Something important.

She stared down at him as he separated offers of used cars guaranteed not to have been driven over a quarter of a million miles from caressing reminders that he still owed half the tuition for the last year of law school and when was he going to pay it?

Came a letter that was neither bill nor ad. Sam's heart momentarily lost interest in the monotonous round of pumping that was its lot as he stared at a strange postmark: Glunt City, Ohio.

Dear Sir:

There is no firm in Glunt City at the present time bearing any name similar to "Bild-A-Man Company" nor do we know of any such organization planning to join our little community. We also have no thoroughfare called "Diagonal"; our north-south streets are named after Indian tribes while our east-west avenues are listed numerically in multiples of five. Glunt City is a restricted residential township; we intend to keep it that. Only small retailing and service establishments are permitted here. If you are interested in building a home in Glunt City and can furnish proof of white, Christian, Anglo-Saxon ancestry on both sides of your family for fifteen generations, we would be glad to furnish further information.

Thomas H. Plantagenet, Mayor.

P.S. An airfield for privately owned jet and propeller-driven aircraft is being built outside the city limits.

That was sort of that. He would get no refills on any of the vials and bottles even if he had a loose slunk or two with which to pay for the stuff. Better go easy on the material and conserve it as much as possible. But no disassembling!

Would the "Bild-A-Man Company" begin manufacturing at Glunt City some time in the future when it had developed into an industrial metropolis against the constricted wills of its restricted citizenry? Or had his package slid from some different track in the human time stream, some era to be born on an other-dimensional earth? There would have to be a common origin to both, else why the English wordage? And could there be a purpose in his having received it, beneficial—or otherwise?

Tina had been asking a question. Sam detached his mind from shapeless speculation and considered her quite-the-opposite features.

"So if you'd still like me to go out with you New Year's Eve, all I have to do is tell Lew that my mother expects to suffer from her gallstones and I have to stay home. Then I think you could buy the Cigale reservations from him cheap."

"Thanks a lot, Tina, but very honestly I don't have the loose cash right now. You and Lew make a much more logical couple anyhow."

Lew Knight wouldn't have done that. Lew cut throats with carefree zest. But Tina did seem to go with Lew as a type.

Why? Until Lew had developed a raised eyebrow where Tina was concerned, it had been Sam all the way. The rest of the office had accepted the fact and moved out of their path. It wasn't only a question of Lew's greater success and financial well-being: just that Lew had decided he wanted Tina and had got her.

It hurt. Tina wasn't special; she was no cultural companion, no intellectual equal; but he wanted her. He liked being with her. She was the woman he desired, rightly or wrongly, whether or not there was a sound basis to their relationship. He remembered his parents before a railway accident had orphaned him: they were theoretically incompatible, but they had been terribly happy together.

He was still wondering about it the next night as he flipped the pages of "Twinning yourself and your friends." It would be interesting to twin Tina.

"One for me, one for Lew."

Only the horrible possibility of an error was there. His mannikin had not been perfect: its arms had been of unequal length. Think of a physically lopsided Tina, something he could never bring himself to disassemble, limping extraneously through life.

And then the book warned: "Your constructed twin, though resembling you in every obvious detail, has not had the slow and guarded maturity you have enjoyed. He or she will not be as stable mentally, much less able to cope with unusual situations, much more prone to neurosis. Only a professional carnuplicator, using the finest equipment, can make an exact copy of a human personality. Yours will be able to live and even reproduce, but cannot ever be accepted as a valid and responsible member of society."

Well, he could chance that. A little less stability in Tina would hardly be noticeable; it might be more desirable.

There was a knock. He opened the door, guarding the box from view with his body. His landlady.

"Your door has been locked for the past week, Mr. Weber. That's why the chambermaid hasn't cleaned the room. We thought you didn't want anyone inside."

"Yes." He stepped into the hall and closed the door behind him. "I've been doing some highly important legal work at home."

"Oh." He sensed a murderous curiosity and changed the subject.

"Why all the fine feathers, Mrs. Lipanti—New Year's Eve party?"

She smoothed her frilled black dress self-consciously. "Y-yes. My sister and her husband came in from Springfield today and we were going to make a night of it. Only . . . only the girl who was supposed to come over and mind their baby just phoned and said she isn't feeling well. So I guess we won't go unless somebody else, I mean unless we can get someone else to take care . . . I mean, somebody who doesn't have a previous engagement and who wouldn't—" Her voice trailed away in assumed embarrassment as she realized the favor was already asked.

Well, after all, he wasn't doing anything tonight. And she had been remarkably pleasant those times when he had to operate on the basis of "Of course I'll have the rest of the rent in a day or so." But why did any one of the earth's two billion humans, when in the possession of an unpleasant buck, pass it automatically to Sam Weber?

Then he remembered Chapter IV on babies and other small humans. Since the night when he had separated the mannikin from its constituent parts, he'd been running through the manual as an intellectual exercise. He didn't feel quite up to making some weird error on a small human. But twinning wasn't supposed to be as difficult.

Only by Gog and by Magog, by Aesculapius the Physician and Kildare the Doctor, he would not disassemble this time. There must be other methods of disposal possible in a large city on a dark night. He'd think of something.

"I'd be glad to watch the baby for a few hours." He started down the hall to anticipate her polite protest. "Don't have a date tonight myself. No, don't mention it, Mrs. Lipanti. Glad to do it."

In the landlady's apartment, her nervous sister briefed him doubtfully.

"And that's the only time she cries in a low, steady way so if you move fast there won't be much damage done. Not much, anyway."

He saw them to the door. "I'll be fast enough," he assured the mother. "Just so I get a hint."

Mrs. Lipanti paused at the door. "Did I tell you about the man who was asking after you this afternoon?"

Again? "A sort of tall, old man in a long, black overcoat?"

"With the most frightening way of staring into your face and talking under his breath. Do you know him?"

"Not exactly. What did he want?"

"Well, he asked if there was a Sam Weaver living here who was a lawyer and had been spending most of his time in his room for the past week. I told him we had a Sam Weber—your first name *is* Sam?—who answered to that description, but that the last Weaver had moved out over a year ago. He just looked at me for a while and said, 'Weaver, Weber—they might have made an error,' and walked out without so much as a good-by or excuse me. Not what I call a polite gentleman."

Thoughtfully Sam walked back to the child. Strange how sharp a mental picture he had formed of this man!

Possibly because the two women who had met him thus far had been very impressionable, although to hear their stories the impression was there to be received.

He doubted there was any mistake: the man had been looking for him on both occasions; his knowledge of Sam's vacation from foolscap this past week proved that. It did seem as if he weren't interested in meeting him until some moot point of identity should be established beyond the least shadow of a doubt. Something of a legal mind, that.

The whole affair centered around the "Bild-A-Man" set, he was positive. This skulking investigation hadn't started until after the gift from 2353 had been delivered—and Sam had started using it.

But till the character in the long, black overcoat paddled up to Sam Weber personally and stated his business, there wasn't very much he could do about it.

Sam went upstairs for his Junior Biocalibrator.

He propped the manual open against the side of the bed and switched the instrument on to full scanning power. The infant gurgled thickly as the calibrator was rolled slowly over its fat body and a section of metal tape un-wound from the slot with, according to the manual, a completely detailed physiological description.

It was detailed. Sam gasped as the tape, running through the enlarging viewer, gave information on the child for which a pediatrician would have taken out at least three mortgages on his immortal soul. Thyroid capacity, chromosome quality, cerebral content. All broken down into neat subheads of data for construction purposes. Rate of skull expansion in minutes for the next ten hours; rate of cartilage transformation; changes in hormone secretions while active and at rest.

This was a blueprint; it was like taking canons from a baby.

Sam left the child to a puzzled contemplation of its navel and sped upstairs. With the tape as a guide, he clipped sections of the molds into the required smaller sizes. Then, almost before he knew it consciously, he was constructing a small human.

He was amazed at the ease with which he worked. Skill was evidently acquired in this game; the mannikin had been much harder to put together. The matter of duplication and working from an informational tape simpli-fied his problems, though.

The child took form under his eyes.

He was finished just an hour and a half after he had taken his first measurements. All except the vitalizing.

A moment's pause, here. The ugly prospect of disassembling stopped him for a moment, but he shook it off. He had to see how well he had done the job. If this child could breathe, what was not possible to him! Besides he couldn't keep it suspended in an inanimate condition very long without running the risk of ruining his work and the materials.

He started the vitalizer.

The child shivered and began a low, steady cry. Sam tore down to the landlady's apartment again and scooped up a square of white linen left on the bed for emergencies. Oh well, some more clean sheets.

After he had made the necessary repairs, he stood back and took a good look at it. He was in a sense a papa. He felt as proud.

It was a perfect little creature, glowing and round with health.

"I have twinned," he said happily.

Every detail correct. The two sides of the face correctly inexact, the duplication of the original child's lunch at the very same point of digestion. Same hair, same eyes—or was it? Sam bent over the infant. He could have sworn the other was a blonde. This child had dark hair which seemed to grow darker as he looked.

He grabbed it with one hand and picked up the Junior Biocalibrator with the other.

Downstairs, he placed the two babies side by side on the big bed. No doubt about it. One was blonde; the other, his plagiarism, was now a definite brunette.

The Biocalibrator showed other differences: Slightly faster pulse for his model. Lower blood count. Minutely higher cerebral capacity, although the content was the same. Adrenalin and bile secretions entirely unalike.

It added up to error. His child might be the superior specimen, or the inferior one, but he had not made a true copy. He had no way of knowing at the moment whether or not the infant he had built could grow into a human maturity. The other could.

Why? He had followed directions faithfully, had consulted the calibrator tape at every step. And this had resulted. Had he waited too long before starting the vitalizer? Or was it just a matter of insufficient skill?

Close to midnight, his watch delicately pointed out. It would be necessary to remove evidences of baby-making before the Sisters Lipanti came home. Sam considered possibilities swiftly.

He came down in a few moments with an old tablecloth and a cardboard carton. He wrapped the child in the tablecloth, vaguely happy that the temperature had risen that night, then placed it in the carton.

The child gurgled at the adventure. Its original on the bed gooed in return. Sam slipped quietly out into the street.

Male and female drunks stumbled along tootling on tiny trumpets. People wished each other a *hic* happy new year as he strode down the necessary three blocks.

As he turned left, he saw the sign: "Urban Foundling Home." There was a light burning over a side door. Convenient, but that was a big city for you.

Sam shrank into the shadow of an alley for a moment as a new idea occurred to him. This had to look genuine. He pulled a pencil out of his breast pocket and scrawled on the side of the carton in as small handwriting as he could manage:

Please take good care of my darling little girl. I am not married.

Then he deposited the carton on the doorstep and held his finger on the bell until he heard movement inside. He was across the street and in the alley again by the time a nurse had opened the door.

It wasn't until he walked into the boarding house that he remembered about the navel. He stopped and tried to recall. No, he had built his little girl without a navel! Her belly had been perfectly smooth. That's what came of hurrying! Shoddy workmanship.

There might be a bit of to-do in the foundling home when they unwrapped the kid. How would they explain it?

Sam slapped his forehead. "Me and Michelangelo. He adds a navel, I forget one!"

Except for an occasional groan, the office was fairly quiet the second day of the New Year.

He was going through the last intriguing pages of the book when he was aware of two people teetering awkwardly, near his desk. His eyes left the manual reluctantly: "New kinds of life for your leisure moments" was really fascinating!

Tina and Lew Knight.

Sam digested the fact that neither of them was perched on his desk.

Tina wore the little ring she'd received for Christmas on the third finger of her left hand; Lew was experimenting with a sheepish look and finding it difficult.

"Oh, Sam. Last night, Lew . . . Sam, we wanted you to be the first—Such a surprise, like that I mean! Why I almost—Naturally we thought this would be a little difficult . . . Sam, we're going, I mean we expect—"

"—to be married," Lew Knight finished in what was almost an undertone. For the first time since Sam had known him he looked uncertain and suspicious of life, like a man who finds a newly-hatched octopus in his breakfast orange juice.

"You'd adore the way Lew proposed," Tina was gushing. "So roundabout. And so shy. I told him afterward that I thought for a moment he was talking of something else entirely. I did have trouble understanding you, didn't I, dear?"

"Huh? Oh yeah, you had trouble understanding me." Lew stared at his former rival. "Much of a surprise?"

"Oh, no. No surprise at all. You two fit together so perfectly that I knew it right from the first." Sam mumbled his felicitations, conscious of Tina's searching glances. "And now, if you'll excuse me, there's something I have to take care of immediately. A special sort of wedding present."

Lew was disconcerted. "A wedding present. This early?"

"Why certainly," Tina told him. "It isn't very easy to get just the right thing. And a special friend like Sam naturally wants to get a very special gift."

Sam decided he had taken enough. He grabbed the manual and his coat and dodged through the door.

By the time he came to the red stone steps of the boarding house, he had reached the conclusion that the wound, while painful, had definitely missed his heart. He was in fact chuckling at the memory of Lew Knight's face when his landlady plucked at his sleeve.

"That man was here again today, Mr. Weber. He said he wanted to see you."

"Which man? The tall, old fellow?"

Mrs. Lipanti nodded, her arms folded complacently across her chest. "Such an unpleasant person! When I told him you weren't in, he insisted I take him up to your room. I said I couldn't do that without your permission and he looked at me fit to kill. I've never believed in the evil eye myself—although I always say where there is smoke there must be fire—but if there is such a thing as an evil eye, he has it."

"Will he be back?"

"Yes. He asked me when you usually return and I said about eight o'clock, figuring that if you didn't want to meet him it would give you time to change your clothes and wash up and leave before he gets here. And, Mr. Weber, if you'll excuse me for saying this, I don't think you want to meet him."

"Thanks. But when he comes in at eight, show him up. If he's the right person, I'm in illegal possession of his property. I want to know where this property originates."

In his room, he put the manual away carefully and told the box to open. The Junior Biocalibrator was not too bulky and newspaper would suffice to cover it. He was on his way uptown in a few minutes with the strangely shaped parcel under his arm.

Did he still want to duplicate Tina, he pondered? Yes, in spite of everything. She was still the woman he desired more than any he had ever known; and with the original married to Lew, the replica would have no choice but himself. Only—the replica would have Tina's characteristics up to the moment the measurements were taken; she might insist on marrying Lew as well.

That would make for a bit of a mad situation. But he was still miles from that bridge. It might even be amusing—

The possibility of error was more annoying. The Tina he would make might be off-center in a number of ways: reds might overlap pinks; like an imperfectly reproduced color photograph she might, in time, come to digest her own stomach; there could very easily be a streak of strange and incurable insanity implicit in his model which would not assert itself until a deep mutual affection had flowered and borne fruit. As yet, he was no great shakes as a twinner and human mimeographer; the errors he had made on Mrs. Lipanti's niece demonstrated his amateur standing.

Sam knew he would never be able to dismantle Tina if she proved defective. Outside of the chivalrous concepts and almost superstitious reverence for womankind pressed into him by a small town boyhood, there was the unmitigated horror he felt at the idea of such a beloved object going through the same disintegrating process as—well, the mannikin. But if he overlooked an essential in his construction, what other recourse would there be?

Solution: nothing must be overlooked. Sam grinned bitterly as the ancient elevator swayed up to his office. If he only had time for a little more practice with a person whose reactions he knew so exactly that any deviation from the norm would be instantly obvious! But the strange, old man would be calling tonight, and, if his business concerned "Bild-A-Man" sets, Sam's experiments might be abruptly curtailed. And where would he find such a person—he had few real friends and no intimate ones. And, to be at all valuable, it would have to be someone he knew as well as himself.

Himself!

"Floor, sir." The elevator operator was looking at him reproachfully. Sam's exultant shout had caused him to bring the carrier to a spasmodic stop six inches under the floor level, something he had not done since that bygone day when he had first nervously reached for the controls.

He felt his craftsmanship was under a shadow as he morosely closed the door behind the lawyer.

And why not himself? He knew his own physical attributes better than he knew Tina's; any mental instability on the part of his reproduced self would be readily discernible long before it reached the point of psychosis or worse. And the beauty of it was that he would have no compunction in dissembling a superfluous Sam Weber. Quite the contrary: the horror in that situation would be the continued existence of a duplicate personality; its removal would be a relief.

Twinning himself would provide the necessary practice in a familiar medium. Ideal. He'd have to take careful notes so that if anything went wrong he'd know just where to avoid going off the track in making his own personal Tina.

And maybe the old geezer wasn't interested in the set at all. Even if he were, Sam could take his landlady's advice and not be at home when he called. Silver linings wherever he looked.

Lew Knight stared at the instrument in Sam's hands. "What in the sacred name of Blackstone and all his commentaries is that? Looks like a lawn mower for a window box!"

"It's uh, sort of a measuring gadget. Gives the right size for one thing and another and this and that. Won't be able to get you the wedding present I have in mind unless I know the right size. Or sizes. Tina, would you mind stepping out into the hall?"

"Nooo." She looked dubiously at the gadget. "It won't hurt?"

It wouldn't hurt a bit, Sam assured her. "I just want to keep this a secret from Lew till after the ceremony."

She brightened at that and preceded Sam through the door. "Hey counselor," one of the other young lawyers called at Lew as they left. "Hey counselor, don't let him do that. Possession is nine points, Sam always says. He'll never bring her back."

Lew chuckled weakly and bent over his work.

"Now I want you to go into the ladies' room," Sam explained to a bewildered Tina. "I'll stand guard outside and tell the other customers that the place is out of order. If another woman is inside, wait until she leaves. Then strip."

"Strip?" Tina squealed.

He nodded. Then very carefully, emphasizing every significant detail of

WILLIAM TENN

operation, he told her how to use the Junior Biocalibrator. How she must be careful to kick the switch and set the tape running. How she must cover every external square inch of her body. "This little arm will enable you to lower it down your back. No questions now. Git."

She was back in fifteen minutes, fluffing her dress into place and studying the tape with a rapt frown. "This is the *strangest* thing—According to the spool, my iodine content—"

Sam snaffled the Biocalibrator hurriedly. "Don't give it another thought. It's a code, kind of. Tells me just what size and how many of what kind. You'll be crazy about the gift when you see it."

"I know I will." She bent over him as he kneeled and examined the tape to make certain she had applied the instrument correctly. "You know, Sam, I always felt your taste was perfect. I want you to come and visit us often after we're married. You can have such beautiful ideas! Lew is a bit too . . . too business-like, isn't he? I mean it's necessary for success and all that, but success isn't everything. I mean you have to have culture, too. You'll help me keep cultured, won't you, Sam?"

"Sure," Sam said vaguely. The tape was complete. Now to get started! "Anything I can do—glad to help."

He rang for the elevator and noticed the forlorn uncertainty with which she watched him. "Don't worry, Tina. You and Lew will be very happy together. And you'll love this wedding present." But not as much as I will, he told himself as he stepped into the elevator.

Back in his room, he emptied the machine and undressed. In a few moments he had another tape on himself. He would have liked to consider it for a while, but being this close to the goal made him impatient. He locked the door, cleaned his room hurriedly of accumulated junk—remembering to grunt in annoyance at Aunt Maggie's ties: the blue and red one almost lighted up the room—ordered the box to open—and he was ready to begin.

First the water. With the huge amount of water necessary to the human body, especially in the case of an adult, he might as well start collecting it now. He had bought several pans and it would take his lone faucet some time to fill them all.

As he placed the first pot under the tap, Sam wondered suddenly if its chemical impurities might affect the end product. Of course it might! These children of 2353 would probably take absolutely pure H_2O as a matter of daily use; the manual hadn't mentioned the subject, but how did he know what kind of water they had available? Well, he'd boil this batch over his chemical stove; when he got to making Tina he could see about getting *aqua* completely *pura*.

Score another point for making a simulacrum of Sam first.

While waiting for the water to boil, he arranged his supplies to positions of maximum availability. They were getting low. That baby had taken up quite a bit of useful ingredients; too bad he hadn't seen his way clear to disassembling it. That meant if there were any argument in favor of allowing the replica of himself to go on living, it was now invalid. He'd have to take it apart in order to have enough for Tina II. (Or Tina prime?)

He leafed through Chapters VI, VII and VIII on the ingredients, completion and disassembling of a man. He'd been through this several times before; but he'd passed more than one law exam on the strength of a last-minute review.

The constant reference to mental instability disturbed him. "The humans constructed with this set will, at the very best, show most of the superstitious tendencies, and neurosis-compulsions of medieval mankind. In the long run they are not normal; take great care not to consider them such." Well, it wouldn't make too much difference in Tina's case—and that was all that was important.

When he had finished adjusting the molds to the correct sizes, he fastened the vitalizer to the bed. Then—very, very slowly and with repeated glances at the manual, he began to duplicate Sam Weber. He learned more of his physical limitations and capabilities in the next two hours than any man had ever known since the day when an inconspicuous primate had investigated the possibilities of ground locomotion upon the nether extremities alone.

Strangely enough, he felt neither awe nor exultation. It was like building a radio receiver for the first time. Child's play.

Most of the vials and jars were empty when he had finished. The damp molds were stacked inside the box, still in their three-dimensional outline. The manual lay neglected on the floor.

Sam Weber stood near the bed looking down at Sam Weber on the bed.

All that remained was vitalizing. He daren't wait too long or imperfections might set in and the errors of the baby be repeated. He shook off a nauseating feeling of unreality, made certain that the big disassembleator was within reach and set the Jiffy Vitalizer in motion.

The man on the bed coughed. He stirred. He sat up. "Wow!" he said. "Pretty good, if I do say so myself!" And then he had leaped off the bed and seized the disassembleator. He tore great chunks of wiring out of the center, threw it to the floor and kicked it into shapelessness. "No Sword of Damocles going to hang over *my* head," he informed an open-mouthed Sam Weber. "Although, I could have used it on you, come to think of it."

Sam eased himself to the mattress and sat down. His mind stopped rearing and whinnied to a halt. He had been so impressed with the helplessness of the baby and the mannikin that he had never dreamed of the possibility that his duplicate would enter upon life with such enthusiasm. He should have, though; this was a full-grown man, created at a moment of complete physical and mental activity.

"This is bad," he said at last in a hoarse voice. "You're unstable. You can't be admitted into normal society."

"I'm unstable?" his image asked, "Look who's talking! The guy who's been mooning his way through his adult life, who wants to marry an over-dressed, conceited collection of biological impulses that would come crawling on her knees to any man sensible enough to push the right buttons—"

"You leave Tina's name out of this," Sam told him, feeling acutely uncomfortable at the theatrical phrase.

His double looked at him and grinned. "O.K., I will. But not her body! Now, look here, Sam or Weber or whatever you want me to call you, you can live your life and I'll live mine. I won't even be a lawyer if that'll make you happy. But as far as Tina is concerned, now that there are no ingredients to make a copy—that was a rotten escapist idea, by the way—I have enough of your likes and dislikes to want her badly. And I can have her, whereas you can't. You don't have the gumption."

Sam leaped to his feet and doubled his fists. Then he saw the other's entirely equal size and slightly more assured twinkle. There was no point in fighting—that would end in a draw, at best. He went back to reason.

"According to the manual," he began, "you are prone to neurosis—"

"The manual! The manual was written for children of four centuries hence, with quite a bit of selective breeding and scientific education behind them. Personally, I think I'm a—"

There was a double knock on the door. "Mr. Weber."

"Yes," they both said simultaneously.

Outside, the landlady gasped and began speaking in an uncertain voice. "Th-that gentleman is downstairs. He'd like to see you. Shall I tell him you're in?"

"No, I'm not at home," said the double.

"Tell him I left an hour ago," said Sam at exactly the same moment.

There was another, longer gasp and the sound of footsteps receding hurriedly.

"That's one clever way to handle a situation," Sam's facsimile exploded. "Couldn't you keep your mouth shut? The poor woman's probably gone off to have a fit."

"You forget that this is my room and you are just an experiment that went wrong," Sam told him hotly. "I have just as much right, in fact more right . . . hey, what do you think you're doing?"

The other had thrown open the closet door and was stepping into a pair of pants. "Just getting dressed. You can wander around in the nude if you find it exciting, but I want to look a bit respectable."

"I undressed to take my measurements . . . or your measurements. Those are my clothes, this is my room—"

"Look, take it easy. You could never prove it in a court of law. Don't make me go into that cliché about what's yours is mine and so forth."

Heavy feet resounded through the hall. They stopped outside the room. Cymbals seemed to clash all around them and there was a panic-stricken sense of unendurable heat. Then shrill echoes fled into the distance. The walls stopped shuddering.

Silence and a smell of burning wood.

They whirled in time to see a terribly tall, terribly old man in a long black overcoat walking through the smoldering remains of the door. Much too tall for the entrance, he did not stoop as he came in; rather, he drew his head down into his garment and shot it up again. Instinctively, they moved close together.

His eyes, all shiny black iris without any whites, were set back deep in the shadow of his head. They reminded Sam Weber of the scanners on the

Biocalibrator: they tabulated, deduced, rather than saw.

"I was afraid I would be too late," he rumbled at last in weird, clipped tones. "You have already duplicated yourself, Mr. Weber, making necessary unpleasant rearrangements. And the duplicate has destroyed the disassembleator. Too bad. I shall have to do it manually. An ugly job."

He came further into the room until they could almost breathe their fright upon him. "This affair has already dislocated four major programs, but we had to move in accepted cultural grooves and be absolutely certain of the recipient's identity before we could act to withdraw the set. Mrs. Lipanti's collapse naturally stimulated emergency measures."

The duplicate cleared his throat. "You are—"

"Not exactly human. A humble civil servant of precision manufacture. I am Census Keeper for the entire twenty-ninth oblong. You see, your set was intended for the Thregander children who are on a field trip in this oblong. One of the Threganders who has a Weber chart requested the set through the chrondromos which, in an attempt at the supernormal, unstabled without carnuplicating. You therefore received the package instead. Unfortunately, the unstabling was so complete that we were forced to locate you by indirect methods."

The Census Keeper paused and Sam's double hitched his pants nervously. Sam wished he had anything—even a fig leaf—to cover his nakedness. He felt like a character in the Garden of Eden trying to build up a logical case for apple-eating. He appreciated glumly how much more than "Bild-A-Man" sets clothes had to do with the making of a man.

"We will have to recover the set, of course," the staccato thunder continued, "and readjust any discrepancies it has caused. Once the matter has been cleared up, however, your life will be allowed to resume its normal progression. Meanwhile, the problem is which of you is the original Sam Weber?"

"I am," they both quavered—and turned to glare at each other.

"Difficulties," the old man rumbled. He sighed like an arctic wind. "I always have difficulties! Why can't I ever have a simple case like a carnuplicator?"

"Look here," the duplicate began. "The original will be—"

"Less unstable and of better emotional balance than the replica," Sam interrupted. "Now, it seems—"

"That you should be able to tell the difference," the other concluded breathlessly. "From what you see and have seen of us, can't you decide which is the more valid member of society?"

What a pathetic confidence, Sam thought, the fellow was trying to display! Didn't he know he was up against someone who could really discern mental differences? This was no fumbling psychiatrist of the present; here was a creature who could see through externals to the most coherent personality beneath.

"I can, naturally. Now, just a moment." He studied them carefully, his eyes traveling with judicious leisure up and down their bodies. They waited, fidgeting, in a silence that pounded.

"Yes," the old man said at last. "Yes. Quite."

He walked forward.

A long thin arm shot out.

He started to disassemble Sam Weber.

"But listennnnn—" began Weber in a yell that turned into a high scream and died in a liquid mumble.

"It would be better for your sanity if you didn't watch," the Census Keeper suggested.

The duplicate exhaled slowly, turned away and began to button a shirt. Behind him the mumbling continued, rising and falling in pitch.

"You see," came the clipped, rumbling accents, "it's not the gift we're afraid of letting you have—it's the principle involved. Your civilization isn't ready for it. You understand."

"Perfectly," replied the counterfeit Weber, knotting Aunt Maggie's blue and red tie.

I had forgotten the bits about the office, but clearly remembered the horrifying conclusion. This still strikes me as a good story, illustrating a pitfall of such an ability. A person's duplicate would have the same physical and mental abilities as the original, and the same instinct of self preservation. He would be, in short, the worst enemy.

  —Piers

GROUND LEAVE
INCIDENT

Rog Phillips

May 1958

I did not like this story when I first read it, for an obvious reason, but was so impressed by its ruthless logic and savage conclusion that it struck me as an outstanding narrative. A housewife is approached and raped by a nastily sure-of-himself man; what does she do? I think she would take the course this one did. Suppose her husband learns of it? He well might take the course this one did. It rings devastatingly true.
    —Piers

To a young country couple on an isolated, hardship planet, a spaceship visit is a special event. There is the trip to town, new clothes, the smell of fresh food and spices . . . . There are also the hot, demanding eyes of the woman-hungry crew.

The sound came to Marvin down the tortuous twists of the pipestem, faint but unmistakable. Behind the transparency of his faceplate his lean face broke into a delighted smile.

Dropping his shovel, he hesitated for a brief second over the almost full bucket of diamond clay, then grabbed the hook and slipped it into the eye on his belt. He caught the small control box swinging on its short flexible cord from the cable, squeezed his thumb down on the black *Go* button, and started walking up the vertical side of the pipestem, pulled along by the hoist cable.

A spaceship was coming!

He was so excited he stumbled a couple of times on the two hundred foot ascent and was dragged along until he could shove out and regain his footing. When he emerged from the pipestem he could see the vapor trail in the blue tinted methane atmosphere. There was no question, the ship was landing.

Marvin skirted the small pile of unsorted clay and ran to his truck. In the ordinary course of things he would have brought up two more buckets of clay, then had his lunch. After that he would have gone through the clay, handful by handful, feeling out the diamonds and sifting the clay into the bucket for dumping.

The phone was ringing in the truck cab. He picked up file mike in the middle of a ring.

"Marv—"

"Thelma!" He drowned out her voice. "Be ready, we're going to town! I'm starting down the mountain this minute."

"I'll be ready, Marvin!" she said excitedly.

Marvin dropped the mike on the hook, and reached under the dashboard to a secret button. A square section of the dash dropped down, revealing a viewscreen and a row of buttons underneath.

He pushed one, and the view of the kitchen sprang onto the screen, with Thelma just disappearing through the door to the hallway. He pushed another. The view of the bedroom appeared, and as he stepped down on the damper rod control and the truck began to move, Thelma came onto the screen, headed toward the clothes closet.

Thelma didn't know he could watch her like this. They had been married just a little over a year, had gotten married as soon as he had put up the prefab bubble. He hadn't liked the idea of her being all alone there. He had pictured her fainting, or being hurt somehow, and lying there suffering until he came home at supper time. So he had put in the spy kits, a couple of electronic eyes to a room, and the screen hidden in the truck. He didn't snoop, he just looked in on her several times a day to be sure she was okay. But he didn't let her know about it because she might not like it.

Marvin sent the truck recklessly down the mountain trail and risked a quick glance at the screen now and then, grinning at Thelma's indecision over what dress to put on.

Filled with excitement, Thelma, having decided on her blue dress with the white bodice, hastened to get ready. There were all sorts of things she wanted to buy, and she and Marvin had quite a bit of money accumulated now. There had been several big diamonds in the past few months. When Marvin arrived she was ready to go, neatly encased in her voluminous transparent plastic sheathe that wouldn't muss her dress, and large plastic helmet that wouldn't muss her hair.

It was sixty miles to town, around Paxton Hill. On their weekly trips to town, Marvin usually closed up the cab and turned on the air supply, and they took their time. But not now. A space ship was down. The speedometer needle pushed up to eighty and the big tires molded to the rocks and bumps with no time for jarring bouncing.

Overhead the twin suns floated, brownish red, in a purple sky. And soon, around the curve of the hill, the city moved into view, from a distance looking like a cardboard box with a mirror lying on top, with a toy ship near it.

City and ship grew in size until the roof of the city was hidden and only the hundred-foot-high walls loomed into the purple haze.

They parked near the wall, went inside, and checked in their gas-tight suits.

They didn't talk much on the expresswalk to the dock area—they were too excited. The platforms at the dock area were already stacked high with goods, and more were being wheeled from the subway elevators. They eagerly sniffed the strange and delightful assortment of spice odors salted with an ozone tang, their eyes trying not to miss anything. They moved slowly, holding hands so as not to become separated, drifting along with the crowd, now and then disengaging themselves from the tide of humanity to make their purchases, checking off their list, making sure their packages were addressed to the right willcall station at the city wall for loading onto the truck.

Thelma was unaware of Claude Mathews for a long time. Marvin was never aware of him.

He was tall, dark-haired, with black eyes and a round face that made him seem a bit fat despite the muscular leanness of his short body and long legs. He was a spaceman.

"Two days. Two lousy days, that's all we've got," he grumbled to his companions as they lifted ten-pound boxes of tea off the conveyor belt. "Six months in space and we get two days. How you gonna get next to a babe in that time?"

"Do like the rest of us, Claude," a short, heavy-set man said without pausing in his work. "Line up at one of the local pro houses or forget it."

"Not me," Claude growled. "None of that grasshopper stuff for me. I'll make out. But two days doesn't give me much time." His eyes roved over the slowly moving crowd as he worked, pausing hungrily here and there.

"You could get shot, you know," the blond man said.

"Not when you size up the right situation," Claude said. About to set down a box of tea, he paused, his eyes on a girl in a blue dress with white bodice that accentuated her slim waist and full hips and breasts. Her hair was a rich golden color, her face pretty, with pale skin and full red lips. Her eyes were large, wideset, and deep blue. His pulse quickened, just looking at her.

The man with her—undoubtedly her husband—was a nothing. The dime-a-dozen solid young citizen type, medium height and build, angular face—an unimaginative worker type.

The couple disentangled themselves from the slowly moving crowd and pushed toward the hawker. Claude slowly set the box of tea down and moved within hearing.

The couple was buying twenty pounds of tea. The girl was taking a pencil out of her purse and crossing off something on her list.

Claude grinned to himself. That kind was a pushover.

He listened while she gave her name to the hawker for the will-call ticket, Mrs. Thelma Lake, will-call station five. Address, bubble seven, Tedrow Valley. He fixed it in his mind.

He leaned against the stacked tea and studied her hungrily. She sensed his stare and turned startled eyes on him. He grinned slowly into her eyes. She tried to look away, her white face slowly growing flushed, her nostrils flaring as her breathing became more rapid.

Suddenly she turned away. He continued staring at the back of her neck, and knew that she felt his stare.

"Me," he said softly to himself, "I've got it made."

Marvin brought the truck in through the big airlock when they got home—an extravagant procedure using up three pounds of oxygen. But, he pointed out, it would take almost two pounds to get everything in through the smaller lock anyway, and this way he could drive the truck right up to the storeroom and unload.

The twin suns were setting when they finished unloading. Thelma and Marvin stood arm in arm beside the truck, watching. It was one of those rare sunsets, with a clear purple sky changing to the indigo of night, Alpha plunging down below the horizon as though in free fall while Beta hung suspended on a sawtooth of the distant Minor Range. It happened that way just once every three years, and it was supposed to bring good luck to see it.

It was an anniversary for Thelma and Marvin. Three years ago they had been standing arm in arm watching Beta rest on the mountains, when Marvin had told her he now had enough money for them to be married and live by themselves . . .

Marvin put an arm around Thelma's shoulders and squeezed lightly.

"Maybe next time, three years from now, there will be three of us standing here."

"I hope so," Thelma said, snuggling closer . . .

Claude Mathews parked at a lookout point on Paxton Hill overlooking Tedrow Valley, and studied his newly bought map for landmarks. After a while he got out of the rented car and studied the valley through his field-scope, turning the light amplifier on full to get a sharp image on the screen. Here and there through the blue, early morning mist were glossy inkblots that he knew must be petroleum pools.

He found bubble seven almost at once, but he also located the other glass domes in the valley, and studied them, to be familiar with their location in relation to number seven. There were ten altogether, scattered out, and the main road took an erratic course that carried it within a mile or two of each of them.

Finally, satisfied that he knew the details of the valley, he settled down to watch bubble seven. There were lights on in the house, and a small truck inside the bubble parked near one wing of the house.

He had learned that most of the men in Tedrow Valley worked diamond mines. Pipestem clay deposits that assayed about five hundred karats a ton, most of it very small, diamond grains suitable only for industrial uses.

If Marvin Lake worked such a mine, he should be leaving soon, and if no one else lived with the Lakes, then Mrs. Thelma Lake would be alone . . .

His round face broke into a smile as he saw a man come out of the house and get into the truck. He watched the truck move into a short extension from the bubble and stop. A truck airlock.

A few minutes later the truck moved away from the bubble. He watched it creep along the valley floor, ignoring the vaguely defined road, and head toward the hills on the other side of the valley.

Claude kept the truck on the viewscreen until it left the valley and vanished part way up a distant hill. Then he got back in the rented car and started down into the valley, driving fast.

The memory of Thelma Lake's face rose in his mind. Wide set large blue eyes, slightly parted full lips—He jerked the wheel, bringing the car away from the edge of the sheer drop on the right side of the road. His heart was pounding violently, but not from his narrow escape.

In the valley he cut off from the road, and parked the rented car in a spot he had picked out where it couldn't be seen.

He continued on foot, checking the landmarks he had picked out from the lookout point. There were ten hours of oxygen left in his rented, light-weight, landside suit. He could not afford to get lost.

He would have preferred his spacesuit. He was used to it and it was more functional. But it would have marked him a mile off as a spaceman to anyone who happened to see him.

After he had walked a mile he stopped at a small pool, dipped a plastic-gloved finger in the black oil, and smeared it over his faceplate, thin enough so he could see out, but thick enough so that it would be difficult for anyone to make out his features.

When he came within sight of his destination he began staggering and stumbling, stopping often to rest. He knew that somewhere, a few hundred yards out from the bubble, he would trip an alarm signal. He had to get into the bubble, and he hoped that Thelma Lake would open up for a stranger apparently in trouble. Of course, she might call her husband before she let him in. The truck certainly would have a radiophone. If she did call, however, there was a good chance Marvin Lake would be down in his mine and not hear the phone. When he was thirty yards from the smaller airlock he saw her come out of the house and look toward him. He staggered and went to one knee, then picked himself up and staggered on toward the airlock.

He saw her half turn, as though to go back into the house. Then she came running toward the airlock. She was wearing a long blue housecoat, and under it, hanging below the housecoat, a sheer pink nightgown.

Claude Mathews grinned. Probably, like many married women left alone, she went back to bed for a while after the old man left in the morning.

He staggered into the airlock and collapsed. He saw her fumbling with the controls, smiling encouragingly at him, and knew that she had not been able to see his face behind the oil on his faceplate.

When Marvin reached the mine he swung the truck around and parked it as usual. Today he felt lazy. He would bring up three more buckets of clay and take things easy.

Before going down he went back to the truck and switched on the secret viewscreen. Thelma wasn't in the kitchen. He looked at the kitchen for a moment. It was very empty without her in it. He switched to the bedroom, and he saw her back in bed, asleep. A tender smile tugged at the corners of his mouth. Thelma had had an exciting time in town, and they hadn't gotten to sleep until after midnight. He hoped she would sleep until noon.

Switching off the screen, Marvin went back to the mine and hooked the cable to his belt. Down at the bottom of the pipe-stem he took the pick and broke loose enough of the whitish clay to fill the bucket twice, his experienced eyes watching for large pebbles that, under their rough opaque surface, would be diamonds of several karats. The hope of finding one of those was the thrilling part of mining.

He had one—he had found it a year ago—that assayed a possible nine karats. He was keeping it as a surprise for Thelma. One of these days he was going to have it cut. It would cost quite a bit to do that, but the finished stone would be worth a small fortune.

He shoveled the bucket full, hooked it onto the cable and sent it up. When it reached the surface the automatic trip would take over and dump it, and send it back down.

While he waited he sifted around in the clay, putting the two or three small stones he found in the pouch at his belt.

The trouble with him, he decided, was that he was lonesome for Thelma. Or maybe he was just lazy this morning.

The bucket came back down. He shoveled clay into it, resisting the desire to go up above.

He would have liked to have stayed home today, but he and Thelma had thrashed that out long ago. Work was work. It would be too easy, when you're your own boss, to goof off once in a while, then oftener and oftener, until you were shiftless like Roul in bubble four.

Of course, if he went home at noon she probably wouldn't make him come back, but she wouldn't like it, and would point out that he had lost most of yesterday.

He finished filling the bucket. He looked at it, wanting to get on it and ride it up. He shook his head, inside his helmet, and firmly pressed the *Go* button, and watched the bucket climb up the pipestem, its rider wheels keeping it away from the walls.

He wished now he had gone up with it.

Suddenly he was impatient. It seemed an eternity until the bucket came into view again.

When it came to rest on the bottom he didn't even bother to unhook it, but stepped into it and pressed the *Go* button. His impatience increased.

As the bucket neared the top, Marvin stood on its rim, holding the taut cable, and leaped off. The bucket kept going, clanging emptily through the tripping setup.

He half ran to the truck, the impatience a driving force in him now. He didn't stop to analyze it or even be curious about it. He just wanted to turn on the screen and see Thelma.

It was still tuned to one of the bedroom eyes, and after a moment the picture of the bedroom flashed into the screen. The bed was empty.

He switched to the other bedroom eye to make sure she wasn't at her dresser. She wasn't.

He switched to one of the kitchen eyes. She wasn't in the kitchen. Probably she was in the bathroom taking a shower or something. He touched the bathroom button, then shook his head.

When he had installed the secret eyes he had hesitated a long time over putting any in the bathroom. Only the realization that lots of accidents happen in bathrooms had decided him. And, even so, he had never used it.

He wasn't worried. Just impatient. Nervously impatient. He passed over the bathroom eyes and punched in one room after another, without finding Thelma.

Finally his finger was back to the bathroom button again. He hesitated. One quick, half a second glance wouldn't do any harm.

He pushed the button and pushed the kitchen button a half second afterwards. The bathroom flashed into the screen and was replaced by the kitchen.

She wasn't in the bathroom.

Wait a minute—she would be in the storeroom working on the load of stuff they had bought in town!

"Why didn't I think of that before?" he said aloud.

He slid over and put one foot to the ground, then changed his mind. He would have part of his lunch now, and a cup of hot tea.

He pulled his leg back in and closed the cab door, and started the air purifier. When the green light flashed on he undamped his faceplate.

He reached to shut off the view of the kitchen on the screen, then decided to leave it on.

The lunch was especially good today. Thelma had bought a lot of new spices and little tidbits from a dozen different planets.

He selected a small sandwich made from a canned bread that he vaguely remembered was made from a flour that was mostly the ground-up roots of a tree from some planet that was lightyears distant.

He bit into the sandwich, chewed thoughtfully, then glanced idly at the viewscreen.

He saw the back door open and Thelma come in. The expression on her face arrested him. She was worried—

He saw the man, suddenly. The round face had a mask of dark stubble—darker than the normal blondness of native born people.

A spaceman? But what would he be doing in Tedrow Valley? Maybe out sightseeing and something had gone wrong with his car.

"I must phone my husband," Thelma said.

The sound of her voice startled Marvin. It was utterly strange for someone to be there, at home with Thelma, when he wasn't.

The man reached out and took Thelma's arm, saying, "Why bother the old man?"

"He's expecting me to call him," Thelma said. "If I don't, he'll be worried and come right home."

At this outright lie Marvin suddenly sat up, feeling icy fear racing through him.

"Forget that guy!" the man said, jerking Thelma around and gripping both sides of her head. He ignored her beating fists, pulling her face toward his.

Marvin was trembling so violently he fumbled several times ineffectively before getting the truck in motion. He slammed down on the damper rod control throttle and was pushed back against the seat.

He risked a glance at the view-screen. Thelma was struggling desperately.

Marvin forced his eyes to the road. It would take twenty minutes to get down the mountain, get home. Twenty minutes!

"That's better," the man's voice erupted in Marvin's ears. "Just relax so I can get this suit off. We're going to have a real good time, baby. A real good time."

"Get out!" Thelma's voice shuddered. "Get out! My husband will kill you."

Marvin risked a glance at the screen. Thelma was on the floor, inching toward the phone. The man, peeling off his suit, was a symbol of nightmare etching into Marvin's mind.

"Kill me?" the man was saying. *"I* don't think so, baby. And do you know why? Because you won't tell him. Not afterwards. You want this as much as I do, but you won't admit it to yourself. I could see it in your eyes when you looked at me yesterday at the docks, baby."

The gloating words seared into Marvin's ears.

At the docks? Absurd!

"That's not true!" Thelma's voice sounded.

Marvin risked another quick glance. Thelma had inched closer to the wall where the phone was. Suddenly she leaped to her feet and darted toward it.

The man leaped after her, the protective suit still hanging to one leg. "Oh no you don't, baby," he said. He seized both her wrists and twisted them behind her, forcing her body to arch against his.

Marvin jerked back to his surroundings with the truck climbing off the road. It nearly overturned as he fought the wheel. Then he was back on the road.

"No!" Thelma screamed.

Marvin risked a look at the screen, and jerked his eyes away from what he saw, sick to the core of his being.

He looked through the windshield. Everything was blurred. He tried to connect his mind to his vision, to see the road. The truck tilted over at a crazy angle again. He was off the road. It should have been the other side, with its two-hundred-foot drop that would mercifully kill him.

He braked to a stop, unable even to see where he was stopping. He wanted to go on. He *had* to go on. It would take another full ten minutes at maximum speed to reach home.

Ten minutes . . . The enormity of time . . .

Like a disembodied spirit, he heard himself crying. Crying . . . lost . . .

It might have been hours that passed, or days. Time had no meaning any more. Maybe Thelma was dead. It would be better for her to be dead, to escape the horror of being still alive.

What insane sounds had come from the speaker? He wasn't sure, He thought Thelma had laughed once, but that couldn't be so. Laughed, and that maddeningly calm male voice had said, "That's it, baby, let yourself go, enjoy it." And the strange, wild, demented laughter spilling into Marvin's ears had changed to sobbing, that became laughter again, then sobbing that drifted into whimpers, and silence.

Silence. The silence had lasted for ages.

Marvin opened his eyes and looked out the windshield. He could see clearly. The road, the haze of the valley below, the twin suns high in the purple sky.

He turned suddenly and looked into the viewscreen. The man stood in the middle of the kitchen, stretching his long lean arms, his long legs widespread, his round face gaping in a huge yawn.

Thelma lay on the floor, on her stomach, her head buried in her arms, unmoving, except for her shoulders which shook with her spasmodic, silent sobs.

"You see, baby," the insanely calm male voice broke the silence. "It wasn't so bad after all, was it? Your old man ever give you such a good time? You know he didn't. And you liked it. You responded. You really wanted it all the time, didn't you? I guessed it when you blushed down at the docks. I could read your mind when you looked at me. You blushed at what you were thinking, didn't you? 'There's a real hunk of man. Wish I could get in bed with him.' That's what you thought, wasn't it? Now admit it to yourself. It was. So I came out and gave you your wish."

The little black eyes in the round face stared down at the back of Thelma's head shrewdly.

"So now what are you going to do?" the man went on, while Marvin listened, unable not to listen.

"Are you going to tell that husband of yours? Don't be foolish. What's done is done, and you liked it. You'll dream about it, baby, believe me. So why ruin things for yourself? What would your husband do if he found out? Kill me? I might have something to say about that if he tried.

"And suppose he did kill me? Then everyone would know. Can't you hear the prosecutor saying, 'Now tell the court once more how the deceased took you on the kitchen floor. Why didn't you struggle harder?' And all your friends—and your husband—will be sitting there, listening to you."

The round face smiled at the back of Thelma's head. "On the other hand, if you keep your mouth shut, he need never know. No one will ever know . . . . And suppose you told him, and I was already gone off the planet? Every time he looked at you he would remember. You would know what he was thinking . . . "

Marvin tried to shut his ears. He wanted to shut off the sound and sight, and couldn't. He tried to shut off his thoughts, and couldn't.

If he rushed down now, he couldn't stop what had already happened.

But—something he hadn't thought of until now—Thelma would then learn of the electronic eyes in all the rooms, know he had been spying on her ever since they were married.

He hadn't thought of it as spying. Certainly he had never even thought of anything but being close to her in secret, watching over her in case she slipped and hurt herself, or fainted, or any one of the many things that could happen . . .

But would she know that?

"Look," the man was saying. "I've got a rented car parked about a mile from here. I'm walking to it now and going back to town. Think it over. I'm a funny kind of a guy. Once, and I've had it. Something goes out of it for me, after I've had a girl the first time. So think of your life ahead, and hold onto it. Keep your mouth shut. After I go, get yourself prettied up for your hubby, and when you're in bed together, think of me, huh?"

A car! Parked about a mile from the bubble! It would take the man half an hour, at least, to get to it. Then he would be going up around Paxton Hill.

Had Thelma heard what the man said to her? What would she do? A lump rose in Marvin's throat. Poor Thelma . . .

He was calm now. He saw the man's back turned to the screen as the man slipped into his gas tight suit again.

Marvin inched the truck down onto the road. When he looked at the screen again the man was gone. Thelma was slowly turning over. Marvin hastily shut off the viewscreen. He couldn't bring himself to see Thelma's face. Not just yet.

He closed up the dashboard and concentrated on driving. Mile after mile, as the mountain fled behind him and he raced toward Paxton Hill, not daring to turn his head to look toward his home.

He had never driven across the valley before without turning to look at his home . . .

Marvin knew exactly what he was going to do. There was a lookout point on Paxton Hill from which he could watch the valley. He would wait there until he saw the car. When he was sure it was coming he would start down the hill at full speed and run head-on into it.

That would solve everything, for him.

For him? The implication of selfishness and self pity in the thought struck him. But Thelma wouldn't have to face him with her shame. She might wonder what he had been doing coming from the direction of town, but she would never suspect that he knew.

The atom-driven turbine whined higher and higher as the speedometer needle passed over into the nineties, but he was unaware of his speed.

What other course was there than to kill the monster and be killed? What was there to live for now?

Suddenly it welled up in him. All that he and Thelma had together, all the future they had looked forward to with such confidence. Was it to be thrown away?

Think of your life ahead, and hold onto it.

What of Thelma. If she wanted to try to hold on to what she had, face life and wait for forgetfulness, didn't she have that right?

Up ahead was the lookout point. Marvin took his foot off the foot control, slammed on the brakes, and made a tight U-turn. Below, Tedrow Valley spread out into the blue haze that lay over it.

Marvin looked at it, then closed his eyes, fighting to still his thoughts.

How selfish he was! Thelma had been raped, her happy life and happy future shattered by an inhuman beast. And he, Marvin Lake, had been about to add to that final blow, an *accident* which took away the only reason she could have left for wanting to live . . .

There was another way. Turn around, drive slowly, and when that car passes, speed up and drive it over the side of the road up where there's a three-hundred-foot drop.

And what if he did kill the man? It would be on all the telecasts and Thelma—would she guess, and know that he knew?

Marvin groaned. If only he had not listened to the terrible reasoning of that monster from hell.

And the horrible doubts he sowed, capitalizing on any guilt feelings his victims might have. Girls naturally admired men other than their husbands, just as men admired girls other than their wives.

In town he found pleasure in seeing all the attractive girls, and Thelma probably found pleasure in seeing tall, manly men walking along—

He was going to kill that spaceman. He wouldn't be able to live with himself if he didn't.

He started to turn the car to head the other way so that he could run the man off the road.

But if he killed the man, Thelma would know he knew . . .

He stopped the car in a torment of indecision.

It was up to Thelma.

That spaceship wouldn't leave until tomorrow morning. Later he could go into town with a knife, find the man, and kill him. Maybe that would be a better way anyway.

A knife. He nodded grimly. There were things he could do with a knife without killing the man. Better things than killing.

He took his foot off the brakes and started slowly back the way he had come, into the valley. When he was almost down to the valley floor he saw the smaller car coming toward him.

He caught a glimpse of the round face with its dark mask of short stubble. Then the car had shot past him.

He continued on another hundred yards, and suddenly he was shaking uncontrollably. He had to stop the truck. He had to put on the handbrake because he was too weak to keep pressure on the foot pedal.

Why was he shaking? Reaction, now that the crisis of his opportunity to kill the man in a crash was past?

Possibly. But it was something else, too. He had seen that face again. It was a symbol to him—the incarnation of everything evil.

But now—He would have to come home at his regular time, be smiling and cheerful as though nothing had happened, and—

Give Thelma a chance for life. That was it. Give Thelma a chance. Everything, no matter what, must be secondary to that.

Suddenly he saw his lunch, spilled out of the lunchbox on the floormat. And the thermos. He picked up the thermos and shook it, hearing the rattle of broken glass. Damn! He'd have to tell Thelma he dropped it and broke it. Good thing they had half a dozen replacements in the store room.

He got out of the cab and went around to the right hand side, and picked up all the little tidbits of his lunch and tossed them over the cliff. He took a whisk broom and swept the floormat carefully.

It was still three hours until his regular time to go home. He would go back to the mine and work. That was the thing to do.

When he reached his mine it looked strange to him—like something familiar he had not seen for years. He began working on the pile of clay, breaking it down a handful at a time, picking out the small diamond granules.

The seconds passed like hours, but slowly the familiar work comforted him. And eventually it was time to go home.

Now that the time had come, he was afraid. As he started the truck he found he was trembling again. He fought it, and it increased.

He slowed down and began to think of that future, the nice things about it, the things worth living for. After a while he wasn't trembling any more.

She would be waiting for him now. How would she be waiting? With a firm grip on herself? Still overcome by shock and horror?

Maybe it would be better if he looked in and found out, so he could know what he had to face. He hesitated, then stopped the truck and turned on the view-screen. The kitchen scene came onto the screen.

She was not there.

The nightmare gnawed at the edge of his mind again. He jabbed the bedroom button in a panic of anxiety. She wasn't there.

He shut off the screen and slammed the panel closed, and sat there, his fists clenched, fighting for control. Thelma was all right. She had to be all right. The whole future depended on it.

Had that—that—come back? What a fool he had been for not keeping the viewscreen on. He had been interested only in his own selfish feelings. God! All afternoon, all he had been interested in was how *he* felt! Not a thought for Thelma. Not once looking in on her to see how she was making out! Not even a thought for the possible danger of that fiend coming back again.

Calm now. Nothing is wrong—Thelma was either in the bathroom or out in the yard at the airlock.

Of course! She was going to be out at the airlock. She was going to wave, force herself to smile! He mustn't be late, force her to stand there longer than necessary,

He started the truck again, and held the vision of Thelma waiting for him, ready to smile and wave to him. It would be a good world. It *was* a good world. Together, he and Thelma would hang onto it.

He speeded up, cutting across the valley floor without paying the re-gard to roads that he usually did. Bubble seven—home—came into view. His heart started to pound painfully. His eyes ached from straining for the first sight of Thelma standing inside the transparent wall of the bubble . . . .

She wasn't there, or if she was he couldn't see her. The truck lurched violently and he brought his eyes back to his driving. Lucky he had only run over a large rock. He could have gone into one of the oil puddles and had a few hours' work cleaning off the sticky stuff.

He pulled up in front of the airlock, leaped out of the truck cab, and ran to the airlock. He punched the button that would close the outer panel and start the air purifier to get rid of the methane. That was always the longest part, that sixty-second wait in the airlock. Usually Thelma was there, scant inches away, smiling at him happily.

Today, he thought, she had remembered that sixty-second wait and realized she couldn't keep smiling as if nothing were wrong. That was why she wasn't here to meet him.

The sixty seconds were up. The inner panel swung open. Marvin started to run toward the house.

At the kitchen door he leaned against the wall, collected himself, and called, "Thelma . . . "

He waited a couple of seconds, then pushed the door open and called again.

When she didn't come he went on in. The kitchen was empty.

The house was empty,

How much later it was, he didn't know. He had run from room to room, shouting her name, searching, searching. In the store room he had run up and down the aisles of canned goods.

Twice hope flared in him—when he thought of the hydroponic house, and when he thought of the emergency underground vault. But she had been in neither place.

There was only one other place she could be. He tried not to think of it.

Against his will he straightened stiffly and looked out through the transparent walls of the bubble to the truck . . . and beyond the truck.

Out there.

People did that. Just a few months ago the telecasts had told about some fellow who had simply walked out into it without a gas tight suit on. And a year ago a woman had run into it and dived into an oil pool. It had taken the police two days to get her body out.

Marvin went into the airlock and on through. There was no sixty second wait going out; you just shut the inner panel and opened the outer one and let the good air out with you. Some alarmists predicted that eventually there would be enough oxygen released in this manner to bring the atmosphere of Jeffries' Planet to an explosive concentration; but that wasn't possible—the oxygen was burned up by ionization produced by the rays from the twin suns.

Funny, to think of a thing like that when Thelma—

Marvin began his search. Somewhere there would be a huddled bundle of clothing, an arm in view above a concealing rise.

How far could she have gone before she dropped? A hundred yards? Not that far. Not even if she ran.

He had never realized before that there were three large oil ponds within running distance of the airlock. Who would ever have a crazy thought like that? He didn't find her. He searched the shores of the three ponds for some sign of a footprint in the rough, baked ground . . . or a slight scraping where Thelma's shoe might have dragged or slipped.

He found a few faint marks—but how could he tell which scratch, if any, had been made by Thelma?

He stared at the gleaming black surfaces of the ponds, trying to sense whether Thelma's body was in this one or that one. It would take a week of dragging operations to get her out. Meanwhile—

He went back to the bubble. He went into the kitchen, into its terrible emptiness. He opened the drawer containing the forks, knives, and spoons.

There were lots of knives. Carving knives, paring knives, steak knives. He selected two. One was a carving knife, long and razor sharp, with a haft. The other was small, a paring knife. He sharpened it until it was razor sharp too. A doctor could perform an operation with it. Anyone could.

At the doorway he paused and looked back. He would never see the kitchen again, perhaps. It didn't matter.

He went out to the truck and began the drive around Paxton Hill to the city.

The twin suns had sunk below the horizon by the time he came within view of the city. The spaceship was still there, with sharp points of light on it here and there. Red, yellow, and green lights from outside, white discs of light from portholes.

Marvin drove into his accustomed parking spot, went through the nearest airlock, and checked his suit. He stuck the tag in his pocket, aware that he would never redeem the suit. Thelma had chosen her way, now he had chosen his. If there were a hereafter they would soon be together. He noticed the rent-a-car booth, On impulse he stopped and went in.

"Hello, Marvin," the girl behind the counter said.

"Hello—Joyce." She had been in one of his classes in school and he had to think a minute before remembering her name.

"What can I do for you?" she said, smiling.

"I'll tell you," Marvin said, trying to be casual. "Did you rent a car to a fellow today, probably off that ship that's in? Tall, dark, sort of round face?"

"Why, yes." She consulted a list. "Claude Mathews. He was out five hours."

"Thanks." Marvin strode out.

Claude Mathews. Knowing the man's name would simplify finding him. For one thing, he had been about to jump onto a moving walk. He changed his mind and went to a sidewalk phone booth. After a few tries he was connected to the spaceship.

"Is Claude Mathews back on board yet?" he asked.

"Just a minute," a male voice said. Then, "No. And, knowing him, I would say he's probably in a poker game somewhere and the L.P.'s will have to bring him aboard at the last minute."

"Thanks," Marvin said.

He left the phone booth, and headed toward the moving walk.

"Hey, Marvin!" a vaguely familiar voice shouted. "Where you going? Long time no see!"

He ignored it and hopped on the walk, skipping over to the successively faster ones. He recalled the owner of the voice after a bit. A casual acquaintance in his single days. A three dimensional chess player with a weakness on Knight defenses and a nasty mind.

Nasty? What had before seemed nasty to Marvin now seemed only a mildly noticeable peculiarity of a decent man. Now Marvin knew about evil, and his values had changed . . .

Once, and I've had it.

The supremely casual evilness of it . . . The rather pleasant, deep voice that had said those words would echo horribly in his ears as long as he lived.

Easy now. It would be so easy to let the dam break. He had to keep control . . . Just a little while longer.

He rode the express walk toward the dock area. In that neighborhood were the card rooms, the pro houses, the alcohol joints and the dope cellars—wide open lures to keep the degenerate and the conscienceless clumped together where they could be controlled.

But one had ignored the honey-baited trap and had gone out into the countryside where decent people lived . . .

Where was he now?

"Want a good time, honey?" Marvin looked without emotion at the ravaged face of the pro girl and moved on, feeling her clutching fingers slide off his sleeve. Had she once . . . ? What had brought her to this—instead of the dark pool of oil in the valley that would have given her eternal peace . . . ?

He turned into another card room. Not there. The street again. "You want happy dream?" Marvin looked down at the short man, his butterball figure, his shiny, jaundiced, fat face and multiple chins, his thick glasses. "You look sad," the grotesque lips said. "You come with me. I show you a happy land where all is lovely,"

Yes, Marvin thought, *that is a way . . .*

To sink into the arms of dope-induced unreality—he could understand *that* need . . .

"No," he said gently. "Not yet."

He pushed on.

Man had spread out to the stars, driven on by a dream. Mankind was a mighty ocean washing against the cliffs of eternity, wearing them away.

But here and there were the tideflats, with distorted shapes crawling under the rocks.

And somewhere near was a thing named Claude Mathews—

A few feet ahead was a sign . . . another card room. It would be the eighth . . . or the eighteenth. Marvin had lost track—he had almost begun to lose hope. This would be like the other places he had entered; there would be no round face on broad lean shoulders, no end to his search.

But he pushed through the swinging doors. And almost immediately he saw the man.

It had once been some kind of store. Shelves still lined the walls, coated with dust. Perhaps thirty by a hundred feet, its asphalt floor was streaked with filth, and a sour smell hung in the smoke-grey air.

There were perhaps two dozen card tables, regularly spaced, all of them filled, eight men to a table. Marvin recognized some of the games. Poker, pan, whiskey . . .

Here and there among the players was a young face that reminded him of himself when he was young and didn't know the meaning of horror. But three fourths of the faces were unmistakably those of spacemen, black men, yellow men, red men, white men—from a dozen parts of the galaxy.

Marvin moved toward the table where Claude Mathews sat. He went unnoticed in the thin crowd.

Would Claude Mathews recognize him? Did the man even know what he looked like?

"I'll take two," the horribly familiar voice said.

Marvin moved closer, until he was so close he could have reached out and touched the man on the shoulder.

The dealer was a yellow-skinned man on the other side of the table. Claude Mathews scooped up his cards, in high good humor. He had plenty of chips in front of him.

He won the pot with two pair.

"You know how it is," he gloated. "Lucky. That's me. Lucky at cards, lucky at love, lucky at everything,"

"Deal 'em," a red man said laconically.

"But none of this grasshopper stuff for me," Claude Mathews went on, sticking up his cards as they were dealt. "Nine out of ten nice women want it, are waiting for it."

When the red man opened, he tossed his cards in and said, "It's that way everywhere. How many husbands give their wife a real good time? None. They don't have what it takes. Nine out of ten married women are just waiting for a guy to walk in the door and give them a thrill they'll never forget."

Marvin clamped a hand on Claude Mathews' shoulder.

The round face turned up, the dark eyes staring at Marvin. No flicker of recognition showed.

"Move on, pal," Claude Mathews said. "No handouts from me. Try someone else,"

"I don't want a handout," Marvin said.

"No?" Claude Mathews shoved out of his chair and half turned. All movement at the table stopped. "What do you want?"

"Those nice women," Marvin said. "One of them was my wife."

"Oh?" Claude Mathews said, glancing up and down Marvin's slight frame with amusement.

"Cut it out," a voice whined. "Let's play cards. The ship lifts at dawn, you know." But no one listened.

"Yes," Marvin said. He was calm now. He was remembering when he was a little boy, with his magic kit and book of instructions that said the secret of magic was to keep them interested in what one hand was doing and they wouldn't notice what the other did.

He pulled out the little paring knife, holding it in his left hand, half raised but not too threatening. All eyes, he knew, were on that little knife. Claude Mathews glanced at it. Marvin could see the gloating confidence in the little black eyes. One threatening move of the little knife and the long armed spaceman could grab the wrist that held it.

"You raped my wife," Marvin said coldly.

"Well now, wait a minute," Claude Mathews said. "Who says so? I don't know who you are, pal, but unless I'm invited—"

Marvin lifted the little paring knife as a left-handed man might draw back to stab downward. Claude Mathews reached to intercept it. He was unaware of the long, broad-bladed carving knife that was thrust point first into his groin, thrust in a twisting slicing motion that stopped only when the point was buried deeply in the upholstery of the chair seat.

The round face was only inches from Marvin's eyes, every pore and whisker magnified. Marvin saw the eyes glaze with shock and knew his thrust had gone where he intended.

He let go the carving knife and stepped back, the little paring knife still in his left hand.

He turned away and walked toward the entrance. Ahead of him, men stepped quickly aside. Behind him, abruptly, Claude Mathews screamed— and screamed again.

Marvin didn't look back. It was over now. Nothing made any difference. If the knife he had just used struck him in the back it would bring him happy oblivion. If Claude Mathews died, and they arrested him for the murder, it didn't matter.

He was not stopped. He walked calmly out the door, unaware even that he had dropped the paring knife.

"Want a good time, darling?" a rather pretty girl asked. She looked into his eyes, then shrank away.

Marvin watched her move on. A man was coming up the street, a bit unsteadily. She hesitated, then moved toward him. The man stopped. They exchanged a few words. Then the man slipped his arm around the girl's waist. Together they walked back toward Marvin.

When they passed, the girl was looking up at the man, smiling. She didn't glance toward Marvin.

It had been one of the spacemen. He had been crooning something to the girl . . . "We lift at dawn."

The song, old as space.

We lift at dawn. Soon we'll be gone. Good bye, my lover, good bye.

"Gods of Space!" a voice said behind Marvin. "He's standing right outside!"

He started to turn. Men in L.P. uniforms and crash helmets moved swiftly to surround him.

His only reaction was a wave of gratitude.

When he had emerged from that door he had had no idea what to do, where to go. There was nothing, anywhere, to draw him.

Now there was purpose. Maybe not his purpose, but something to carry him along so he wouldn't have to think of anything.

"What're we gonna do with him?" one of them said. "He's a hot potato. Why didn't he have sense enough to lam?"

"Let's get him out of here before the police get here," another said urgently. "Gil, go back in and pass the word around that nobody saw nothin'."

"Let's get him on the ship," someone said. "The cops can't find him there. Last place they'd think of, on the ship."

Marvin let himself be moved along.

He caught a fleeting glimpse of the little fat man looking at him owlishly through his thick lensed glasses. The happy dreams man. He was pushed into a car that jerked into motion a moment later. In the distance he heard the moan of sirens. After a few blocks one passed by, rising to a peak of deafening sound and dwindling away.

He felt the car make several turns, then lurch up onto something and stop. He felt the car dropping swiftly and knew he was on an elevator. He knew where he was—in the dock area, dropping down into the underground tubes leading out into the spaceport.

He had never been on a spaceship but he knew that they settled with exact precision so that their elevator shafts could connect to the subway elevator shafts.

In a few moments the car got into motion again. Then there was a fast lift upward. Up up up, higher than he had ever gone in an elevator.

Suddenly the very atmosphere around him seemed different, alien.

The car stopped rising. The car doors opened. He was pushed out gently but firmly.

"Let's stick him in J room," one of the L.P.'s said.

Marvin went along without protest.

He lifted his feet over a hatchway and was in a room with four of the strange, bulky forms that he had seen in pictures, and which were called crash boxes. There were also several conventional chairs, welded to the floor.

"Sit down," he was told.

He sat down.

Two of the landside policemen stayed with Marvin. The others went away. Marvin closed his eyes and leaned back. His body tingled with fatigue. His mind floated in pools of darkness where the past and the future did not intrude.

After a while he was listening to the conversation of the two L.P.'s. Not what they talked about, but the words, their voices. Their accent was subtly different, the tempo of speech more rapid than he was used to.

Twice during the long wait the phone on the wall shrilled and one of the L.P.'s answered it. Marvin opened his eyes and watched, and knew the conversation was about him.

At last the wait was over. A man in the uniform of a space officer came in. Marvin knew nothing about the meanings of the insignia on the uniform, whether the man was the ship's Captain or some minor officer. He dismissed the L.P.'s and closed the door.

He was lean faced with a strong chin. His hair was iron gray. Marvin felt a liking for him.

"I'm Dr. Cavendish," the man said abruptly.

"I'm Marvin Lake."

"One name is as good as another," Dr. Cavendish said with a twisted smile.

"Oh, but it is!" Marvin said.

"If you say so," Dr. Cavendish said. "Have you ever been in space?"

"No. I've never even been on a ship until now."

Dr. Cavendish smiled. "It probably seems as strange to you then as Jeffries' Planet seems to me. What do you do for a living?"

"I have a diamond mine."

"Oh? How many work with you in the mine?"

"I work it by myself. You see, the clay deposits are like long fingers sticking deep in the ground. We call them pipestems. They go down at very steep angles and are never more than six or eight feet in diameter, and usually about four feet. One man is all that can work comfortably. Besides, it's against the law to make a crew operation out of a mine. Inspectors make regular visits to make sure we clean the pipestem as we go down and don't let the cheap stuff go to waste."

"Cheap stuff?"

"The grains that assay under a tenth of a karat."

Dr. Cavendish nodded. "I see," he said. "You work alone then, day after day."

"That's right."

"What do you think about while you're working alone, day after day?"

"Oh, I don't know," Marvin said. "I have a lot of interests. But mainly, when you're working, you have to concentrate on what you're doing."

"But you do think about things, at times?" Dr. Cavendish said.

"Oh, sure."

"Like your wife being home alone, and a spaceship in, with the crew on ground leave?"

"So that's your line," Marvin said. "Look." He took a deep breath. "Let's get something straight. I did something. I don't regret it. I'm ready to take my punishment. Is that good enough for you?"

"But you haven't done anything," Dr. Cavendish said quietly. "That's the point. *You haven't done anything.*"

Marvin blinked at the ship's officer. "What do you mean?" he asked with a sinking feeling. "Are you trying to tell me I missed?" He leaped to his feet. "Where is he?" he said. "I'll get him—"

"Listen to me," Dr. Cavendish said firmly. "Two members of our crew had a knife fight in a land-side card room. You, as one of the hundred or so spectators of that fight, saw it. You projected yourself into the fight, in your imagination, and *imagined* you were one of the two men."

Marvin stared at the man unbelievingly.

"It's not a serious mental condition," Dr. Cavendish went on. "It's well known that for every crime there are usually two or three people who come in and confess to it. It has to do with the urge to *be* somebody. Such confessions have to be checked against the facts. . . . We have witnesses, several dozen of them in fact, willing to swear to the fact that the fight occurred between two members of our crew."

Dr. Cavendish leaned forward. "Don't you see what your story, if told to the police, could do to us? You would charge that one of our crew went out into the countryside and attacked a citizen of Jeffries' Planet. Our ship would be grounded for weeks. If the courts of this planet believed your testimony—and I doubt that they would without your wife's testimony and a doctor's examination, and probably not even then—the most Claude Mathews could get would be two years in your local jail. That would be mild punishment compared to the damage that has already been done to him. On the other hand, it would cost us a lot of money and wreck our schedule. Other planets on our route—"

"Did I cut him, then?" Marvin interrupted.

"The crew member who knifed him did a very thorough job. He will live, but he would be much better off dead. I am not the one to say if he deserved what he got—there have been reports that he talked a pretty dirty game, only no one believed it was more than talk. However, that's beside the point. We intend to lift on schedule at dawn and deal with the matter in our own way in space. I would suggest you forget the whole thing. What could you do? Do you want your wife on the witness stand?"

"My wife is dead," Marvin said quietly.

"I'm sorry," Dr. Cavendish said. He looked away, uncomfortably. "But that still doesn't change the picture." He stood up. "I understand now. I wish there were something I could do for you. All I can do is say, go home. Let time bring forgetfulness, as it will."

The doctor went to the door and opened it.

"Take this man groundside," he said. "Escort him to wherever his car is. See that he starts for home. And hurry back—We're at zero minus two hours right now."

Marvin fished in his pocket for the claimcheck—the check he had been sure he would never be using. The L.P.'s helped him get into his suit, shook hands with him, and watched while he went to the airlock.

He could, he knew, wait outside until they had gone, then come back in. But what was there for him inside the city? What was there anywhere, for that matter?

But yes, there was something. Out across Paxton Hill, down in Tedrow Valley, fifty yards from bubble seven. A dark pool was waiting for him, and he was ready for it now.

A dark pool, little different than the surrounding darkness except that it reflected the stars. And when it had welcomed him it would ripple sluggishly, then become smooth again.

When he was well up Paxton Hill he stopped the truck and looked back. The city at night captured a strange sort of beauty, its transparent flat ceiling and dark outer wall making it appear to be a cauldron of molten fire in the night, as the lights of the city escaped upward into the darkness.

And the ship. There were lights on it. Red, blue, and green riding lights. Luminous discs of white that were portholes. Behind which ones was the room he had been in?

He felt a tinge of regret that his life was over. Some day he would have liked to have taken a trip somewhere out among the stars. With Thelma.

He started the truck again, and went on around Paxton Hill without looking back again, and down the long grade into Tedrow Valley.

Overhead in the indigo night sky stars shone feebly. In the close confines of the truck cab the high pitched whine of the turbines was lulling, peaceful.

Strange, how peaceful it was when life was over.

Bubble seven loomed in the light from the headlights all too soon.

He glanced at his watch. Zero minus forty-five minutes for the ship. Should he wait? Should he watch it soar into the morning sky, as he and Thelma had watched similar ships before?

No.

That was for the living.

He opened the cab door and stepped out onto the ground. Unconsciously, he had parked where he always parked. The airlock was only a few feet away.

The house was dark. Marvin turned away from it with a sob of torment. He should not have looked at it. He would not look at it again.

He walked out into the darkness toward the pool, the largest and deepest of the three. It would be the one Thelma had chosen.

He reached up and fumbled at the release clamp of his faceplate.

He was calm now. He would open up his faceplate. He would take several deep breaths of the natural atmosphere of Jeffries' Planet. It was supposed to have an opiate effect that would deaden the pain to come later.

He stilled the panic within him and stiffened his fingers for the final act.

And a sound broke into his consciousness.

The shrill, strident ringing of the phone in his truck.

His first reaction was anger.

Who would be calling at a time like this? To release his faceplate, to breathe in the lethal atmosphere of the planet, to dive into the depths of the dark pool, with the sound of a phone ringing. . .

He made a strange sound, a mixture of a sob and a snort. Then he ran to the truck, stumbling and sprawling halfway there, and picking himself up again and running on.

He jerked the hand mike off its hook and said, "Hello!"

"Is that you, Marvin? My lands, where have you been? I've been trying to reach you for hours!"

It was the voice of his mother-in-law.

"What do you want?" he said dully.

"What do I *want?*" she said. "That's a fine question for you to ask. Don't you even care about your wife? I suppose when you got home and found out she was over here you went into town and got in a card game or something. A lot you care that she's sick, and going to have a baby."

"What?" Marvin croaked.

"Sure," Thelma's mother said smugly. "She got sick this afternoon and called me, and we came over there and got her and brought her home with us, and then called the doctor."

Marvin sagged against the seat.

"What have you been doing?" the voice went on. "Didn't you get her note? I saw her tape it to the inner door of the airlock myself. Maybe it fell off."

"The baby—" Marvin croaked.

"Two months along, and doing fine. Thelma slipped and fell this noon, and felt dizzy afterwards. It made her afraid . . ."

The words droned on and on, but Marvin was no longer listening.

Thelma had decided to live. She was going to have a baby.

And for the baby, for him, for herself, Thelma had decided to live, to fight for what she held dear, to protect him from the knowledge of what had happened.

" . . . and she can't sleep. If you don't get over here right away, you no good fool . . . "

Dear, wonderful mother-in-law.

"Okay," Marvin said, laughing and crying. "Okay, I'll come right away. You're right. I'm a fool. I was in town—gambling. I'll be right there. And mother-in-law . . . "

"What is it, you addle-pated son-in-law?"

"Did I ever tell you I love you?"

"Go on, now," the shrill voice snorted.

The carrier tone ended. She had hung up.

Marvin started to get into the truck, glanced toward the airlock, hesitated, then went over to it. There was no note stuck to the inner door, but after a moment he saw it inside the bubble on the ground, vague in the semi-darkness.

He stepped into the airlock and closed the door. He waited impatiently for the air to clear, then opened the inner door and picked up the envelope. It was grimy with oily dirt where he had stepped on it again and again in his blind torment an eternity ago. He opened it with great tenderness.

"Darling," it read. "Mama and papa have come to get me. I took sick and didn't want to worry you. Fix your dinner and I will call you or have mama call you later. Love, Thelma."

Cautiously worded. He could see her as she wrote it. Brave, protecting him, not sure whether the baby would live or die after what had happened . . .

He could do nothing but be equally brave. She would never know that he knew, never know what he had done.

He went back outside.

Suddenly Paxton Hill took on faint detail, and with it the valley around Marvin. One of the twin suns was shooting into sight. Alpha, from its color.

And then came the thunder. It grew deeper, more steady.

Marvin looked up over Paxton Hill into the purpling morning sky. In a moment the ship rose into sight.

A needle shape gleaming in the rays of the suns, riding upward with gathering momentum on a tail of fire.

It grew smaller and smaller, and then he lost it.

Out into the void. Out among the stars. Keeping to its schedule. Connecting the worlds of man, itself a small world, peopled with men who had found their souls—or lost them.

Marvin turned. A few feet away was his truck, the door standing open.

Without hesitation, he went to it and got in.

I was in the US Army in Oklahoma in 1958 when I read this, living off-post with my wife of two years. There's a certain similarity to the setting of this story that perhaps made me relate to it. No, my wife did not get raped, but she did suffer a grueling miscarriage that had her a month in the hospital, as I recall. I remember once I had guard duty during visiting hours, and was able to go to visit her only as the open time ended, and they would not let me see her. She could hear me talking to the impervious nurse in the hall, but I had to go. The machine schedule of the military does not allow for the feelings of real folk. We did go on from there to a better life together. So maybe there were reasons I re-membered this story. Rereading it in 2010 I find it taut, compelling, horrible, and excellently done. The insidious logic of the rapist, followed by that of the ship's doctor—both make infernal sense. Crime, punishment, redemption fitted to the crucifix of the situation. Beautiful.
    —Piers

DREAMS ARE SACRED

Peter Phillips

September 1948

I remember the opening history of the boy afraid of nightmares, and his father has him practice with a heavy gun, which then joins him in his dreams. I simply loved that; think it is marvelous psychology. I also loved the lucid dreaming, wherein he enters another person's dream and starts changing it about. How good a story it actually is I don't remember, but those two aspects were enough to make me cherish it for life.
—Piers

When I was seven, I read a ghost story and babbled of the consequent nightmare to my father.

"They were coming for me, Pop," I sobbed. "I couldn't run, and I couldn't stop 'em, great big things with teeth and claws like the pictures in the book, and I couldn't wake myself up, Pop, I couldn't come awake."

Pop had a few quiet cuss words for folks who left such things around for a kid to pick up and read; then he took my hand gently in his own great paw and led me into the six-acre pasture.

He was wise, with the canny insight into human motives that the soil gives to a man. He was close to Nature and the hearts and minds of men, for all men ultimately depend on the good earth for sustenance and life.

He sat down on a stump and showed me a big gun. I know now it was a heavy Service Colt .45. To my child eyes, it was enormous. I had seen shotguns and sporting rifles before, but this was to be held in one hand and fired. Gosh, it was heavy. It dragged my thin arm down with its sheer, grim weight when Pop showed me how to hold it.

Pop said: "It's a killer, Pete. There's nothing in the whole wide world or out of it that a slug from Billy here won't stop. It's killed lions and tigers and men. Why, if you aim right, it'll stop a charging elephant. Believe me, son, there's nothing you can meet in dreams that Billy here won't stop. And he'll come into your dreams with you from now on, so there's no call to be scared of anything."

He drove that deep into my receptive subconscious. At the end of half an hour, my wrist ached abominably from the kick of that Colt. But I'd seen heavy slugs tear through two-inch teakwood and mild steel plating. I'd looked along that barrel, pulled the trigger, felt the recoil rip up my arm and seen the fist-size hole blasted through a sack of wheat.

And that night, I slept with Billy under my pillow. Before I slipped into dreamland, I'd felt again the cool, reassuring butt.

When the Dark Things came again, I was almost glad. I was ready for them. Billy was there, lighter than in my waking hours—or maybe my dream-hand was bigger—but just as powerful. Two of the Dark Things crumpled and fell as Billy roared and kicked, then the others turned and fled.

Then I was chasing them, laughing, and firing from the hip.

Pop was no psychiatrist, but he'd found the perfect antidote to fear—the projection into the subconscious mind of a common-sense concept based on experience.

Twenty years later, the same principle was put into operation scientifically to save the sanity—and perhaps the life—of Marsham Craswell.

"Surely you've heard of him?" said Stephen Blakiston, a college friend of mine who'd majored in psychiatry.

"Vaguely," I said. "Science-fiction, fantasy . . . I've read a little. Screwy."

"Not so. Some good stuff." Steve waved a hand round the bookshelves of his private office in the new Pentagon Mental Therapy Hospital, New York State. I saw multicoloured magazine backs, row on row of them. "I'm a fan," he said simply. "Would you call me screwy?"

I backed out of that one. I'm just a sports columnist, but I knew Blakiston was tops in two fields—the psycho stuff and electronic therapy.

Steve said: "Some of it's the old 'peroo, of course, but the level of writing is generally high and the ideas thought-provoking. For ten years, Marsham has been one of the most prolific and best-loved writers in the game.

"Two years ago, he had a serious illness, didn't give himself time to convalesce properly before he waded into writing again. He tried to reach his previous output, tending more and more towards pure fantasy. Beautiful in parts, sheer rubbish sometimes.

"He forced his imagination to work, set himself a wordage routine. The tension became too great. Something snapped. Now he's here."

Steve got up, ushered me out of his office. "I'll take you to see him. He won't see you. Because the thing that snapped was his conscious control over his imagination. It went into high gear, and now instead of writing his stories, he's living them—quite literally, for him.

"Far-off worlds, strange creatures, weird adventures—the detailed phantasmagoria of a brilliant mind driving itself into insanity through the sheer complexity of its own invention. He's escaped from the harsh reality of his strained existence into a dream world. But he may make it real enough to kill himself.

"He's the hero of course," Steve continued, opening the door into a private ward. "But even heroes sometimes die. My fear is that his morbidly overactive imagination working through his subconscious mind will evoke in this dream world in which he is living a situation wherein the hero must die.

"You probably know that the sympathetic magic of witchcraft acts largely through the imagination. A person imagines he is being hexed to death—and dies. If Marsham Craswell imagines that one of his fantastic creations kills the hero—himself—then he just won't wake up again.

"Drugs won't touch him. Listen."

Steve looked at me across Marsham's bed. I leaned down to hear the mutterings from the writer's bloodless lips.

". . . . We must search the Plains of Istak for the Diamond. I, Multan, who now have the Sword, will lead thee; for the Snake must die and only in virtue of the Diamond can his death be encompassed. Come."

Craswell's right hand, lying limp on the coverlet, twitched. He was beckoning his followers.

"Still the Snake and the Diamond?" asked Steve. "He's been living that dream for two days. We only know what's happening when he speaks in his role of hero. Often it's quite unintelligible. Sometimes a spark of consciousness filters through, and he fights to wake up. It's pretty horrible to watch him squirming and trying to pull himself back into reality. Have you ever tried to pull yourself out of a nightmare and failed?"

It was then that I remembered Billy, the Colt .45. I told Steve about it, back in his office.

He said: "Sure. Your Pop had the right idea. In fact, I'm hoping to save Marsham by an application of the same principle. To do it, I need the co-operation of someone who combines a lively imagination with a severely practical streak, boss-sense—and a sense of humour. Yes—you."

"Uh? How can I help? I don't even know the guy."

"You will," said Steve, and the significant way he said it sent a trickle of ice water down my back. "You're going to get closer to Marsham Craswell than one man has ever been to another.

"I'm going to project you—the essential you, that is, your mind and personality—into Craswell's tortured brain."

I made pop-eyes, then thumbed at the magazine-lined wall. "Too much of yonder, brother Steve," I said. "What you need is a drink."

Steve lit his pipe, draped his long legs over the arm of his chair. "Miracles and witchcraft are out. What I propose to do is basically no more miraculous than the way your Pop put that gun into your dreams so you weren't afraid any more. It's merely more complex scientifically.

"You've heard of the encephalograph? You know it picks up the surface neural currents of the brain, amplifies and records them, showing the degree—or absence—of mental activity. It can't indicate the kind or quality of such activity save in very general terms. By using comparison-graphs and other statistical methods to analyze its data, we can sometimes diagnose incipient insanity, for instance. But that's all—until we started work on it, here at Pentagon.

"We improved the penetration and induction pickup and needled the selectivity until we could probe any known portion of the brain. What we were looking for was a recognizable pattern among the millions of tiny electric currents that go to make up the imagery of thought, so that if the subject thought of something—a number, maybe—the instruments would react accordingly, give a pattern for it that would be repeated every time he thought of that number.

"We failed, of course. The major part of the brain acts as a unity, no one part being responsible for either simple or complex imagery, but the activity of one portion inducing activity in other portions—with the exception of those parts dealing with automatic impulses. So if we were to get a pattern we should need thousands of pickups—a practical impossibility. It was as if we were trying to divine the pattern of a coloured sweater by putting one tiny stitch of it under a microscope.

"Paradoxically, our machine was too selective. We needed, not a probe, but an all-encompassing field, receptive simultaneously to the multitudinous currents that made up a thought-pattern.

"We found such a field. But we were no further forward. In a sense, we were back where we started from—because to analyze what the field picked up would have entailed the use of thousands of complex instruments. We had amplified thought, but we could not analyze it.

"There was only one single instrument sufficiently sensitive and complex to do that—another human brain."

I waved for a pause. "I'm home," I said. "You'd got a thought-reading machine."

"Much more than that. When we tested it the other day, one of my assistants stepped up the polarity-reversal of the field—that is, the frequency—by accident. I was acting as analyst and the subject was under narcosis.

"Instead of 'hearing' the dull incoherencies of his thoughts, I became part of them. I was inside that man's brain. It was a nightmare world. He wasn't a clear thinker. I was aware of my own individuality. . . . When he came round, he went for me bald-headed. Said I'd been trespassing inside his head.

"With Marsham, it'll be a different matter. The dream world of his coma is detailed, as real as he used to make dream worlds to his readers."

"Hold it," I said. "Why don't you take a peek?"

Steve Blakiston smiled and gave me a high-voltage shot from his big grey eyes. "Three good reasons: I've soaked in the sort of stuff he dreams up, and there's a danger that I would become identified too closely with him. What he needs is a salutary dose of common sense. You're the man for that, you cynical old whisky-hound.

"Secondly, if my mind gave way under the impress of his imagination, I wouldn't be around to treat myself; and thirdly, when—and if—he comes round, he'll want to kill the man who's been heterodyning his dreams. You can scram. But I want to stay and see the results."

"Sorting that out, I gather there's a possibility that I shall wake up as a candidate for a bed in the next ward?"

"Not unless you let your mind go under. And you won't. You've got a cast-iron non-gullibility complex. Just fool around in your usual iconoclastic manner. Your own imagination's pretty good, judging by some of your fight reports lately."

I got up, bowed politely, said: "Thank you, my friend. That reminds me—I'm covering the big fight at the Garden tomorrow night. And I need sleep. It's late. So long." Steve unfolded and reached the door ahead of me. "Please," he said, and argued. He can argue. And I couldn't duck those big eyes of his. And he is—or was—my pal. He said it wouldn't take long—(just like a dentist)—and he smacked down every "if" I thought up.

Ten minutes later, I was lying on a twin bed next to that occupied by a silent, white-faced Marsham Craswell. Steve was leaning over the writer adjusting a chrome-steel bowl like a hair-drier over the man's head. An assistant was fixing me up the same way.

Cables ran from the bowls to a movable arm overhead and thence to a wheeled machine that looked like something from the Whacky Science Section of the World's Fair, A.D. 2,000.

I was bursting with questions, but the only ones that would come out seemed crazily irrelevant.

"What do I say to this guy? 'Good morning, and how are all your little complexes today?' Do I introduce myself?"

"Just say you're Pete Parnell, and play it off the cuff," said Steve. "You'll see what I mean when you get there."

Get there. That hit me—the idea of making a journey into some nut's nut. My stomach drew itself up to softball size.

"What's the proper dress for a visit like this? Formal?" I asked. At least, I think I said that. It didn't sound like my voice.

"Wear what you like."

"Uh-huh. And how do I know when to draw my visit to a close?"

Steve came round to my side. "If you haven't snapped Craswell out of it within an hour, I'll turn off the current." He stepped back to the machine. "Happy dreams." I groaned.

It was hot. Two high summers rolled into one. No, two suns, blood-red, stark in a brazen sky. Should be cool underfoot—soft green turf, pool table smooth to the far horizon. But it wasn't grass. Dust. Burning green dust—

The gladiator stood ten feet away, eyes glaring in disbelief. All of six-four high, great bronzed arms and legs, knotted muscles, a long shining sword in his right hand. But his face was unmistakable. This was where I took a good hold of myself. I wanted to giggle.

"Boy!" I said. "Do you tan quickly! Couple of minutes ago, you were as white as the bed sheet."

The gladiator shaded his eyes from the twin suns. "Is this yet another guise of the magician Garor to drive me insane—an Earthman here, on the Plains of Istak? Or am I already—mad?" His voice was deep, smoothly modulated.

My own was perfectly normal. Indeed, after the initial effort, I felt perfectly normal, except for the heat.

I said: "That's the growing idea where I've just come from—that you're going nuts."

You know those half-dreams, just on the verge of sleep, in which you can control your own imagery to some extent? That's how I felt. I knew intuitively what Steve was getting at when he said I could play it off the cuff. I looked down. Tweed suit, brogues—naturally. That's what I was wearing when I last looked at myself. I had no reason to think I was wearing—and therefore to be wearing—anything else. But something cooler was indicated in this heat, generated by Marsham Craswell's imagination.

Something like his own gladiator costume, perhaps.

Sandals—fine. There were my feet—in sandals.

Then I laughed. I had nearly fallen into the error of accepting his imagination.

"Do you mind if I switch off one of those suns?" I asked politely. "It's a little hot."

I gave one of the suns a very dirty look. It disappeared.

The gladiator raised his sword. "You are—Garor!" he cried. "But your witchery shall not avail you against the Sword!"

He rushed forward. The shining blade cleaved the air towards my skull.

I thought very, very fast.

The sword clanged, and streaked off at a sharp tangent from my G.I. brain-pan protector. I'd last worn that homely piece of hardware in the Argonne, and I knew it would stop a mere sword. I took it off.

"Now listen to me, Marsham Craswell," I said. "My name's Pete Parnell, of the Sunday *Star*, and—"

Craswell looked up from his sword, chest heaving, startled eyes bright as if with recognition. "Wait! I know now who you are—Nelpar Retrep, Man of the Seven Moons, come to fight with me against the Snake and his ungodly disciple, magician and sorceress, Garor. Welcome, my friend!"

He held out a huge bronzed hand. I shook it.

It was obvious that, unable to rationalize—or irrationalize—me, he was writing me into the plot of his dream! Right. It had been amusing so far. I'd string along for a while. My imagination hadn't taken a licking—yet.

Craswell said: "My followers, the great-hearted Dok-men of the Blue Hills, have just been slain in a gory battle. We were about to brave the many perils of the Plains of Istak in our quest for the Diamond—but all this, of course, you know."

"Sure," I said. "What now?"

Craswell turned suddenly, pointed. "There," he muttered. "A sight that strikes terror even into my heart—Garor returns to the battle, at the head of

her dread Legion of Lakros, beasts of the Overwork!, drawn into evil sym-
biosis with alien intelligences—invulnerable to men, but not to the Sword,
or to the mighty weapons of Nelpar of the Seven Moons. We shall fight
them alone!"

Racing across the vast plain of green dust towards us was a horde of . . .
er . . . creatures. My vocabulary can't cope fully with Craswell's imagination.
Gigantic, shimmering things, drooling thick ichor, half-flying, half-lolloping.
Enough to say I looked around for a washbasin to spit in. I found one, with
soap and towels complete, but I pushed it over, looked at a patch of green dust
and thought hard.

The outline of the phone booth wavered a little before I could fix it. I
dashed inside, dialed. "Police H.Q.? Riot squad here—and quick!"

I stepped outside the booth. Craswell was whirling the Sword round
his head, yelling war cries as he faced the onrushing monsters.

From the other direction came the swelling scream of a police siren.
Half a dozen good, solid patrol cars screeched to a dust-spurting stop outside the phone booth. I don't have to think hard to get a New York cop car
fixed in my mind. These were just right. And the first man out, running to
my side and patting his cap on firmly, was just right, too.

Michael O'Faolin, the biggest, toughest, nicest cop I know.

"Mike," I said, pointing. "Fix 'em."

"Shure, an' it's an aisy job f'the bhoys I've brought along," said Mike,
hitching his belt.

He deployed his men.

Craswell looked at them fanning out to take the charge, then staggered
back towards me, hand over his eyes. "Madness!" he shouted. "What madness is this? What are you doing?"

For a moment, the whole scene wavered. The lone red sun blinked out,
the green desert became a murky transparency through which I caught a
split-second glimpse of white beds with two figures lying on them. Then
Craswell uncovered his eyes.

The monsters began to diminish some twenty yards from the riot squad.
By the time they got to the cops, they were man-size, and very amenable
to discipline—enforced by raps over their horny noggins with nightsticks.
They were bundled into the squad cars, which set off again over the plains.

Michael O'Faolin remained. I said: "Thanks, Mike. I may have a couple of spare tickets for the big fight tomorrow night. See you later."

"Just what I was wantin', Pete. 'Tis me day off. Now, how do I get
home?"

I opened the door of the phone booth. "Right inside." He stepped in.
I turned to Craswell.

"Mighty magic, O Nelpar!" he exclaimed. "To creatures of Garor's mind you opposed creatures of your own!"

He'd woven the whole incident into his plot already.

"We must go forward now, Nelpar of the Seven Moons—forward to the Citadel of the Snake, a thousand lokspans over the burning Plains of Istak."

"How about the Diamond?"

"The Diamond—?"

Evidently, he'd run so far ahead of himself getting me fixed into the landscape that he'd forgotten all about the Diamond that could kill the Snake. I didn't remind him.

However, a thousand lokspans over the burning plains sounded a little too far for walking, whatever a lokspan might be.

I said: "Why do you make things tough for yourself, Craswell?"

"The name," he said with tremendous dignity, "is Multan."

"Multan, Sultan, Shashlik, Dikkidam, Hammaneggs or whatever poly-syllabic pooh-bah you wish to call yourself—I still ask, why make things tough for yourself when there's plenty of cabs around? Just whistle."

I whistled. The Purple Cab swung in, perfect to the last detail, includ-ing a hulking-backed, unshaven driver, dead ringer for the impolite gorilla who'd brought me out to Pentagon that evening.

There is nothing on earth quite so unutterably prosaic as a New York Purple Cab with that sort of driver. The sight upset Craswell, and the green plains wavered again while he struggled to fit the cab into his dream.

"What new magic is this! You are indeed mighty, Nelpar!"

He got in. But he was trembling with the effort to maintain the struc-ture of this world into which he had escaped, against my deliberate at-tempts to bring it crashing round his ears and restore him to colourless—but sane—normality.

At this stage, I felt curiously sorry for him; but I realized that it might only be by permitting him to reach the heights of creative imagery before dousing him with the sponge from the cold bucket that I could jerk his drifting ego back out of dreamland.

It was dangerous thinking. Dangerous—for me.

Craswell's thousand lokspans appeared to be the equivalent of ten blocks. Or perhaps he wanted to gloss over the mundane near-reality of a cab ride. He pointed forward, past the driver's shoulder: "The Citadel of the Snake!"

To me, it looked remarkably like a wedding cake designed by Dali in red plastic: ten stories high, each storey a platter half a mile thick, each platter diminishing in size and offset to the one beneath so that the edifice spiraled towards the glossy sky.

The cab rolled into its vast shadow, stopped beneath the sheer, blank precipice of the base platter, which might have been two miles in diameter.

Or three. Or four. What's a mile or two among dreamers?

Craswell hopped out quickly. I got out on the driver's side.

The driver said: "Dollar-fifty."

Square, unshaven jaw, low forehead, dirty-red hair straggling under his cap. I said: "Comes high for a short trip."

"Lookit the clock," he growled, squirming his shoulders. "Do I come out and get it?"

I said sweetly: "Go to hell."

Cab and driver shot downward through the green sand with the speed of an express elevator. The hole closed up. The times I've wanted to do just that—

Craswell was regarding me open-mouthed. I said: "Sorry. Now I'm being escapist, too. Get on with the plot."

He muttered something I didn't catch, strode across to the red wall in which a crack, meeting place of mighty gates, had appeared, and raised his sword.

"Open, Garor! Your doom is nigh, Multan and Nelpar are here to brave the terrors of this Citadel and free the world from the tyranny of the Snake!" He hammered at the crack with the sword-hilt.

"Not so loud," I murmured. "You'll wake the neighbours. Why not use the bell-push?" I put my thumb on the button and pressed. The towering gates swung slowly open.

"You. . . you have been here before—"

"Yes—after my last lobster supper." I bowed. "After you." I followed him into a great, echoing tunnel with fluorescent walls. The gates closed behind us. He paused and looked at me with an odd gleam in his eyes. A gleam of—sanity. And there was anger in the set of his lips. Anger for me, not Garor or the Snake.

It's not nice to have someone trampling all over your ego. Pride is a tiger—even in dreams. The subconscious, as Steve had explained to me, is a function or state of the brain, not a small part of it. In thwarting Craswell, I was disparaging not merely his dream, but his very brain, sneering at his intellectual integrity, at his abilities as an imaginative writer. In a brief moment of rationality, I believe he was strangely aware of this.

He said quietly: "You have limitations, Nelpar. Your outward-turning eyes are blind to the pain of creation; to you the crystal stars are spangles on the dress of a scarlet woman, and you mock the God-blessed unreason that would make life more than the crawling of an animal from womb to grave. In tearing the veil from mystery, you destroy not mystery— for there are many mysteries, a million veils, world within and beyond worlds—but beauty. And in destroying beauty, you destroy your soul."

These last words, quiet as they sounded, were caught up by the curving walls of the huge tunnel, amplified then diminished in pulsing repetition, loud then soft, a surging hypnotic echo: "Destroy your SOUL, DESTROY your soul. SOUL—"

Craswell pointed with his sword. His voice was exultant. "There is a veil, Nelpar—and you must tear it lest it become your shroud! The Mist— the Sentient Mist of the Citadel!"

I'll admit that, for a few seconds, he'd had me a little groggy. I felt— subdued. And I understood for the first time his power as a word-spinner.

I knew that it was vital for me to reassert myself.

A thick, grey mist was rolling, wreathing slowly towards us, filling the tunnel to roof-height, puffing out thick, groping tentacles.

"It lives on Life itself," Craswell shouted. "It feeds, not on flesh, but on the vital principle that animates all flesh. I am safe, Nelpar, for I have the Sword. Can your magic save you?"

"Magic!" I said. "There's no gas invented yet that'll get through a Mark 8 mask."

Gas-drill—face-piece first, straps behind the ears. No, I hadn't forgotten the old routine.

I adjusted the mask comfortably. "And if it's not gas," I added, "this will fix it." I felt over my shoulder, unclipped a nozzle, brought it round into the "ready" position.

I had only used a one-man flame-thrower once—in training—but the experience was etched on my memory.

This was a deluxe model. At the first thirty-foot oily, searing blast, the Mist curled in on itself and rolled back the way it had come. Only quicker.

I shucked off the trappings. "You were in the Army for a while, Craswell. Remember?"

The shining translucency of the walls dimmed suddenly, and beyond them I glimpsed, as in a movie close-up through an unfocused projector, the square, intense face of Steve Blakiston.

Then the walls re-formed, and Craswell, still the bronzed, naked-limbed giant of his imagination, was looking at me again, frowning, worried. "Your words are strange, O Nelpar. It seems you are master of mysteries beyond even my knowing."

I put on the sort of face I use when the sports editor queries my expenses, aggrieved, pleading. "Your trouble, Craswell, is that you don't want to know. You just won't remember. That's why you're here. But life isn't bad if you oil it a little. Why not snap out of this and come with me for a drink?"

"I do not understand," he muttered. "But we have a mission to perform. Follow." And he strode off.

Mention of drink reminded me. There was nothing wrong with my memory. And that tunnel was as hot as the green desert. I remembered a very small pub just off the street-car depot end of Sauchiehall Street, Glasgow, Scotland. A ginger-whiskered ancient, an exile from the Highlands, who'd listened to me enthusing over a certain brand of Scotch. "If ye think that's guid, mon, ye'll no' tasted the brew from ma own private deestillery. Smack yer lips ower this, laddie—" And he'd produced an antique silver flask and poured a generous measure of golden whisky into my glass. I had never tasted such mellow nectar before or since. Until I was walking down the tunnel behind Craswell.

I nearly envisaged the glass, but changed my mind in time to make it the antique flask. I raised it to my lips. Imagination's a wonderful thing.

Craswell was talking. I'd nearly forgotten him.

". . . near the Hall of Madness, where strange music assaults the brain, weird harmonies that enchant, then kill, rupturing the very cells by a mixture of subsonic and supersonic frequencies. Listen!"

We had reached the end of the tunnel and stood at the top of a slope which, broadening, ran gently downward, veiled by a blue haze, like the smoke from fifty million cigarettes, filling a vast circular hall. The haze eddied, moved by vagrant, sluggish currents of air, and revealed on the farther side, dwarfed by distance but obviously enormous, a complex structure of pipes and consoles.

A dozen Mighty Wurlitzers rolled into one would have appeared as a miniature piano at the foot of this towering music-machine.

At its many consoles which, even at that distance, I could see consisted of at least half a dozen manuals each, were multi-limbed creatures—spiders or octopuses or Polilollipops—I didn't ask what Craswell called them—I was listening. The opening bars were strange enough, but innocuous. Then the multiple tones and harmonies began to swell in volume. I picked out the curious, sweet harshness of oboes and bassoons, the eldritch, rising ululation of a thousand violins, the keen shrilling of a hundred demonic flutes, the sobbing of many cellos. That's enough. Music's my hobby, and I don't want to get carried away in describing how that crazy symphony nearly carried me away.

But if Craswell ever reads this, I'd like him to know that he missed his vocation. He should have been a musician. His dream-music showed an amazing intuitive grasp of orchestration and harmonic theory. If he could do anything like it consciously, he would be a great modern composer.

Yet not too much like it. Because it began to have the effects he had warned about. The insidious rhythm and wild melodies seemed to throb inside my head, setting up a vibration, a burning, in the brain tissue.

Imagine Puccini's "Recondita Armenia" re-orchestrated by Stravinsky then re-arranged by Honegger, played by fifty symphony orchestras in the Hollywood Bowl, and you might begin to get the idea.

I was getting too much of it. Did I say music was my hobby? Certainly—but the only instrument I play is the harmonica. Quite well, too. And with a microphone, I can make lots of nice noise.

A microphone—and plenty of amplifiers. I pulled the harmonica from my pocket, took a deep breath, and whooped into "Tiger Rag," my favourite party-piece.

The stunning blast-wave of jubilant jazz, riffs, tiger-growls and tremolo discords from the tiny mouth organ, crashed into the vast hall from the amplifiers, completely swamping Craswell's mad music.

I heard his agonized shout even above the din. His tastes in music were evidently not as catholic as mine. He didn't like jazz.

The music-machine quavered, the multi-limbed organists, ludicrous in their haste to escape from an unreal doom, shrank, withered to scuttling black beetles; the lighting effects that had sprayed a rich, unearthly effulgence over the consoles died away into pastel, blue gloom; then the great machine itself, caught in swirl upon wave of augmented chords complemented and reinforced by its own outpourings, shivered into fragments, poured in a chaotic stream over the floor of the hall.

I heard Craswell shout again, then the scene changed abruptly. I assumed that, in his desire to blot out the triumphant paean of jazz from his mind, and perhaps in an unconscious attempt to confuse me, he had skipped a part of his plot and, in the opposite of the flashback beloved of screen writers, shot himself forward. We were—somewhere else.

Perhaps it was the inferiority complex I was inducing, or in the transition he had forgotten how tall he was supposed to be, but he was now a mere six feet, nearer my own height.

He was so hoarse, I nearly suggested a gargle. "I . . . I left you in the Hall of Madness. Your magic caused the roof to collapse. I thought you were—killed."

So the flash-forward wasn't just an attempt to confuse me. He'd tried to lose me, write me out of the script altogether.

I shook my head. "Wishful thinking, Craswell old man," I said reproachfully. "You can't kill me off between chapters. You see, I'm not one of your characters at all. Haven't you grasped that yet? The only way you can get rid of me is by waking up."

"Again you speak in riddles," he said, but there was little confidence in his voice.

The place in which we stood was a great, high-vaulted chamber. The lighting effects—as I was coming to expect—were unusual and admirable—many coloured shafts of radiance from unseen sources, slowly moving, meeting and merging at the farther end of the chamber in a white, circular blaze which seemed to be suspended over a throne-like structure.

Craswell's size-concepts were stupendous. He'd either studied the biggest cathedrals in Europe, or he was reared inside Grand Central Station. The throne was apparently a good half-mile away, over a completely bare but softly resilient floor. Yet it was coming nearer. We were not walking. I looked at the walls, realized that the floor itself, a gigantic endless belt, was carrying us along.

The slow, inexorable movement was impressive. I was aware that Craswell was covertly glancing at me. He was anxious that I should be impressed. I replied by speeding up the belt a trifle. He didn't appear to notice.

He said: "We approach the Throne of the Snake, before which, his protector and disciple, stands the female magician and sorceress, Garor. Against her, we shall need all your strange skills, Nelpar, for she stands invulnerable within an invisible shield of pure force.

"You must destroy that barrier, that I may slay her with the Sword. Without her, the Snake, though her master and self-proclaimed master of this world, is powerless, and he will be at our mercy."

The belt came to a halt. We were at the foot of a broad stairway leading to the throne itself, a massive metal platform on which the Snake reposed beneath a brilliant ball of light.

The Snake was—a snake. Coil on coil of overgrown python, with an evil head the size of a football swaying slowly from side to side.

I spent little time looking at it. I've seen snakes before. And there was something worth much more prolonged study standing just below and slightly to one side of the throne.

Craswell's taste in feminine pulchritude was unimpeachable. I had half-expected an ancient, withered horror, but if Flo Ziegfeld had seen this baby, he'd have been scrambling up those steps waving a contract, force-shield or no force-shield, before you could get out the first glissando of a wolf-whistle.

She was a tall, oval-faced, green-eyed brunette, with everything just so, and nothing much in the way of covering—a scanty metal chest-protector and a knee-length, filmy green skirt. She had a tiny, delightful mole on her left cheek.

There was a curious touch of pride in Craswell's voice as he said, rather unnecessarily: "We are here, Garor," and looked at me expectantly.

The girl said: "Insolent fools—you are here to die."

Mm-m-m—that voice, as smooth and rich as a Piati-gorski cello-note. I was ready to give quite a lot of credit to Craswell's imagination, but I couldn't believe that he'd dreamed up this baby just like that. I guessed that she was modeled on life; someone he knew; someone I'd like to know—someone pulled out of the grab bag of memory in the same way as I had produced Mike O'Faolin and that grubby-chinned cab driver.

"A luscious dish," I said. "Remind me to ask you later for a phone number of the original, Craswell."

Then I said and did something that I have since regretted. It was not the behaviour of a gentleman. I said: "But didn't you know they were wearing skirts longer, this season?"

I looked at the skirt. The hem line shot down to her ankles, evening-gown length.

Outraged, Craswell glared at his girl-friend. The skirt became knee-length. I made it fashionable again.

Then that skirt-hem was bobbing up and down between her ankles and her knees like a crazy window blind. It was a contest of wills and imaginations, with a very pretty pair of well-covered tibiae as battleground. A fascinating sight, Garor's beautiful eyes blazed with fury. She seemed to be strangely aware of the misbecoming nature of the conflict.

Craswell suddenly uttered a ringing, petulant howl of anger and frustration—a score of lusty-lunged infants whose rattles had been simultaneously snatched from them couldn't have made more noise—and the intriguing scene was erased from view in an eruption of jet-black smoke.

When it cleared, Craswell was still in the same relative position but his sword was gone, his gladiator rig was torn and scorched, and thin trickles of blood streaked his muscular arms.

I didn't like the way he was looking at me. I'd booted his super-ego pretty hard that time.

I said: "So you couldn't take it. You've skipped a chapter again. Wise me up on what I've missed, will you?" Somehow it didn't sound as flippant as I intended.

He spoke incisively. "We have been captured and condemned to die, Nelpar. We are in the Pit of the Beast, and nothing can save us, for I have been deprived of the Sword and you of your magic.

"The ravening jaws of the Beast cannot be stayed. It is the end, Nelpar. The End—"

His eyes, large, faintly luminous, looked into mine. I tried to glance away, failed.

Irritated beyond bearing by my importunate clowning, his affronted ego had assumed the whole power of his brain, to assert itself through his will—to dominate me.

The volition may have been unconscious—he could not know why he hated me—but the effect was damnable.

And for the first time since my brash intrusion into the most private recesses of his mind, I began to doubt whether the whole business was quite—decent.

Sure, I was trying to help the guy, but . . . but dreams are sacred.

Doubt negates confidence. With confidence gone, the gateway is open to fear.

Another voice, sibilant. Steve Blakiston saying ". . . unless you let your mind go under." My own voice ". . . wake up as a candidate for a bed in the next ward—" No, not—". . . not unless you let your mind go under—" And Steve had been scared to do it himself, hadn't he? I'd have something to say to that guy when I got out. If i got out . . . if—

The whole thing just wasn't amusing any more.

"Quit it, Craswell," I said harshly. "Quit making goo-goo eyes, or I'll bat you one—and you'll feel it, coma or no coma."

He said: "What foolish words are these, when we are both so near to death?"

Steve's voice: ". . . sympathetic magic . . . imagination. If he imagines that one of his fantastic creations kills the hero—himself—he just won't wake up again."

That was it. A situation in which the hero must die. And he wanted to envisage my death, too. But he couldn't kill me. Or could he? How could Blakiston know what powers might be unleashed by the concept of death during this ultramundane communion of minds?

Didn't psychiatrists say that the death-urge, the will to die, was buried deep, but potent, in the subconscious minds of men? It was not buried deep here. It was glaring, exultant, starkly displayed in the eyes of Marsham Craswell.

He had escaped from reality into a dream, but it was not far enough. Death was the only full escape—

Perhaps Craswell sensed the confusion of thought and speculation that laid my mind wide open to the suggestions of his rioting, perfervid, death-intent imagination. He waved an arm with the grandiloquent gesture of a Shakespearean Chorus introducing a last act, and brought on his monster.

In detail and vividness it excelled everything that he had dreamed up previously. It was his swan-song as a creator of fantastic forms, and he had wrought well.

I saw, briefly, that we were in the centre of an enormous, steep-banked amphitheatre. There were no spectators. No crowd scenes for Craswell. He preferred that strange, timeless emptiness which comes from using a minimum number of characters.

Just the two of us, under the blazing rays of great, red suns swinging in a molten sky. I couldn't count them.

I became visually aware only of the Beast.

An ant in the bottom of a washbowl with a dog snuffling at it might feel the same way. If the Beast had been anything like a dog. If it had been anything like *anything*.

It was a mass the size of several elephants. An obscene hulking gob of animated, semi-transparent purple flesh, with a gaping, circular mouth or vent, ringed inside with pointed beslimed tusks, and outside with—eyes.

As a static thing, it would have been a filthy envenomed horror, a thing of surpassing dread in its mere aspect; but the most fearsome thing was its nightmarish mode of progression.

Limbless, it jerked its prodigious bulk forward in a series of heaves—and lubricated its lath with a glaucous, viscid fluid which slopped from its mouth with every jerk.

It was heading for us at an incredible pace. Thirty yards—Twenty—

The rigidity of utter fear gripped my limbs. This was true nightmare. I tried desperately to think . . . flame-thrower . . . how . . . I couldn't remember . . . my mind was slipping away from me in face of the onward surging of that protoplasmic juggernaut . . . the slime first, then the mouth, closing . . . my thoughts were a screaming turmoil—

Another voice, a deep, drawling, kindly voice, from an unforgettable hour in childhood—"There's nothing in the whole wide world or out of it that a slug from Billy here won't stop. There's nothing you can meet in dreams that Billy here won't stop. He'll come into your dreams with you from now on. There's no call to be scared of anything." Then the cool, hard butt in my hand, the recoil, the whining irresistible chunk of hot, heavy metal—deep in my subconscious. "Pop!" I gasped. "Thanks, Pop."

The Beast was looming over me. But Billy was in my hand, pointing into the mouth. I fired.

The Beast jerked back on its slimy trail, began to dwindle, fold it on itself. I fired again and again.

I became aware once more of Craswell beside me. He looked at the dying Beast, still huge, but rapidly diminishing, then at the dull metal of the old Colt in my hand, the wisp of blue smoke from its uptilted barrel.

And then he began to laugh.

Great, gusty laughter, but with a touch of hysteria.

And as he laughed, he began to fade from view. The red suns sped away into the sky, became pin points; and the sky was white and clean and blank—like a ceiling.

In fact—what beautiful words are "in fact"—in fact, in sweet reality, it *was* a ceiling.

Then Steve Blakiston was peering down, easing the chromium bowl off the rubber pads round my head.

"Thanks, Pete," he said. "Half an hour to the minute. You worked on him quicker than an insulin shock."

I sat up, adjusting myself mentally. He pinched my arm. "Sure—you're awake. I'd like you to tell me just what you did—but not now. I'll ring you at your office."

I saw an assistant taking the bowl off Craswell's head.

Craswell blinked, turned his head, saw me. Half a dozen expressions, none of them pleasant, chased over his face.

He heaved upright, pushed aside the assistant.

"You lousy bum," he shouted. "I'll murder you!"

I just got clear before Steve and one of the others grabbed his arms.

"Let me get at him—I'll tear him open!"

"I warned you," Steve panted. "Get out, quick." I was on my way. Marsham Craswell in a nightshirt may not have been quite so impressive physically as the bronzed gladiator of his dreams, but he was still passably muscular.

That was last night. Steve rang this morning.

"Cured," he said triumphantly. "Sane as you are. Said he realized he'd been overworking, and he's going to take things easier—give himself a rest from fantasy and write something else. He doesn't remember a thing about his dream-coma—but he had a curious feeling that he'd still like to do something unpleasant to a certain guy who was in the next bed to him when he woke up. He doesn't know why, and I haven't told him. But better keep clear."

"The feeling is mutual," I said. "I don't like his line in monsters. What's he going to write now—love stories?"

Steve laughed. "No. He's got a sudden craze for Westerns. Started talking this morning about the sociological and historical significance of the Colt revolver. He jotted down the title of his first yarn—'Six-Gun Rule.' Hey—is that based on something you pulled on him in his dream?"

I told him.

So Marsham Craswell's as sane as me, huh? I wouldn't take bets.

Three hours ago, I was on my way to the latest heavyweight match at Madison Square Garden when I was buttonholed by an off-duty policeman.

Michael O'Faolin, the biggest, toughest, nicest cop I know. "Pete, m'boy," he said. "I had the strangest dream last night. I was helpin' yez out of a bit of a hole, and when it was all over, you said, in gratitude it may have been, that yez might have a couple of spare tickets for the fight this very night, and I was wondering whether it could have been a sort of telepathy like, and—"

I grabbed the corner of the bar doorway to steady myself. Mike was still jabbering on when I fumbled for my own tickets and said: "I'm not feeling too well, Mike. You go. I'll pick my stuff up from the other sheets. Don't think about it, Mike. Just put it down to the luck of the Irish."

I went back to the bar and thought hard into a large whisky, which is the next best thing to a crystal ball for providing a focus of concentration. "Telepathy, huh?"

No, said the whisky. Coincidence. Forget it. Yet there's something in telepathy. Subconscious telepathy—two dreaming minds in rapport. But I wasn't dreaming. I was just tagging along in someone else's dream. Minds are particularly receptive in sleep. Premonitions and what-have-you. But I wasn't sleeping either. Six and four makes minus ten, strike three—you're out. You're nuts, said the whisky.

I decided to find myself a better-quality crystal ball. A Scotch in a crystal glass at Cevali's club.

So I hailed a Purple Cab. There was something reminiscent about the back of the driver's head. I refused to think about it. Until the pay-off.

"Dollar-fifty," he growled, then leaned out. "Say—ain't I seen you some place?"

"I'm around," I said, in a voice that squeezed with reluctance past my larynx. "Didn't you drive me out to Pentagon yesterday?"

"Yeah, that's it," he said. Square unshaven jaw, low forehead, dirty red hair straggling under his cap. "Yeah—but there's something else about your pan. I took a sleep between cruises last night and had a daffy dream. You seemed to come into it. And I got the screwiest idea you already owe me a dollar-fifty."

For a moment, I toyed with the idea of telling him to go to hell. But the roadway wasn't green sand. It looked too solid to open up. So I said, "Here's five," and staggered into Cevali's.

I looked into a whisky glass until my brain began to clear, then I phoned Steve Blakiston and talked. "It's the implications," I said finally. "I'm driving myself bats trying to figure out what would have happened if I'd conjured up a few score of my acquaintances. Would they all have dreamed the same dream if they'd been asleep?"

"Too diffuse," said Steve, apparently through a mouthful of sandwich. "That would be like trying to broadcast on dozens of wavelengths simultaneously with the same transmitter. Your brain was an integral part of that machine, occupying the same position in the circuit as a complexus of recording instruments, keyed in place with Craswell's brain—until the pick-up frequency was raised. What happened then I imagined purely as an induction process. It was—as far as the Craswell hook-up was concerned, but—"

I couldn't stand the juicy champing noises any longer, and said: "Swallow it before you choke." The guy lives on sandwiches.

His voice cleared. "Don't you see what we've got? During the amplification of the cerebral currents, there was a backsurge through the tubes and the machine became a transmitter. These two guys were sleeping, their unconscious minds wide open and acting as receivers; you'd seen them during the day, envisaged them vividly—and got tuned in, disturbing their minds and giving them dreams. Ever heard of sympathetic dreams? Ever dreamed of someone you haven't seen for years, and the next day he looks you up? Now we can do it deliberately—mechanically assisted dream telepathy, the waves reinforced and transmitted electronically! Come on over. We've got to experiment some more."

"Sometimes," I said, "I sleep. That's what I intend to do now—without mechanical assistance. So long."

A nightcap was indicated. I wandered back to the club bar. I should have gone home.

She hipped her way to the microphone in front of the band, five-foot ten of dream wrapped up in a white, glove-tight gown. An oval-faced, green-eyed brunette with a tiny, delightful mole on her left cheek. The gown was a little exiguous about the upper regions, perhaps, but not as whistle-worthy as the outfit Craswell had dreamed on her.

Backstage, I got a double shot of ice from those green eyes. Yes, she knew Mr. Craswell slightly. No, she wasn't asleep around midnight last night. And would I be so good as to inform her what business it was of mine? College type, ultra. How they do drift into the entertainment business. Not that I mind.

When I asked about the refrigeration, she said: "It's merely that I have no particular desire to know you, Mr. Parnell."

"Why?"

"I'm hardly accountable to you for my preferences." She frowned as if trying to recall something, added: "In any case—I don't know. I just don't like you. Now if you'll pardon me, I have another number to sing—"

"But, please . . . let me explain—"

"Explain what?"

She had me there. I stumble-tongued, and got a back view of the gown.

How can you apologize to a girl when she doesn't even know that you owe her an apology? She hadn't been asleep, so she couldn't have dreamed about the skirt incident. And if she had—she was Craswell's dream, not mine. But through some aberration a trickle of thought-waves from Blakiston's machine had planted an unreasonable antipathy to me in her subconscious mind. And it would need a psychiatrist to dig it out. Or—

I phoned Steve from the club office. He was still chewing. I said: "I've got some intensive thinking to do—into that machine of yours. I'll be right over."

She was leaving the microphone as I passed the band on my way out. I looked at her hard as she came up, getting every detail fixed.

"What time do you go to bed?" I asked.

I saw the slap coming and ducked.

I said: "I can wait. I'll be seeing you. Happy dreams."

The story is as I remembered it, though I had not realized it was such a parody, and I did not remember the followup where real people had been touched by the reverse surge of telepathy. That fills it out somewhat. The essence remains: lucid dreaming, becoming increasingly real.
　　—Piers

WHEREVER YOU MAY BE

James Gunn

May 1953

I remember this as sheer fun, with a winsome girl, a somewhat unscrupulous man, psi powers galore, and a really neat conclusion. He conspires to evoke her mental powers, succeeds, but then there's hell to pay. I remember a string of sausages plunging down the décolletage of a buxom waitress. Quite different in mood from James Gunn's other story here, "Breaking Point," but worthy in its own way. Psi powers are one of the staples of the science fiction genre, and this is a good job of showing them.
      —Piers

Matt refused to believe it. Vacant incredulity paralyzed him for a moment as he stared after the fleeing, bounding tire. Then, with a sudden release, he sprinted after it.

"Stop!" he yelled futilely. "Stop, damn it!"

With what seemed like sadistic glee, the tire bounced high in the air and landed, going faster than ever. Matt pounded down the hot dusty road for a hundred yards before he pulled up even with it. He knocked it over on its side. The tire lay there, spinning and frustrate, like a turtle on its back. Matt glared at it suspiciously. Sweat trickled down his neck.

A tinkling of little silver bells. Laughter? Matt looked up quickly, angrily. The woods were thin along the top of this Ozark ridge. Descending to the lake, sparkling cool and blue far below, they grew thicker, but the only one near was the young girl shuffling through the dust several hundred yards beyond the crippled car. And her head was bent down to watch her way.

Matt shrugged and wiped the sweat from his forehead with his shirt sleeve. A late June afternoon in southern Missouri was too hot for this kind of work, for any kind of work. Matt wondered if it had been a mistake.

In shimmering heat waves and a slowly settling haze of red dust, he righted the tire and began to roll it back toward the green Ford with one bare metal wheel drum pointing upward at a slight angle. The tire rolled easily, as if it repented its brief dash for freedom, but it was a dirty job and Matt's hands and clothes were soiled red when he reached the car.

With one hand clutching the tire, Matt studied the road for a moment. He could have sworn that he had stopped on one of the few level stretches in these hills, but the tire had straightened up from the side of the car and started rolling as if the car were parked on a steep incline.

Matt reflected bitterly on the luck that had turned a slow leak into a flat only twenty-five miles from the cabin. It couldn't have happened on the highway, ten miles back, where he'd have been able to pull into a service station. No, it had to wait until he couldn't get out of this rutted cow track. The tire's escapade had been only the most recent of a series of annoyances and irritations to which bruised shins and scraped knuckles were painful affidavits.

He sighed. After all, he had wanted isolation. Guy's offer of a hunting cabin in which to finish his thesis had seemed like a godsend at the time, but now Matt wasn't so certain. If this was a fair sample, Matt was beginning to see how much of his time would be wasted just on the problems of existence.

Cautiously, Matt rolled the tire to the rear of the car, laid it carefully on its side, and completed pulling the spare from the trunk. Warily, he maneuvered the spare to the left rear wheel, knelt, lifted it, fitted it over the bolts, and stepped back. He sighed again, but this time with relief.

Kling-ng! Klang! Rattle!

Matt hastily looked down. His foot was at least two inches from the hub cap, but it was rocking now, empty. Matt saw the last nut roll under the car.

Matt's swearing was vigorous, systematic, and exhaustive. It concerned itself chiefly with the perversity of inanimate objects.

There was something about machines and the things they made which was basically alien to the human spirit. They might disguise themselves for a time as willing slaves, but eventually, inevitably, they turned against their masters. At the psychological moment, they rebelled.

Or perhaps it was the difference in people. For some people, things always went wrong—their cakes fell; their lumber split; their golf balls sliced into the rough. Others established a mysterious sympathy with their tools.

Luck? Skill? Coordination? Experience?

It was, he felt, something more conscious and malignant.

Matt remembered a near-disastrous brush with chemistry; he had barely passed qualitative analysis. For him the tests had been worse than useless. Faithfully he had gone through every step of the endless ritual: precipitate, filter, dissolve, precipitate . . . And then he would take his painfully secured, neatly written results to—what was his name?—Wads-worth, and the little chemistry professor would study his analysis and look up, frowning.

"Didn't you find any whatyoumaycallit oxide?" he would ask.

"Whatyoumaycallit oxide?" Startled. "Oh, there wasn't any whatyoumaycallit oxide."

And Wadsworth would make a simple test and, sure enough, there would be the whatyoumaycallit oxide.

There was the inexplicably misshapen gear Matt had made on the milling machine, the drafting pen that would not draw a smooth line no matter how much he sanded the point . . .

It had convinced Matt that his hands were too clumsy to belong to an engineer. He had transferred his ambitions to a field where tools were less tangible. Now he wondered.

Kobolds? Accident prones?

Some time he would have to write it up. It would make a good paper for the *Journal of*—

Laughter! This time there was no possible doubt. It came from right behind him.

Matt whirled, The girl stood there, hugging her ribs to keep the laughter in. She was a young little thing, not much over five feet tall, in a shapeless, faded blue dress. Her feet were small and bare and dirty. Her hair, in long braids, was mouse-colored. Her pale face was saved from plainness only by her large, blue eyes.

Matt flushed. "What the devil are you laughing at?"

"You!" she got out between chuckles. "Whyn't you get a horse?"

"Did that remark just arrive here?"

He swallowed his irritation, turned, and got down on his hands and knees to peer under the car. One by one he gathered up the nuts, but the last one, inevitably, was out of reach. Sweating, he crawled all the way under.

When he came out, the girl was still there. "What are you waiting for?" he asked bitingly.

"Nothin'." But she stood with her feet planted firmly in the red dust.

Kibitzers annoyed Matt, but he couldn't think of anything to do about it. He twirled the nuts onto the bolts and tightened them up, his neck itching. It might have been the effect of sweat and dust, but he was not going to give the girl the satisfaction of seeing him rub it. That annoyed him even more. He tapped the hub cap into place and stood up.

"Why don't you go home?" he asked sourly.

"Cain't," she said.

He went to the rear of the car and released the jack. "Why not?"

"I run away." Her voice was quietly tragic.

Matt turned to look at her. Her blue eyes were large and moist. As he watched, a single tear gathered and traced a muddy path down her cheek.

Matt hardened his heart. "Tough." He picked up the flat and stuffed it into the trunk and slammed the lid. The sun was getting lower, and on this forgotten lane to nowhere it might take him the better part of an hour to drive the twenty-five miles.

He slid into the driver's seat and punched the starter button. After one last look at the forlorn little figure in the middle of the road, he shook his head savagely and let in the clutch.

"Mister! Hey, mister!"

He slammed on the brakes and stuck his head out the window. "Now what do you want?"

"Nothin'," she said mournfully. "Only you forgot your jack."

Matt jammed the gear shift into reverse and backed up rapidly. Silently, he got out, picked up the jack, opened the trunk, tossed in the jack, slammed the lid. But as he brushed past her again, he hesitated. "Where are you going?"

"No place," she said.

"What do you mean 'no place'? Don't you have any relatives?" She shook her head. "Friends?" he asked hopefully. She shook her head again.

"All right, then, go on home!"

He slid into the car and banged the door. She was not his concern. The car jerked into motion. No doubt she would go home when she got hungry enough. He shifted into second, grinding the gears. Even if she didn't, someone would take her in. After all, he was no welfare agency.

He grudgingly slowed, then angrily backed up and skidded to a stop beside the girl.

"Get in," he said.

Trying to keep the car out of the ruts was trouble enough, but the girl jumped up and down on the seat beside him, squealing happily.

"Careful of those notes," he said, indicating the bulging manila folders on the seat between them. "There's over a year's work in those."

Her eyes were wide as she watched him place the folders in the back seat on top of the portable typewriter that rested between the twenty-pound sack of flour and the case of eggs.

"A year's work?" she echoed wonderingly.

"Notes. For the thesis I'm going to write."

"You write stories?"

"A research paper I have to do to get my degree." He glanced at her blank expression and then looked back at the road. "It's called," he said with a nasty superior smile, "'The Psychodynamics of Witchcraft, with Special Reference to the Salem Trials of 1692.'"

"Oh," she said wisely. "Witches." As if she knew all about witches.

Matt felt unreasonably annoyed. "All right, where do you live?"

She stopped bouncing and got very quiet. "I cain't go home."

"Why not?" he demanded. "And don't tell me 'I run away,'" he imitated nasally.

"Paw'd beat me again. He'd purty nigh skin me alive, I guess."

"You mean he *hits you?*"

"He don't use his fists—not often. He uses his belt mostly. Look." She pulled up the hem of her dress and the leg of a pair of baggy drawers that appeared to be made from some kind of sacking.

Matt looked quickly and glanced away. Across the back of one thigh was an ugly dark bruise. But the leg seemed unusually well rounded for a girl so small and young. Matt frowned thoughtfully. Did girls in the hills *mature* that early?

He cleared his throat. "Why does he do that?"

"He's just mean."

"He must have some reason."

"Well," she said thoughtfully, "he beats me when he's drunk 'cause he's drunk, and he beats me when he's sober 'cause he ain't drunk. That covers it mostly."

"But what does he say?"

She glanced at him shyly. "Oh, I cain't repeat it."

"I mean what does he want you to do?"

"Oh, that!" She brooded over it. "He thinks I ought to get married. He wants me to catch some strong young feller who'll do the work when he moves in with us. A gal don't bring in no money, he says, leastwise not a good one. That kind only eats and wants things."

"Married?" Matt said. "But you're much too young to get married."

She glanced at him out of the corner of her eye. "I'm sixteen," she said. "Most girls my age got a couple of young 'uns. One, anyways."

Matt looked at her sharply. Sixteen? It seemed impossible. The dress was shapeless enough to hide almost anything—but sixteen! Then he remembered the thigh.

She frowned. "Get married, get married! You'd think I didn't want to get married. 'Tain't my fault no feller wants me."

"I can't understand that," Matt said sarcastically.

She smiled at him. "You're nice."

She looked almost pretty when she smiled. For a hill girl.

"What seems to be the trouble?" Matt asked hurriedly.

"Partly Paw," she said. "No one'd want to have him around. But mostly I guess I'm just unlucky." She sighed. "One feller I went with purty near a year. He busted his leg. Another nigh drownded when he fell in the lake. Don't seem right they should blame me, even if we did have words."

"Blame you?"

She nodded vigorously. "Them as don't hate me say it's courtin' disaster 'stead of a gal. The others weren't so nice. Fellers stopped comin'. One of 'em said he'd rather marry up with a catamount. You married, Mister— Mister—?"

"Matthew Wright. No, I'm not married."

She nodded thoughtfully. "Wright. Abigail Wright. That's purty."

"Abigail *Wright?*"

"Did I say that? Now, ain't that funny? My name's Jenkins."

Matt gulped. "You're going home," he said with unshakable conviction. "You can tell me how to get there or you can climb out of the car right now."

"But Paw—"

"Where the devil did you think I was taking you?"

"Wherever you're going," she said, wide-eyed.

"For God's sake, you can't go with me! It wouldn't be decent."

"Why not?" she asked innocently.

In silence, Matt began to apply the brakes.

"All right," she sighed. She wore an expression the early Christians must have worn before they were marched into the arena. "Turn right at the next crossroad."

Chickens scattered in front of the wheels, fluttering and squawking; pigs squealed in a pen beside the house. Matt stopped in front of the shanty, appalled. If the two rooms and sagging porch had ever known paint, they had enjoyed only a nodding acquaintance, and that a generation before.

A large brooding figure sat on the porch, rocking slowly in a rickety chair. He was dark, with a full black beard and a tall head of hair.

"That's Paw," Abigail whispered in fright.

Matt waited uneasily, but the broad figure of her father kept on rocking as if strangers brought back his daughter every day. *Maybe they do,* Matt thought with irritation.

"Well," he said nervously, "here you are."

"I cain't get out," Abigail said. "Not till I find out if Paw's goin' to whale me. Go talk to him. See if he's mad at me."

"Not me," Matt stated with certainty, glancing again at the big, black figure rocking slowly, ominously silent. "I've done my duty in bringing you home. Good-by. I won't say it's been a pleasure knowing you."

"You're nice and mighty handsome. I'd hate to tell Paw you'd taken advantage of me. He's a terror when he's riled."

For one horrified moment, Matt stared at Abigail. Then, as she opened her mouth, he opened the door and stepped out. Slowly he walked up to the porch and put one foot on its uneven edge.

"Uh," he said. "I met your daughter on the road."

Jenkins kept on rocking.

"She'd run away," Matt went on.

Jenkins was silent. Matt studied the portion of Jenkins' face that wasn't covered with hair. There wasn't much of it, but what there was Matt didn't like.

"I brought her back," Matt finished desperately.

Jenkins rocked and said nothing. Matt spun around and walked quickly back to the car. He went around to the window where Abigail sat. He reached through the window, opened the glove compartment, and drew out a full pint bottle.

"Remind me," he said, "never to see you again." He marched back to the porch. "Care for a little drink?"

One large hand reached out, smothered the pint, and brought it close to faded blue overalls. The cap was twisted off by the other hand. The bottle was tilted toward the un-painted porch ceiling as soon as the neck disappeared into the matted whiskers. The bottle gurgled. When it was lowered, it was only half full.

"Weak," the beard said. But the hand that held the bottle held it tight.

"I brought your daughter back," Matt said, starting again.

"Why?" he asked.

"She had no place to go. I mean—after all, this is her home."

"She run away," the beard said. Matt found the experience extremely unnerving.

"Look, Mr. Jenkins, I realize that teen-age daughters can be a nuisance, and after meeting your daughter I think I can understand how you feel. Still in all, she is your daughter."

"Got my doubts."

Matt gulped and tried once more. "A happy family demands a lot of compromise, give-and-take on both sides.

"Your daughter may have given you good cause to lose your temper, but beating a child is never sound psychology. Now if you—"

"Beat her?" Jenkins rose from his chair. It was an awesome thing, like Neptune rising out of the sea in all his majesty, gigantic, bearded, and powerful. Even subtracting the height of the porch, Jenkins loomed several inches over Matt's near six feet. "Never laid a hand to her. Dassn't."

My God, thought Matt, *the man is trembling!*

"Come in here," said Jenkins. He waved the pint toward the open door, a dark rectangle.

Uneasily, Matt walked into the room. Under his feet, things gritted and cracked.

Jenkins lit a kerosene lamp and turned it up. The room was a shambles. Broken dishes littered the floor. Wooden chairs were smashed and splintered. In the center of the room, a table on its back waved three rough legs helplessly in the air; the fourth leg sagged pitifully from its socket.

"She did this?" Matt asked weakly.

"This ain't nothin'." Jenkins' voice quavered; it was a terrible sound to come from that massive frame. "You should see the other room."

"But how? I mean *why?*"

"I ain't a-sayin' Ab done it," Jenkins said, shaking his head. His beard wobbled near Matt's nose. "But when she gets onhappy, things happen. And she was powerful onhappy when that Duncan boy tol' her he wan't comin' back. Them chairs come up from the floor and slam down. That table went dancin' round the room till it fell to pieces. Then dishes come a-flyin' through the air. Look!"

His voice was full of self-pity as he turned his head around and parted his long, matted hair. On the back of his head was a large, red swelling. "I hate to think what happened to that Duncan boy."

He shook his head sorrowfully. "Now, mister, I guess I got ever' right to lay my hand to that gal. Ain't I?" he demanded fiercely, but his voice broke.

Matt stared at him blankly.

"But whop her? Me? I sooner stick my hand in a nest of rattlers."

"You mean to say that those things happened all by themselves?"

"That's what I said. I guess it kinder sticks in your craw. Wouldn't have believe it myself, even seein' it and feelin' it—" he rubbed the back of his head—"if it ain't happen afore. Funny things happen around Ab, ever since she started fillin' out, five-six year ago."

"But she's only sixteen," Matt objected.

"Sixteen?" Jenkins glanced warily around the room and out the door toward the car. He lowered his voice to a harsh whisper. "Don't let on I tol' you, but Ab allus was a fibber. She's past eighteen!"

From a shelf, a single unbroken dish crashed to the floor at Jenkins' feet. He jumped and began to shake.

"See?" he whispered plaintively.

"It fell," Matt said.

"She's witched." Jenkins took a feverish swallow from the bottle. "Maybe I ain't been a good Paw to her. Ever since her Maw died, she run wild and got all kinda queer notions. 'Tain't allus been bad. For years I ain't had to go fer water. That barrel by the porch is allus filled. But ever since she got to the courtin' age and started bein' disappointed in fellers round about, she been mighty hard to live with. No one'll come nigh the place. And things keep a-movin' and a-jumpin' around till a man cain't trust his own chair to set still under him. It gets you, son. A man kin only stand so much!"

To Matt's dismay, Jenkins' eyes began to fill with large tears. "Got no friend no more to offer me a drink now and again, sociable-like, or help me with the chores, times I got the misery in my back. I ain't a well man, son. Times it's more'n I kin do to get outa bed in the mornin'.

"Look, son," Jenkins said, turning to Matt pleadingly. "Yore a city feller. Yore right nice-lookin' with manners and edyacation. I reckon Ab likes you. Whyn't you take her with you?" Matt started retreating toward the door. "She's right purty when she fixes up and she kin cook right smart. You'd think a skillet was part of her hand, the way she kin handle one, and you don't even have to marry up with her."

Matt backed away, white-faced and incredulous. "You must be mad. You can't give a girl away like that." He turned to make a dash for the door.

A heavy hand fell on Matt's shoulder and spun him around. "Son," Jenkins said, his voice heavy with menace, "any man that's alone with a gal more'n twenty minutes, it's thought proper they should get married up quick. Since yore a stranger, I ain't holdin' you to it. But when Ab left me, she stopped bein' my daughter. Nobody asked you to bring her back. That gal," he said woefully, "eats more'n I do."

Matt reached into his hip pocket. He pulled out his billfold and extracted a five-dollar bill.

"Here," he said, extending it toward Jenkins, "maybe this will make life a little more pleasant."

Jenkins looked at the money wistfully, started to reach for it, and jerked his hand away.

"I cain't do it," he moaned. "It ain't worth it. You brought her back. You kin take her away."

Matt glanced out the doorway toward the car and shuddered. He added another five to the one in his hand.

Jenkins sweated. His hand crept out. Finally, desperately, he crumpled the bills into his palm. "All right," he said hoarsely. "Them's ten mighty powerful reasons."

Matt ran to the car as if he had escaped from bedlam. He opened the door and slipped in. "Get out," he said sharply. "You're home."

"But Paw—"

"From now on, he'll be a doting father." Matt reached across and opened the door for her. "Good-by."

Slowly Abigail got out. She rounded the car and walked up to the porch, dragging her feet. But when she reached the porch, she straightened up. Jenkins, who was standing in the doorway, shrank back from his five-foot-tall daughter as she approached.

"Dirty, nasty old man," Abigail hissed.

Jenkins flinched. After she had passed, he raised the bottle hastily to his beard. His hand must have slipped. By some unaccountable mischance, the bottle kept rising in the air, mouth downward. The bourbon gushed over his head.

Pathetically, looking more like Neptune than ever, Jenkins peered toward the car and shook his head.

Feverishly, Matt turned the car around and jumped it out of the yard. It had undoubtedly been an optical illusion. A bottle does not hang in the air without support.

Guy's cabin should not have been so difficult to find. Although the night was dark, the directions were explicit. But for two hours Matt bounced back and forth along the dirt roads of the hills. He got tired and hungry.

For the fourth time, he passed the cabin which fitted the directions in every way but one—it was occupied. Lights streamed from the windows into the night. Matt turned into the steep driveway. He could, at least, ask directions.

As he walked toward the door, the odor of frying ham drifted from the house to tantalize him. Matt knocked, his mouth watering. Perhaps he could even get an invitation to supper.

The door swung open. "Come on in. What kept you?"

Matt blinked. "Oh, no!" he cried. For a frantic moment, it was like the old vaudeville routine of the drunk in the hotel who keeps staggering back to knock on the same door. Each time he is more indignantly ejected until finally he complains, "My God, are you in *all* the rooms?"

"What are you doing here?" Matt asked faintly. "How did you—How *could* you—?"

Abigail pulled him into the cabin. It looked bright and cheerful and clean. The floor was newly swept; a broom leaned in the corner. The two lower bunks on opposite walls were neatly made up. Two places were laid at the table. Food was cooking on the wood stove.

"Paw changed his mind," she said.

"But he couldn't! I gave him—"

"Oh, that." She reached into a pocket of her dress. "Here."

She handed him the two crumpled five-dollar bills and a handful of silver and copper that Matt dazedly added up to one dollar and thirty-seven cents.

"Paw said he'd have sent more, but it was all he had. So he threw in some vittles."

He sat down in a chair heavily. "But you couldn't—I didn't know where the place was myself, exactly. I didn't tell you—"

"I always been good at finding things," she said. "Places, things that are lost. Like a cat, I guess."

"But—but—" Matt spluttered, "how did you get here?"

"I rode," she said. Instinctively, Matt's eyes switched to the broom in the corner. "Paw loaned me the mule. I let her go. She'll get home all right."

"But you can't stay here. It's impossible!"

"Now, Mr. Wright," Abigail said soothingly. "My Maw used to say a man should never make a decision on a empty stomach. You just sit there and relax. Supper's all ready. You must be nigh starved."

"There's no decision to be made!" Matt said, but he watched while she put things on the table—thick slices of fried ham with cream gravy, corn on the cob, fluffy biscuits, butter, homemade jelly, strong black coffee that was steaming and fragrant. Abigail's cheeks were flushed from the stove, and her face was peaceful. She looked almost pretty.

"I can't eat a bite," Matt told her.

"Nonsense." Abigail filled his plate.

Glumly, Matt sliced off a bite of ham and put it in his mouth. It was so tender, it almost melted. Before long he was eating as fast as he could shovel the food into his mouth. The food was delicious; everything was cooked just as he liked it. He had never been able to tell anyone how to fix it that way. But that was the way it was.

He pushed himself back from the table, teetering against the wall on the back legs of his chair, lit a cigarette and watched Abigail pour him a third cup of coffee. He was swept by a wave of contentment.

"If I'd had time I'd a made a peach pie. I make real good peach pie," Abigail said.

Matt nodded lazily. There would be compensations in having someone around to—

"No!" he said violently, thumping down on the two front legs of his chair. "It won't work. You can't stay here. What would people say?"

"Who'd care?—Paw don't. Anyways, I could say we was married."

"No!" Matt said hoarsely. "Please don't do that!"

"Please, Mr. Wright," she pleaded, "let me cook and clean for you. I wouldn't be no trouble, Mr. Wright, honest I wouldn't."

"Look, Abbie!" He took her hand. It was soft and feminine. She stood beside his chair obediently, her eyes cast down. "You're a nice girl, and I like you. You can cook better than anyone I've ever known, and you'll make some man a good wife. But I think too much of you to let you ruin your name by staying here alone with me. You'll have to go back to your father."

The life seemed to flow out of her. "All right," she said, so low that it was difficult to hear her.

Dazed at his sudden success, Matt got up and walked toward the door. She followed him, and Matt could almost feel the tears welling in her eyes.

Matt opened the car door for her and helped her in. He circled the front of the car and slid into the driver's seat. Abbie huddled against the far door, small and forlorn.

Since Matt's speech, she hadn't said a word. Suddenly, Matt felt very sorry for her and ashamed, as if he had hit a child. *The poor little thing!* he thought. Then he caught himself. He shook his head. For a poor little thing, she had certainly managed to browbeat her father.

He thumbed the starter button, and the motor growled, but it didn't catch. Matt let it whine to a stop and pressed again. The motor moaned futilely. Matt checked the ignition. It was on. Again and again he pushed in the button. The moans got weaker. He tried to roll the car—but the brakes locked.

He glanced suspiciously at Abigail. *But that's absurd,* he thought. Since he had met Abbie, his thoughts had taken a definite paranoid tinge. It was foolish to blame everything that went wrong on the girl.

But the car wouldn't move. He gave up.

"All right," he sighed. "I can't put you out this far from home. You can sleep here tonight."

Silently, she followed him into the cabin. She helped him tack blankets to the upper bunks on each side of the cabin. They made an effective curtain around the lower beds. As they worked, Matt discovered that he was unusually sensitive to her nearness. There was a sweet, womanly smell to her, and when she brushed against him the spot that was touched came to life—tingling awareness.

When they finished, Abbie reached down and grasped the hem of her dress to pull it off over her head.

"No, no," Matt said hurriedly. "Don't you have any modesty? Why do you think we tacked up those blankets?" He gestured to the bunk on the left-hand wall. "Dress and undress in there."

She let the hem of her dress fall, nodded meekly, and climbed into the bunk.

Matt stared after her for a moment and released his breath. He turned and climbed into his own bunk, undressed, and slipped under the blanket. Then he remembered that he had forgotten to turn out the lamps.

He rose on one elbow and heard a soft padding on the floor. The lamps went out, one by one, and the padding faded to the other side of the room. Rustling sounds. Darkness and silence.

"Good night, Mr. Wright." It was a little child's voice in the night.

"Good night, Abbie," he said softly. And then after a moment, firmly, "But don't forget—back you go first thing in the morning."

Before the silence wove a pattern of sleep, Matt heard a little sound from the other bunk. He couldn't quite identify it.

A sob? A snore? Or a muffled titter?

The odor of frying bacon and boiling coffee crept into Mart's nightmare of a terrifying pursuit by an implacable and invisible enemy. Matt opened his eyes. The bunk was bright with diffused sunlight; the dream faded. Matt sniffed hungrily and pushed aside the blanket to look out.

All the supplies from the car had been unloaded and neatly stowed away. On a little corner table by the window were his typewriter and precious manila folders, and a stack of blank white paper.

Matt dressed hurriedly in his cramped quarters. When he emerged from his cocoon, Abbie was humming happily as she set breakfast on the table. She wore a different dress this morning—a brown calico that did horrible things for her hair and coloring, but fitted better than the blue gingham.

The dress revealed a slim but unsuspectedly mature figure.

How would she look, he wondered briefly, in good clothes and nylons, shoes, and make-up?

The thought crumbled before a fresh onslaught to his senses of the odor and sight of breakfast. The eggs were cooked just right, sunny side up, the white firm but not hard. It was strange how Abbie anticipated his preferences. At first he thought that she had overestimated his appetite, but he stowed away three eggs while Abbie ate two, heartily.

He pushed back his plate with a sigh. "Well," he began. She got very quiet and stared at the floor. His heart melted. He felt too contented; a few hours more wouldn't make any difference. Tonight would be time enough for her to go back. "Well," he repeated, "I guess I'd better get to work."

Abbie sprang to clear the table. Matt walked to the corner where the typewriter was waiting. He sat down in the chair and rolled in a sheet of paper. The table was well arranged for light; it was the right height. Everything considered, it was just about perfect for working.

He stared at die blank sheet of paper. He leafed through his notes. He resisted an impulse to get up and walk around. He rested his fingers lightly on the keys and after a moment lifted them, crossed one leg over the other knee, put his right elbow on the raised leg, and began to finger his chin.

There was only one thing wrong: he didn't feel like working.

Finally he typed in the middle of the page:

THE PSYCHODYNAMICS OF WITCHCRAFT
With Special Reference to the
Salem Trials of 1692

He double-spaced and stopped.

It wasn't that Abbie was noisy; she was too quiet, with a kind of purposeful restraint that is worse than chaos. With one ear Matt listened to the sounds of dishwashing and stacking. And then silence.

Matt stood it as long as he could and turned. Abbie was seated at the table. She was sewing up a hole in the pocket of his other pair of pants. He could almost see the aura of bliss that surrounded her.

Like a child, Matt thought, *playing at domesticity.* But there was something mature about it, too; a mature and basic fulfillment. *If we could all be happy with so little. It's a pity, with so small an ambition, to have the real thing so elusive.*

As if she felt him looking at her, Abbie glanced around and beamed. Matt turned back to his typewriter. It still wouldn't come.

Witchcraft, he began hesitantly, *is the attempt of the primitive mind to bring order out of chaos. It is significant, therefore, that belief in witchcraft fades as an understanding of the natural workings of the physical universe grows more prevalent.*

He let his hands drop. It was all wrong, like an image seen in a distorted mirror. He swung around. "Who wrecked your father's house?"

"Libby," she said.

"Libby?" Matt echoed. "Who's Libby?"

'The other me," Abbie said calmly. "Mostly I keep her bottled up inside, but when I feel sad and unhappy I can't keep her in. Then she gets loose and just goes wild. I can't control her."

Good God! Matt thought, *Schizophrenia!* "Where did you get an idea like that?" he asked cautiously.

"When I was born," Abbie said, "I had a twin sister, only she died real quick. Maw said I was stronger and just crowded the life right out of her. When I was bad, Maw used to shake her head and say Libby'd never have been mean or cross or naughty. So when something happened, I started saying Libby done it. It didn't stop a licking, but it made me feel better."

What a thing to tell a child! Matt thought.

"Purty soon I got to believing it, that Libby done the bad things that I got licked for, that Libby was part of me that I had to push deep down so she couldn't get out and get me in trouble. After I"—she blushed—"got older and funny things started happening, Libby come in real handy."

"Can you see her?" Matt ventured.

"Course not," Abbie said reproachfully. "She ain't real."

"Isn't."

"Isn't real," Abbie said. "Things happen when I feel bad. I can't do anything about it. But you got to explain it somehow . . . I use Libby."

Matt sighed. Abbie wasn't so crazy—or stupid either. "You can't control it—ever?"

"Well, maybe a little. Like when I felt kind of mean about that liquor you gave Paw, and I thought how nice it would be if Paw had something wet on the outside for a change."

"How about a tire and a hub cap full of nuts?"

She laughed. Again that tinkling of little silver bells. "You did look funny."

Matt frowned. But slowly his expression cleared and he began to chuckle. "I guess I did."

He swung back to the typewriter before he realized that he was accepting the events of the last eighteen hours as physical facts and Abbie's explanation as theoretically possible. Did he actually believe that Abbie could—how was he going to express it?—move objects with some mysterious, intangible force? By wishing? Of course he didn't. He stared at the typewriter. Or did he?

He called up a picture of a pint bottle hanging unsupported in midair, emptying its contents over Jenkins' head. He remembered a dish that jumped from a shelf to shatter on the floor. He thought of a hub cap that dumped its contents into the dirt when his foot was two inches away. And he saw a tire straighten up and begin to roll down a level road.

You can't just dismiss things, he thought. *In any comprehensive scheme of the universe, you must include all valid phenomena. If the accepted scheme of things cannot find a place for it, then the scheme must change.*

Matt shivered. It was a disturbing thought.

The primitive mind believed that inanimate objects had spirits that must be propitiated. With a little sophistication came mythology and its personification—nymphs and sprites, Poseidon and Aeolus—and folklore, with its kobolds and poltergeists.

Sir James Frazer said something about the relationship between science and magic. Man, he said, associates ideas by similarity and by contiguity in space or time. If the association is legitimate, it is science; if illegitimate, it is magic, science's bastard sister.

But if the associations of magic are legitimate, then those of science must be illegitimate, and the two reverse their roles and the modern world is standing on its head.

Matt felt a little dizzy.

Suppose the primitive mind is wiser than we are. Suppose you can insure good luck by the proper ritual or kill your enemy by sticking a pin in a wax doll. Suppose you can prove it.

You had to have some kind of explanation of unnatural events, the square pegs that do not fit into any of science's round holes. Even Abbie recognized that.

Matt knew what the scientific explanation would be: illusion, delusion, hypnosis, anything which demanded the least possible rearrangement of accepted theory, anything which, in effect, denied the existence of the phenomenon.

But how could you really explain it? How could you explain Abbie? Did you believe in the spirits of inanimate objects, directed by Abbie when she was in the proper mood? Did you believe in poltergeists which Abbie ordered about? Did you believe in Libby, the intangible projectable, manipulative external soul?

You had to explain Abbie or your cosmology was worthless.

That man at Duke—Rhine, the parapsychologist—he had a word for it. Telekinesis. That was one attempt to incorporate psychic phenomena into the body of science, or, perhaps, to alter the theoretical universe in order to fit those phenomena into it.

But it didn't explain anything.

Then Matt thought of electricity. *You don't have to explain something in order to use it. You don't have to understand it in order to control it. It helps, but it isn't essential. Understanding is a psychological necessity, not a physical one.*

Matt stared at the words he had written. The seventeenth century. Why was he wasting his time? Here was something immediate. He had stumbled on something that would set the whole world on its ear, or perhaps stand it on its feet again. It would not molder away, as the thesis would in a university library.

Matt turned around. Abbie was sitting at the table, her mending finished, staring placidly out the open doorway. Matt stood up and walked toward her. She turned her head to look at him, smiling slowly. Matt turned his head, searching the room.

"Kin I get you something?" Abbie asked anxiously.

Matt looked down at her. "Here!" he said. He plucked the needle from the spool of darning thread. He forced it lightly into the rough top of the table so that the needle stood upright. "Now," he said defiantly, "make it move."

Abbie stared at him. "Why?"

"I want to see you do it," Matt said firmly. "Isn't that enough?"

"But I don't want to," Abbie objected. "I never wanted to do it. It just happened."

"Try!"

"No, Mr. Wright," Abbie said firmly. "It never brung me nothing but misery. It scared away all my fellers and all Paw's friends. Folks don't like people who can do things like that. I don't ever want it to happen again."

"If you want to stay here," Matt said flatly, "you'll do as I say."

"Please, Mr. Wright," she begged. "Don't make me do it. It'll spoil everything. It's bad enough when you can't help it, but it's worse when you do it a-purpose—something terrible will come of it."

Matt glowered at her. Her pleading eyes dropped. She bit her lip. She stared at the needle. Her smooth, young forehead tightened.

Nothing happened. The needle remained upright.

Abbie took a deep breath. "I cain't, Mr. Wright," she wailed. "I just cain't do it."

"Why not?" Matt demanded fiercely. "Why can't you do it?"

"I don't know," Abbie said. Automatically her hands began to smooth the pants laid across her lap. She looked down and blushed. "I guess it's 'cause I'm happy."

After a morning of experimentation, Matt's only half-conscious need was still unsatisfied. He had offered Abbie an innumerable assortment of objects: a spool of thread, a fountain pen cap, a dime, a typewriter eraser, a three-by-five note card, a piece of folded paper, a bottle . . . The last Matt considered a stroke of genius. But tip it as he would, the bottle, like all the rest of the objects, remained stolidly unaffected.

He even got the spare tire out of the trunk and leaned it against the side of the car. Fifteen minutes later, it was still leaning there.

Finally, frowning darkly, Matt took a cup from the shelf and put it down on the table. "Here," he said. "You're so good at smashing dishes, smash this."

Abbie stared at the cup hopelessly. Her face seemed old and haggard. After a moment, her body seemed to collapse all at once. "I cain't," she moaned. "I cain't."

"Can't," Matt shouted. "Can't! Are you so stupid you can't say that? Not 'cain't'—can't!"

Her large blue eyes lifted to Matt's in mute appeal. They began to fill with tears. "I can't," she said. A sob broke from her throat. She put her head down on her arms. Her thin shoulders began to quiver.

Moodily, Matt stared at her back. Was everything that he had seen merely an illusion? Or did this phenomenon only evidence itself under very rigid conditions? Did she have to be unhappy?

It was not without a certain logic. Neurotic children had played a large part in the history of witchcraft. In one of the English trials, children had reportedly fallen into fits and vomited crooked pins. They could not pronounce such holy names as "Lord," "Jesus," or "Christ," but they could readily speak the names "Satan" or "Devil." Between the middle of the fifteenth century and the middle of the sixteenth, 100,000 persons had been put to death for witchcraft. How many had come to the rack, the stake, or the drowning pool, through the accusations of children? A child saw a hag at her door. The next moment she saw a hare run by and the woman had disappeared. On no more convincing evidence than that, the woman was accused of turning herself into a hare by witchcraft.

Why had the children done it? Suggestibility? A desire for attention?

Whatever the reason, it was tainted with abnormality.

In the field of psychic phenomena as well, the investigations of the Society of Psychical Research were full of instances in which neurotic children or neurotic young women played a distinct if inexplicable role.

Did Abbie have to be unhappy? Matt's lips twisted. *If it was true, it was hard on Abbie.*

"Get your things together," Matt said harshly. "You're going home to your father."

Abbie stiffened and looked up, her face tear-streaked but her eyes blazing. "I ain't."

"You are not," Matt corrected sharply.

"I are not," Abbie said fiercely. "I are not. I are not."

Suddenly the cup was sailing toward Matt's head. Instinctively, he put out his hand. The cup hit it and stuck. Matt looked at it dazedly and back at Abbie. Her hands were still in her lap.

"You did it!" Matt shouted. "It's true."

Abbie looked pleased. "Do I have to go back to Paw?"

Matt thought a moment. "No," he said. "Not if you'll help me."

Abbie's lips tightened. "Ain't—isn't once enough, Mr. Wright? You know I can do it. Won't you leave it alone now? It's unlucky. Something awful will happen. I got a feeling." She looked up at his implacable face. "But I'll do it, if you want."

"It's important," Matt said gently. "Now. What did you feel just before the cup moved toward me?"

"Mad."

"No, no. I mean what did you feel physically or mentally, not emotionally."

Abbie's eyebrows were thick. When she knit them, they made a straight line across the top of her nose. "Gosh, Mr. Wright, I cain't—" She looked at him quickly. "I can't find the words to tell about it. It's like I wanted to pick up the nearest thing and throw it at you, and then it was like I had thrown it. Kind of a push from all of me, instead of just my hand."

Matt frowned while he put the cup back on the table. "Try to feel exactly like that again."

Obediently, Abbie concentrated. Her face worked. Finally she sagged back in her chair. "I cai—I can't. I just don't feel like it."

"You're going back to your father!" Matt snapped.

The cup rocked.

"There!" Matt said quickly. "Try it again before you forget!"

The cup spun around.

"Again!"

The cup rose an inch from the table and settled down.

Abbie sighed. "It *was* just a trick, wasn't it, Mr. Wright? You aren't really going to send me back?"

"No, but maybe you'll wish I had before we're through. You'll have to work and practice until you have full conscious control of whatever it is."

"All right," Abbie said submissively. "But it's terrible tiring work when you don't feel like it."

"Terribly," Matt corrected.

"Terribly," Abbie repeated.

"Now," Matt said. "Try it again."

Abbie practiced until noon. Her maximum effort was to raise the cup a foot from the table, but that she could do very well.

"Where does the energy come from?" Matt asked.

"I don't know," Abbie sighed, "but I'm powerful hungry."

"Very," Matt said.

"Very hungry," Abbie repeated. She got up and walked to the cupboard. "How many ham sandwiches do you want—two?"

Matt nodded absently. When the sandwiches came, he ate in thoughtful silence.

It was true, then. Abbie could do it, but she had to be unhappy to have full power and control.

"Try it on the mustard," he said.

"I'm so full," Abbie explained contentedly. She had eaten three sandwiches.

Matt stared at the yellow jar, unseeing. It was quite a problem. There was no sure way of determining just what Abbie's powers were, without getting some equipment. He had to find out just what it was she did, and what effect it had on her, before he could expect to fully evaluate any data.

But that wasn't the hardest part of it. He should be able to pick up the things he needed in Springfield. It was what he was going to have to do to Abbie that troubled him.

All he had been able to find out about Abbie's phenomena was that they seemed to occur with the greatest frequency and strength when the girl was unhappy.

Matt stared out through the cabin window.

Gradually, he was forming a plan to make Abbie un-happier than she had ever been.

All afternoon Matt was very kind to Abbie. He helped her dry the dishes, although she protested vigorously. He talked to her about his life and about his studies at the University of Kansas. He told her about the thesis and how he had to write it to get his master's degree in psychology and what he wanted to do when he was graduated.

"Psychology," he said, "is only an infant science. It isn't really a science at all but a metaphysics. It's a lot of theorizing from insufficient data. The only way you can get data is by experimentation, and you can't experiment because psychology is people, living people. Science is a ruthless business of observation and setting up theories and then knocking them down in laboratories. Physicists can destroy everything from atoms to whole islands; biologists can destroy animals; anatomists can dissect cadavers. But psychologists have no true laboratories; they can't be ruthless because public opinion won't stand for it, and cadavers aren't much good. Psychology will never be a true science until it has its laboratories where it can be just as ruthless as the physical sciences. It has to come."

Matt stopped. Abbie was a good listener; he had forgotten he was talking to a hill girl.

"Tell me more about K.U.," she sighed.

He tried to answer her questions about what the coeds wore when they went to classes and when they had dates and when they went to dances. Her eyes grew large and round.

"Guess it would be romantic," Abbie sighed. "How far do they let a fellow go if they ain't—aren't serious?"

Matt thought Abbie's attempt to improve her English was touching—almost pathetic. He puzzled about her question for a moment. "I guess it depends on the girl."

Abbie nodded understandingly. "Why do they go to college?"

"To get married," Matt said. "Most of them."

Abbie shook her head. "All those pretty clothes. All those men. They must be awful—very slow not to get married quick. Can't they get married at home without waiting so long?"

Matt frowned perplexedly. Abbie had a talent for asking questions which reached down to basic social relationships. "The men they meet at college will make more money for them."

"Oh," Abbie said. She shrugged. "That's all right, I guess, if that's what you want."

So it went. Matt paid Abbie little compliments on her appearance, and she blushed and looked pleased. He told her he couldn't understand why she wasn't besieged by suitors and why she hadn't been married long ago. She blushed deeper. He dwelt expansively on the supper she cooked and swore that he had never tasted better.

Abbie couldn't have been happier. She hummed through her tasks. Everything worked well for her. The dishes were done almost as soon as they were started.

Matt walked out on the porch. He sat down on the edge. Abbie settled herself beside him, quietly, not touching him, her hands in her lap.

The cabin was built on the top of a ridge. It was night, but the moon had come up big and yellow, and they could look far out over the valley. Silvery, in a dark green setting of trees, the lake glimmered far below.

"Ain't—isn't it purty?" Abbie sighed, folding her hands.

"Pretty," Matt said absently.

"Pretty," Abbie sighed.

They sat in silence. Matt sensed her nearness in a way that was almost physical. It stirred him. There was something intensely feminine about Abbie that was very appealing at times, in spite of her plain face and shapeless clothes and bare feet and lack of education. Even her single-minded ambition was a striving to fulfill her true, her basic function. In a way it was more vital and understandable than all the confused sublimations of the girls he had known.

Abbie, at least, knew what she wanted and what she would pay to get it. She would make someone a good wife. Her one goal would be to make her husband happy. She would cook and clean for him and bear his strong, healthy children with a great and thrilling joy. She would be silent when he was silent, unobtrusive when he was working, merry when he was gay, infinitely responsive when he was passionate. And the transcendent wonder of it was that she would be fulfilling her finest function in doing it; she would be serenely happy, blissfully content.

Matt lit a cigarette in an attempt to break the mood. He glanced at her face by the light of the match. "What is courting like here in the hills?" he asked.

"Sometimes we walk," Abbie said dreamily, "and look at things together, and talk a little. Sometimes there's a dance at the school house. If a fellow has a boat, you can go out on the lake. There's huskin' bees an' church socials an' picnics. But mostly when the moon is a-shinin' an' the night is warm, we just sit on a porch an' hold hands and do whatever the girl's willin' to allow."

Matt reached out and took one of her hands and held it in his. It was cool and dry and strong. It clung to his hand.

She turned her face to him, her eyes searching for his face in the darkness. "Do you like me a little bit, Mr. Wright?" she asked softly. "Not marryin'-like, but friendly-like?"

"I think that you're the most feminine girl I've ever met," he said, and realized it was true.

Almost without volition on either part, they seemed to lean together, blending in the night. Matt's lips sought her pale little-girl lips and found them, and they weren't pale or little-girlish at all, but warm and soft and passionate. He broke away, breathing quickly.

Abbie half turned to nestle against his shoulder, his arm held tightly around her. She sighed contentedly. "I reckon I wouldn't be unwillin'," she said tremulously, "whatever you wanted to do."

"I can't understand why you didn't get married long ago," he said.

"I guess it was me," Abbie said reflectively. "I wasn't rightly satisfied with any of my fellows. I'd get mad at them for no reason at all, and then something bad would happen to them and pretty soon no one would come courtin'. Maybe I expected them to be what they weren't. I guess I wasn't really in love with any of them. Anyways, I'm glad I didn't get married up." She sighed.

Matt felt the stirrings of something that felt oddly like compunction. *What a louse you are, Matthew Wright!*

"What happened to them—your fellows?" he asked. "Was it something you did?"

"Folks said it was," Abbie said. There was a trace of bitterness in her voice. "They said I had the evil eye. I don't see how. There isn't anything wrong with my eyes, is there?" She looked up at him; her eyes were large and dark blue, with little flecks of silvery moonlight in them.

"Not a thing," Matt said. "They're very beautiful."

"I don't see how it could have been any of my fault," Abbie said. "Of course, when Hank was late that evening, I told him he was so slow he might as well have a broken leg. Right after that he was nailing shingles on a roof, and he fell off and broke his leg. But I reckon he'd have broke it anyways. He was always right careless.

"And then Gene, he was so cold I told him he should fall in the lake and warm up. But a person who does a lot of fishin', I guess he falls in a lot anyways."

"I guess so," Matt said. He began to shiver.

"You're shivering, Mr. Wright," Abbie said solicitously. "Let me go get your jacket."

"Never mind," Matt said. "It's about time for bed anyway. You go in and get ready. Tomorrow—tomorrow we're going to drive to Springfield for some shopping."

"Really, Mr. Wright? I haven't never been to Springfield," Abbie said incredulously. She got up, her eyes shining. "Really?"

"Really," Matt said. "Go on in, now."

She went in. She was almost dancing.

Matt sat on the porch for a few minutes longer, thinking. It was funny what happened to the fellows that disappointed Abbie. When he lit a cigarette, his hand was shaking.

Abbie had a way of being many different persons. Already Matt had known four of them: the moody little girl with braids down her back shuffling along a dusty road or bouncing gleefully on a car seat; the happy, placid housewife with cheeks rosy from the stove; the unhappy vessel of strange powers, tearful and reluctant; the girl with the passionate lips in the moon-streaked darkness. Which one was Abbie, the true Abbie?

The next morning Matt had a fifth Abbie to consider. Her face was scrubbed and shining until it almost rivaled her eyes. Her braided hair was wound in a coronet around her head. She was wearing a different dress made of a shiny blue quilted material with a red lining. Matt scanned his small knowledge of dress materials. Taffeta? The color did terrible things to her hair. The dress had a V-shape neck and back and fitted better than anything she had worn yet. On one hip was a large artificial rose. Her stockingless feet were enclosed in a pair of black, patent-leather sandals.

My God! Matt thought. *Her Sunday best! I'll have to walk with that down the streets of Springfield.* He shuddered, and resisted the impulse to tear off that horrible rose.

"Well," he said, "all ready?"

Abbie blushed excitedly. "Are we really going to Springfield, Mr. Wright?"

"We are if the car will start."

"Oh, it'll start," Abbie said confidently.

Matt gave her a thoughtful sidelong glance. That was another thing.

After the usual hearty breakfast, with fried potatoes on the side, they got into the car. The brakes released without hesitation.

The drive was more than fifty miles, half of it over dirt roads that were roller-coaster washboards, and they drove it in silence. Every few miles Matt would glance at Abbie out of the corner of his eye and shudder. As excited as she was, like a child, Abbie was contented to sit quietly and enjoy the ride, particularly when they swung off the dirt road onto Highway 665.

When they came to Springfield, Abbie's face was glowing. She stared at the buildings as if they had sprung magically into being especially for her. Then she began to inspect the people walking along the streets. Matt noticed that it was the women who received her closest attention.

Suddenly Matt noticed that Abbie was very quiet. He glanced toward her. She was still, staring down at her hands resting in her lap.

"What's the matter?" Matt asked.

"I guess," she said, her voice a little unsteady, "I guess I look pretty funny. I guess you'll feel ashamed having me along. If it's all right with you, Mr. Wright, I'll just sit in the car."

"Nonsense," Matt said heartily. "You look fine." *The little devil,* he thought. *She has an uncanny talent for understanding things. She's either unusually perceptive or—What?* "Besides, I'll need you to try on some clothes."

"Clothes, Mr. Wright!" she exclaimed. She seemed to find it hard to speak. "You're going to buy some clothes."

Matt nodded. He parked the car in front of Springfield's biggest department store. He came around to Abbie's door and helped her out. For a moment Abbie's face was level with his; her blue eyes locked with his dark ones in a look that Matt refused to analyze. They walked into the store, Abbie clinging to his arm. He could feel her heart beating swiftly. Matt stopped a moment to study the directory.

"Second floor," he said.

Abbie held back as Matt started off. "Kin we—can we look around here—for just a second?" Abbie asked hesitantly.

Matt glanced at her and shrugged. "I suppose so."

Abbie started off determinedly toward some mysterious, unseen destination, leading Matt down innumerable aisles. All the way to the back of the store they went, and emerged miraculously into the kitchenware department. Abbie stopped on the threshold, gazing rapturously at the gleaming pots and pans, beaters, knives, and gadgets, as if they were jewels. She dismissed with a glance the stoves and electrical appliances, but the cooking utensils brought forth long sighs. After a moment she moved among them, staring at them, touching them with one timid finger. She made little crooning sounds deep in her throat.

Matt had to drag her away.

They were almost to the stairs when Matt noticed that she was holding something to her breast. He stopped. He stared aghast. She was hugging a tiny frying pan of shiny aluminum and dully gleaming copper.

"Where did you get that?" he demanded.

"Back there," she said innocently. "They got so many. They'll never miss a little thing like this,"

"But you can't do that!" Matt said. "That's stealing."

"'Tain't stealing when they got so much and I got so little," she explained.

"You've got to take it back!" Matt made a futile grab for the frying pan. Abbie hugged it to her breast with both arms.

"Don't take it away from me!" she wailed. "Please don't make me take it back!"

Matt glanced around nervously. So far no one seemed to be watching them. He turned back to Abbie. "Sh-h-h!" he said. "Be quiet now. Please be quiet." He looked at her pleadingly. She hugged the frying pan tighter. "All right," he sighed. "Stay here! Don't move! Don't say anything!"

Quickly he walked back to kitchenwares. He caught the attention of the clerk. "How much are those?" he said, pointing to the frying pans.

"Four-fifty, sir. Shall I wrap one up?"

"Four-fifty!"

"Yes, sir," the man said. "We have some cheaper ones in all aluminum—"

"Never mind," Matt said hurriedly. He pulled out his billfold. "Here. Give me a receipt and a sack."

The clerk picked up a frying pan.

"No, no," Matt said. "I don't want one. I just want a receipt and a sack."

"But, sir," the man said bewilderedly. "You said—"

"Don't argue with me," Matt said. "Just give me a receipt and a sack!"

The clerk rang up the sale, tore off the receipt, dropped it in a sack, and handed it to Matt with a very dazed expression on his face.

"Anything else, sir?" he asked automatically.

"I hope not," said Matt, and hurried away. When he looked back the clerk was still staring after him.

Abbie was standing by the stairs where he had left her. "Put the frying pan in here," he whispered.

She gave him a look of admiration. "Oh, that was real clever of you."

Matt mopped his forehead. "Yes, wasn't it?" He took her arm and hurried her up the stairs. At the top Matt came to a halt and looked around. Abbie stared with big eyes at the racks upon racks of dresses.

"I never knew," she whispered, "there was so many dresses in the world."

Matt nodded absently. He had to get away long enough to find a laboratory from which to rent some testing apparatus.

He saw a saleswoman, and drew her aside.

"The girl over there," he said. "I want you to take her to the beauty parlor and give her the works. Haircut, shampoo, setting, facial, eyebrows thinned and shaped and a make-up job. Then get her a new outfit from the skin out. Can you do all that?"

The saleswoman looked quite pleased. "We'll be very happy to help you."

Matt took out his billfold and peered into it. Slowly he extracted one traveler's check for one hundred dollars and then another. It left him only three hundred dollars, and he still had to get the equipment and live for the rest of the summer. Matt sighed and countersigned the checks. "Try to keep it under this," he said heavily. "If you can."

"Yes, sir," said the saleswoman and hesitated, smiling. "Your fiancée?"

"Good God, no," Matt blurted out. "I mean—she's my—niece. It's her birthday."

He walked over to Abbie, breathing heavily. "Go with this woman, Abbie, and do what she tells you."

"Yes, Mr. Wright," Abbie said dazedly. And she walked away as if she were entering into fairyland.

Matt turned, biting his lip. He felt slightly sick. He had one more thing to do before he could leave the store. Making sure Abbie was gone, he went into the lingerie department. He regretted it almost immediately. Once he had seen a woman come into a pool hall; he must, he thought, wear the same sheepish, out-of-place expression.

He swallowed his qualms—they were a hard lump in his throat—and walked up to the counter.

"Yes, sir," said the young woman brightly, "what can I do for you?"

Matt avoided looking at her. "I'd like to buy a negligee," he said in a low voice.

"What size?"

Matt began a motion with his hands and then dropped them hastily at his sides. "About five feet tall. Slim."

The woman led him along the counter. "Any particular color?"

"Uh—black," Matt said hoarsely.

The clerk brought out a garment that was very black, very lacy, very sheer. "This is thirty-nine ninety-eight."

Matt stared at it. "That's awfully black," he said.

"We have some others," the clerk began, folding the negligee.

"Never mind," Matt said quickly. "Wrap it up." Furtively, he slipped the money over the counter.

When he came out, the package under his arm, he was sweating freely.

He put the box in his car and looked at his watch. He had about two and a half hours, at least. He should be able to find everything he needed in that time.

He pulled a list of things out of his pocket, and found a telephone directory in a drugstore.

Springfield had a laboratory supply house. He called the number, asked for the equipment he'd need, was told they had it for rent, and drove over to pick it up. The rental didn't seem like much by the day, but it was, he discovered on figuring it out, a lot by the month—enough to break him fast if he didn't get something like a controlled series of tests, very fast.

Feeling like a child-slayer, he drove back to the department store and parked.

Only one hour had gone by. He went into the store and browsed about.

Two hours. He put another nickel in the parking meter. He sat down in a red leather chair and tried to look as if he were testing it for size and comfort.

Three hours. He fed the parking meter again, and began to feel hungry. He went back to the chair. From it, he could keep an eye on the stairs.

Women went up and came down. None of them was Abbie. He wondered, with a flash of fear, if she had been caught trying to make off with something else.

Matt tried not watching the stairs on the theory that a watched pot never boils. Never again, he vowed, would he go shopping with a woman. Where the devil was Abbie?

"Mr. Wright." The voice was tremulous and low.

Matt looked up and leaped out of his chair. The girl standing beside him was blonde and breath-taking. The hair was short and fluffed out at the ends; it framed a beautiful face. A soft, simple black dress with a low neckline clung to a small but womanly figure. Slim, long legs in sheer stockings and small black shoes with towering heels.

"Good God, Abbie! What have they done to you?"

"Don't you like it?" Abbie asked. The lovely face clouded up.

"It's—it's marvelous," Matt spluttered. "But they bleached your hair!"

Abbie beamed. "The woman who worked on it called it a rinse. She said it was natural, but I should wash it every few days. Not with laundry soap, either." She sighed. "I didn't know there was so much a girl could do to her face. I've got so much to learn . . . Why, she—"

Abbie prattled on happily while Matt stared at her, incredulous. Had he been sleeping in the same cabin with this girl? Had she been cooking his meals and darning the holes in his pockets? Had he really kissed her and held her in his arms and heard her say, "I reckon I wouldn't be unwillin'—"

He wondered if he would act the same again.

Matt had expected a difference but not such a startling one. She wore her clothes with a becoming sureness. She walked on the high heels as if she had worn them all her life. She carried herself as if she was born to beauty. But then, things always worked well for Abbie.

Abbie opened a small black purse and took out five dollars and twenty-one cents. "The woman said I should give this back to you."

Matt took it and looked at it in his hand and back at Abbie. He shrugged and smiled. "The power of money. Have you got everything?"

Under her arm she carried a large package that contained, no doubt, the clothes and shoes she had worn. Matt took it from her. She refused to give up the package that held the frying pan.

"I couldn't wear this," she said. She reached into her purse and pulled out something black and filmy. She held it up by one strap. "It was uncomfortable."

Matt shot nervous glances to the right and the left. "Put it away." He crammed it back into the purse and snapped the purse shut. "Are you hungry?"

"I could eat a hog," Abbie said.

Coming from this blonde creature, the incongruity set Matt to laughing. Abbie stared with wide eyes. "Did I say something wrong?" she asked plaintively.

"No." Matt got out and led her toward the door.

"You got to tell me," Abbie said appealingly. "There's so much I don't know."

Matt located the most expensive restaurant in town. It had a romantic atmosphere but he had chosen it because it specialized in sea food. He wanted to be sure that Abbie had things to eat she had never tasted before.

Matt ordered for both of them: shrimp cocktail, assorted relishes, chef's salad with Roquefort dressing, broiled lobster tails with drawn butter, french fried potatoes, broccoli with a cheese sauce, frozen éclair, coffee. The food was good, and Abbie ate everything with great wonderment, as if it were about to disappear into the mysterious place from which it came.

She stared wide-eyed at the room and its decorations and the other diners and the waiter, and seemed oblivious of the fact that other men were staring admiringly at her. The waiter puzzled her. "Is this all he does?" she asked timidly. Matt nodded. "He's good at it," Abbie conceded.

"Try to move the coffee cup," Matt said when they finished.

Abbie stared at it for a moment. "I can't," she said softly. "I tried awful—very hard, but I can't. I'd do anything you wanted, Mr. Wright, but I can't do that."

Matt smiled. "That's all right. I just wanted to see if you could."

Matt found a place they could dance. He ordered a couple of drinks. Abbie sipped hers once, made a face, and wouldn't touch it again.

She danced lightly and gracefully in her high-heeled shoes. They brought the top of her head level with his lips. She rested her head blissfully against his shoulder and pressed herself very close. For a moment Matt relaxed and let himself enjoy the pleasures of the aftermath of a good meal and a beautiful girl in his arms. But Abbie seemed to be in a private Eden of her own, as if she had entered a paradise and was afraid to speak for fear the spell would break.

During the long drive home, she spoke only once. "Do people live like that all the time?"

"No," Matt said. "Not always. Not unless they have a lot of money."

Abbie nodded. "That's the way it should be," she said softly. "It should only happen a long ways apart."

When they reached the cabin, Matt reached into the back seat for the package he had bought.

"What's that?" Abbie asked.

"Open it," Matt said.

She held it up a little, lacy and black in the moonlight. Then she turned to look at Matt, her face transparent, her eyes glowing. "Wait out here a minute, will you?" she asked breathlessly.

"All right." Matt lit a cigarette and stood on the porch looking out over the valley, hating himself.

After a few minutes, he heard a little whisper. "Come in, Mr. Wright."

He opened the door, started in and stopped, stunned. One kerosene lamp lit the room dimly. The new clothes were draped carefully over the edge of a chair. Abbie was wearing the negligee. That was all. Through its lacy blackness she gleamed pink and white, a lovely vision of seductiveness. She stood by the table, staring at the floor. When she looked up, her cheeks were flushed.

Suddenly she ran lightly across the floor and threw her arms around Matt's neck and kissed him hard on the lips. Her lips moved. She drew back a little, looking up at him.

"There's only one way a girl like me can thank a man for a day as wonderful as this," she whispered. "For the clothes and the trip and the dinner and the dancing. And for being so nice. I never thought anything like this would ever happen to me. I don't mind. I guess it isn't bad when you really like someone. I like you awful—very well. I'm glad they made me pretty. If I can make you happy—just for a moment—"

Gently, feeling sick, Matt took her hands from around his neck. "You don't understand," he said coldly. "I've done a terrible thing. I don't know how you can ever forgive me. Somehow you misunderstood me. Those clothes, the negligee—they're for another girl—the girl I'm going to marry—my fiancée. You're about her size and I thought—I don't know how I could have misled . . . "

He stopped. It was enough. His plan had worked. Abbie had crumpled. Slowly, as he spoke, the life had drained out of her, the glow had fled from her face, and she seemed to shrink in upon herself, cold and broken. She was a little girl, slapped across the face in her most spiritual moment by the one person she had trusted most.

"That's all right," she said faintly. "Thanks for letting me think they was mine—that it was for me—only for a little. I'll never forget."

She turned and went to the bunk and let the blanket fall back around her.

It was the sobbing that kept Matt from going to sleep that night. Or maybe it was the way the sobs were so soft and muffled that he had to strain to hear them.

Breakfast was a miserable meal. There was something wrong with the food, although Matt couldn't quite pin down what it was. Everything was cooked just the same, but the flavor was gone. Matt cut and chewed mechanically and tried to avoid looking at Abbie. It wasn't difficult; she seemed very small today, and she kept her eyes on the floor.

She was dressed in the shapeless blue gingham once more. She toyed listlessly with her food. Her face was scrubbed free of make-up, and everything about her was dull. Even her newly blonde hair had faded.

Several times Matt opened his mouth to apologize again, and shut it without saying anything. Finally he cleared his throat and said, "Where's your new frying pan?"

She looked up for the first time. Her blue eyes were cloudy. "I put it away," she said lifelessly, "do you want it back?"

"No, no," Matt said hurriedly. "I was just asking." Silence fell again, like a sodden blanket. Matt sat and chain-smoked while Abbie cleaned up the table and washed the dishes.

When she finished she turned around with her back to the dishpan. "Do you want me to move things for you? I can do it real good today."

Matt saw the little pile of packages in the corner and noticed for the first time that the new clothes were gone. He steeled himself. "How do you know?"

"I got a feeling."

"Do you mind?"

"I don't mind. I don't mind anything." She came forward and sat down in the chair. "Look!"

The table between them lifted, twisted, tilted on one leg, and crashed on its side to the floor.

"How did you feel?" Matt said excitedly. "Can you control the power? Was the movement accidental?"

"It felt like it was land of a part of me," Abbie said. "Like my hand. But I didn't know exactly what it was going to do."

"Wait a minute," Matt said. "I'm going to get some things out of the car. Maybe we can learn a little more about what makes you able to do things like this. You don't mind, do you?"

"What's the good of it?" she asked listlessly.

Matt dashed out to the car and pulled the two cartons of equipment out of the trunk. He carried them into the shack and laid the apparatus out on the table. He went back to the car and brought in the bathroom scales he'd bought in the drugstore in Springfield.

"All right, Abbie. First, let's find out a few things about you before we try moving anything else."

Abbie complied automatically while he took her temperature and pulse, measured her blood pressure and weighed her. "I wish I could set up controls to measure your basal metabolism," he muttered as he worked, "but this will have to do. I wish this shack had a generator."

"I could get you electricity," Abbie said without much interest.

"Hmmm—you could at that, I guess. But that would make these tests meaningless, if you had to devote energy to keeping the equipment running."

He cursed the limited knowledge that was undoubtedly making him miss things that a man who had studied longer would have known more about.

But there wasn't anything he could do about that. Once he'd reached some preliminary conclusions, more experienced researchers could take over the job.

Working carefully, he wrote down the results. "Now, Abbie, would you please pick that chair up off the floor, and hold it up for a few minutes? No—I mean really go over and pick it up."

He let her hold it for exactly five minutes, then ran her through the same tests as before, noting the changes in temperature, blood pressure, pulse rate, respiration, and then he weighed her again.

"All right. Take a rest now. We'll have to wait until these readings drop down to what they were before we do anything else," Matt said.

Still not displaying anything more than acquiescence, Abbie sat down in another chair and stared at the floor.

"Abbie, do you mind helping me?" Matt asked. "It's for your benefit, too. If you can control these powers all the time, maybe the fellows around here will stop breaking legs and falling into lakes."

Abbie's dull expression did not change. "I don't care," she said.

Matt sighed. For a moment, he considered dropping his experiments and just getting out of Abbie's life—packing his thesis notes and typewriter in the car and driving back to the university. But he couldn't stop now. He was too close to the beginnings of an answer.

He checked Abbie again, and found his readings coincided with the first set. The short rest had dropped her heartbeat and respiration back to normal.

"Let's try all over again," Matt said. "Lift that chair to the same height you were holding it, please."

The chair jerked upward, hesitantly. "Easy. Just a little more." It straightened, then moved more steadily. "Hold it there." The chair hovered motionless in the air, maintaining its position. Matt waited five minutes. "All right. Let it down easy. Slow." The chair settled gently to the floor, like a drifting feather.

Once more, he checked Abbie.

Her heartbeat was below what it had been. Her blood pressure was lower. Her respiration was shallow—her breast was barely rising to each breath. Her temperature was low—dangerously so, for an ordinary human being.

"How do you feel?" he asked apprehensively. If this was what always happened, then Abbie was in real danger every time she used her powers.

"All right," she said with no more than her previous disinterest. Matt frowned, but she was showing no signs of discomfort.

"Are you sure?" he asked.

"Yes," she said. "You want me to try some more?"

"If you're sure you're not in danger. But I want you to stop if you feel any pain or if you're uncomfortable. Now, lift the table just this far . . ."

They practiced with the table for an hour. At the end of that time, Abbie had it under perfect control. She could raise it a fraction of an inch or rocket it to the ceiling where it would remain, legs pointing stiffly toward the floor, until she lowered it. She balanced it on one leg and set it spinning like a top.

Distance did not seem to diminish Abbie's control or power. She could make the table perform equally well from any point in the room, from outside the cabin, or from a point to which she shuffled dispiritedly several hundred yards down the road.

"How do you know where it is and what it's doing?" Matt asked, frowning.

Abbie shrugged listlessly. "I just feel it."

"With what?" Matt asked. "Do you see it? Feel it? Sense it? If we could isolate the sense—"

"It's all of those," Abbie said.

Matt shook his head in frustration. "You look a little tired. You'd better lie down."

She lay in her bunk, not moving, her face turned to the wall, but Matt knew that she wasn't asleep. When she didn't get up to fix lunch, Matt opened a can of soup and tried to get her to eat some of it.

"No, thanks, Mr. Wright," Abbie said. "I ain't hungry."

"I'm not hungry," Matt corrected.

Abbie didn't respond. In the evening she got out of her bunk to fix supper, but she didn't eat more than a few mouthfuls. After she washed the dishes, she went back into her bunk and pulled the blanket around it.

Matt sat up, trying to make sense out of his charts. Despite their readings, Abbie hadn't reacted dangerously to what should have been frightening physiological changes. He could be fairly safe in assuming that they always accompanied the appearance of her parapsychological powers—and she had certainly lived through those well enough.

But why was there such a difference in the way she reacted when she was happy and when she wasn't? The first morning, when she had barely been able to assume conscious control, she'd been ravenously hungry. Today, when she had performed feats that made the others insignificant she was neither hungry nor abnormally exhausted. She was tired, yes, but there *had* been a measurable, though slight, expenditure of energy with each action, which, accumulated through their numerous experiments, could be expected to equal that required for an afternoon's normal work.

What was different? Why, when she tried with what amounted to willpower alone, was it harder for her to move an object telekinetically than it would have been to do so physically? Why was the reverse true when she was unhappy?

Unless she was tapping a source of energy somewhere.

The thought sounded as though there might be something behind it. He reached for a blank sheet of paper and began jotting down ideas.

Disregarding the first morning's experiments, when she was obviously succeeding despite this hypothetical force, what source of energy could she be contacting?

Well, what physical laws was she violating? Gravity? Inertia?

When Abbie was unhappy, she could nullify gravity—no, not exactly gravity—mass. Once she had done that, a process that might not require much energy at all, the object rose by itself, and, having no mass, could be pushed around easily. Somehow, by some unconscious mechanism, she could restore measured amounts of mass and—there was an idea trying to come to the surface of his thinking—of course! The energy created by the moving or falling body when mass was restored and gravity reasserted itself was channeled into her body. She stopped being a chemical engine sustained by food burned in the presence of oxygen, and became a receiver for the power generated by the moving bodies.

Writing quickly, he systematized what he had learned. Obviously, the energy restored when the manipulated objects fell or swooped back into place couldn't quite balance the energy required to move them. She did get tired—but nowhere near as tired as she should have been. If she empathized with her feelings at such times, she retained a bare margin of control even when happy, but she lost the delicate ability to tap the energy thus liberated, and had to draw on her own body for the power.

Matt grimaced. If that was true—and his charts and graph confirmed it, then she could never use her powers unless she was miserable.

And the key to that lay buried in the childhood of a little hill girl, who probably had been scolded and beaten, as hill children were when they were bad. In this case "bad" meaning a little girl who could move things without touching them, who had been confronted with the example of "Libby," the perfect little girl who would always have minded her mother, until she had come to associate the use of her powers only with unhappiness, with not being wanted, with rejection on the part of the people whom she loved.

Matt winced. *You louse, Wright!*

But it was too late to do anything about it now. He had to go on with what he was doing.

Abbie's appetite wasn't any better in the morning. She looked tired, too, as if she hadn't slept. Matt stared at her for a moment thoughtfully, then shrugged and put her to work.

In a few minutes, Abbie could duplicate her feats with the table of the day before with a control that was, if anything, even finer. Matt extended his experiment to her subjective reactions.

"Let's isolate the source," he said. "Relax. Try to do it with the mind alone. Will the table to move."

Matt jotted down notes. At the end of half an hour he had the following results:

Mind alone—negative.
Body alone—negative.
Emotions alone—negative.

It was crude and uncertain. It would take days or months of practice to be able to use the mind without a sympathetic tension of the body, or to stop thinking or to wall off an emotion. But Matt was fairly sure that the telekinetic ability was a complex of all three and perhaps some others that he had no way of knowing about, which Abbie couldn't describe. But if any of the primary three were inhibited, consciously or unconsciously, Abbie could not move a crumb of bread.

Two of them could be controlled. The third was a product of environment and circumstances. Abbie had to be unhappy.

A muscle twitched in Matt's jaw, and he told Abbie to try moving more than one object. He saw a cup of coffee rise in the air, turn a double somersault without spilling a drop, and sit down gently in the saucer that climbed to meet it. Matt stood up, picked the cup out of the air, drank the coffee, and put the cup back. The saucer did not wobble.

There were limits to Abbie's ability. The number of dissimilar objects she could manipulate seemed to be three, regardless of size; she could handle five similar objects with ease, and she had made six slices of bread do an intricate dance in the air. It was possible, of course, that she might improve with practice.

"My God!" Matt exclaimed. "You could make a fortune as a magician."

"Could I?" Abbie said without interest. She pleaded a headache and went to bed. Matt said nothing. They had worked for an hour and a half.

Matt lit a cigarette. The latent telekinetic power could explain a lot of things, poltergeist phenomena, for instance, and in a more conscious form, levitation and the Indian rope trick and the whole gamut of oriental mysticism.

He spent the rest of the day making careful notes of everything Abbie did, the date and time, the object and its approximate weight and its movements. When he finished, he would have a complete case history. Complete except for the vital parts which he did not dare put down on paper.

Several times he turned to stare at Abbie's still, small form. He was only beginning to realize the tremendous potentialities locked up within her. His awareness had an edge of fear. What role was it he'd chosen for himself. He had been fairy godmother, but that no longer. Pygmalion? He felt a little like Pandora must have felt before she opened the box. Or, perhaps, he thought ruefully, he was more like Doctor Frankenstein.

Abbie did not get up at all that day, and she refused to eat anything Matt fixed. Next morning, when she climbed slowly from her bunk, his apprehension sharpened.

She was gaunt, and her face had a middle-aged, haggard look. Her blonde hair was dull and lifeless. Matt had already cooked breakfast, but she only went through the motions of eating. He urged her, but she put her fork down tiredly.

"It don't matter," she said.

"Maybe you're sick," Matt fretted. "We'll take you to a doctor."

Abbie looked at Matt levelly and shook her head. "What's wrong with me, a doctor won't fix."

That was the morning Matt saw a can of baking powder pass through his chest. Abbie had been tossing it to Matt at various speeds, gauging the strength of the push necessary. Matt would either catch it or Abbie would stop it short and bring it back to her. But this time it came too fast, bullet-like. Involuntarily, Matt looked down, tensing his body for the impact.

He saw the can go in . . .

Abbie's eyes were wide and frightened. Matt turned around dazedly, prodding his chest with trembling fingers. The can had shattered against the cabin wall behind him. It lay on the floor, battered, in a drift of powder.

"It went in," Matt said. "I saw it, but I didn't feel a thing. It passed right through me. What happened, Abbie?"

"I couldn't stop it," she whispered, "so I just sort of wished it wasn't there. For just a moment. And it wasn't."

That was how they found out that Abbie could teleport. It was as simple as telekinesis. She could project or pull objects through walls without hurting either one. Little things, big things. It made no difference. Distance made no difference either, apparently.

"What about living things?" Matt asked. Abbie concentrated. Suddenly there was a mouse on the table, a brown field mouse with twitching whiskers and large, startled black eyes. For a moment it crouched there, frozen, and then it scampered for the edge of the table, straight toward Abbie.

Abbie screamed and reacted. Twisting in the air, the mouse vanished. Matt looked up, his mouth hanging open. Abbie was three feet in the air, hovering like a hummingbird. Slowly she sank down to her chair.

"It works on people, too," Matt whispered. "Try it again. Try it on me."

Matt felt nauseated, as if he had suddenly stepped off the Earth. The room shifted around him. He looked down. He was floating in the air about two feet above the chair he had been sitting on. He was turning slowly, so that the room seemed to revolve around him.

He looked for Abbie, but she was behind him now. Slowly she drifted into view. "That's fine," he said. Abbie looked happier than she had looked for days. She almost smiled.

Matt began to turn more rapidly. In a moment he was spinning like a top; the room flashed into a kaleidoscope. He swallowed hard. "All right," he shouted, "that's enough."

Abruptly he stopped spinning and dropped. His stomach soared up into his throat. He thumped solidly into the chair and immediately hopped up with a howl of anguish. He rubbed himself with both hands.

"Ouch!" he shouted. And then accusingly, "You did that on purpose."

Abbie looked innocent. "I done what you said."

"All right, you did," Matt said bitterly. "From now on, I resign as a guinea pig."

Abbie folded her hands in her lap. "What shall I do?"

"Practice on yourself," Matt said.

"Yes, Mr. Wright." She rose steadily in the air. "This is wonderful." She stretched out as if she were lying in bed. She floated around the room. Matt was reminded of shows in which he had seen magicians producing the same illusion, passing hoops cleverly around their assistant's body to show that there were no wires. Only this wasn't magic; this wasn't illusion; this was real.

Abbie settled back into the chair. Her face was glowing. "I feel like I could do anything," she said. "Now what shall I try?"

Matt thought for a moment. "Can you project yourself?"

"Where to?"

"Oh, anywhere," Matt said impatiently. "It doesn't matter."

"Anywhere?" she repeated. There was a distant and unreadable expression in her eyes.

And then she vanished.

Matt stared at the chair she had been in. She was gone, indisputably gone. He searched the room, a simple process. There was no sign of her. He went outside. The afternoon sun beat down, exposing everything in a harsh light.

"Abbie!" Matt shouted. "Abbie!" He waited. He heard only the echo drifting back from the hills across the lake. For five minutes he roamed about the cabin, shouting and calling, before he gave up.

He went back into the cabin. He sat down and stared moodily at the bunk where Abbie had slept. Where was she now? Was she trapped in some extra dimension, weird and inexplicable to the senses, within which her power could not work.

There had to be some such explanation for teleportation—a fourth-dimensional shortcut across our three. Why not—if she could nullify mass, she could adjust atoms so that they entered one of the other dimensions.

As he brooded, remorse came to him slowly, creeping in so stealthily that awareness of it was like a blow. The whole scheme had been madness. He could not understand now the insane ambition that had led to this tinkering with human lives and the structure of the Universe. He had justified it to himself with the name of science. But the word had no mystic power of absolution.

His motive had been something entirely different. It was only a sublimated lust for power, and thinly disguised at that. The power of knowledge. And for that lust, which she could never understand, an innocent, unsophisticated girl had suffered.

Was Abbie dead? Perhaps that was the most merciful thing.

Ends can never justify means, Matt realized now. They are too inextricably intertwined ever to be separated. The means inevitably shape the ends. In the long view, there are neither means nor ends, for the means are only an infinite series of ends, and the ends are an infinite series of means . . .

And Abbie appeared. Like an Arabian genie, with gifts upon a tray, streaming a mouth-watering incense through the air. Full-formed, she sprang into being, her cheeks glowing, her eyes shining.

"Abbie!" Matt shouted joyfully. His heart gave a sharp bound, as if it had suddenly been released from an unbearable weight. "Where have you been?"

"Springfield."

"Springfield!" Matt gasped. "But that's over fifty miles."

Abbie lowered the tray to the table. She snapped her fingers. "Like that, I was there."

Matt's eyes fell to the tray. It was loaded with cooked food: shrimp cocktail, broiled lobster tails, french fried . . .

Abbie smiled. "I got hungry."

"But where—?" Matt began. "You went back to the restaurant," he said accusingly, "you took the food from there."

Abbie nodded happily. "I was hungry."

"But that's stealing," Matt moaned. And he realized for the first time the enormity of the thing he had done, what he had let loose upon the world. Nothing was safe. Neither money nor jewels nor deadly secrets. Nothing at all.

"They won't ever miss it," Abbie said, "and nobody saw me." She said it simply, as the ultimate justification.

Matt was swept by the staggering realization that where her basic drives were concerned Abbie was completely unmoral. There was only one small hope. If he could keep her from realizing her civilization-shattering potentialities! They might never occur to her.

"Sure," Matt said. "Sure."

Abbie ate heartily, but Matt had no appetite. He sat thoughtfully, watching her eat, and he experienced a brief thankfulness that at least she wasn't going to starve to death.

"Didn't you have any trouble?" he asked. "Getting the food without anyone seeing you?"

Abbie nodded. "I couldn't decide how to get into the kitchen. I could see that the cook was all alone . . ."

"You could see?"

"I was outside, but I could see into the kitchen, somehow. So finally, I called 'Albert!' And the cook went out and I went in and took the food that was sitting on the tray and came back here. It was really simple, because the cook was expecting someone to call him."

"How did you know that?"

"I thought it," Abbie said, frowning. "Like this." She concentrated for a moment. He watched her, puzzled, and then knew what she meant. Panic caught him by the throat. There were things she shouldn't know. Because he was trying so hard to bury them deep, they scuttled across his consciousness. Telepathy!

And as he watched her face, he knew that he was right. Her eyes grew wide and incredulous. Slowly, something hard and cruelly cold slipped over her face like a mask. *Oh, Abbie! My sweet, gentle Abbie!*

"You—" she gasped. "You devil! There ain't nothin' too bad for anyone who'd do that!" *I'm a dead man,* Matt thought.

"You with your kindness and your handsome face and your city manners," Abbie said pitifully. "How could you do it? You made me fall in love with you. It wasn't hard, was it? All you had to do was hold a little hill girl's hand in the moonlight an' kiss her once, an' she was ready to jump into bed with you. But you didn't want anything as natural as that. All the time you was laughing and scheming. Poor little hill girl!

"You make me think you like me so well you want me to look real purty in new clothes and new hair and a new face. But it's just a trick. All the time it's a trick. When I'm feeling happiest and most grateful, you take it all away. I'd sooner you hit me across the face. Poor little hill girl! Thinking you wanted her. Thinking maybe you were aiming to marry her. I wanted to die. Even Paw was never that mean. He never done anything a-purpose, like you."

White-faced, Matt watched her, his mind racing.

"You're thinking you can get around me somehow," Abbie said, "and I'll forget. You can make me think it was all a mistake. 'Tain't no use. You can't, not ever, because I know what you're thinking."

What *had* he been thinking? Had he actually thought of marrying her? Just for a second? He shuddered. It would be hell. Imagine, if you can, a wife who is all-knowing, all-powerful, who can never be evaded, avoided, sighed to, lied to, shut out, shut up. Imagine a wife who can make a room a shambles in a second, who can throw dishes and chairs and tables with equal facility and deadly accuracy. Imagine a wife who can be any place, any time, in the flicker of a suspicion. Imagine a wife who can see through walls and read minds and maybe wish you a raging headache or a broken leg or aching joints.

It would be worse than hell. The torments of the damned would be pleasant compared to that.

Abbie's chin came up. "You don't need to worry. I'd as soon marry up with a rattlesnake. At least he gives you warning before he strikes."

"Kill me!" Matt said desperately. "Go ahead and kill me!"

Abbie smiled sweetly. "Killing's too good for you. I don't know anything that ain't too good for you. But don't worry, I'll think of something. Now, go away and leave me alone."

Thankfully, Matt started to turn. Before he could complete it, he found himself outside the cabin. He blinked in the light of the sinking sun. He began to shiver. After a little he sat down on the porch and lit a cigarette. There had to be some way out of this. There was always a way.

From inside the cabin came the sound of running water. *Running water!* Matt resisted an impulse to get up and investigate the mystery. "Leave me alone," Abbie had said, in a tone that Matt didn't care to challenge.

A few minutes later he heard the sound of splashing and Abbie's voice lifted in a sweet soprano. Although he couldn't understand the words, the tune sent chills down his back. And then a phrase came clear:

Root-a-toot-toot
Three times she did shoot
Right through that hardwood door.
He was her man,
But he done her wrong. . . .

Matt began to shake. He passed a trembling hand across his sweaty forehead and wondered if he had a fever. He tried to pull himself together, for he had to think clearly. The situation was obvious. He had done a fiendishly cruel thing—no matter what the excuse—and he had been caught and the power of revenge was in the hands of the one he had wronged, never more completely.

The only question was: What form would the revenge take? When he knew that, he might be able to figure out a way to evade it. There was no question in his mind about waiting meekly for justice to strike.

The insurmountable difficulty was that the moment he thought of a plan, it would be unworkable because Abbie would be forewarned. And she was already armed. He had to stop thinking.

How do you stop thinking? he thought miserably. *Stop thinking!* he told himself. *Stop thinking, damn you!*

He might be on the brink of the perfect solution. But if he thought of it, it would be worthless. And if he couldn't think of it, then—

The circle was complete. He was back where he started, staring at its perfect viciousness. There was only one possi—

Mary had a little lamb with fleece as white as snow and everywhere that Mary went (Relax) *the lamb* (Don't think!) *was sure* (Act on the spur of the moment) *to go. Mary had a* . . .

"Well, Mr. Wright, are you ready to go?" Matt started. Beside him were a pair of black suede shoes filled with small feet. His gaze traveled up the lovely, nylon-sheathed legs, up the clinging black dress that swelled so provocatively, to the face with its blue eyes and red lips and blonde hair.

Even in his pressing predicament, Matt had to recognize the impact of her beauty. It was a pity that her other gifts were too terrible.

"I reckon your fiancée won't mind," Abbie said sweetly. "Being as you ain't got a fiancée. Are you ready?"

"Ready?" Matt looked down at his soiled work clothes. "For what?"

"You're ready," Abbie said.

A wave of dizziness swept him, followed by a wave of nausea. Matt shut his eyes. They receded. When he opened his eyes again, he had a frightening sensation of disorientation. Then he recognized his surroundings. He was on the dance floor in Springfield.

Abbie came into his arms. "All right," she said, "dance!"

Shocked, Matt began to dance, mechanically. He realized that people were staring at them as if they had dropped through a hole in the ceiling. Matt wasn't sure they hadn't. Only two other couples were on the small floor, but they had stopped dancing and were looking puzzled.

As Matt swung Abbie slowly around he saw that the sprinkling of customers at the bar had turned to stare, too. A waiter in a white jacket was coming toward them, frowning determinedly.

Abbie seemed as unconcerned about the commotion she had caused as the rainbow-hued juke box in the corner. It thumped away just below Matt's conscious level of recognition. Abbie danced lightly in his arms.

The waiter tapped Matt on the shoulder. Matt sighed with relief and stopped dancing. Immediately he found himself moving perkily around the floor like a puppet. Abbie, he gathered, did not care to stop.

The waiter followed doggedly. "Stop that!" he said bewilderedly. "I don't know where you came from or what you think you're doing, but you can't do it in here and you can't do it dressed like that."

"I—I c-can-n't s-st-stop-p!" Matt said jerkily.

"Sure you can," the waiter said soothingly. He plodded along after them. "There's lots of things a man can't do, but he can always stop whatever you're doing. I should think you'd be glad to stop."

"W-w-would," Matt got out. "S-st-stop-p!" he whispered to Abbie.

"Tell the man to go 'way," Abbie whispered back.

Matt decided to start dancing again. It was easier than being shaken to pieces. "I think you'd better go away," he said to the waiter.

"We don't like to use force," the waiter said, frowning, "but we have to keep up a standard for our patrons. Come along quietly"—he jerked on Matt's arm—"or—"

The grip on Matt's arm was suddenly gone. The waiter vanished. Matt looked around wildly.

The juke box had a new decoration. Dazed, opaque-eyed, the waiter squatted on top of the box, his white jacket and whiter face a dark fool's motley in the swirling lights.

Abbie pressed herself close. Matt shuddered and swung her slowly around the floor. On the next turn, he saw that the waiter had climbed down from his perch. He had recruited reinforcements. Grim-faced and silent, the waiter approached, followed by another waiter, a lantern-jawed bartender, and an ugly bulldog of a man in street clothes. The manager, Matt decided.

They formed a menacing ring around Matt and Abbie. "Whatever your game is," growled the bulldog, "we don't want to play. If you don't leave damn quick, you're going to wish you had."

Matt, looking at him, believed it. He tried to stop. Again his limbs began to jerk uncontrollably.

"I-I c-can-n't," he said. "D-d-don't y-you th-think I-I w-would if I-I c-could?"

The manager stared at him with large, awed, bloodshot eyes. "Yeah," he said. "I guess you would." He shook himself. His jowls wobbled. "Okay, boys. Let's get rid of them."

"Watch yourself," said the first waiter uneasily. "One of them has a trick throw."

They closed in. Matt felt Abbie stiffen against him. They vanished, one after the other, like candles being snuffed. Matt glanced unhappily at the juke box. There they were on top of the box, stacked in each other's laps like a totem pole. The pile teetered and collapsed in all directions. Dull thuds made themselves heard even above the juke box. Matt saw them get up, puzzled and wary. The bartender was rubbing his nose. He doubled his fists and started to rush out on the floor. The manager, a wirier sort, grabbed his arm. The four of them went into consultation. Every few seconds one of them would raise his head and stare at Matt and Abbie. Finally the first waiter detached himself from the group and with an air of finality reached behind the juke box. Abruptly the music stopped; the colored lights went out. Silence fell. The four of them turned triumphantly toward the floor.

Just as abruptly, the lights went back on; the music boomed out again. They jumped.

Defiantly, the manager stepped to the wall and pulled the plug from the socket. He turned, still holding the cord. It stirred in his hand. The manager looked down at it incredulously. It wriggled. He dropped it hurriedly, with revulsion. The plug rose cobra-like from its coils and began a slow, deadly, weaving dance. The manager stared, hypnotized with disbelief.

The cord struck. The manager leaped back. The bared, metal fangs bit into the floor. They retreated, all four of them, watching with wide eyes. Contemptuously, the cord turned its back on them, wriggled its way to the socket, and plugged itself in.

The music returned. Matt danced on with leaden legs. He could not stop. He would never stop. He thought of the fairy tale of the red shoes. Abbie seemed as fresh and determined as ever.

As the juke box came into sight again, Matt noticed some commotion around it. The bartender was approaching the manager with an axe, a glittering fire axe. For one whirling moment, Matt thought the whole world had gone mad. Then he saw the manager take the axe and approach the juke box cautiously, the axe poised in one hand ready to strike.

He brought it down smartly. The cord squirmed its coils out of the way. The manager wrenched the axe from the floor. Bravely he advanced closer. He looked down and screamed. The cord had a loop around one leg; the loop was tightening. Frantically the manager swung again and again. One stroke hit the cord squarely. It parted. The music stopped. The box went dark. The headless cord squirmed in dying agonies.

Abbie stopped dancing. Matt stood still, his legs trembling, sighing with relief.

"Let's go, Abbie," he pleaded. "Let's go quick."

She shook her head. "Let's sit." She led him to a table which, like the rest of the room, had been suddenly vacated of patrons. "I reckon you'd like a drink."

"I'd rather leave," Matt muttered.

They sat down. Imperiously, Abbie beckoned at the waiter.

He came toward the table cautiously. Abbie looked inquiringly at Matt.

"Bourbon," Matt said helplessly. "Straight." In a moment the waiter was back with a bottle and two glasses on a tray. "The boss said to get the money first," he said timidly.

Matt searched his pockets futilely. He looked at the manager, standing against one wall, glowering, his arms folded across his chest. "I haven't got any money on me," Matt said.

"That's all right," Abbie said. "Just set the things down."

"No, ma'am," the waiter began, and his eyes rolled as the tray floated out of his hand and settled to the table. He stopped talking, shut his mouth, and backed away.

Abbie was brooding, her chin in one small hand. "I ain't been a good daughter," she said. "Paw would like it here."

"No, no," Matt said hurriedly. "Don't do that. We've got enough trouble—"

Jenkins was sitting in the third chair, blinking slowly, reeking of alcohol. Matt reached for the bottle and sloshed some into a glass. He raised it to his lips and tossed it off. The liquor burned his throat for a moment and then was gone. Matt waited expectantly as he lowered the glass to the table. He felt nothing, nothing at all. He looked suspiciously at the glass. It was still full.

Jenkins focused his eyes. "Ab!" he said. He seemed to cringe in his chair. "What you doin' here? You look different. All fixed up. Find a feller with money?"

Abbie ignored his questions. "If I asked you to do some-thin', Paw, would you do it?"

"Sure, Ab," Jenkins said hurriedly. His eyes lit on the bottle of bourbon. "Anything." He raised the bottle to his lips. It gurgled pleasantly and went on gurgling.

Matt watched the level of amber liquid drop in the bottle, but when Jenkins put it down and wiped his bearded lips with one large hairy hand, the bottle was half empty and stayed that way. Jenkins sighed heavily.

Matt raised his glass again and tilted it to his lips. When he lowered it, the glass was still full and Matt was still empty. He stared moodily at the glass.

"If I asked you to hit Mr. Wright in the nose," Abbie went on, "I reckon you'd do it?"

Matt tensed himself.

"Sure, Ab, sure," Jenkins said. He turned his massive head slowly. He doubled his fist. The expression behind the beard was unreadable, but Matt decided that it was better that way. "Ain't you been treatin' mah little gal right?" Jenkins demanded. "Say, son," he said with concern, "you don't look so good." He looked back at Abbie. "Want I should hit him?"

"Not now," Abbie said. "But keep it in mind."

Matt relaxed and seized the opportunity to dash the glass to his mouth. Futilely. Not a drop of liquor reached his stomach. Hopelessly, Matt thought of Tantalus.

"Police!" Jenkins bellowed suddenly, rising up with the neck of the bottle in one huge hand.

Matt looked. The bartender was leading three policemen into the front of the room. The officers advanced stolidly, confident of their ultimate strength and authority. Matt turned quickly to Abbie.

"No tricks," he pleaded. "Not with the law."

Abbie yawned. "I'm tired. I reckon it's almost midnight."

Jenkins charged, bull-like, bellowing with rage. And the room vanished.

Matt bunked, sickened. They were back in the cabin, Abbie and he. "What about your father?" Matt asked.

"Next to liquor," Abbie said, "Paw likes a fight best. I'm going to bed now. I'm real tired."

She left her shoes on the floor, climbed into her bunk, and pulled the blanket around herself.

Matt walked slowly to his bunk, *Mary had a little lamb* . . . He sat down on it and pulled off his shoes, letting them thump to the floor . . . *with fleece as white as snow* . . . He pulled the blanket around his bunk and made rustling sounds, but he lay down without removing his clothes . . . *and everywhere that Mary went* . . . He lay stiffly, listening to the immediate sounds of deep breathing coming from the other bunk . . . *the lamb was sure to go* . . .

Two tortured hours crawled by. Matt sat up cautiously. He picked up his shoes from the floor. He straightened up. Slowly he tiptoed toward the door. Inch by inch, listening to Abbie's steady breathing, until he was at the door. He slipped it open, only a foot. He squeezed through and drew it shut behind him.

A porch board creaked. Matt froze. He waited. There was no sound from inside. He crept over the pebbles of the driveway, suppressing exclamations of pain. But he did not dare stop to put on his shoes.

He was beside the car. He eased the door open and slipped into the seat. Blessing the steep driveway, he released the brake and pushed in the clutch. The car began to roll. Slowly at first, then picking up speed, the car turned out of the driveway into the road.

Ghostlike in the brilliant moon, it sped silent down the long hill. After one harrowing tree-darkened turn, Matt switched on the lights and gently clicked the door to its first catch.

When he was a mile away, he started the motor.

Escape!

Matt pulled up to the gas pump in the gray dawn that was already sticky with heat. Through the dusty, bug-splattered windshield the bloodshot sun peered at him and saw a I dark young man in stained work clothes, his face stubbled blackly, his eyes burning wearily. But Matt breathed deep; he drew in the wine of freedom.

Was this Fair Play or Humansville? Matt was too tired and hungry to remember. Whichever it was, all was well.

It seemed a reasonable assumption that Abbie could not find him if she did not know where he was, that she could not teleport herself anywhere she had not already been. When she had disappeared the first time, she had gone to the places in Springfield she knew. She had brought her father from his two-room shanty. She had taken him back to the cabin.

The sleepy attendant approached, and with him came a wash of apprehension to knot his stomach. Money! He had no money. Hopelessly he began to search his pockets. Without money he was stuck here, and all his money was back in his cabin with his clothes and his typewriter and his manila folder of notes.

And then his hand touched something in his hip pocket. Wonderingly, he pulled it out. It was his billfold. He peered at its contents. Four dollars in bills and three hundred in traveler's checks. "Fill it up," he said.

When had he picked up the billfold? Or had he had it all the time? He could have sworn that he had not had it when he was in the cocktail lounge in Springfield. He was almost sure that he had left it in his suit pants. The uncertainty made him vaguely uneasy. Or was it only hunger? He hadn't eaten since toying with Abbie's stolen delicacies yesterday afternoon.

"Where's a good place to eat?" he asked, as the attendant handed him change.

It was an old fellow in coveralls. He pointed a few hundred feet up the road. "See those trucks parked outside that diner?" Matt nodded. "Usual thing, when you see them outside, you can depend on good food inside. Here it don't mean a thing. Food's lousy. We got a landmark though. Truckers stop to see it." The old fellow cackled. "Name's Lola."

As Matt pulled away, the old man called after him. "Don't make no difference, anyway. No place else open."

Matt parked beside one of the large trailer trucks. Lola? He made a wry face as he got out of the car. He was through with women.

The diner, built in the shape of a railroad car, had a long counter running along one side, but it was filled with truckers in shirt sleeves, big men drinking coffee and smoking and teasing the waitress. Tiredly, Matt slipped into one of the empty booths.

The waitress detached herself from her admirers immediately and came to the booth with a glass of water in one hand, swinging her hips confidently. She had a smoldering, dark beauty, and she was well aware of it. Her black hair was cut short, and her brown eyes and tanned face were smiling. Her skirt and low-cut peasant blouse bulged generously in the right places. Some time—and not too many years in the future—she would be fat, but right now she was lush, ready to be picked by the right hand. Matt guessed that she would not be a waitress in a small town long. As she put the water on the table, she bent low to demonstrate just how lush she was.

The neckline drooped. Against his will, Matt's eyes drifted toward her.

"What'll you have?" the waitress said softly.

Matt swallowed. "A couple of—hotcakes," he said, "with sausages."

She straightened up slowly, smiling brightly at him. "Stack a pair," she yelled, "with links." She turned around and looked enticingly over her shoulder. "Coffee?"

Matt nodded. He smiled a little to show that he appreciated her attentions. There was no doubt about the fact that she was an attractive girl. In anyone's mind. Any other time . . .

"Ouch!" she said suddenly and straightened. She began to rub her rounded bottom vigorously and cast Matt a hurt, reproachful glance. Slowly her pained expression changed to a roguish smile. She waggled a coy finger at Matt. "Naughty, naughty!" the finger said. Matt stared at her as if she had lost her senses. He shook his head in bewilderment as she vanished behind the counter. And then he noticed that a couple of the truckers had turned around to glower at him, and Matt became absorbed in contemplating the glass of water.

It made him realize how thirsty he was. He drank the whole glassful, but it didn't seem to help much. He was just as thirsty, just as empty.

Lola wasted no time in bringing Mart's cup of coffee. She carried it casually and efficiently in one hand, not spilling a drop into the saucer. But as she neared Matt the inexplicable happened. She tripped over something invisible on the smooth floor. She stumbled. The coffee flew in a steaming arc and splashed on Mart's shirt with incredible accuracy, soaking in hotly.

Lola gasped, her hand to her mouth. Matt leaped up, pulling his shirt away from his chest, swearing. Lola grabbed a handful of paper napkins and began to dab at his shirt.

"Golly, honey, I'm sorry," she said warmly. "I can't understand how I came to trip."

She pressed herself close to him. Matt could smell the odor of gardenias.

"That's all right," he said, drawing back. "It was an accident."

She followed him, working at his shirt. Matt noticed that the truckers were all watching, some darkly, the rest enviously. He slipped back into the booth.

One of the truckers guffawed. "You don't have to spill coffee on me, Lola, to make me steam," he said. The rest of the truckers laughed with him.

"Oh, shut up!" Lola told them. She turned back to Matt. "You all right, honey?"

"Sure, sure," Matt said wearily. "Just bring me the hot-cakes." The coffee had cooled now. His shirt felt clammy. Matt thought about accident prones. It had to be an accident. He glanced uneasily around the diner. The only girl here was Lola.

The hotcakes were ready. She was bringing them toward the booth, but it was not a simple process. Matt had never seen slippery hotcakes before this. Lola was so busy that she forgot to swing her hips.

The hotcakes slithered from side to side on the plate. Lola juggled them, tilting the plate back and forth to keep them from sliding off. Her eyes were wide with astonishment; her mouth was a round, red "O"; her forehead was furrowed with concentration. She did an intricate, unconscious dance step to keep from losing the top hotcake.

As Matt watched, fascinated, the sausages, four of them linked together, started to slip from the plate. With something approaching sentience, they spilled off and disappeared down the low neck of Lola's blouse.

Lola shrieked. She started to wriggle, her shoulders hunched. While she tried to balance the hotcakes with one hand, the other dived into the blouse and hunted around frantically. Matt watched; the truckers watched. Lola hunted and wiggled. The hand that held the plate flew up. The hot-cakes scattered.

One hit the nearest trucker in the face. He peeled it off, red and bellowing. "A joker!" He dived off the stool toward Matt.

Matt tried to get up, but the table caught him in his stomach. He climbed up on the seat. The hotcake the trucker had discarded had landed on the head of the man next to him. He stood up angrily.

Lola had finally located the elusive sausages. She drew them out of their intimate hiding place with a shout of triumph. They whipped into the open mouth of the lunging trucker. He stopped, transfixed, strangling.

"Argh-gh-uggle!" he said.

A cup crashed against the wall, close to Matt's head. Matt ducked. If he could get over the back of this booth, he could reach the door. The place was filled with angry shouts and angrier faces and bulky shoulders approaching. Lola took one frightened look and grabbed Matt around the knees.

"Protect me!" she said wildly.

The air was filled with missiles. Matt reached down to disengage Lola's fear-strengthened arms. He glanced up to see the trucker spitting out the last of the sausages. With a maddened yell, the trucker threw a heavy fist at Matt. Hampered as he was, Matt threw himself back hopelessly. Something ripped. The fist breezed past and crashed through a window.

Matt hung over the back of the booth, head downward, unable to get back up, unable to shake Lola loose. Everywhere he looked he could see rage-inflamed faces. He closed his eyes and surrendered himself to his fate.

From somewhere, above the tumult, came the sound of laughter, like the tinkling of little silver bells.

Then Matt was outside with no idea of how he had got there. In his hand was a strip of thin fabric. Lola's blouse. *Poor Lola,* he thought, as he threw it away. What was his fatal fascination for girls?

Behind him the diner was alive with lights and the crash of dishes and the smacking of fists on flesh. Before long they would discover that he was gone.

Matt ran to his car. It started to life when he punched the button. He backed it up, screeched it to a stop, jerked into first, and barreled onto the driveway. Within twenty seconds, he was doing sixty.

He turned to look back at the diner and almost lost control of the car as he tried to absorb the implications of the contents on the back seat.

Resting neatly there were his typewriter, notes, and all his clothes.

When Matt pulled to a stop on the streets of Clinton, he was feeling easier mentally and much worse physically. The dip in a secluded stream near the road, the change of clothes, and the shave—torturing as it had been in cold water—had refreshed him for a while. But that had worn off, and the lack of a night's sleep and twenty-four hours without food were catching up with him.

Better that, he thought grimly, than Abbie. He could endure anything for a time.

As for the typewriter and the notes and the clothes, there was probably some simple explanation. The one Matt liked best was that Abbie had had a change of heart; she had expected him to leave and she had made his way easy. She was, Matt thought, a kind-hearted child underneath it all.

The trouble with that explanation was that Matt didn't believe it.

He shrugged. There were more pressing things—money, for instance. Gas was getting low, and he needed to get something in his stomach if he was to keep up his strength for the long drive ahead. He had to cash one of his checks. That seemed simple enough. The bank was at the corner of this block. It was eleven o'clock. The bank would be open. Naturally they would cash a check.

But for some reason Matt felt uneasy. Matt walked into the bank and went directly to a window. He countersigned one of the checks and presented it to the teller, a thin little man with a wispy mustache and a bald spot on top of his head. The teller compared the signatures and turned to the shelf at his side where bills stood in piles, some still wrapped. He counted out four twenties, a ten, a five, and five ones.

"Here you are, sir," he said politely.

Matt accepted it only because his hand was outstretched and the teller put the money in it. His eyes were fixed in horror upon a wrapped bundle of twenty-dollar bills which was slowing rising from the shelf. It climbed leisurely over the top of the cage.

"What's the matter, sir?" the teller asked in alarm. "Do you feel sick?"

Matt nodded once and then tore his eyes away and shook his head vigorously. "No," he gasped. "I'm all right." He took a step back from the window.

"Are you sure? You don't look well at all."

With a shrinking feeling, Matt felt something fumble its way into his right-hand coat pocket. He plunged his hand in after it. His empty stomach revolved in his abdomen. He could not mistake the touch of crisp paper. He stooped quickly beneath the teller's window. The teller leaned out. Matt straightened up, the package of bills in his hand.

"I guess you must have dropped this," he muttered.

The teller glanced at the shelf and back at the sheaf of twenties. "I don't see how—But thank you! That's the funniest—"

Matt pushed the bills under the grillwork. "Yes, isn't it," he agreed hurriedly. "Well, thank you."

"Thank you!"

Matt lifted his hand. The money lifted with it. The package stuck to his hand as if it had been attached with glue.

"Excuse me," he said feebly. "I can't seem to get rid of this money." He shook his hand. The money clung stubbornly. He shook his hand again, violently. The package of bills did not budge.

"Very funny," the teller said, but he was not smiling. From his tone of voice, Matt suspected that he thought money was a very serious business indeed. The teller reached under the bars and caught hold of one end of the package. "You can let go now," he said. "Let go!"

Matt tried to pull his hand away. "I can't!" he said, breathing heavily.

The teller tugged, Matt tugged. "I haven't time to play games," the teller panted. "Let go!"

"I don't want it," Matt said frantically. "But it seems to be stuck. Look!" He showed his hand, fingers spread wide.

The teller grabbed the bundle of bills with both hands and braced his feet against the front of his cubicle. "Let go!" he shouted.

Matt pulled hard. Suddenly the tension on his arm vanished. His arm whipped back. The teller disappeared into the bottom of the cubicle. Something clanged hollowly. Matt looked at his hand. The bills were gone.

Slowly the teller's head appeared from the concealed part of the cubicle. It came up, accompanied by groans, with a red swelling in the middle of the bald spot. After it came the teller's hand, waving the package of twenties triumphantly. The other hand was rubbing his head.

"Are you still here?" he demanded, slamming the bills down at his side. "Get out of this bank. And if you ever come back I'll have you arrested for—for disturbing the peace."

"Don't worry," Matt said. "I won't be back." His face suddenly grew pale. "Stop," he said frantically, waving his arms. "Go back!"

The teller stared at him, fearfully, indecisively. The bundle of twenties was rising over the top of the cage again. Instinctively, Matt grabbed them out of the air. His mind clicked rapidly. If he was to keep out of jail, there was only one thing to do. He advanced on the teller angrily, waving the bills in the air.

"What do you mean by throwing these at me!"

"Throwing money?" the teller said weakly. "Me?" Matt shook the bills in front of the teller's nose. "What do you call this?"

The clerk glanced at the money and down at his side. "Oh, no!" he moaned.

"I have a good mind," Matt said violently, "to complain to the president of this bank." He slammed the bills down. He closed his eyes in a silent prayer. "Tellers throwing money around!"

He took his hand away. Blissfully, the money stayed where it was on the counter. The teller reached for it feebly. The package shifted. He reached *again*. The bills slid away. He stuck both hands through the slot and groped wildly. The money slipped between his arms into the cage.

Matt stood shifting his weight from foot to foot, paralyzed between flight and fascination. The bundle winged its way around in the cage like a drunken butterfly. Wide-eyed and frantic, the teller chased it from side to side. He made great diving swoops for it, his hands cupped into a net. He crept up on it and pounced, catlike, only to have it slip between his fingers at the last moment. Suddenly he stopped, frozen. His hands flew to his head.

"My God!" he screamed. "What am I doing? I'm mad!" Matt backed toward the door. The other clerks and tellers were running toward the center of the disturbance. Matt saw a dignified gentleman with a paunch stand up inside a railed-in office and hurdle the obstacle with fine show of athletic form.

Matt turned and ran, dodging the guard at the gate. "Get the doctor," he yelled.

From somewhere came the sound of a tinkling of little silver bells.

There was no doubt in Matt's mind as he gunned his car out of Clinton. Abbie was after him. He had not been free a moment. All the time she had known where to find him. He was the fleeing mouse, happy in his illusion of freedom—until the cat's paw comes down on his back. Matt thought of the Furies—awful Alecto, Tisiphone, Megaera—in their bloodstained robes and serpent hair pursuing him across the world with their terrible whips. But they all had Abbie's face.

Matt drove north toward Kansas City, thirsty, starving, half dead from fatigue, wondering hopelessly where it would end.

Darkening shades of violet were creeping up the eastern sky as Matt reached Lawrence, Kansas. He had not tried to stop in Kansas City. Something had drawn him on, some buried hope that still survived feebly, and when, five miles from Lawrence, he had seen Mount Oread rise against the sunset, the white spires and red tile roofs of the university gleaming like beacons, he had known what it was.

Here was a citadel of knowledge, a fortress of the world's truth against black waves of ignorance and superstition. Here, in this saner atmosphere of study and reflection, logic and cool consideration, here, if anywhere, he could shake off this dark conviction of doom that sapped his will. Here, surely, he could think more clearly, act more decisively, rid himself of this demon of vengeance that rode his shoulders. Here he could get help.

He drove down Massachusetts Street, his body leaden with fatigue, his eyes red-rimmed and shadowed, searching restlessly from side to side. His hunger was only a dull ache; he could almost forget it. But his thirst was a live thing. Somewhere—he could not remember where—he had eaten and drunk, but the meal had vanished from his throat as he swallowed.

Is there no end? he thought wildly. *Is there no way out?* There was, of course. There always is. *Always—Mary had a little lamb . . .*

Impulse swung his car into the diagonal parking space. First he was going to drink and eat, come what may. He walked into the restaurant. Summer students filled the room, young men in sport shirts and slacks, girls in gay cotton prints and saddle shoes, laughing, talking, eating . . .

Swaying in the doorway, Matt watched them, bleary-eyed. *Once I was like them,* he thought dully. *Young and alive and conscious that these were the best years I would ever know. Now I am old and used up, doomed . . .*

He slumped down at a table near the front, filled with a great surge of sorrow that all happiness was behind him. He was conscious that the waitress was beside him. "Soup," he mumbled. "Soup and milk." He did not look up.

"Yes, sir," she said. Her voice sounded vaguely familiar, but they are all the same, all the voices of youth. He had eaten here before. He did not look up.

Slowly he raised the glass of water to his lips. It went down his throat in dusty gulps. It spread out in his stomach in cool, blessed waves. Matt closed his eyes thankfully. The hunger pains began to return. For a moment Matt regretted the soup and wished he had ordered steak. *After the soup,* he thought.

The soup came. Matt lifted a spoonful. He let it trickle down his throat.

"Feelin' better, Mr. Wright?" said the waitress. Matt looked up. He strangled. It was Abbie! Abbie's face bending over him. Matt choked and spluttered. Students turned to stare. Matt gazed around the room wildly. The girls—they all looked like Abbie. He stood up, almost knocking over the table as he ran to the front door.

With his hand on the doorknob, he stopped, paralyzed. Staring in at him, through the glass, was a pair of bloodshot eyes set above an unruly black nest. Stooped, powerful shoulders loomed behind the face. As Matt stared back, the eyes lighted up as if they recognized him. "Argh-gh!" Matt screamed.

He staggered back and turned on trembling leers. He tottered toward the back of the restaurant. The aisle seemed full of feet put out to trip him. He stumbled to the swinging kitchen door and broke through into odors of frying and baking that no longer moved him.

The cook looked up, startled. Matt ran on through the kitchen and plunged through the back door. The alley was dark. Matt barked his shins on a box. He limped on, cursing. At one end of the alley a street light spread a pool of welcome. Matt ran toward it. He was panting. His heart beat fast. Then it almost stopped. A shadow lay along the mouth of the alley. A long shadow with huge shoulders and something that waved from the chin.

Matt spun. He ran frantically toward the other end of the alley. His mind raced like an engine that has broken its governor. Nightmarish terror streaked through his arms and legs; they seemed distant and leaden. But slowly he approached the other end. He came nearer. Nearer.

A shadow detached itself from the dark back walls. But it was no shadow. Matt slowed, stopped. The shadow came closer, towering tall above him. Matt cowered, unable to move. Closer. Two long arms reached out toward him. Matt quivered. He waited for the end. The arms wrapped around him. They drew him close.

"Son, son," Jenkins said weakly. "Yore the first familiar face I seen all day."

Matt's heart started beating again. He drew back, extracting his face from Jenkins' redolent beard.

"Cain't understand what's goin' on these days," Jenkins said, shaking his head sadly, "but I got a feelin' Ab's behint it. Just as that fight got goin' good, the whole shebang disappeared and here I was. Where am I, son?"

"Kansas," Matt said. "Lawrence, Kansas."

"Kansas?" Jenkins wobbled his beard. "Last I heard, Kansas was dry, but it cain't be half as dry as I am. I recollect hearin' Quantrill burned this town. Too bad it didn't stay burned. Here I was without a penny in my pocket and only what was left in the bottle I had in my hand to keep me from dyin' of thirst. Son," he said sorrowfully, "somethin's got to be done. It's Ab, ain't it?"

Matt nodded.

"Son," Jenkins went on, "I'm gettin' too old for this kind of life. I should be sittin' on my porch with a jug in my lap, just a-rockin' slow. Somethin's got to be done about that gal."

"I'm afraid it's too late for that," Matt said. "That's the trouble," Jenkins said mournfully. "Been too late for these six years. Son, yore an edycated man. What we gonna do?"

"I can't tell you, Jenkins," Matt said. "I can't even think about it." *Mary had a little lamb* . . . "If I did, it wouldn't work. But if you want to hit me, go ahead. I'm the man who's responsible."

Jenkins put a large hand on his shoulder. "Don't worry about it, son. If it weren't you, it would've been some other man. When Ab gets a notion, you cain't beat it out of her. I learned that years ago."

Matt pulled out his billfold and handed Jenkins a five-dollar bill. "Here. Kansas isn't dry any more. Go get something and try to forget. Maybe when you're finished with that, things will have changed."

"Yore a good boy, son. Don't do nothin' rash." *Mary had a little lamb* . . .

Jenkins turned, raising his hand in a parting salute. Matt watched the mountainous shadow dwindle, as if it was his last contact with the living. Then Jenkins rounded the corner and was out of sight.

Matt walked slowly back to Massachusetts Street. There was one more thing he had to do.

As he reached the car, Matt sensed Abbie's nearness. The awareness was so sharp that it was almost physical. He felt her all around, like dancing motes of dust that are only visible under certain conditions, half angel, half devil, half love, half hate. It was an unendurable mixture, an impossible combination to live with. The extremes were too great.

Matt sighed. It was not Abbie's fault. If it was anyone's fault, it was his. Inevitably, he would pay for it. The Universe has an immutable law of action and reaction.

It was dark as Matt drove along Seventh Street. The night was warm, and the infrequent street lights were only beacons for night-flying insects. Matt turned a corner and pulled up in front of a big old house surrounded by an ornamental iron fence. The house was a two-story stucco, painted yel-low—or perhaps it had once been white—and the fence sagged in places.

Most of the houses in Lawrence are old. The finest and the newest are in the west, on the ridge overlooking the Wakarusa Valley, but university professors cannot afford such sites or such houses.

Matt rang the bell. In a moment the door opened. Blinking out of the light was Professor Franklin, his faculty adviser.

"Matt!" Franklin said. "I didn't recognize you for a second. What are you doing back so soon? I thought you were secluded in the Ozarks. Don't tell me you have your thesis finished already?"

"No, Dr. Franklin," Matt said wearily, "but I'd like to talk to you for a moment if you can spare the time."

"Come in, come in. I'm just grading some papers." Franklin grimaced. "Freshman papers."

Franklin led the way into his book-cluttered study off the living room. His glasses were resting on top of a pile of papers. He picked them up, slipped them on, and turned to Matt. He was a tall man, a little stooped now in his sixties, with gray, unruly hair.

"Matt!" he exclaimed. "You aren't looking well. Have you been sick?"

"In a way," Matt said, "you might call it that. How would you treat someone who believes in the reality of psychic phenomena?"

Franklin shrugged. "Lots of people believe in it and are still worth-while, reliable members of society. Conan Doyle, for instance—"

"And could prove it," Matt added.

"Hallucinations? Then it becomes more serious. I suppose psychiatric treatment would be necessary. Remember, Matt, I'm a teacher, not a practi-tioner. But look here, you aren't suggesting that—?"

Matt nodded. "I can prove it, and I don't want to. Would it make the world any better, any happier?"

"The truth is always important—for itself if for nothing else. But you can't be serious—"

"Dead serious." Matt shivered. "Suppose I could prove that there were actually such things as levitation, teleportation, telepathy. There isn't any treatment, is there, Professor, when a man goes sane?"

"Matt! You are sick, aren't you?"

"Suppose," Matt went on relentlessly, "that your glasses should float over and come to rest on my nose. What would you say then?"

"I'd say you need to see a psychiatrist," Franklin said worriedly. "You do, Matt."

His glasses gently detached themselves and floated leisurely through the air and adjusted themselves on Matt's face. Franklin stared blindly.

"Matt!" he exclaimed, groping. "That isn't very funny." Matt sighed and handed the glasses back. Franklin put them back on, frowning.

"Suppose," Matt said, "I should float in the air?" As he spoke, he felt himself lifting.

Franklin looked up. "Come down here!" Matt came back into his chair.

"These tricks," Franklin said sternly, "aren't very seemly. Go to a doctor, Matt. Don't waste any time. And," he added, taking off his glasses and polishing them vigorously, "I think I'll see my oculist in the morning."

Matt sighed again. "I was afraid that was the way it would be. Abbie?" Franklin stared.

"Yes, Mr. Wright." The words, soft and gentle, came out of mid-air.

Franklin's eyes searched the room frantically. "Thanks," Matt said.

"Leave this house!" Franklin said, his voice trembling. "I've had enough of these pranks!"

Matt got up and went to the front door. "I'm afraid Dr. Franklin doesn't believe in you. But I do. Good-by, Dr. Franklin. I don't think a doctor would cure what I've got." When he left, Franklin was searching the living room. There was something strangely final about the drive through the campus. Along Oread Street on top of Mount Oread, overlooking the Kaw Valley on the north and the Wakarusa on the south, the university buildings stood dark and deserted. Only the Student Union was lighted and the library and an occasional bulletin board. The long arms of the administration building were gloomy, and the night surrounded the white arches of Hoch Auditorium . . .

He pulled into the parking area behind the apartment building and got out and walked slowly to the entrance. He hoped that Guy wouldn't be in.

Matt opened the door. The apartment was empty. He turned on a living room lamp. The room was in typical disarray. A sweater on the davenport, books in the chair.

In the dark, Matt went to the kitchen. He bumped into the stove and swore, and rubbed his hip. *Mary had a little lamb* . . . Somewhere around here . . .

Some hidden strength kept Matt from dropping in his tracks. He should have collapsed from exhaustion and hunger long ago. But soon there would be time to rest . . . *and everywhere that Mary went* . . . He stooped. There it was. The sugar. The sugar. He had always liked blue sugar.

He found a package of cereal and got the milk from the refrigerator. He found a sharp knife in the drawer and sliced the box in two. He dumped the contents into a bowl and poured the milk over it and sprinkled the sugar on top. The blue sugar . . . *with fleece as white as snow* . . . He was very sleepy.

He lifted a spoonful of the cereal to his mouth. He chewed it for a moment. He swallowed. . .

And it was gone.

He grabbed the knife and plunged it toward his chest.

And his hand was empty.

He was very sleepy. His head drooped. Suddenly it straightened up. The hissing had stopped. A long time ago. He turned on the light and saw that the burner was turned off, the one that never lighted from the pilot, the one he had stumbled against.

The blue insect poison had failed and the knife and the gas.

He felt a great wave of despair. It was no use. There was no way out.

He walked back to the living room, brushed the sweater off the davenport, and sat down. The last hope—beyond which there is no hope—was gone. And yet, in a way, he was glad that his tricks had not worked. Not that he was still alive but because it had been the coward's way. All along he had been trying to dodge the only solution that faced him at every turn. He had refused to recognize it, but now there was no other choice.

It was the hard way, the bitter way. The way that was not a quick death but a slow one. But he owed it to the world to sacrifice himself on the altar he had raised, under the knife he had honed, wielded by the arm that he had given strength and skill and consciousness.

He looked up. "All right, Abbie," he sighed. "I'll marry you."

The words hung in the air. Matt waited, filled with a fear that was half hope.

Was it too late for anything but vengeance?

But Abbie filled his arms, cuddled against him in homely blue gingham, scarcely bigger than a child but with the warmth and softness of a woman. She was more beautiful than Matt had remembered. Her arms crept around his neck.

"Will you, Mr. Wright?" she whispered. "Will you?"

A vision built itself up in his mind. The omniscient, omnipotent wife, fearsome when her powers were sheathed, terrible in anger or disappointment. No man, he thought, was ever called upon for greater sacrifice. But he was the appointed lamb.

He sighed. "God help me," he said, "I will."

He kissed her. Her lips were sweet and passionate.

Matthew Wright was lucky, of course, far luckier than he deserved to be, than any man deserves to be.

The bride was beautiful. But more important and much more significant—

The bride was happy.

This story is every bit as fabulous a romp as I remembered. It is also a fine study of the dangers in evoking supernatural powers. The conclusion makes perfect sense. The man is such a turd, while the girl is trying so desperately to win him, and she really would make a good wife. She is dedicated to the wifely arts, and good at them. Her pain is completely understandable, as is her outrage when she discovers how he has manipulated her. But she does love him, and forgives him the moment he agrees to marry her. I suspect she is too good for him, but that's her choice. She finishes happy, and we may be sure he will do everything in his power to keep her that way. It seems like a perfect story.
—Piers

MYRRHA

Gary Jennings

September 1962

I remember this as an utterly savage story of revenge for a personal slight, phenomenally out of proportion to the offense. I remember Myrrha as a beautiful magical princess, or the equivalent. It has subtleties I'll discuss in the Afternote. I regard it as a classic of horror.

  —Piers

Excerpts from the report of the court-appointed psychiatrist, concurring in the commitment of Mrs. Shirley Makepeace Spencer to the Western State Hospital at Staunton, Virginia:

To all stimuli applied, subject remains blind, deaf, mute and paralyzed . . .

Catatonic schizophrenia . . .

. . . complete withdrawal. . .

Briefly, subject's formerly uneventful domestic life was recently disrupted by two tragic circumstances. Two loved ones died violently; but by indisputable accident, as attested by attending physicians.

To judge from her diary, subject reacted rationally enough to the *fact* of these deaths. Traumatic withdrawal appears to have developed from her inability to accept them as accidental. Although an intelligent, educated woman, she mentions toward the end of her diary, "a blight, a curse." When Mrs. Spencer hints at suspecting her innocent house guest of complicity in the tragedies, the textbook syndrome is complete.

Events leading up to her psychogenic deterioration are set down in subject's daily journal. The appended extractions have been arranged in narrative form, edited only in the excision of extraneous matter and repeated datelines.

NOTE: The last, unfinished sentence, which subject wrote just before the onset of catatonia, is inexplicable. In the absence of any other indication that she was obsessed with classical mythology, the final entry can only be dismissed as hysteric incoherence.

Excerpts from the journal of Mrs. Shirley Spencer, dated at intervals, May 10, 1960 to final entry, sometime in July, 1961. Intervals of one day or more are indicated by asterisks:

I had forgotten how beautiful Myrrha Kyronos was. Is, I should say. When she arrived this morning, I just had to get out the old Southern Seminary annual and look up her picture. She hasn't changed an iota. She was a year ahead of me at school, probably a year older. That would make her 31 now, and she might just have doffed the cap and gown! And after that long ocean crossing, and the ride in the trucks and all, and having to mother a dozen horses and half a dozen helpers the whole way!

Tom's mouth fell open when he met her. Afterwards he said if he'd known what a "temptation" I was putting in his way he'd never have agreed to let Myrrha come for the summer. Pooh to the temptation; Myrrha's interested in nothing but her horses. And lovely creatures they are; she must have rounded them up on Mount Olympus. By comparison, our gentle old saddle jades here on the farm appear as torpid as tortoises.

Myrrha has certainly brought excitement. Right from the start, when her letter came. I don't believe Mr. Tatum bothered to stop at any mailbox between Warrenton and here, he was so anxious to deliver that letter from Greece. And I was just about as amazed as he was. Myrrha and I hadn't been "close" at school, and I'd had no reason to give her a thought since then.

And now here she is. And here I am, dabbling in international relations or whatever you'd call it. This is the first time Greece has ever competed in the National Horse Show. When I told Myrrha we were honored to play hosts to a representative of the Greek team, she laughed and said, *"I am* the Royal Hellenic Team."

Of course the Show doesn't come off until November. Myrrha brought the horses here now to get them used to American weather and atmosphere and feed—apparently foreign horses are a sensitive lot.

In just 24 hours, Myrrha has become undisputed queen of the Spencer acres, at least as far as our Dorrie is concerned. Dorrie, who can hardly speak "Virginian" yet, is beginning to imitate Myrrha's exotic speech. A slight accent, disarming rather than distracting, that I don't remember her having, way-back-when.

Even if we weren't just thrilled to have Myrrha herself here, we'd enjoy basking in her reflected glory. The horses are the showpiece and envy of the neighborhood, and she is the cynosure of all the local young men. Cars drive by hourly, full of sightseers either openly ogling or pretending a nonchalant interest.

For the first time today I tried to strike up a conversation with one of Myrrha's—whatever they are; she has a Greek word for them—herders, I suppose. And I can say truthfully it was all Greek to me. None of them speak English.

All are dark, saturnine, hairy little men. They keep strictly to themselves—and the horses, of course. They seem to have made provision for their keep. Whatever it is they cook for themselves down there by the barn smells like singed hair and is eaten wrapped in a grape leaf. At night they amuse themselves with a sonorous and inharmonious tweedling; Pan-pipes, is my guess.

Good old bumbling Tom got familiar enough to ask her why her husband hadn't come over. When she admitted there was none, he essayed gallantry and said he would expect her to be married to a prince. She told him quite seriously, "King Paul has only daughters."

It does appear that Myrrha hails from one of the wealthiest families in her country, which somehow I never realized in the old days at school. Her father owns all these horses she brought, and is underwriting the expenses of the whole venture, all for the greater glory of Greece.

Myrrha told us, on arrival, that we must try to overlook any of her "so-strange" customs. I'd call them superstitions. Why, when we went walking in the woods, did she refuse to cross the branch? She said the still water would reflect her image; so what? And why, when I resurrected my old class ring, did she recoil and say she had a horror of wearing rings?

Dorrie, who has always treated our own horses with a sort of lazy, familiarity-bred contempt looks on Myrrha's as if they were Santa's reindeer. It gives me turn, sometimes, to see her dodging in and out among their sharp hoofs, or brazenly braiding one's tail. But hair-triggered and wall-eyed as they are at any other intrusion, they suffer her as benignly as if she were their own frisky colt.

And Myrrha doesn't seem to mind, any more than she minds Tom's tomfoolery. Nowadays he pretends to be a horseflesh expert. He's forever down at the stable or the paddock, looking wise, or expounding on some trick-of-the trade known only to him, and getting in the little Greek herder's way, and one of these times he's going to get kicked in the head.

Was admiring Myrrha' steeds today, for the umptieth time, and she scolded me gently about my own Merry Widow. Said she could have made a show-horse if I'd spent a little time and effort instead of letting her turn out to be just—"A drudge?" I laughed, "Like me?" and said that Merry and I suited each other.

Tom said maybe it wasn't too late; how about Myrrha letting one of her stallions service Merry Widow after the Show doing were over? I thought, and told him so, that that was an indelicate suggestion. He and Myrrha laughed.

First friction tonight.

My fault. We were rehashing schooldays. Thinking it was the typical hair-letting-down hen session, I humorously confided to Myrrha that I and the other girls had considered her rather too "queenly" in her demeanor.

Myrrha was not amused; she practically demanded to know what were the necessary qualifications for queenliness. Somewhat flustered, I said, "Well, after all, the only other Greek any of us knew was the little man at the depot fruitstand over in Lexington."

Black, an artist friend once told me, is considered a "cold" color. Myrrha's eyes are black, but they flared out like heat-lightning. I shouldn't have said what I did.

I shouldn't have said what I did. Things have been very awkward and a little awful for the past two days. Myrrha is being queenly in earnest, now, and I guess I'm in the role of the Court Fool. Tom has chided me for my "inhospitality," and even Dorrie turns an occasional melancholy gaze on Mommy for tilting at her idol.

Myrrha unbent a little tonight; at least far enough to contribute a decanter of wine for the dinner, and invite me, too, to partake. I could have done without it. I forget what it's called—some Greek name—but its proudest feature is that it's spiced with resin (and tastes to me like old socks). Tom liked it fine; he and Myrrha had quite a high time. Quite high. Just one of their customs, she called it, but I've been gargling mouthwash all evening.

I wondered a little, at the time, when I saw her take the stone away from Laddie. It was just a plain old pebble; the dog had been idly chewing on it. She wheedled it away from him, stuck it in her pocket and walked away. Laddie didn't seem to care, and I soon forgot the incident.

Then tonight she and Tom insisted I have some more of that wretched resin wine. Tom was quite set on my not being a "party-pooper"—I think he must have had a little something previously. So I choked down a sip, then nearly choked for real. In the bottom of the decanter was the pebble Laddie had been mouthing.

There must be some reason, but she didn't even pretend to vouchsafe one. Now I come to think, she didn't taste the wine tonight.

Bad to worse. Perhaps I really shouldn't have made such a fuss about that pebble; all the conflict seems to date from that night. Or was it from the time I made that thoughtless remark about the fruit peddler? Anyway, Tom has taken Myrrha's side whenever there's been the slightest brush between us. There've been more than a few, and not all of them slight.

The worst was at Dorrie's bedtime, when she refused to kiss me good-night, because I'd "been bad" to her adored Myrrha. Finally, by promising to mend my ways, I bought a reluctant kiss—and tasted that damnable resin wine on my child's lips!

Don't know what to do. First that horrible scene, when I found what was left of Laddie, down by the herders' campfires. And then the horrible scene when I confronted Myrrha—and Tom leaped to her defense.

And now both of them gone. Gone all day, and here it is after mid-night. Dorrie upstairs, still awake, crying for Myrrha to come and kiss her goodnight.

Surely there can be no more   horrible day in my life. Tom's confession was enough to chill my soul. And then Myrrha's denial of it—and his confusion. Is he losing his mind, or is she driving me out of mine?

He came to me, crying, pleading forgiveness "for what happened in the hayloft," pleading that *she* had been the seducer. Then she, so cool, so self-possessed, said, "Do you think I'd give myself to *that?*" and I smelled the reek of resin on his breath.

She called our own old faithful Wheeler to witness, and he nodded wit-lessly and stammered yes, that Miss Kyronos had spent all night doctoring a croupy mare at the stable.

Tom, Tom, you were so bewildered. Did you confess to a dream? A wish?

324

Poor Myrrha. I've been so shaken by what has happened in these last couple days that haven't thought what they might have meant to her. It was my mare Merry Widow, she spent that night nursing. And here I was all ready and willing to believe—

Anyway, today we've been close friendly and forgiving, and more or less re-cemented our friendship Tom—chastened, remorseful and shame-faced—has spent all day down at the stable, taking over the care of Merry Widow. When he comes up, I'll tell him he's forgiven, too.

Tomorrow is the funeral. How many days has it been since I last wrote here? Why am I writing now? I look back over the pages and marvel at having written "there can be no more horrible day in my life." I must force my self not to write that again here in mortal fear that I may thereby call down another blow from fate.

If only I could have said good bye, but he'll be buried in a sealed coffin. Dr. Carey says the stallion did it because, when Tom went among Myrrha's herd, he still had the smell of the sick mare on him

I don't know what I'd have done all this time without Myrrha here to help me. Bless her she realized that I wanted only seclusion. She has even neglected her duties with the horses, to keep Dorrie occupied and out of the way, and leave me to meander alone through the empty house.

But I must come back to myself. Dorrie will need me. Sooner or later she will be asking why Daddy hasn't come back "from town."

I think I have lost all capacity for grief, all vulnerability to horror. I know I have lost all sense of time. All I have left is a mild wonder that there really can be such a thing as a blight, a curse—and wonder, why me? Why us?

I can't think when it was—it wasn't recently, because I am sure she's been gone for quite a long time. Whenever it was, she came running up the hill from the wooded place down near the branch. She was chewing happily, eating from the little paper bag she carried, and calling, "Marsh-mallows, Mommy!"

Whenever that was, she died that night in convulsions. The doctor—

not Dr. Carey; we couldn't get him; and it was an emergency—whoever the doctor was, he said she had eaten Amanita-something. Not a marshmallow, a mushroom that they call the Death Angel.

Haven't written. Things so seldom, so far between I don't remember at the time, and when I think to write, by then they've lost all meaning. But write that farm now is empty as an echo. Whatever it is about this place that made Myrrha and the herders take their horses and leave, whatever it is seems to keep everybody else away as well.

Everything suffers. My bay mare Merry Widow foaled this morning after whole night of painful labor, screamed like a woman, I not much help and no one here with me but simple old Wheeler, not much help either.

Merry Widow unmotherly, refused to lick foal clean at birth. Today ignores, even shuns the poor trembly thing. Wheeler won't touch it either, says it can't live long. I don't care, going to keep it anyway. Somebody, it reminds me so of somebody, somebody I loved.

Its dear little hands are

Yes, I remembered it correctly. For those who may find it confusing, here is the summary as I see it: Myrrha was furious about the slight on her character she believed Shirley had made, and conspired for drastic revenge. She arranged the deaths of the dog and Shirley's daughter. She either seduced Tom and saved the semen to artificially impregnate the mare, or caused Tom to think he was having sex with Myrrha when it was actually with the mare. The jealous stallion then killed Tom for that offense. The result was the birthing of a man/horse crossbreed, a baby centaur. When Shirley realized what had happened, she lost her mind. What horror!

    —Piers

Editor's Note

Evan Filipek

I first encountered the magical world of Piers Anthony's Xanth at the awkward age of twelve. At the time, I was in the desperate throes of unrequited love with a girl named Isis, and immediately came to identify with the young Prince Dolph. Xanth and her inhabitants became my constant friends, and Dolph and I matured together. As I devoured Anthony's works, I scoured local antiquarian bookstores, libraries and antique shops for every science fiction and horror story I could find, discovering as I went the works of Poul Anderson, Isaac Asimov, Ray Bradbury, Robert Heinlein, Edgar Allan Poe, Arthur Conan-Doyle, H. P. Lovecraft, Douglas Preston, Lincoln Child and Neil Gaiman as well as my own knack for locating difficult-to-find items.

Many years later, I found myself working a third-shift job in a basement with no radio reception. In those long and lonely hours hunched over a copy machine, I rekindled my love for Piers Anthony's work. Using my Xanthine talent of acquisition, I found all the Xanth titles on audiobooks on an online auction website and dove right in. As an adult, I understood the books differently. Though the stories were familiar to me, I now noticed their layered complexity; I picked up on a broader range of associations. And though my youthful associations with Dolph persisted, I also found myself relating to other, older characters. As a child, Xanth audiobooks helped me to overcome my trouble sleeping. Years later, they made those long nights in the basement bearable.

From an early age, my mother taught me to appreciate someone's hard work and talent, so it seemed only natural that I would write a letter to Piers Anthony to express my gratitude for the tremendous positive impact his writing has had on my life. To my great surprise and elation, I received a reply. Mr. Anthony was pleased by how much his stories meant to me, but also informed me that the audiobooks I had been listening to were pirated. Horrified by such news, I offered a heartfelt apology, promised to return the offending copies, and vowed to purge all evidence of piracy of his work, from the internet. Mr. Anthony insisted that I keep them, and surprised me once more by telling me he had a better idea for my talents. He explained his desire to compile an anthology of a dozen or so stories that had most influenced him as a young author. Most were long out of print, but he suggested if I were able to track down the stories in question, I could edit the volume for publication. As I began acquiring and reading original copies of each story, Piers & I discussed his memories of each. I was particularly astonished at some of their similarities to today's gritty and cutting edge horror as well as Science Fiction blockbusters like The Matrix Trilogy and Inception. In some cases his *memory* of the stories differed from what I read and I asked that before re-reading the stories, Piers write a Note to precede each, summarizing his memory and perceptions. He did so, and after re-reading the stories he wrote the included Afternotes. I quickly tracked down all those long out-of-print volumes and set to work assembling, scanning, negotiating publishing rights for, and editing them. The book you now hold is the result.

So to all you true believers out there, I say this: When you get the chance to thank your heroes, take it! I extend my heartfelt thanks for all their support to my wife, Isis Cowling Filipek (yes, *that* Isis), Kate, Paul, and Jesse Filipek, Josh and Todd Gannon, Don Renuart, Martha Pontoni, Bud Webster, Dan and Jason Bryan, Erik Kjell Johnson, and Cameron Pierce. A special thanks to Noah Carter Sees and my children Marcus Anakin, Bodhi Rider, and Isla Florin Evangeline, to whom I want to show the world's magic. And, of course, I offer my deepest appreciation to Piers Anthony for this once-in-a-lifetime opportunity.

PIERS ANTHONY:
AN AUTOBIOGRAPHICAL SKETCH

I was born in Oxford, England, in AwGhost, 1934. My parents both graduated from the university at Oxford, but I was slow from the outset. I spent
time with relatives and a nanny while my parents went to do relief work
in Spain during the Spanish Civil War of 1936-39. They were helping to
feed the children rendered hungry by the devastation of the war. When
that ended, my sister and I joined them in Spain. I left my native country
at the age of four—and never returned. The new government of General
Franco in Spain, evidently error-prone and suspicious of foreigners doing
good works, arrested my father in 1940. They refused to admit that they
had done so, making him in effect a "disappeared" person, but he was able
to smuggle out a note. Then rather than admit error, they let him out on
condition that he leave the country. World War II was then in progress, so
instead of returning to England, we went to my father's country. In this
manner I came to America at age six, on what I believe was the last ship
out. Though I was too young to understand what was going on, in time I
learned, and I retain an abiding hostility to dictatorships.

My parents' marriage grew strained and finally foundered. Suffering
the consequences of separation from my first country and my second country as well as the stress of a family going wrong, I showed an assortment of
complications such as nervous tics of head and hands, bed-wetting, and
inability to learn. It required three years and five schools to get me through
first grade. I later gained intellectual ground, but lost physical ground.
When I entered my ninth school in ninth grade I was at the proper level
but not the proper size, being the smallest person, male or female, in my
class. However, boarding school, and later college, became a better home
for me than what I had, and I managed to grow almost another foot by the
time I got my BA in writing at Goddard College, Vermont, in 1956. This
was just as well, because I married a tall girl I met in college; I had to grow,

literally, to meet the challenge.

When I was discharged from the Army in 1959, my wife and I decided to move to Florida. We had family there, and the winters were warm. I had spent several years going to school in the cold winters in Vermont and I do not like the cold weather. I do like the mountainous scenery so we live in north-central Florida where it is hilly, rather than flat.

I had the hodgepodge of employments typical of writers. Of about fifteen types of work I tried, ranging from aide at a mental hospital to technical writer at an electronics company, only one truly appealed: the least successful. But the dream remained. Finally in 1962 my wife agreed to go to work for a year, so that I could stay home and try to write fiction full time. The agreement was that if I did not manage to sell anything, I would give up the dream and focus on supporting my family. As it happened, I sold two stories, earning $160. But such success seemed inadequate to earn a living. So I became an English teacher, didn't like that either, and in 1966 retired again to writing. This time I wrote novels instead of stories, and with them I was able to earn a living. As with the rest of my life, progress was slow, but a decade later I got into light fantasy with the first of my ongoing Xanth series of novels, A Spell for Chameleon, and that proved to be the golden ring. And I wrote two other fantasy series: the Adept novels and the Incarnations of Immortality. My sales and income soared, and I became one of the most successful writers of the genre, with twenty-one NEW YORK TIMES paperback bestsellers in the space of a decade. This enabled us to send our two daughters to college, and drove the wolf quite far from our door. We now live on a tree farm, and would love to have a wolf by our door, but do have deer and wild cat and other wildlife. I am an environmentalist.

But a writer does not live by frivolous fantasy alone. I turned back to serious writing with direct comment on sexual abuse in Firefly, and on history in novels like Tatham Mound, which relates to the fate of the American Indians, and the Geodyssey series, covering man's past three and a half million years to the present, and Volk (available via the Internet), which shows love and death in Civil War Spain and World War II Germany. So I close the circle, returning in my writing to the realm I left as a child. And I have a new, less frivolous fantasy series, ChroMagic, that begins with Key to Havoc. There has always been a serious side to my writing, even in my fantasy, and my readers respond to it. They tell me that I have taught many to read, by showing them that reading could be fun, and that I have saved the lives of some, by addressing concerns such as suicide. I take my readers as seriously as I take my writing, a number of them have become collaborators in a series of joint novels. My autobiography to age 50, Bio of an Ogre, is now out-of-print; there is a sequel, How Precious Was That While. I have had 140 books published, with more in the pipeline.

In fact I am a workaholic, and I love my profession. I have, of course, an ongoing battle with critics, who see only the frivolous level; it is doubtful whether my work will ever in my lifetime receive much critical applause, but I believe in its validity for the longer haul. So do my readers.

ALSO FROM FANTASTIC PLANET
AND ERASERHEAD PRESS

WAVE OF MUTILATION

BY DOUGLAS LAIN

"The universe has a hole in it and reality is leaking out. Who knew it would be this much fun? Doug Lain's *Wave of Mutilation* is the story of Christian and Samantha; a story that generates itself as it devours itself. Its characters and surreal scenes are rendered with an engaging style and seem to have truths to tell us about relationships, politics, sex, the history of furniture. At the same time, they convince us they are insubstantial, errant, nothing but the illusion of the world. Terrific writing, good laughs, and the flawless execution of a fictional tightrope walk between "reality" and nothing. Wonderfully original!" **—JEFFREY FORD**, World Fantasy Award winner

THE PICKLED APOCALYPSE OF PANCAKE ISLAND

BY CAMERON PIERCE

"Weird, wicked, wonderful." —**PIERS ANTHONY**

A demented fairy tale about a pickle, a pancake, and the apocalypse.

It is Gaston Glew's sixteenth Sad Day – the sixteenth anniversary of his birth – and his parents have just committed suicide. Fed up with the sadness of Pickled Planet, Gaston Glew builds a rocket ship and blasts off into outer space, hoping to escape his briny fate.

Meanwhile, on Pancake Island, Fanny Fod, the most beautiful pancake girl in the world, nurses a secret sadness as she guards the origin of all happiness: the mysterious Cuddlywumpus. When Gaston's rocket ship crash-lands in the sea of maple syrup that surrounds Pancake Island, nothing will ever be the same for him, or for Fanny Fod.

SPACE WALRUS
BY KEVIN L. DONIHE

Space: the final frontier . . . these are the voyages of . . . a walrus?

Meet Walter. He is the first walrus in a revolutionary space program. Someday, his blubbery form will float past asteroids, stars, and planets as he journeys through the dark beyond to become a Master of Space. But for now, Walter's dream is to win the heart of his lifelong love, Dr. Stephanie, who happens to be the scientist assigned to conduct experiments on him. The problem is Dr. Stephanie does not love Walter. She views him as a test subject and nothing more. To make matters worse, Dr. Stephanie appears to be in love with the abusive head scientist, Dr. Ron.

From Wonderland Book Award-winner Kevin L. Donihe comes a tragic comedy of unrequited love and inspired determination.

THE SOPATHS

THE MOST CONTROVERSIAL BOOK
BY NY TIMES BESTSELLER PIERS ANTHONY